Saint of the Shadows

SAINT OF THE SHADOWS

Jonesy Elise

Cover Design: Sweet 'N Spicy Designs

Editor: The Editing Hall

Formatting: Anessa Books

CONTENT NOTES

Shenanigans are afoot in this book—from run-of-the-mill injuries one might find in an ER to blood and guts one might find in a horror comic, not to mention an undead furry critter. All these pair well with consensual domme-sub play and other BDSM antics such as edging, denial, spankings, and bindings.

With all the fun stuff, there's the not-so fun stuff: systemic racism, classism, drug dealing, gang activity, gun violence, gentrification, wealth-hoarding, homicide, and living on the stolen lands of tribes decimated by the cruelty of European invaders.

Or as I like to call it, just another day in an American city.

I

The Legend Of The Overworked Nurse

Marisol Novotny pushed against the bouncy, good vein in the man's arm. The portly fellow's sweat had smeared his eyeliner into raccoon eyes. He yanked at the handcuff around his thick and freckled wrist, seething. "I was chasing a robber."

Unfortunately, that wasn't how the police saw it when they found him trespassing.

Marisol arched an eyebrow toward the gauze, as bulky as an old school maxi-pad, covering the stitches on the man's forehead. "Promise not to fight a dumpster with your head next time." Though next time, he shouldn't lead the police on a chase wearing a Halloween costume in February.

The other cuff scraped against the bed rail. "Listen here, Nurse. Something big is coming, and I'll send it to the gutter with all the other vermin."

Right... Shadowhaven always had some guy in a mask pretending to be a crime fighter. Grown men playing dress-up in sweatpants and ski masks came with the city's charter, and a lot of them ended up in the ER of the Varian Family and Research Hospital during her third shift. With a quick stab, she drew a vial of blood and released the tourniquet from his arm. She passed the vial to the arresting officer hovering nearby. The bloodwork most likely would come back positive for B'Lee, the city's own new and improved brand of heroin.

The officer said, "You're good at tapping a vein on a moving target. Did you serve?"

She wrapped the patient's arm with medical tape and forced a laugh. "No, but I suppose I've seen combat. Westside Shadowhaven, born and raised." She threw away her gloves and ran her hands under the faucet.

Her city wasn't exactly a war zone, but outsiders compared the Westside to some bombed-out pile of rubble. Nothing so epic happened there, just the slow-detonating bomb of poverty. If a similar squalor riddled a city abroad, someone powerful would send forces, but Shadowhaven, the world's forgotten city, handled it on its own.

The police officer took the patient away. Bed one cleared. Marisol dried her hands and bemoaned her ragged cuticles. They were long overdue for a manicure. She'd make time for that on the eighth day of the week.

She barely had time to adjust the dark hair of her ponytail before the patient in her second bed hit the call button. A shelf had fallen and crushed his leg earlier that night. Screwed and stitched together, he rode high out of trauma surgery, screaming, "An angel saved me!"

She checked his vitals and administered acetaminophen. As soon as she finished, the old man grabbed her hand. His eyes shined, and he repeated, "An angel saved me."

"I'm sure." She dismissed the assertion. More likely? Some guys came to rob his place, ransacked the register, and then called 911.

"It was the Patron Saint. The real one. Not those foolish pretend ones," the old man said.

She patted his wrinkled hand. "I bet your surveillance cameras captured good footage of him for the news."

The old man waved a crooked finger as if giving a lesson. "My shelves are strong. I only wanted the best. No one man can lift my shelves. That's what the forklift is for. But the Patron Saint? He single-handedly lifted the shelf. He saved me." The man grimaced, breathed in, and the floodgates opened, unleashing sob after sob.

Occasionally, a kook would come into the ER claiming a man in all black rescued or attacked him. A favorite account came from some strung-out mobsters who said a masked man, the Patron Saint, jumped out of a sixth-story window in a hail of gunfire and ran off. These stories served as

Shadowhaven's brand of fairy tales like The Man-Eating Mega Rats of the Sewers or The Immortal Cockroach. But an official Patron Saint never existed. Only imitators of imitators who needed as much stitching and stapling as the people they saved. Actual heroes—let alone super ones—were just another piece of fiction.

Marisol lowered her voice and gently shushed the old man. "You're going to be fine."

He blinked, his expression tense with lucidity. "You remind me of my wife."

She rolled her shoulders back, readying to quash a potentially horny old patient. With his tears fresh along his laugh lines, she caved. What about her reminded him of his wife?

She imagined a woman like her abuelita in sensible heels and a shirtdress, heading off to Mass. And the fictional wife would look at Marisol's chapped lips and tired eyes and balk at the comparison. "She's a lucky woman with a husband who only gets the best shelves."

"She died a couple of years ago. Cancer. Had a personality like boxed chocolate. Hard shell, soft and sweet center."

All these described her abuelita. "I'm sorry."

"Are you married?" He barely finished the question before she shook her head. "Your boyfriend needs some sense knocked into him."

"No boyfriend to knock. Or anyone for that matter." A relationship was like a manicure—an indulgence that didn't fit in her life. If someone wedged themselves in, her life shoved them back out.

"With those gentle doe eyes? What's wrong with these men?" the old man asked.

The explanation that, most days, singlehood was the better option would take too long. College guys split as soon as the "urban" lifestyle lost its novelty, and the few Westsiders, who her gangster brother hadn't chased off, would inch out the door when their typical macho bag of tricks failed to impress her. She was too much work, and if it wasn't for her best friend, Annie, doomed to be alone. "I guess they don't make them like they used to," she said.

She didn't dwell on her lack of a love life for long. Another patient arrived. A middle-aged woman raced into the ER, pushing her elderly mother in front of her in a borrowed wheelchair. The mother moaned, *"Estoy muriendo"* amid bouts of coughing.

As soon as she heard the woman moan about dying, Marisol took over the wheelchair. She soothed into the patient's ear, "Señora, no morirá. Lo prometo."

A weak smile crept across her pale face, perhaps holding on to Marisol's promise that she would not die. But it did not last long. Señora's shoulders heaved with another cough attack.

Dr. Foster, who looked like a princess but was definitely the ogre of the ER, popped through the partition curtain with her laptop precariously balanced on one forearm. She already tapped her foot as she clicked through the standard questionnaire. Maybe tonight her microaggressions would become full-on macro. Trading in "You speak English so well!" for "Those people always exaggerate their symptoms."

The patient's daughter explained that her mother had recurring bronchitis but insisted her recent cough was the worst yet. On top of that, a bad hip limited Señora's mobility, and she always ached. The patient's stark white hair, in contrast to her crepey brown skin, reminded Marisol of her abuelita, so Marisol lingered in the treatment room. Dr. Foster needed to be careful with a too-quick diagnosis. The cough and sedentary lifestyle could mean deep-vein thrombosis developing into a pulmonary embolism. Though it had been a few years since dropping out of med school, Marisol never shut off her wanna-be doctor. Dr. Foster would probably order a CT scan and put Señora on a blood thinner.

Dr. Foster wiggled her upturned nose like a bunny while staring at her laptop. "Bronchitis. We'll prescribe a nebulized steroid," she announced without looking up.

The daughter whispered to herself. She appeared to be translating the words before she said, "*Mamá, necesitas un inhalador.*"

Marisol's tightly drawn brow wasn't going to stand much against a patient's wrongful death, so she opted for her own professional suicide. "Steroid? Are you sure, Dr. Foster? Señora's daughter said her cough is worse than before. Might be good to rule out a blood clot traveling to her lungs and—"

"And?!" Dr. Foster finally looked up from the screen.

"If we are wrong, it could be deadly."

The daughter translated Marisol's words to her mother.

"Are you questioning me in front of a patient? Nurse?"

Marisol swallowed. "I'm pointing out information important to her diagnosis, Doctor."

Dr. Foster wiggled her nose again. "Go get me the steroid."

"No!" Then a flood of words rushed from the elderly patient. Her daughter patted her shoulder and repeated, "*Yo sé*," only when the patient took a breath between her sentences. Both actions seemed to be feeble attempts to calm Señora.

The daughter asked, "Can we please check if it's a blood clot?" She looked at Marisol as if she was the one in charge.

Dr. Foster sighed. "Very well. We'll order the CT scan and give her an infusion of heparin." She shut her laptop close with a clap. "If the scan is clear, it's off the blood thinner and home with an inhaler."

Marisol pursed her lips together, holding back her smile, which she couldn't hold for long as Dr. Foster snatched her into the hallway. The doctor guided Marisol around the corner, away from patients' prying ears. "Are you trying to make me look bad?"

"I'm just advocating for my patient—"

"My patient. You are aware that we follow a chain of command here."

"Yes, Dr. Foster."

"If every nurse made diagnoses, there would be chaos. For the safety of our patients, if you can't contribute to the order of my ER, I will have you removed. You'll be taking nothing but blood pressure and temperatures in the clinics!"

Marisol stared past a tendril of Dr. Foster's blonde hair, focusing on the wall. There was nothing worse than the predictable routine of the clinics.

"If you wanted to be in charge, you should've received the proper education like the rest of us." Dr. Foster stormed down the hallway.

And beliefs like that chafed Marisol's butt raw. She had received the proper education: college, a couple years of nursing, the MCAT, a year-and-change of medical school, and throughout, jerks would ask, "How did you know that?" or any other loaded but superficially innocuous expression that said Marisol had no business knowing what she knew because she didn't go to the best schools... because Mom was a first-generation immigrant...

because Dad lost his stevedore job... because she grew up on the Westside in row housing... because her brother, Caz, wound up in prison.

She wrongly figured entering a third decade would get her the respect she deserved. Nope. More time on the planet meant she knew more jerks, but dammit if she didn't hold on to the fantasy of one day calling the shots.

Marisol ducked into the linen closet to release a string of curse words, only to find Nurse Rossi there with an armload of sheets. Rossi greeted her with, "Want a good laugh?"

Not now. Marisol grunted, straining the tendons of her neck. "What's up?"

"Check out the thread count on these bed sheets."

The tag read 1000 count, a little fancy for absorbing a third of the city's mucus, sweat, blood, vomit, urine, feces, and whatever else the human body squeezed or spurted out.

"The man posed for photos during the first shift to promote his fundraiser. Apparently, he brought a set decorator and left behind an ample supply of these."

The man was Vincent Varian, Shadowhaven's golden boy. If he wasn't on some exotic adventure, with or without his companion of the month, he'd make brief appearances at the hospital with cameras in tow. Luckily with working the night shift, Marisol never had to be sickened from witnessing the pageantry. Instead, she experienced it secondhand, happily recycling worn magazines and tabloids scattered all over the cafeteria, waiting room, and treatment areas. Cover after cover displayed his square jaw, dusky blue eyes, and stylish dark golden coif. Occasionally, he'd pose with a sick child to "raise awareness." Awareness of *what* was beyond her. In Shadowhaven, children still got sick, and their parents still struggled to pay the bills. The only thing people remained aware of was Vincent.

That inflamed her anger further. The urge to curse escalated to needing to punch something. "Are your beds full?"

"Almost, but I have a discharge coming up. Why?" A mousy brown lock of hair had escaped from Rossi's elastic headband. She tried to flick it back out of her face.

"I have half occupied. Could you watch my beds for a moment?"

"Is it Opposite Day?" Rossi shifted the load in her arms like a squirming toddler to free one of her hands. She touched Marisol's forehead. "You're not coming down with something?"

"I'm fine." A lie. Marisol had better mix it with the truth, so Rossi would buy it. "Just haven't eaten much."

"Get going."

Then Marisol ran. Ran past the treatment rooms. Ran down the winding hallways. She burst through the double doors and continued into the closed portions of the clinics.

In the cover of darkness, she punched the wall. *Ow!* It didn't make things better. And now she needed a bandage for the broken skin on her knuckle. She'd swipe one from a treatment room.

She bound into the treatment room, flung open the cabinets, and groped around the lower shelf for—*voila!*—bandages. As she taped her finger by the murky outline of streetlights, she realized the motion sensors hadn't turned on the lights. Strange. She'd better let maintenance know of an electrical issue.

She closed the cabinets. An inky splotch near the cabinet handle shimmered, reflecting the yellow glow from outside. Upon further inspection, the splotch was a handprint.

In fresh blood.

Her stomach muscles tightened. She spun around to see an empty, undisturbed exam table.

However, on the floor next to it, a beam of light landed on a pulsating black heap.

"Hello?" Marisol called out a greeting fit for de-escalation rather than *I know where the scalpels are and how to use them.*

The heap struggled to stand and collapsed back onto the floor.

"You're injured. I'm a nurse." The job had a way of overriding the typical fight-flight response.

It grabbed the exam table and hoisted itself up. An impossibly tall figure stood wearing all black, resembling the Patron Saint. Or rather a Patron

Saint. He wore a molded suit that hugged his heavyweight form. He flicked back his cape, caught by some unseen wind. At last, his head tilted upright. A leather half-hood encased his face, emphasizing his square jaw. But the most remarkable sight was his eyes. Even in the darkness, they were a penetrating blue, like the sun through stained glass. His gloved hands glistened with blood. His blood?

Marisol pressed her back into the cabinets. "I can help you. If you follow me to the ER–"

"I can't do that!" He groaned and immediately hugged his wound. An object stuck into his injured side. He gripped it and breathed through his teeth. "People can't... know about... me. They'll want to... know who... I am."

Even straining, he had a velvet-rich baritone voice. It soothed her enough to release her white-knuckle grip from the counter edges. Marisol reached toward the light switch above the counter. *Click.* In the light, she saw his blood pool around a large gash. Like trauma surgery, ruptured organs, and rapid infusion gash. She couldn't let a patient bleed to death on an account of his pride. "Seriously, man. You need to come with me. It's pretty bad."

The man recoiled. "Forget it. I can do this myself." He grunted and fidgeted with the object in his side.

"Not by the looks of it." Marisol touched his arm. "You can't do this on your own." The physical contact between them crackled like static electricity, standing the hair on her arm on end. Her eyes caught onto his, and those blues seared into her. She went rigid.

What was it about him? He was different. Taller and fitter than the other dressed-up patients. And he added an electric charge to the air? How authentic.

She held his gaze, and his breath quieted to a calm and even rhythm. "I got you," she whispered. The tension in his body relaxed under the pressure of her hand; their breathing synced. As she rubbed her lips together, her fear subsided.

Time to get to work.

Marisol washed her hands, keeping the man in her view. She pulled gloves from the boxes lined against the wall and snapped them on. "I need to remove your shirt... thing."

He unclasped his cape and nodded toward his back. Marisol ran her hands over his back in search of the zipper. His costume seemed like an enhanced wetsuit. Once she found the hidden zipper, she undid the top half. She pulled it away from his body, careful not to hurt him more. He helped her by shrugging the layer off.

The suit was heavy with what looked to be Kevlar, neoprene, and metal plating. All those major layers practically doubled his size. Compared to a pair of sweatpants and a ski mask, this costume was official.

More impressive than the suit, his naked upper body revealed him to be both a weapon and a thing of beauty, with broad, sinewy shoulders and muscular ridges carved into his torso. Unlike the other masked loons, this one had worked out. A lot. She'd have to grab some paper towel to wipe the drool from the corners of her mouth.

The metallic object protruding from his side yanked back her focus. Buried in his side was a large pair of forceps.

A renewed sense of urgency sucked the moisture from her mouth. She plucked the forceps from his side and kneeled, studying the wound closer. The forceps failed to grip on to a sharp piece of metal. "If I pull that out now, I'm afraid you'll bleed out. At the ER, a surgeon could—"

He put his hand on top of hers. "It digs... in deeper... when I move. If you get... it out... I will... go to... the ER."

She needed to help him soon, or the shard would bore a hole through him, and he'd bleed out of two places rather than one. Marisol turned around, gathered gauze and antiseptic, and removed a skinny pair of forceps from sealed plastic, placing the supplies ceremoniously out on a stainless-steel tray. Returning to her mysterious patient, she dabbed the wound with the gauze and antiseptic. Marisol grabbed the smaller forceps and hovered them over the gash. Another wave of doubt hit her. "Sure you wouldn't like some topical anesthetic?"

He clenched his teeth. "Get it out!"

Let's hope he keeps up his end of the bargain. Marisol dug the smaller forceps into his side. "Okay. Here..." She gripped the metallic object. "We..." Then she leaned her weight on her right leg, pressing her foot against the table. "Go!" Marisol pushed her leg against the table, pulled the forceps, and–squelch!–yanked out the blade. The man collapsed onto the exam table. Marisol dropped the broken blade into the metal tray, where it landed with a clank. The hilt was missing.

Marisol pressed more gauze against his side, and her eyes met his. Her head rushed with warmth. Adrenaline. That had to be adrenaline. She parted her lips, inhaling and exhaling.

He turned up one side of his mouth; she realized he mirrored her own awkward smile. Between ragged breaths, he said, "Thank you, Nurse Novotny."

Her fixation broke. "You know my name?"

He pointed to her badge clipped to her shirt. *M. Novotny, RN* was barely discernible in the room's limited light.

Of course. "People who owe me big favors call me Marisol."

He repeated her name, and it sent a tingle of dopamine throughout her body. Marisol's chest heaved. "Hm."

He echoed, "Hm."

She shifted her weight, rubbing her thighs together as the tremors of his low voice rumbled through her. Too much dopamine...

"You hurt your hand," he said.

Her busted knuckle appeared as a slight discoloration in her gloves, practically lost in the angry red of his blood. How did he know? She blurted, "I'm fine."

"Swiping a single bandage in the dark because you're fine."

A chill like a sudden nakedness whispered over her. Most people failed to pry past her half-truths. She looked down, concentrating on suppressing the bleeding. "I will call someone to bring a gurney, and we can look at you in the ER. Can you keep the pressure on the wound?"

He nodded.

When she moved her hand, the gauze fell away. The gash didn't seem that deep or wide, more like a paper cut. As she held fresh gauze against the wound, she attempted a second look at it, but the Patron Saint snatched the gauze and took over once again.

She turned around and whipped her bloody gloves off into the trash. While she washed her hands, he slipped the top part of his costume back on. She held her hand up for him to stop. "Keep pressure on it!"

Without the knife in his side holding him back, he zipped his costume with ease. But with an admonishing look from her, he cradled his side again and nodded his head.

Marisol turned around again and pressed the call button. She waited for a click and a beep. A voice returned, "How may I help you?"

She looked over her shoulder. The sight squeezed the air from her lungs. He was gone. "Never mind." She ran to the window, opened it, and stuck her head outside. Nothing but an empty alley. He couldn't have jumped and sprinted, not with that wound. She sighed and shut the window. "I'm having a weird night."

Before returning to the ER, she remembered what he had said. People couldn't know about him. For some reason, those eyes earned her loyalty. She pulled on a fresh set of gloves and wiped the blood from the cabinet, cleaned the forceps, dispensed them in the bin to be sanitized, and emptied the bio-waste. She gave the room another scan. No sign of a break-in or a clandestine treatment. All traces of this Patron Saint converted into a memory, a tale—*The Sexy Vigilante and the Mysterious Knife Wound.*

Interlude

Whenever someone needs blood squeezed from a rock, they hire me. Business turning in zero profit? I know how and where to apply pressure, even on whom. And since adversity begets creativity, sometimes people don't know what they're capable of until I arrive.

Hello, Shadowhaven, welcome to your true potential. It'll be uncomfortable at first, but I swear you will like it. I'm a real hero that way.

Consequently, I get a little offended when you say I've gone too far. You're really going to argue that you made too much money? That the drug works too well? That I was too literal when I got rid of the competition?

There are two types of people: those who bend to change and those who break. Refuse to accept change, and you pay the price.

To my dear friend Signore Romano, last of the mobsters, I'm afraid it's your time to pay. How do you want to break? An injection of jubilation? You might live through it. No? A knife, then? You'd go out fighting. But I see the worry twitch in your upper lip. You're old and out of shape. There's always the simple third option. The gun. Resign yourself to the fact you aged out of this New World.

You make your choice. I like it. It's hopeful. They called you Red Romano, but now you're white, practically exsanguinated.

And that's why they hire me. Because I'm efficient and effective.

That's why they call me the Bloodsucker.

2

Familiar Faces

Marisol covered her yawn with her hand, noting her newly bandaged finger. As she headed back to the ER, the heightened adrenaline from earlier had faded and weighed down her limbs. So much for a break. She pushed through the double-doors into the main entryway to turbulent clashing and shouting, which stifled her second yawn.

Code frickin' gray. A detective guy she recognized from Caz's sentencing was in a typical third-shift kerfuffle. He, Dr. Foster, and an EMT struggled to strap a large patient with a bleeding head wound down. Another B'Lee overdose, by the look of it. Marisol picked a perfect time to return. "Here we go," she muttered.

Right as the detective strapped one arm down, the patient swung at Dr. Foster, knocking her across the corridor into an empty hospital bed.

Marisol grabbed a container from the nurse's station and ran toward the fray.

With his giant paw, the patient pulled the detective by his tie, choking him. The security guard tried to pry the patient's fingers from the tie, now a drum-tight string of silk. The patient swung his arm back, ready to strike the detective with a right hook. Marisol leaped, landed on the bed, jabbed the patient with a dose of naloxone—and another ER miracle!—crazed patient number infinity flopped onto the bed. She jumped down and strapped in the patient.

"Thanks, Novotny," Dr. Foster murmured as she fixed her hair.

Marisol nodded. Since Dr. Foster expressed gratitude, maybe she could use this moment to demand her title and validating CT scans. Don't forget who saved you from an assault and a malpractice suit, Marisol Novotny, RN.

"You're my hero," the detective said as he loosened the killer piece of menswear from his neck.

Marisol shrugged. She wanted to say, "No problem," but was uncertain if it was true. Especially when the patient chattered like a small train.

Another doctor commandeered the gurney. "We're taking him up to psych."

Marisol helped the doctor and the EMT push the gurney to the elevators. She noticed the man in the tie trailed close behind them. Second by second, the patient's mantra became clearer and louder. "Teeth and teeth and teeth and teeth."

The EMT shook his head. "The antidote couldn't wear off that fast."

The doctor said, "B'Lee. Sometimes they hallucinate when they come down. Regardless, we need to do a blood draw to confirm. Go back to the emergency floor, nurse. We have it from here."

As Marisol moved to head back to the ER, sandpaper-like fingers dug into her skin. Oh Lord, they were seconds from another code gray with a patient impervious to antidotes. The gurney rattled as the patient pulled against the straps. "Teeth and teeth and teeth and teeth!"

Marisol yanked her hand from the patient's grip and backed away. "Why is he talking about teeth?" She rubbed the top of her hand because the patient's touch burned like a brand. The doctor and the EMT's continued silence fed her worry.

The elevator arrived with a ding! The doctor and EMT pushed the gurney onto it, though the patient's flailing shook it off a smooth trajectory.

While the doctor entered a code to enter a secure floor, the gurney rattled, frantic and violent. The patient sobbed. "I swatted a fly because he ordered it."

Marisol wanted those elevator doors to close and drown out his sobs, specifically, when they turned into shrieks. "The teeth! Rows of teeth! The Bloodsucker! He's coming for me! He's coming for you! He's coming for the whole damn city! The Bloodsucker!"

The doors closed. Marisol could feel herself breathe again, but a sliver of fear lingered right under her ribs. Sure, the patient was crazy, but something about tonight made all of Shadowhaven's fairy tales become real. She rubbed the hollow spot at her clavicle bone.

Marisol pivoted to walk back to the ER and jumped with a start as the detective wearing his loosened tie stood behind her. His black trench coat billowed in the HVAC breeze.

"What do you think got into him?" he asked.

Marisol's body shivered, so she hugged herself. "Sounded like the Bloodsucker." She rubbed her arms and said, "Maybe we should check his blood for parasites."

The detective chuckled. "That's Red Romano. Last of the Mob's bosses. Seeing him wheeled off like that? Almost makes me want to sing 'Danny Boy.' Found him tied to a streetlight outside the precinct. It broke my heart to see the big guy stand there and bleed."

From their brief interactions at court, she hadn't noticed his voice, a broad working-class accent so gruff that it felt put on. But that strong jawline of his had her wishing she remembered his name. Started with a K? Kelley? Her nerves challenged her to rub the small area just above her sternum raw. "Tied up?" she asked.

"Yeah. This town's crazy." The detective straightened, growing taller. He grunted and held his side.

Marisol said, "You're hurt."

"Yeah. The bastard sucker-punched me after I untied him."

"Would you let me look at it?" She reached toward his right side.

He stepped away. "I'm fine. Took up boxing in order to take punches." The detective smiled. Charming crow's feet surrounded his eyes colored with flecks of amber, floating in a sea of blue. No, his name was Qu... Qui...

Blue. Marisol thought of the blue eyes of the Patron Saint. She studied the detective longer. Towering height. Square jaw. Side injury. A build that could pack a punch. Suddenly the images of naked, well-defined muscles and a taped wound entered Marisol's mind. She must be making a stupid face again because the detective raised an eyebrow and grinned.

The grin flexed into a grimace when he strained to reach into his back pocket. He drew out a beat-up business card. "If anyone comes looking for our crazed crime boss. You can leave a message at my desk."

Marisol toyed with the card in her fingers. Detective Tobias Quinlan. Quinlan, that was his name! His wallet had dulled its corners. They started to walk to the main entrance of the ER. Marisol said, "You know, if you need to work on your boxing rhythm, you should stop by my dad's boxing club. I usually work out there before heading here."

"I haven't spoken to ole Pete since... since..."

Marisol braced for the awkward mention of Caz's sentencing, the orange jumpsuit-sporting elephant in the room.

"Since I arrested him for public intox back when I worked a beat."

Oh. The other elephant in the room. As a cop, he probably had so many run-ins with Dad and her brother that the wide hospital hallway suddenly became a clown car of the unmentionable Novotny elephants. She was too much work, indeed. She held out the business card to return it. "Actually, I don't know anything useful."

"You could call about something else." He pushed her hand carrying the card back. The moment his fingers bristled against hers, he jerked his touch away and scrubbed his hand through his salt and pepper hair. "God, I don't know why I said that. If it helps, we dropped the charges."

Marisol laughed at that shot of comfort. Life dropped nothing when it came to her family.

"Well, I'm gonna cut out before I mess this up anymore, Nurse Novotny."

"Marisol," she reminded him.

He repeated her name, and his face lit up. The dopey grin didn't last long as Tobias gripped his side and hobbled out of the ER.

"Wait!" Marisol ran to the nurse's station and reached into the mini refrigerator. She drew out an ice pack and wrapped it in paper towels before running it back to Tobias. "For your side." She offered him the ice.

Tobias unbuttoned the bottom half of his dress shirt and tucked the cold pack through the opening. He backed out of the ER, his gaze never leaving Marisol's direction until the automatic doors opened.

Heat rose to her cheeks. The Florence Nightingale effect gave her lots of luck tonight. She watched Tobias until he walked out of her sight down the sidewalk.

After she tucked the business card into her front pocket, Marisol headed to the old shopkeeper fresh from an orthopedic technician's visit. He rested with his new cast up in a sling.

Marisol squeezed his hand, which prodded her bandaged knuckle, burning with her own memory of the Patron Saint. "Tell me about the Patron Saint again."

"I thought no one heard me. I thought I was going to die. He was an angel."

"He is," she answered.

But as much as Hallmark moments like these kept her in the job, optimism was a foreign body attacked by an unexpected dread. Goodness sprang from luck, and luck should always be treated with suspicion, the dread warned, because the bad always accompanies the good.

Because if the Patron Saint was real, the Bloodsucker could be real as well.

3

RICH, RADIOACTIVE, OR ALIEN?

Marisol clasped the silver chain around her neck and shifted the cross pendant forward. She had lost the greater meaning of the cross, but because it was Abuelita's, she ached a bit every time she had to take it off. Her latest shift was a case-in-point that looping things around one's throat was not recommended at the ER. She ran her thumb over the pendant and let go. The pendant hung right under the V of her clavicle, shining against her own brown skin the way it shined against Abuelita's.

Rossi collapsed on the bench in front of the lockers. "What're you up to this weekend?" She shoved one foot into a wool-lined boot.

Marisol slid into her shabby overcoat. The pilled fabric turned the herringbone pattern into disarrayed zigzags. A pull of an oncoming smile threatened to give her surprise away. "Have a hot date to the children's hospital ball Saturday."

"I didn't know you were seeing anyone." Rossi's hazel eyes widened. "Do I know him?" she asked before she grunted, jamming her other foot into its respective boot.

"You do. Her name is Annie Park." Marisol slammed the locker shut. "She said she's above performances of hetero normativity. In other words, we're having a girl's night out." She fluttered her eyes, joking.

Marisol wasn't exactly straight as an arrow, but if she ever did come out, she imagined there would be cake, tequila, and a smidge more sacrilege to make Mom go apoplectic, not the beat-up locker room after a long third shift. Nope, Ma Novotny's disappointment in Marisol would come from wasting the childbearing hips she inherited with her standard case of spinsterhood.

Rossi pulled on her trapper hat. "A trip to the Varian estate? Could you spill a glass of really expensive champagne for me? Or chew up and spit out some caviar?" Finished with her layers, Rossi resembled a snowman.

All Marisol had to withstand the cold were pockets. "You got it," she said.

Beyond the automatic doors, the air bit into her already dry skin. Rossi nodded to her and headed in the opposite direction. The morning sun blasted against Marisol's back as she hunched her shoulders to her ears and stuffed her hands inside her pockets. First stop was the corner store to get her sunrise special.

The electric bell sounded as she stepped inside the store. It stank of old cooking oil and brewed coffee. Not the freshest coffee, but it was the best zap of caffeine for a person's dollar. She filled one large paper cup with it and the second with hot water.

To Marisol's amusement, the spirited conversation between the cashier and a customer overpowered the twang of the Greek guitar playing over the store's speakers. She plopped a bag of chamomile tea into the second cup, sealed the drinks with a lid, and headed to the counter to pay, having assembled her sunrise special.

"Who reads actual newspapers, anyway?" the cashier said in an exasperated tone. "People read the news on their phones."

"I still read it!" The customer tapped his finger against the counter—the counter he blocked. If Marisol waited any longer, she'd receive third-degree burns holding her beverages. The kook continued, "You can always tell what the rich and powerful are hiding from you with a physical paper. Not so with algorithms, links, and headlines they control."

The cashier motioned for Marisol to step forward. She scooched behind the dramatic customer and dropped a few bucks in the metal tray under the scratched plexiglass partition.

The customer shook his wrinkled copy of the day's paper. "Backpage and below the fold. That's where the real news is. That's what will screw us over."

The cashier tossed the change into the tray. Marisol mouthed, "Thanks" and moved on.

"Look here," the customer continued, "not even two inches of text about the W.H.O. losing a virus in Manila. Mark my words! That's what we should pay attention to, not Vincent Varian and whoever he's bringing to a party."

Vincent Varian again! Marisol couldn't escape his vapid idiocy. The less space he occupied in the news or in her mind, the happier she'd be. She exited the store with the same sing-song bell that greeted her. The winter air provided welcome relief to her bare hands from the piping hot drinks. Though outside, she heard the conversation inside, building to a crescendo of a full-blown argument. Something about free refills being free as long as someone didn't annoy the cashier.

Marisol hurried down an alleyway next to the hospital. Not too long ago, she and Annie would usually meet for a post-shift breakfast on one of the hospital's well-hidden fire escapes. That was, until the morning Vincent Varian interrupted them, dry heaving over the ledge.

Annie's heart-shaped face poked out of the cocoon of her thickly knitted scarf. With a mouthful of breakfast, she shouted, "Dude! Are you okay?"

In sunglasses and a wool coat, he was the epitome of refined cool despite his failure at ejecting his stomach's contents. A half-chewed morsel of English muffin dropped from Annie's lips as she whispered, "Holy Mother of God. It's Vincent Varian."

Marisol handed him the last of her lotion tissues to wipe his mouth. She had splurged on the fancier ones to help her during Abuelita's time in hospice and Caz's arraignment. As she offered them, she said, "Some days you need the good stuff. If you swipe the toilet paper from here, you'll sand your nose clean off."

He gaped, dumbfounded, as if the help had never spoken to him before. "Just a hangover," he said.

Her tissues had been there for her during the hardest part of her year, and their final use was assisting this rich bitch, who couldn't party like a grownup. He mumbled a thank you and left.

Annie had finally swallowed her bite. "I feel like I just saw Santa Claus."

Marisol and Annie agreed to meet in Annie's lab, far from interruptions.

Now Marisol found an unmarked door and used her keycard to unlock it. The electronic screen welcomed in an unnatural cadence, "Hello, Marisol Novotny," and she entered the research labs of the Varian Family and Research Hospital.

As a lowly nurse, her keycard should never have given her access, but she discovered the glitch in security shortly after her Varian sighting when she inadvertently leaned against the door, waiting for Annie after a shift. It always worked, and no one cared to wonder why a nurse visited the labs.

Inside, she walked a few paces before smacking on a set of lights and stormed through the empty hallway toward the elevator. The elevator doors, scuffed and dented by carts and gurneys, opened feebly. After elbowing the up button, Marisol reached the sixth floor, and she followed the meager light from the lab of Dr. Annie Park.

Marisol tapped at the wired glass of the window and watched Annie's pineapple-stem of an up-do bob while she continued at her computer.

The bespectacled doctor clicked an image of a chromosome pair. With each strand she clicked, a box of different molecular structures appeared in the screen's corner. Marisol attempted another desperate knock. Finally, Annie noticed her and scooted her office chair to the entrance of her lab and opened the door without standing.

"Morning. I thought I'd find you here." Marisol handed Annie the coffee.

Annie snatched the drink before wheeling back to her computer. "Morning? I always lose track of time." She sipped the coffee, uttered a thanks, and returned to clicking.

Marisol sauntered around the counter island behind Annie. Notes and scientific journals scattered among rainbow-colored gossip magazines graced with the handsome mug of Vincent Varian. Some covers varied—his shit-eating grin on one, his posh pout on the other. Marisol read over the headline *VINCENT VARIAN: LATE BLOOMER OR AFFLUENZA?* and felt like setting it afire with the Bunsen burner. She picked up a magazine, dangling it like dirty underwear. "Really Annie? These rags?"

"I'm the woman who has it all. I can have my serious science discoveries and my celebrity gossip too." Annie glided back in her chair and yanked the magazine from Marisol's hands. Annie continued, "I'm actually following Varian's secret off-the-books side project, and the media tend not to write about Vincent Varian in Scientific American, unfortunately." She moved her bejeweled cat-eye glasses up from her face and rubbed her eyes.

Marisol shook her head and mocked in a fake deep voice, "Secret side project?"

"My ego would like to think the project they refer to is my work, but most think he's funding the police's super-cop program."

The chamomile hadn't kicked in yet, so Marisol had time for an Annie rant. "What do you actually think?"

"One of those rags said he has a home outside town deep in the Micah National Forest, never filmed nor seen." Annie exaggerated her facial expressions like she was telling a spooky campfire story. "Now, none of those magazines have said it, but I think it's home to his secret lab where he's developing a weapon. Consider it the Manhattan Project's sequel."

Marisol grazed her finger across a photo of Vincent and drew an invisible mustache. "Sounds diabolical. He doesn't seem to have the brains for that kind of project."

"He doesn't. But he can buy the brains." Annie leaned toward her computer. The massive, messy topknot on her head pulled her closer to the monitor.

The computer screen shuffled through the squiggly shapes of chromosomes and the geometric shapes of molecules. Chromosomes, molecules, chromosomes, molecules.

The pattern scrambled Marisol's brain. She failed to imagine how Annie spent hours staring and clicking. "Can't you get an intern to do all that mindless work for you?" Marisol asked, teasing, unsure how electronically filing old samples propelled the medicine world forward.

"I want the utmost control." Annie patted the keyboard.

"I just wouldn't want to go through years of an M.D.-Ph.D. just to file."

"You say file. I say coding genetic traits into chemical compounds. Tomato, tomahto."

Marisol set her cup of tea down and covered Annie's eyes to pull her away from the computer. Annie pushed Marisol's hands away and whirled away from the desk on the chair. She cocked her head. "I've told you my theory."

Marisol lip-synced the next words, ones she heard time in and time out.

Annie said, "The cures for most ailments have been around for many years, but a global conspiracy suppresses the research." Marisol stopped her mockery before Annie said, "By going through important past research of Dr. Victor Varian, I will find the exact point in time that the cure suppression occurred. I found one of Dr. Varian's promising formulas, though the mice metabolized it quickly. Not to mention the unpleasant side effects. But if I learn the right combination..."

"You'll discover the cure to end all cures," Marisol said. She unbuttoned her coat and flicked it behind her as she hoisted herself up on a counter next to a glass cage where a white mouse scurried. The mouse mattered more than the Varians, and the poor thing plodded around with tumors drooping like swollen teats. Speaking of giant boobs devoid of life: the Varians. "Victor... which one is he?"

"Vincent's long-dead father. The doctor. Not to be confused with the nuclear physicist grandpa who died last year." Annie coasted to a file cabinet and traded one box of slides for another, loading them into the computer. "I'm nearly a year into this project. I'd be further into this thing if the law would allow some stinkin' human cloning."

Oh, no. Annie warned Marisol to slap her if she sounded too much like a mad scientist. Instead of a slap, Marisol asked, "What's our mission, Dr. Park?"

"People over ambition." Annie sank into herself and sighed. "But I will get my eureka in the bathtub by god." She waved her finger in the air for emphasis.

Marisol looked up from the mouse cage. "I met a guy last night."

Annie stopped clicking and reclined in her chair, swallowing one gulp of her coffee. "Do tell."

"We had another Patron Saint in the hospital last night. But this time, he snuck into the clinic. I caught him trying to treat his own stab wound." Her brain crackled with another rush of dopamine, revisiting the images of a well-built torso and scorching blue eyes. "I helped him like some back-alley surgeon."

Annie choked on her coffee. "Are you insane?"

"There was something about him." Marisol nibbled her lip to counter her rising embarrassment. "I'm about to risk professionalism, but this is my safe space, right?"

Annie signaled for Marisol to confess in a parody of a priest's blessing.

Marisol breathed through her teeth and shook her head. "No man has ever given me that spark."

Annie released a low, throaty laugh. "It's the mask thing. Behind it, anyone can be anything, and you hate when things get familiar."

"I don't"—Marisol prepared for the oncoming rebuttal—"always hate when things get familiar." She looked at her dry nail beds. "I work too much to get close with anyone."

"That's a pattern. Now that you're a woman of a certain age, you're escalating. I just didn't think your kink journey would take this long to begin. First, it's masks, then ropes, and then, 'Oh Annie, don't go back there. That's the sexy playroom.'"

"Ha ha. The world's escalating. I pulled a blade out of him. A whole blade." Marisol raised her hands with a six-inch gap to show how long the knife had been. "He should've bled out or at least ruptured his spleen or kidney, but he was fine. A knife wound was nothing but a paper cut. And when I turned my back, he disappeared into the night."

"Let me guess. You're picking up extra shifts?"

"I am."

"You're hallucinating."

Marisol's skin tingled from the lingering memory. She rubbed her arms for warmth. To be warm and solid like him. "He was real."

"Or he's rich, radioactive, or alien." There went Annie, committing a continental shift in conversation.

Failing to follow along, Marisol asked, "What?"

"Superheroes in the movies. They're rich, radioactive, or alien." Annie shrugged. "Which one is he?"

"I'd sooner believe in the latter two than the rich giving even the most constipated and tiniest of shits about Shadowhaven. Besides, our man's middle class." Marisol drew out the beat-up business card the detective gave her. She handed it to Annie.

"The crazy person gave you his business card?"

"I think so." But after Marisol said it, she wasn't so sure.

Annie read the card. "Detective Tobias Quinlan is your Patron Saint? Why would a detective play dress up?"

"Because there are too many rules to follow and too many boxes to check. Maybe by putting on a costume, he finally serves Justice." Marisol plopped her empty cup loudly on the counter for emphasis. "My brother's rotting up at the Hill because they can always scrounge up a case against the pawn but never the king."

Although the state had charged Caz with at least one murder he had actually committed, the string of murders he confessed to was not his handiwork. He took the fall for the gang, so everyone else in the Shadows stayed clean. And the free birds were always Shadowhaven's worst: sinister and powerful men who had the right family names to keep their dirty meat hooks jabbed into the city for over a century.

Despite the huge hole Caz's absence had ripped into her family, nothing changed in the city. A new enforcer, who dirtied his hands with blood, took his spot. That guy would inevitably be caught or killed himself, and the cycle repeated. The shitty ouroboros of it all tugged so hard that Marisol rested her elbows on her lap until her hair fell into her eyes.

Annie's chair glided over the vinyl floor. She brushed the hair away from Marisol's face. "You really think a mask makes a difference?"

Marisol lifted her head and attempted a pathetic smile. What did she have to lose?

Annie pushed her glasses to her nose and peered over the top of them. "Maybe I should wear one." She laughed and handed back the card. "Call him. At least he's not boring."

Maybe Marisol would in a few days—to let the intensity from last night wane a bit. She wouldn't want this Tobias Quinlan to believe that all it took was a mask and a quick-to-heal knife wound to bring out her clingy side.

Buzz! Annie's cell phone rattled next to Marisol's leg. She picked it up but noticed the message.

I need it. Give it to me now.

"Your phone. I didn't mean to read it." Marisol held it out. Annie turned red and snatched it from her.

Annie, a self-described asexual, exchanged embarrassing, saucy texts? Who was the messenger? The reincarnation of Rosalind Franklin? Marisol teased, "Who is she?"

Silence.

"They?"

No response again.

"He?!"

"It's nothing."

"What'd he do to get you to join the dark side? Whisper sweet nothings about the human genome? Show you his long, thick strand of DNA he isolated? Spit on your dry, neglected petri dish?"

"I minored in double entendres, and you're grossing me out."

"Are you sure you want to go to the ball with me? Your messenger doesn't want to take you?"

Annie tucked her phone in her lab coat. "I'm sure." The redness lingered in splotches down her neck. She clicked louder through more chromosomes and hexagonal molecular compounds.

Obviously, the messenger was a sensitive subject. Marisol rubbed her lips together and uttered the beginnings of an apology.

In the middle of Marisol's first vowel sound, Annie kicked her chair back until it slammed into the island with a *thwack*! "Holy shit! Uh, I mean eureka? This specimen only has forty-four chromosomes!"

Despite Annie's excitement, some humans existed absent a pair of chromosomes, twenty-two pairs versus the typical twenty-three. "Could be fused—"

"Nothing's fused. Look at it. It's gorgeous."

Marisol bent over the computer screen too. Her shoulder bristled against Annie's. On the monitor, there was nothing but slightly bent chromosomes resembling larvae. "And?"

"The chemical compound at its fifteenth chromosome? Haven't seen that level of cellular regeneration in humans. Starfish, however..."

Ridiculous. Marisol chortled. "This person is part starfish?" She faced Annie's profile.

"This person might not be homo sapien. What we might be looking at is the next step in our evolution." Annie turned to Marisol. Behind her glasses, a single eye twitched. It probably was from screen strain or a nutrient deficiency from living off microwavable noodles and sugary yogurt, but Marisol shuddered to think the twitch meant Annie found her loophole in stinkin' human cloning.

"Remember the mission," Marisol reminded Annie, tapping her friend's nose before stretching her arms overhead. With the amount of energy spent on the stretch, she was due for some shut-eye. "See you tomorrow."

"I rented a gown for you. They're delivering it right to your door."

"You didn't have to do that."

"I did. You'd get so busy, you'd forget." Annie adjusted herself back in the chair.

Marisol hugged Annie, resting her chin against Annie's shoulder. "You're the only one who looks out for me."

Without breaking her focus on the computer, Annie said, "That's because the last time I remember a man giving you an orgasm, I wasn't dyeing my grays."

Marisol stepped back and cataloged her love life. "I've had..." Nope. Flatline. "Didn't you say science made men obsolete?"

"I said *almost* obsolete. Don't cherry-pick what a doctor says to you."

Marisol laughed. "You don't have gray hair."

"Because I dye it."

Marisol kissed the top of Annie's head and straightened up, readjusting her coat before heading out into the cold.

"I'm not putting on a mask for you," Annie said. "I'm not prepared to escalate our friendship. Yet. And don't be stupid. Help detectives play dress up off the clock."

Marisol nodded and left. Ultimately with Annie around, men, even the ones dressed like the Patron Saint, could go suck eggs. Marisol lived her best life—the opinion of ailing old shopkeepers be damned.

In the hallway, she tapped the button for the elevator. The sorry doors opened, and she stepped in until—Jesus! Her heart leaped to her throat as she gripped the door frame. Her foot hovered over nothing but metal cables and a long, dark drop. Vincent Varian, or whoever was in charge, really needed to fix this thing.

She rushed back to the lab and smacked the glass.

Annie cracked the door open and spoke through the space. "Elevator again?"

"That thing is a deathtrap."

"I'll put in another maintenance request. They insist nothing's wrong. It only happens to you. You're probably irradiated."

"That might explain it. I'm not rich or an alien." Marisol headed for the stairs.

4

Daddy Issues

The sun lowered in the evening sky. Clad in hoodie and leggings, Marisol ran through the city. But not in a straight line. If there was a retaining wall to climb or a cement post to jump over, she took that path.

She hopped off the curb. The No Parking sign rang as she swung around it. She landed in a lot outside her dad's gym. Her mom always had an opinion about how often she worked out, claiming the free-running and boxing made her look ponchado. That insult was of the exaggerated, devastating variety that only mothers like hers could spout. Marisol was athletic, not muscular, and begrudgingly had to wear industrial strength Spandex to hold back her boobs.

While entering, she finished stretching her triceps behind her head. After she unzipped her hoodie, she placed it on a hook over her duffle bag. From her bag, she pulled out some kickboxing gloves and a roll of gauze. Wrapped and strapped, she moved her way to a freestanding punching bag. She began a series of slow, alternating jabs to get the blood pumping into her arms.

The Westside Boxing Club was a converted warehouse with a tin roof and walls. A few boxing bags, some patched with duct tape, hung from the scaffolding in the ceiling, and a handful of freestanding bags circled the single ring in the gym. Though her apparent mission was a good workout, she made it routine to drop in and see how Dad was doing. After he sank his measly retirement into the place, she needed to double-check if the business made out the way he claimed.

As she switched her punch to alternating cross-hooks, she observed her dad in the ring with mitts on his hands, coaching a tall heavyweight boxer. The boxer already had a stream of sweat trailing down his tank top. When he ducked under Dad's rudimentary swing, she recognized the boxer instantly. Detective Tobias Quinlan. She pretended not to check out his glistening shoulder muscles, but she slowed down her punching pace so she could pay more attention to the action. Tobias waved to her, and she flickered a quick smile to play it cool.

Tobias wiggled his hand out of a glove, shook Dad's hand, and crawled out of the ring. Marisol showed off with a jab and cross hook combination.

"I was hoping to see you here," Tobias said.

She stifled a squee, striking the bag with a hinge kick. "Looks like my dad's working you up a sweat."

"This?" He gestured to the sweat soaking his shirt. "All nerves. I'm an Eastsider on the Westside learning how to punch from the dad of the woman I'm interested in."

Her laugh came out so loud that it practically shook the rafters. She forgot she was in a gym—Dad's gym. An embarrassment confirmed by the face Dad made at her. The face that said, "Who is this guy?"

"We should move over to the hanging bag. See if you can actually throw a punch," Tobias said.

"Surprised to see you moving so spryly after you limped out of the emergency room." Marisol pushed the bag to have momentum to work with. She shuffled in place, gearing up for a big swing.

"I had a good nurse."

She rolled her eyes before she showed off with another combination topped with a kick. The bag swung and twirled. Tobias steadied it. "Remind me to never make you mad." He held it against his rippling shoulder and motioned for her to attack.

Between punches and kicks, she asked, "Why are you really here?"

Tobias traded places with her. She held the bag still while he punched. "I like boxing. Gets all life's shit out of the system."

"A lot of that is going around. What's yours?"

Every few words he spoke, the force of his punches pushed his voice louder. "I'm tired of a sixty percent clearance rate putting me near the top of my department." Tobias stood up and wiped the sweat off his forehead. "Every year the city gets 300 murders, and a little over half of them get solved. It's a little disheartening when that's the best we can do."

"I get that. The hospital board is more invested in creating a beautiful brochure to hand out at the latest conference. It's like ever since Grandaddy Varian died, so did the last brain cell of the Varian family. If Vincent just stepped down from his tower..."

"They wouldn't be bosses without being pains in our asses."

"It makes those guys who dress up to fight crime make sense. No one to answer to, just take control and put the law in your own hands." She returned to punching the bag.

"I wouldn't be much of a cop if I condoned vigilantes running the streets in their pjs, but that isn't what's bugging me right now."

"What's bugging you?"

"I didn't get your number. Wouldn't want you to think that my interest in you is strictly business." He smirked, revealing the handsome signs of age around his eyes.

She hoped her workout glow covered up the flattered blush on her cheeks. "That's a little fast. Sure you don't want to leave me hanging for a bit?"

"I'm old-fashioned. When I like someone, I do something about it."

Though he had a carbon-dated flirting style, he wasn't exactly old. Tobias was in decent enough shape to not wear a brace over any of his joints. Was he a fit forty or foolishly hate himself tomorrow because his knees hurt forty? Marisol, no longer punching, asked, "Are you trying to ask me out, old man?"

"Something like that, kid."

Bold and matched her blow for blow? He had to be kidding. "In front of my dad?" Marisol brushed away sweat from her face with her forearm.

"I was thinking when you're done working up a sweat, we could grab a couple of refreshments, and I'd ask you then." He leaned against the bag again and winked.

In his eyes, she saw a hint of blue, a reminder of the Patron Saint. And there was that rush of dopamine again. She shifted her weight from side to side and resumed her jabs and hooks. "Your eyes. They change color. What's up with that?"

"Sectoral heterochromia. They're brown and blue."

"That's a pair of big words coming from a cop," Marisol said.

"I'm a dumb guy that sometimes stumbles into some smart things."

"I'm a smart gal who lets quite a few dumb things into my life."

"Then we'll get along well."

As he grunted and sweated, Marisol shivered from the sudden curiosity of the other noises he made when he was worked up. Particularly, what did she need to do to get him to "Hm" in that growling deep voice he put on?

After the workout, Tobias leaned against his green and rusted sedan, draining the last of the contents of an orange sports drink. "I know a food cart eight blocks from here that makes the best cheesesteaks. Whaddya say? You. Me. A couple of beers. Sit along the Riverwalk and watch the lights?"

Marisol twisted the cap on and off her bottle. "You think I'd like street food and beer on a date?"

"I've been thinking a lot about you. I think if I took you someplace where we can't pronounce half the menu, you'd label me a try-hard dork. I might get a second date if you felt sorry for me. But you, you like things to be real, and I'd really like to take you out for some street food and beers. You'd like that, wouldn't you?"

Marisol nodded as her curiosity from earlier shimmered below her belly. "I would. When?"

"How about right now?"

Marisol's face scrunched up. In a couple more hours, her shift would start. Maybe she'd raincheck the beers and dig into the cheesesteak, but she was soaked in sweat and stunk. She wanted a chance to prove that she could be a knockout outside the ring. Now? It would be all too real. "Maybe some other time—"

"Saturday?"

A night of formal wear and Annie formed into a small disappointment that tugged a tiny fiber of muscle in her chest. "I'm going to Varians' fundraising ball with my bestie."

"I'll tell you what, I got tickets to Rooks' semi-finals, the Legacy Game, next week."

Before she could muster an answer, a black Escalade drove into the gym's parking lot. Four men exited the vehicle. Three men surrounded one, and none came to work out. Marisol recognized the man in the middle with his bald head and sparse mustache above his crookedly molded lips as Izzy, leader of the Westside Shadows. He was the one whose hands stayed clean while Caz served multiple sentences. They entered Dad's gym.

"That's Izzy." Tobias crossed his arms and clenched his jaw.

More muscles in her body threatened to snap. "I know."

"We got some detail monitoring him. Not the greatest guy. But we can't seem to nab him. These kings are never put in check."

There was one thing Izzy's presence meant: Another Novotny man got himself into something he'd have a hell of a time getting out of. "I gotta go." Marisol pulled her hoodie closer around herself.

"I could come with you. Make sure they don't cause any trouble."

"My family is trouble." Tobias's clueless face prompted her to continue, "Casimir's doing multiples up at the Hill for the Shadows."

"The walking scowl, Caz."

Marisol grew heavy with shame. "My brother." She recognized the shock on Tobias's face. Too much work. "You should go. If they know I'm hanging out with a cop, I don't know what they'll do."

"We all got black sheep," Tobias said.

Marisol heard him but didn't listen. She stormed back toward the gym. In the entrance, she crossed her arms over her chest and ground her teeth together.

The Westside Shadows hadn't stayed long. Marisol watched as Izzy shook Dad's hand. Although she stepped to the side to not impede them, the men moved around her before they exited, and Izzy made a kissy face. She squeezed herself tighter and refused to look him in the eye. The heat prickling her skin wasn't her recent cardio, but her blood reaching 212 degrees Fahrenheit. She held her tongue until the Shadows loaded into the Escalade. She turned and stared at Dad, her gaze throwing knives at him.

He put his hands on his hips, his dark eyes shifting and belying his confrontational stance. "What, Mare?"

"What were they doing here?"

"It's nothing." Dad grabbed a bottle of cleaner dangling out of a bucket set on the boxing ring. He sprayed down a standing bag and wiped it.

Marisol would not let him off so easily. She followed him at his every move. "Caz is serving multiple life sentences for them, and it's nothing?"

"Okay, some partners pulled out of the gym, and I'm short on some bills this month. After Caz took the fall for them, Izzy always said he'd look out for us." Dad threw his cleaning rag to the floor.

"How much?"

"Don't worry about it!"

"How much?"

"A couple grand."

She had a little over half of that in her savings. "Two grand? We don't need them!"

"Easy for you to say, Mare. Your life didn't fall out from under you!" Dad ran his chubby fingers through his thinning hair.

"Did you even think to ask if I could help you out?"

"I couldn't do that. I'm not asking my daughter for money."

"But getting the Westside Shadows hooked more into our lives seemed like a good idea? Are you even hearing yourself?"

"I figured I could use Caz for leverage. Get something out of this miserable muck we're in." Dad leaned against the ring. He held his face in his hands. "Just don't tell your mom."

"I won't. I don't want another murderer in the family." Marisol left the gym, disappointed yet not surprised to find an empty parking lot. No Tobias. Bad with the good put her life back into that dour balance she always expected. She pulled her hood up and strapped her gym bag tightly across her chest.

She jogged, slipping around crowds with a jump or a climb. At the nearest ATM, she reached her withdrawal limit. She stuffed the wad of cash in her hoodie pocket and boarded a bus that took her deeper into the west side of Shadowhaven. Buildings with hand-painted signs and bars in the window soon became decaying brick mounds covered in graffiti. She hopped off the bus and continued running before reaching a deli.

Dingy yellow, fluorescent lights cast a jaundiced pall over the deli's worn vinyl booths and peeling pictures of sandwiches. Marisol walked past the counter. A few people recognized her. "Yo Mare!" But she didn't even acknowledge them as she pushed her way past an Employee's Only door.

In the back room, Izzy sat at a table with the men who flanked him at the gym. He ate a torta that left globs of food in the corners of his mouth. One of the bigger men stopped Marisol before she came closer. He flashed the gun in his waistband, a warning to not try anything. It didn't scare her like they intended. A gun was just a fact, like a patient's gushing wound. Freaking out about it did nothing.

"She's cool," Izzy said.

Marisol stepped up to the table and slammed down a wad of cash. One thousand dollars.

"What's up, Mare?" Izzy asked, his voice garbled with bits of sandwich.

"That's part one. I'll have more for you tomorrow." She'd squeeze part two from a payday loan. "Don't come near my family again."

"Pete came to me." He wiped his hands on a napkin and eased back in his chair.

Marisol leaned on the table, hovering over Izzy. "Let's operate like the Novotny men are too stupid to make any decisions. As far as you're concerned, I'm my dad's power of attorney. If he does it again, you see me first. I don't want anyone in my family in your pocket anymore."

Izzy shook his head. "Girl, you act like you're above it, but you're in this. You think your ass got out of this game because you got grit?" Izzy stared at her like a shark circling chum. She said nothing and kept her gaze latched onto Izzy's. "Nah. People left you alone because Caz earned our respect. Caz got you this life, whether you like it or not. And someday, you'll be glad you're in my pocket."

She wasn't sure if she wanted to shout or throw a punch. Her arm muscle spasmed, and she swallowed while deciding.

But fate made the decision. One of the guard's cell phones lit up. "Izzy, Teeth Man is at the car shop."

"Teeth Man?" Izzy wrinkled his nose.

Marisol sighed and headed out of the deli. In the corner of her eye, she caught Izzy and his men unloading a safe with guns.

Outside, the air felt thick. She smelled the change in the atmosphere as flashes of lightning streaked the sky. A storm had arrived, and she needed to head home before work. She ran. Past the graffiti. Past the barred windows. Past the bus stops. Anger fueled her speed. Her feet hit the pavement with power, propelling her faster and farther. Izzy nagged her. She wanted to be free of his grasp. His power. His arrogance. His money. As she ran, she swore she heard angel wings flying above her. What would the Patron Saint do?

At her apartment, she took out Tobias's business card and called the number while she toyed with the pendant on her necklace. "Detective Quinlan? I think something big is about to go down."

5

A Rooftop, A Tear

Marisol reached the end of the sandwich rotation in the vending machine. Dammit, no egg salad, which meant she'd have to go back empty-handed to Shopping Cart Zeke to see if a tuna sandwich could convince him to play nice with the social worker and, more importantly, empty a bed for the next patient.

Luckily, Dr. Foster poked her head around the corner. "Novotny, we got some tough with a broken nose behind curtain two. He's got quite the mouth on him. Thinking you could handle it." Marisol turned the opportunity to an exchange of the pain-in-our-asses. Though Dr. Foster might regret the trade-off—tuna and Zeke versus the curse words personified.

She pulled back the polyester curtain to find Izzy cuffed to the table with a newly splinted nose oozing dark, coagulated blood. Her nerves forgot to move. An officer waited in the corner while Izzy pulled at his cuffs.

"Yo Mare, long time no see," Izzy greeted with a smile. Blood filled in the grooves between his teeth.

Her brain spun like a stuck tire. Whenever she felt this overwhelmed, she broke tasks into increments. Blood. Teeth. Got it. Even an enemy deserved some dignity. Marisol snapped on her gloves and held a small cup of water to Izzy's lips, motioning for him to drink. She held out a pan to spit in. "You look worse for wear."

"They won't be able to keep me in bracelets for long when word gets out that the Shadowhaven PD uses a costumed psychopath to do their dirty work." Izzy scowled in the direction of the police officer, who waited in the corner.

"Costumed?" Marisol asked. Her heart fluttered. Could it be him?

"Alarms sounded off at the car shop. Turns out, something set one of my cars on fire." He spat his words toward the police officer, "I expect someone to investigate that." The officer shrugged in response. Izzy continued, "So, I'm putting out the fire, and before I knew it, something came out of the dark and attacked us. Like a robot or something. Its hand crushed my gun. My legally registered gun crumbled into pieces, but they're trying to nail me with drug trafficking, possessing illegal firearms, and destroying evidence. I'd like to see those howlers stick."

Marisol's mind drifted. Her Patron Saint had flown through the flames and vanquished his foes. Her foes.

She jammed more cotton inside of his nostrils.

"Ow!" Izzy shrieked. "Woman, why are you going all Nurse Ratched?"

The textbook case of schadenfreude dared to wipe the concern off her face. "You will have swelling. Keep it iced and dry. Acetaminophen can help with the pain. In a couple of weeks, we can take this off you."

Izzy pulled at his handcuff. "It was made of the darkness. The police got something working for them."

"We got no such thing," the officer who watched piped up.

Marisol nodded in the officer's direction. He freed Izzy from the exam table and cuffed him behind his back. She slowly removed her gloves and took extra time to wash her hands. As the officer left with Izzy, she called after him, "Where's Detective Quinlan?"

"I haven't seen him."

She followed the officer and Izzy out of the room and out of the ER. Watching the officer guide Izzy into the back of a police car seemed to close a chapter in her life. The car pulled away, and finally, something went right.

A wind gusted around her. The air soon tasted electric. Her gaze followed up the glowing sign bearing the hospital's name. Something moved underneath it. Was it…? Marisol ran into the hospital and retraced her steps back into the darkened clinic, into the room where she had first seen the Patron Saint. She opened the window and stuck her head out. Above her, a figure climbed toward the roof. "Hey!" she shouted.

Marisol bolted out of the room and up the stairs. At each new floor level, her face muscles hurt from her widening smile. Her family was free of Izzy thanks to him. And she needed to see him.

She reached the rooftop and walked out onto the empty helipad. Happy tears trickled down her face. The wind whipped her hair out of its tie, and the strands danced about her face. She stepped to the edge of the roof, searching. Footsteps landed on the helipad.

Marisol turned and faced the figure, the Patron Saint, and instinctively hugged herself for protection. "It was you. You got Izzy."

He nodded. His cape flew behind him in the wind.

"I thought I would never see the day." She stepped closer to him. The cold chilled her tears. "Thank you."

Without a word, he touched her face. His gloved hand wiped the tear from her cheek.

Marisol's mouth parted as she searched for words to say. But she hesitated with the awe of someone stepping into an elaborate sanctuary for the first time. Her heart beat inside her ears. *Badum, badum, badum!*

A helicopter swooped down, the blades roared in her ears and lights scorched her retinas. She ducked, holding her arms to her ears and squeezing her eyes shut. After it landed, she blinked away the spots in her eyes and faced the darkness again. Yet the Patron Saint was gone.

6

The Worst Date

Marisol checked her reflection in the mirror. She couldn't believe that Annie picked this number out, and at this hour on a Saturday night, no place would be open to offer a more sensible alternative. The silver sequin gown hugged her body, displaying every curve, crease, and the divot of her belly button. The neckline's deep V exposed the tops of her breasts, and the string-like straps crisscrossed her back, ending at the dimples above her buttocks. She adjusted her abuelita's cross necklace at her collarbone. "That's right. You need Jesus wearing this dress in public," she said to her reflection.

Marisol tossed her straightened hair back. She finished her look with blood-red lipstick. Now for the real blood. She selected Annie's number on her cell with the full intention of harassing her over the ridiculous dress, but it went straight to voicemail. "Annie! Pick up your phone!"

The only other gown-adjacent attire she owned was a tennis dress with attached shorts. Though showing up in that might be a good laugh, she settled for half naked in silver. With one more glance in the mirror, she put on her worn, oversized coat, officially de-glamorizing her appearance. Her phone rang, and she answered it. "Annie?"

"This is Mr. Varian's driver. I am waiting for you downstairs," an oddly modulating but pleasant feminine voice greeted.

Maybe Annie was already with their ride to the ball. "Does there happen to be an over-caffeinated woman in that car with you?"

"I do not understand the question."

"I'll be right down." She hung up the phone.

During the walk down the stairs to the car, she constructed reasons why Annie didn't pick up. She was in the middle of sticking on eyelashes, or the psychic death glares Marisol sent out because the dress had actually killed Annie.

The backseat of the town car was empty, so Marisol tapped the tinted partition in search of answers.

The glass lowered, and she gasped as it revealed nothing. A voice spoke from all sides of the car. "Your driver aims to serve. How may I help you?"

The wave of the future hadn't exactly reached Marisol's side of Shadowhaven. She had read about driverless cars, but to see an unmanned dashboard in action stunned her like a ghost sighting. "Can you take me to 8th and Chavez?"

"Your driver aims to serve," the voice said. The partition rolled up, and the car took off.

The driver stopped at Annie's apartment. With the spare set of keys, Marisol entered the place. Annie's ball gown hung on her closet door. She hadn't been home. Marisol's stomach knotted, but it was too early to worry. For now. If she hadn't been home, there was only one other place Annie could be—her true home.

The car arrived at the alley behind Varian Family and Research Hospitals near the back entrance. Marisol followed the typical path down the dingy hallway and up the beat-up elevator to the lab, dragging Annie's garment bag behind her. Why hadn't she been answering her phone? Why hadn't she been home today? When Marisol finally turned the corner, she saw Annie through the window. Disheveled and dressed in the same clothes she had worn the morning before, Annie stooped over a stack of old papers. Marisol caught her attention with a wave.

Annie opened the door. "Ball time?"

Marisol said, "You're the worst date, you know?"

Annie resumed her perch over the scattered papers with a grunt.

"Why weren't you answering your phone? I thought something horrible happened." And the dreadful moment arrived—Marisol became her mother.

Annie said, "Phone dead. Can't charge. Been busy." Hours in the lab had worn away her ability to produce multisyllabic words. She studied a paper with brown edges and chewed the end of her pencil.

Marisol put her hands over Annie's eyes, but backed away when she discovered over a day and a half in the lab coated Annie in a funk. "You need a bottle of dry shampoo and a shower."

"I need to read one more thing." Annie gripped onto the sheet of paper.

"We're already late! And I'm dying to tell you about yesterday's shift." Marisol retreated to the counter and attempted to hop on top of it to take her usual seat by the mouse, but the gown impeded any movement that wasn't sultry or graceful. In the cage on the counter, the mouse had a smooth, tumor-free body. "Did you get a new mouse?"

"No." Annie kept her head bowed over the papers.

"Where did its tumors go?"

"Cured. I think." Annie's blank tone belied the scientific revelation.

"What?"

"I think I cured it?" Annie finally looked up.

Suddenly the temperature-controlled room grew hot and stuffy, and Marisol pulled at the collar of her coat. "Oh. That's what I thought you said."

Annie and Marisol raced out of the hospital, having primped with miraculous speed. Annie had showered away the funk of her research bender in the doctor's locker room, and she styled her hair into a simple chignon. Unlike the spectacular gown she had ordered for Marisol, she wore a relatively simpler deep purple sheath gown. Yet Marisol's anger over their dress discrepancy retreated behind the excitement of a possible new discovery.

They entered the town car, and Annie flipped on the overhead light to put on some makeup.

"So?" Marisol prodded. "How'd you do it?"

"The other day, after you saw those beautiful chromosomes. I clo—synthesized the molecular structure of the fifteenth chromosome. Eureka! Put it in my little mousy friend. To my surprise, its tumors disappeared before my eyes."

Marisol laughed and shook her head. "You're pulling my leg. It's a new mouse."

"I swear it's the same one! But I haven't told you the best part."

Marisol mimed zipping her mouth shut.

"I dug up old records. I wanted to know who or what owned those chromosomes. Dr. Varian wrote something down but scribbled over it. Kind of like a government redaction? So, I traced my pencil over it and found out who the chromosomes belonged to." Annie swallowed. She eyed the active dashboard and lowered her voice. "Dr. Varian."

"His chromosomes created a cure-all? We should tell people. Heck, we'll see Vincent tonight."

"Not so fast." Annie placed her index finger over her lips. She gestured her head toward the driverless front seat and whispered, "No cellular decay and hyper-regeneration? Either Dr. Varian did something to himself, or the Varians are some kind of superhuman. A different species, even. Hence, the fewer chromosomes. No matter which option is true, both are reasons for a cover-up." Annie gripped Marisol's arm. "Do you know how Dr. Varian died?"

Marisol shrugged.

"Skiing accident in the Alps almost fifteen years ago." Annie air-quoted on the word accident. "News said an avalanche threw his body, along with his wife's, down a steep crevasse. They never found them. You can read all about it. I know I have." Annie stopped putting on makeup and pulled her faux fur stole close around her. "Their caskets were empty at the funeral. Dr. Varian became something or was something. Something worth hiding. And the conspiracy got him."

Perhaps rich and radioactive?

"You're next then?" Marisol teased before chuckling to herself.

"I'm not paranoid," Annie said, returning to a normal volume. She looked out the dimmed windows of the car. "But I bought a gun a while back."

"It's Occam's razor. The easiest explanation is the right one. Who really benefits from hiding research? Conspiracy theorists always say follow the money. If Varian had an ability or genetic component that could be replicated for therapeutic benefits, there would be so much money. Why would they want it to go away? It makes zero sense."

"Who benefits?" Annie counted on her fingers. "Population control. The world economy. Shadow governments." Annie sighed and put her compact in her purse. "How much longer until we're there?"

The sprawl of the city faded as space grew between streetlights. "Reaching city limits. Five minutes?"

"Good. I have five minutes to rehearse in my head exactly how I'm going to ask *the* Vincent Varian for a sample of his DNA." Annie sighed. "What did you want to say about your day?"

Marisol shrugged. "Nothing." She never imagined someone outdoing her Patron Saint versus Izzy story, but compared to Annie's, her story felt small.

The car pulled into the Varian estate, joining a short line of other latecomers in the roundabout driveway. A row of hulking Corinthian pillars marked the palatial home's main entrance like a behemoth's smile. Marisol and Annie walked up the entrance's stairs. Marisol's gaze traveled up the pillars to a phrase carved above them. AUT VIAM

INVENIAM AUT FACIAM. The words emblazoned the estate with something ancient and ominous. They should've entered a darkened cave, but, to Marisol's surprise, the foyer inside radiated gold.

Annie handed a uniformed attendant her invitation. "Dr. Park and guest." The attendant crossed them off a list. To be known only as "guest" hit Marisol like a small jab—the continuing tradition of anonymous recognition of Marisol and people like her always received.

The invitation attendant's white-gloved twin offered to take their coats. Marisol unbuttoned her coat, realizing that some of her buttons hung by a thread. As the attendant helped Marisol out of her coat, she felt a twinge of shame. She should've ditched her shabby coat eons ago like a real grownup. "Sorry we're late," Marisol said, actually apologizing for her coat.

"It's okay. Mr. Varian isn't even here yet." The attendant held Marisol's coat away like a soiled diaper before hanging it up.

A belch rumbled from Annie's stomach. "I need food. Stat." Annie dragged Marisol inside the ballroom. Marisol stared at the room's domed ceiling around the massive chandelier. Every item in the room appeared in shades of gold and cream, except for the grand, red-carpeted staircase. The staircase, where two wings of the estate met, split the ballroom in two. Multiple sets of French doors adorned with heavy tasseled curtains stood perpendicular to the staircase. The doors opened to a terrace that overlooked a garden. Above the treetops, Shadowhaven's skyline glowed in the distance. The riches and excess here mocked those who had so little back in the city. The disparity told Marisol to keep her eyes down and her mouth closed. Although she had to fight the oohs and aahs that threatened to escape her lips at the sight of flaxen swirls of marble shimmering in the soft, warm light.

Most of the attendees gathered around the long tables boasting spreads of fine food or collected around cocktail tables dotted along the room's edges. Like a soggy puzzle piece to the classical ambience, a DJ played a mix of haunted jazz strings with a hip-hop beat, music far too trendy for this older, stuck-up crowd.

And the crowd was a sea of somber—men in traditional black and white tuxedos and women in dark gowns. Marisol's sequins reflected fractals of light that buzzed around her like fruit flies. Dressed for the disco, she searched for a good hiding spot.

Marisol tugged Annie into the nook under the staircase. A server followed them, offering a tray of food. Annie took two canapés, stopped the server from leaving, and took two more, balancing a pile in her hand.

Annie stuffed two of them in her face. With her mouth full, she said, "I knew you could pull that dress off."

"This dress is obnoxious."

"Please. You wear less when you work out." Annie looked forlornly at her empty hand and waved over another server. She chowed down on another canapé. "You don't realize how much you got it. One promenade around here, you'll have someone offering to take you to Bermuda."

Marisol crossed her arms to hide her cleavage. "So, you wanted to pimp me out tonight."

"No! You're the bravest person I know, and I thought you should wear something, well, brave." She popped another morsel of food into her mouth and pushed it into the inside of her cheek. "And you're wearing it, so a part of you thinks it's a killer dress too."

"I'm the only one here dressed for a party."

"In all fairness, I imagined this crowd would be exponentially more festive."

"Doctors, scientists, and the people who fund them are festive?"

"Don't poke holes in my logic. I either invented a wonder drug, discovered a new species, or all the above. I want to celebrate."

Marisol relaxed her arms and chuckled. "Congratulations."

Inside the nook's protection, a series of family portraits of the Varian family hanging on the wall drew Marisol's focus. In one, a balding man resembled Albert Einstein's hairless twin with sagging jowls and sad, brown puppy dog eyes. He sat on a chair and looked straight ahead while a young blue-eyed man stood behind him with his hand placed on the old man's shoulder. It was labeled Leonard and Vincent.

Annie studied the portrait. "The Varians had a legacy of discovery and scientific progress. This one, Leonard, the nuclear physicist, was a wunderkind of the Manhattan Project and started the hospital. Before him, great-grandad Varian worked with Marie Curie. It's all so cool. And Victor was an amazing medical doctor, but Vincent... gave operational control to the board a little over a year ago. Everything but the side project, some say. All he knows is how to spend the family money. How the mighty have fallen." Annie sighed and positioned herself before a photo of Dr. Victor Varian and his wife, Staci. Annie's gaze lingered over the photo, showing how much she admired the doctor.

Marisol squinted at the portrait of the two men. "They look nothing alike."

"Looks must've skipped that generation because they are definitely strong with the doctor. He could be Vincent's twin, except," Annie lowered her volume to a whisper, "he'd be the smart one."

The portrait hypnotized Marisol. "It must've been painted after the ski accident. Their eyes. They look so sad."

"Let's move. There's shrimp cocktail." Annie yanked Marisol away.

Before making it too far into the ballroom, Annie stopped and gasped. "Don't look. My kind-of, sort-of archnemesis from undergrad is over there."

"What?"

"Frickin' Sandra Farraday. Dr. Farraday. I only had a few classes with her, but she had this interpretation of string theory that was positively..." Annie's eyes crossed.

Marisol spotted a woman with a sharply angled bob in a black velvet gown. "That good, huh?"

"I thought she was all the way in Switzerland working for that particle accelerator." Annie's eyes widened, and she gripped Marisol's arm. "What if she's working on Varian's secret project? I'll find out." Annie cleaned her glasses and smoothed her chignon just so. "She probably doesn't remember me." She headed toward Dr. Farraday.

Marisol stuck by the spread of food and watched as Annie grew livelier and less aware of her growing distance between them. Annie's laugh traveled across the room, a sign that she and the other doctor had recalled an inside joke. One that Marisol would never get.

Vulnerable in the middle of the room, Marisol snuck to its edge and resolved to walk along the shadows, away from the crowd.

Flashes from photographers' cameras popped over and over into a roar. The crowd applauded. Vincent Varian and his date, a young model made famous on social media, descended the stairs. She looked like a confection. Her hair dyed bright baby blue with a matching tight satin dress.

Although Marisol disdained the billionaire, in person and free of the armor of a coat, gloves, and sunglasses, he appeared all-the-more dashing. His tuxedo was tailored close to his body, emphasizing his broad shoulders. Definitely a middleweight. And the small cleft in his chin, Marisol couldn't help but admit, was especially charming.

From the stairs, Vincent announced, "I hosted this party to emphasize the many ways our hospital and research have saved lives." After years of prep school and surrounding himself with the country's elites, he sounded like no one else in Shadowhaven with his crisp consonants and the occasional elongated vowel. Though deep and full, his voice grated her ears as he seemed to try so hard to sound sophisticated. He continued, "We're here to raise awareness and fund treatment for our world's most precious lives—children. In bringing together our doctors, our researchers, and Shadowhaven's elite, we hope to raise enough money so that no child who walks in the doors of our hospital, regardless of ability to pay, is without the finest care. Cheers to you and your hard work. To the finer people!"

People cheered, and the music continued to play. Vincent's date posed awkwardly against the ballroom's filigree. A dutiful photographer snapped multiple angles of the blue-haired woman. It seemed she would've been willing to be anyone's date as long as she got a good photo. Annie would find this hilarious. Where was she? Marisol traipsed the room to find her.

She found Annie finishing a flute of champagne and grabbing another from the conveniently stationed server's tray. A semi-circle of stately elderly people hovered around Annie, as if she was the hired entertainment for the night. Annie's face had gone pale, and she fidgeted with her champagne glass. If Annie's nerves and the air of nobility from these people were any indication, Annie stood before the board. And their names were Fluffy Brows, Jowly Paunch, White Updo, Skeleton, and Dad 'Stache. Not really, but Marisol rolled with the information available to her.

Fluffy Brows threw his head back and laughed. He pushed Skeleton toward Annie. "Meet this wonderful young lady who continues Dr. Varian's research."

"Hi, I'm Dr. An Jung Park or Annie, rather. I experiment in pharmaceuticals but specialize in coding chemical compounds to particular genetic traits." Annie offered her hand to Skeleton, who shook it. And squeezed it and shook it again.

Marisol fluttered her eyes at Annie, psychically communicating, *These people are weird.*

Skeleton clenched his teeth together in a forced smile. To be all the more skeletal, my dear.

"How do you align chemicals with genetic traits?" Fluffy Brows waved his hands in the air as if he conjured the answer from Annie.

Annie sipped the champagne and rubbed her lips together. "In my work, we've looked at the genetic properties of superhumans. Not the type you'd read fantastical stories about in the comics, but you know, people with exaggerated physical characteristics such as overactive muscle development or extra lung capacity. We've studied the molecular properties of their DNA to synthesize and replicate those traits to help chronically ill lab mice. We haven't been successful so far because cellular respiration loses any gains. But if I found the right molecular compound that made cells impervious? Varian Research could possibly create noninvasive, consumable gene therapy. Or a shot of perfection." Annie finished her champagne. "Disease-free. Ageless. We could do it. In my lifetime. Maybe even within the year."

Every one of the board members stifled a laugh. All but Skeleton. Annie's head drooped. Afraid that Annie felt insulted, Marisol touched her back. "What is it?" Annie asked.

Marisol whispered in Annie's ear, "I thought you wanted to keep your whole cure-all on the down-low."

"I said it was possible. Under promise, over deliver. Or do you need a lesson on how to suck up to these blue bloods?" Annie whispered back.

Marisol forced a closed-mouth smile in the board's direction and guided Annie to another part of the floor. "Those people creep me out. Especially Skeleton."

"Skeleton?"

"That one with the slicked back hair, thin lips, and exaggerated zygomatic bones? He looked like a walking skeleton and touched you for way too long." Marisol pointed in the direction of the member who she had named "Skeleton."

"Zygomatic? Look who's still proud of her higher gross anatomy grade. You can say cheekbone like the rest of us. And that's Mr. Ruthven."

"The C.O.O.?"

"He's actually the second most powerful man in the room. If he wants to touch me with his clammy, white hands, I'd let him if it means I keep my funding." Annie stopped a waiter with champagne and helped herself to another glass. "I think if I talk to him long enough, I'll get the courage to ask Varian for his tissue. Even if that courage is liquid." Annie moved her way through the crowd, disappearing from Marisol's sight.

Marisol picked at her freshly painted red nails. When she looked up, she saw Vincent Varian, who was stuck in a tuned-out stare at the margins of the party, ignored by his blue-haired date. Marisol's gaze must've snapped him into the present. She watched him blink away his blank stare, and he returned a smile in her direction.

Heat rose from her chest to her cheeks, an embarrassing, visceral reaction. It frustrated her that handsome looks in a tuxedo overrode her repulsed feelings. To cover up her reaction, she gazed down again.

She searched for comfort and found it in the background music. Marisol bobbed her head to the beat and grew irritated at the partygoers who were far too occupied chatting and seeming important to appreciate the music. If this was a block party, there would be people dancing. Here, it seemed people didn't want to give away that they could be joyful.

Marisol caught herself moving a bit too rhythmically. Uh-oh, guess who else noticed? Vincent. He looked at her and seemed to chuckle. After adjusting his bowtie and buttoning his jacket, he headed in her direction. Marisol bolted to Annie and jerked her away from her conversation. She dragged Annie to a large vanity room, safe from Vincent Varian.

7

Ready For Battle

The door to the vanity room closed with a click. Annie broke from Marisol's grasp. "Are you going to be like this all night?"

"Everyone here gives me the creeps," Marisol said.

"They're harmless. I invited you because I thought you'd have a good time."

Marisol crossed her arms. "I didn't think I'd spend the night watching you yukking it up with every Ph.D. and M.D. in the room." She looked down at her feet, sinking from her loose-button shame that melted into the root cause: the shame of quitting. "I'm sorry I'm not good enough for your little club."

"You are good enough, Marisol, damn it! Just because you don't have a doctorate, doesn't mean you're not twice as smart as those people out there." Annie put a hand on each of Marisol's shoulders.

"But you can't turn your nose up at them and expect them to include you."

Marisol pursed her lips together. She didn't come with a crank for a reason. She shouldn't have to wind herself up and perform to matter.

"If it bothers you so much, you should go back to med school," Annie said.

"I can't." Marisol could taste the quickly forming tears. She sat on a padded bench in front of a vanity mirror.

Annie sat next to Marisol and nudged her. "Why? You're Miss Shark, always swimming forward, never looking back?" Annie's laughing face met Marisol's somber face in the mirror. Her expression changed to match Marisol's, and she sighed.

"Who is going to waste another chance on someone who already had one?" The jagged edges of Marisol worry lodged inside her throat.

"You left for good reasons," Annie mumbled.

"I'm not going back to med school."

"Then relax. Grab a glass of champagne. You seem like you could use one." Annie patted Marisol's back as she stood.

Marisol, stuck in a powder room licking her pride wounds, ensured she would not relax. "I won't," she warned in a bratty singsong.

Annie threw her head back. "Ugh." She opened the door to go back to the ballroom. "Stay in here the entire night for all I care, Novotny."

Marisol turned to the bathroom mirror and touched away the tears in her eyes with a tissue, careful not to smudge her mascara. In the mirror, she noticed Vincent's date stretched out on a lounger, clicking through her phone in a drone-like fashion.

Marisol turned to his date and swallowed back her tears. "I know you from somewhere."

The all-blue woman rolled her eyes and set down her phone. "Whit DeWinter, content creator and influencer."

"Marisol Novotny, nurse. So, you're dating Vincent Varian?"

"Dating is such an antiquated term. We are consciously intertwining lifestyles."

Hearing the ridiculous phrase lifted Marisol's spirits. She smirked. "What's that like?"

"We met last summer taking 'shrooms and dancing at that one desert musical festival. So much fun. Highly recommend. I heard all the colors of the rainbow." Whit held her phone to her heart, snorted, and looked back at her phone. "But tonight…"

Morbidly curious, Marisol asked, "What's wrong tonight?"

"The last I saw him we were smoking peyote in his air-conditioned tent. Tonight, he's so boring." Whit stopped scanning her phone and furrowed her eyebrows. "I think he's a little sad. It must be all the old people here. Their idea of a party is eating something gross that costs a lot. I'm telling you, knowing Vincent Varian is a head trip. It's like meeting two different people."

Marisol nodded. The Patron Saint awakened every one of her nerves. One set tingled with admiration, another with fear. As Tobias, she felt the admiration and fear at the quietest volume level. It was as if the costume brought out the alluring element—the part that she desired.

"Who are you avoiding here?" Whit asked.

Marisol grimaced, unsure of how to answer the question because her answer could've been "Everyone" or "Vincent Varian." She chose the safe answer. "Not avoiding. I'm just touching up my makeup."

Marisol needed out. She hurried through the ballroom. Her heels unfortunately clomped as she escaped through the French doors and onto the empty terrace. As she leaned against the balustrade, she focused on the lights of Shadowhaven. That's where she belonged, and the terrace was the closest thing to home in Varian's estate. Although she shivered, the cold equally invigorated her compared to the inside's stuffiness. Marisol could stay out here forever, admiring the city lights from afar.

The hair on her arms stood on end. She touched her cheek, reliving her tear being wiped away by his hand. She closed her eyes. He'd hold her against his body, a solid wall of warmth.

A voice shattered Marisol's dream. "It's too cold of a night to be standing out here alone." A familiar voice. Vincent Varian.

She hiked up her shoulders to protect her ears. "Sorry. I came out here to be alone. I don't think I'll make good small talk."

"No small talk? Big talk it is then. The meaning of life, geopolitics… that dress."

Marisol looked over her shoulder. The light from the ballroom highlighted half of his mischievous, cat-like grin. She bit her cheek to stop her smile from forming. She appreciated a smart aleck retort but not from him.

"That dress fits you well," he said.

She turned back to face the skyline and sighed. The muscles in her back tensed, preparing for a cheesy come-on.

He added, "It looks like chain mail. Like you're ready for battle. Fitting for a bold risk-taker like yourself, Nurse Novotny."

The fancy-tissue and hangover incident must've left an impression. She released the inside of her cheek, and the tiny smile she had held back crept across her face. "You remembered my name."

"I saw it on the guest list."

Her name wasn't there. He must have asked about her. Marisol played into the ruse. Let this playboy think he made a slam dunk before he fell flat on his back. "Not many nurses on your guest list. For a hospital ball."

"And not too many bold risk-takers. For being Shadowhaven's finer people."

"Maybe you should invite more nurses."

"If they look like you, I'll consider it."

Marisol scowled, skin burning from Vincent's caustic irritation. "Why should someone's appearance tell you their worth?"

Vincent dumped his champagne over the balustrade. "We choose how the world sees us."

"Like how you want the world to see you in your tuxedo and ballroom when you could easily donate a hundred times the amount this party could raise and wouldn't look twice at your bank statement? It's almost like this ball isn't for saving sick children but for everyone's ego."

"If our egos offend you so, why are you here?"

"Good question." Marisol turned around. "Good night, Mr. Varian." She headed toward the door.

"Please don't go." Vincent followed her. "I'm enjoying the conversation."

He had a funny view of enjoyable conversation. Fine. She needed a verbal punching bag, and Vincent seemed up for the challenge. "You don't understand. If you walked a mile on the Westside—or hell, a block—in your dress shoes that haven't seen the crease of a day's work, you wouldn't be among the elites, congratulating yourselves on a job well done. You'd hang your head in shame because there are plenty of children left behind in my city.

Left behind by a system that leaves them fighting for scraps and rewards you with obscene wealth."

Vincent put his hand on the door handle. "Long live the revolution. Give me a moment to lock up the silverware." His tone oozed with sarcasm.

If he went inside, she was definitely staying outside. She stomped back to the edge of the terrace. "That's what you all think. We point out injustice, and you think we're going to storm your palace with pitchforks."

"Pitchfork doesn't seem your style. Your dress suggests that you'd lure me with your beauty and stab me in the back."

Oh please. She narrowed her eyes.

"Stab me in the front?"

"I wouldn't do that." Marisol had been particularly prickly to him, but then, had she been prickly to everyone tonight? She toyed with Abuelita's cross necklace to chase away her discomfort. Any second now, he would leave, and she'd return to normal—alone on a terrace in the dead of winter. She whispered, "Si no puedes decir nada bueno, no digas nada en absoluto."

Vincent walked back to her at the balustrade. "You were saying?"

"Something my abuelita would say to me. Sort of like if you can't say anything nice, don't say anything at all."

"Which is why you're out here alone at a party."

"Something like that." Marisol looked up from her necklace.

He looked down at his empty glass. "Tenía que ser dicho y tu lo dijiste."

It needed to be said, and you said it. Marisol straightened. Despite the gossip noise, she knew nothing about Vincent Varian. "My friend and I talked about you. You don't make a lick of sense to us. How could someone from such a line of scientists and doctors become... you?" Vincent's expression seemed to relish the implied insult. However, Marisol's gaze focused back on the city lights above the trees, toward home. "If I had what you had, I'd want to change the world." Marisol faced Vincent, who looked at her as if a defensive layer had shed away, from sparring to surrendering. Did she wound him? "I'll take that as my cue to shut up."

He chortled and smoothed his hands over the top of the balustrade. "I don't mind. Keeps my ego in check."

Marisol looked back inside the ballroom. Whit DeWinter played around with the DJ's headphones and turntable. She laughed, and the DJ seemed happy, too. "Seems like your date is accomplishing that just as well."

Vincent shook his head. "Ah yes. A match made in PR Heaven."

"She's making you look like a chump."

His expression turned steely. "I can handle it."

His sonorous voice rattled her nerves. A shiver traveled through her body and ended in a tight sensation below her belly. The cold must be getting to her, not Vincent's voice. She squeezed her thighs together. Please, not that voice.

Annie stumbled onto the terrace. "There you are." She sounded joyous. Perhaps the champagne killed enough brain cells to forget their argument. "And I see you've found—Holy Mother of God—Mr. Varian."

Thank the Lord. Drunk Annie offered the escape she needed from the siren allure of Vincent. "C'mon Annie. We should get you home." Marisol grabbed Annie by the arm and pulled her toward the door.

Annie finagled away from Marisol and staggered toward Vincent. "Mr. Varian, I would like a sample of your DNA."

"Annie, we're leaving!" Marisol had to stop Annie before she further embarrassed herself.

"I'd be interested in replicating an experiment of your father's. With your DNA."

"For what ends?" Vincent laughed, but the tremor in it signaled that he might call security.

"For scientific progress!" Annie raised her arms to the sky, and her declaration echoed through the night.

Marisol turned to Vincent, apologizing. "Did I mention we're leaving?"

"Stop by my lab, anytime. If I need to twist your arm, I'm sure I could get Marisol to come along. Make it a date." Annie snorted with laughter.

Marisol struggled to maneuver Annie through the party, but she gathered their belongings in the foyer and dragged her drunken companion inside the car home.

And safe from Vincent Varian.

Interlude

You strike out. The beautiful woman in the silver dress leaves the party, and your young blue-haired date snuggles up to the floppy-haired DJ. Shouldn't you go lick your wounds in booze and drugs like any other poor little rich kid?

Maybe you are high, though. You say you want more control. All this time, you've stepped away from your responsibilities. You've cried about living in the shadow of two dead men, father and grandfather. What shadow? I was in charge of your most successful year. Reined in your wasteful spending. It should be my name on that hospital. Bloodsucker would look great in lights.

It doesn't have to be this way. If you opened up about your secret project, we could build an empire. We could be the richest men on earth. I shouldn't have to coax desperate doctors to tell me your secrets. I want to stay on the straight path, but you keep stepping on me.

The world needs your secret project and the goofy little doctor at the center of it. If you only cared about your future the way you care about gaining the attention of beautiful women.

And you say, "Since I do care about my future, perhaps I enjoy beautiful women more than I enjoy money. Live a little."

Sooner than later, you'll wish you hadn't easily dismissed me. Do you know what's coming? A big sandpaper dick from Manila to fuck everyone. I'm bringing it, of course, but I could also end it. And that secret side project sounds like the perfect ending. See how I bring out everyone's best?

8

Chemical Reactions

Marisol pulled Annie out of the car. "Wait twenty minutes," she said to the empty driver's seat.

"Your driver aims to please," the computerized voice replied.

She hobbled inside, bolstering a barely conscious Annie. Safe in the apartment, Marisol flopped Annie onto her bed, leaving her in her evening gown. She helped take off her shoes, filled a glass of water, and set it and two capsules of ibuprofen on Annie's nightstand.

She sat next to the bed and flipped open a gossip magazine she found. Marisol pored over an article about Vincent buying an overripe banana duct taped to a wall at an art auction for over a hundred grand. She twisted her face. The idiot in this article didn't remotely resemble the man at the ball tonight.

Annie's breath became steady and deep. She would make it through the night but hate her morning. Marisol put on her worn, oversized coat and headed outside to an empty street. She checked the time on her phone. She'd been twenty-two minutes. Artificially intelligent drivers were excruciatingly literal.

According to the app on her phone, a hired car would be awhile. She could make the walk four times while she waited. As long as she kept to the main street, she'd have an uneventful and brief walk home.

Outside, the streetlight flickered on and off again to her annoyance. Interludes of darkness quickened her pace. Her high heels clicked louder.

She toyed with her phone in the pocket of her coat. She should call Tobias. Maybe he'd invite her over, but she'd keep the dress on. If he saw her in it, he'd flip.

Even the next streetlight went light, dark, light, dark, light, dark.

A gangly man emerged from the shadows. His hood draped over his face and a handkerchief over his mouth. "Gimme the purse."

She scoffed but handed over the tiny purse she used just for that night. It only held her lipstick and a twenty. The guy wasn't going to make out with a lot.

"And your coat."

"This old thing?" Or actually the phone in her pocket?

"The coat!" He pointed at her with an object. The strobing streetlight reflected off the edge of a knife.

As if she were the artificial intelligence, she immediately unbuttoned her coat. The night's cold grew sharp against her exposed skin, and in that dress, she exposed a lot of skin. Her coat felt like armor, and she would not lose her dignity any more than she already had. She unbuttoned the penultimate button and shifted her body weight lower and swung her right fist, landing a hook in the man's jaw. As he reeled back, she started to run. Her delicate heels and hugging dress painfully reminded her they could not handle her typical gazelle-like strides.

She stopped to undo the strap of her heel. Bare feet might fare better on cold, uneven cement. Before she freed the strap from the tiny buckle, she felt a strong tug at her coat and ripped herself free, thanks to those loose buttons. The coat flew behind her. Marisol didn't enjoy a long enough of an escape before rough hands grabbed the back of her neck and squeezed the breath from her throat. Marisol gasped for oxygen. The man swung Marisol's body into a brick wall of a building, slamming her head against the bricks.

She staggered back in pain and reached to touch her head. But something stabbed into her neck. She reflexively grabbed at the object. The mugger pulled at her abuelita's necklace. With another yank, the strand broke. Her vision grew fuzzier and fuzzier. Blood trickled into her eyes. Her legs turned into jelly, and she hit the ground.

A dark blur jumped on top of the mugger.

"Are you okay?" the Patron Saint asked.

"I'm peachy." She passed out to the sound of fists beating flesh.

She woke up with a pounding headache, so she touched the source of the pain, feeling a bandage. Someone had good first aid skills. She rubbed her neck. Her abuelita's necklace was gone. Opening her eyes, she searched for something familiar. Her roving gaze confirmed she lay on a wrought-iron bench bolted to the roof of her apartment, and a blanket draped over her. A gust of cold wind pierced her, so she drew her blanket closely around her.

It wasn't a blanket but a cape.

She jolted up. Sitting on the opposite side of the rooftop was the Patron Saint. He appeared like a floating jawline and a set of eyes. His body blended into the shadows, but his eyes glimmered blue. He was her Patron Saint.

His voice was deep and husky like a growl. "Glad to see you're okay."

"I almost got him," she said. A joke, but he didn't laugh.

"Foolish to pick a fight with someone strung-out on B'Lee, but you're talking coherently. I doubt you have a severe concussion. You should get some rest." He stood upon the ledge. "Keep the cape." He rocked his weight back to prepare to jump. And disappear from her again.

"Wait!"

He hesitated.

"I want to thank you." She stood, dropping the cape to the ground. Her deep breath heaved her breasts upward. Every vein in her pulsed with wanting. His gaze moved down and quickly back up. She cracked a smile, finally glad that Annie rented her this dress.

He stepped down from the ledge and cleared his throat. "Your words are enough."

"Sure." She rolled her shoulders back and held out her hand. "But I want to shake your hand. A little contact doesn't hurt anybody." Though it might hurt her. Hand on hand wasn't the contact she talked about.

"You were in danger. In danger, your brain releases chemicals that make you experience a rush of feelings." He stepped closer to her. "Lust, for instance. I couldn't take advantage of you after being in danger."

"That's what this is? A chemical reaction?"

He moved even closer. "Most certainly." She felt the heat of his breath.

"Did you feel a chemical reaction? When I saved you? Don't you want to thank me?" She lowered her eyelids and tilted her chin, offering her lips to him.

"Or shake your hand?" His gloved hand took hers.

She opened an eye, searching for a clue to tell her where her kiss had gone. He pulled her hand to his face. Then, on the inside of her wrist against her pulse, he kissed her. His lips felt warm and soft against her cold skin. A sigh traveled from her mouth, vaporizing into the air.

He moved from her to the edge of the rooftop. She reached out. "Could I convince you to stay awhile? You and me? A couple of beers? Like you talked about?"

"Like I talked about? I'll have to take a rain check." He smirked before taking a running leap off the ledge.

She gasped and ran to the ledge. No way could a man handle that kind of jump. As she looked down, she watched him sprint into the shadows. "Tobias?"

9

Head Wounds All Around

Marisol needed a real day off. Not a day off consisting of numbing her headache with pills and scrounging the last of her cash to replace her stolen phone.

After couch diving and a trip to the coin machine at the supermarket, she had her new phone in hand, but she wouldn't complete her mission until she headed in the direction of the police precinct to file a report. Probably for her insurance agent to do nothing but wipe his ass with, but it was one of those things. If she didn't file a report, there would be hell to pay. Or a grand. But hell felt more accurate as the recent events of her life depleted her savings account. She pulled her black stocking cap lower to cover the bandage on her head and wore an oversized gray Shadowhaven Rooks' basketball sweatshirt that an ex-boyfriend left behind in her apartment long ago.

The memory of the Patron Saint mere hours before warmed the inside of her wrist. Was Tobias at the precinct? Don't be a little girl. Of course, he wouldn't be working. It was Sunday.

Before crossing the street to the precinct, she glimpsed her reflection in a parked car's window. What if she saw Tobias? Compared to her dress the night before, she appeared a sorry sight. She had to think quickly, so she ran her fingers through the ends of her hair and put on lip balm. The bulky ex-boyfriend's sweatshirt had to go, so she took it off and tied it around her waist. Her Henley, a utilitarian layer, served little against the cold. She rubbed her arms together as she marched up the stairs into the precinct.

Inside, the dull greeting from the officer at the front desk calmed her foolish notion of Tobias being there. But after the officer handed her a copy of the filed report, she dared to ask, "Is Detective Quinlan in today?"

The officer walked her over to Homicide and opened the door a crack. Marisol peered inside the department. Everything inside appeared gray and reeked of stale coffee. The overhead lights were off, clouding the room in shadows and the smoggy haze of veiled daylight. With the way the sparse Sunday crew slumped at their desks, they all must've been nursing hangovers.

Surrounded by piles of file folders, Tobias bent over a computer keyboard, stabbing away at the keys.

Marisol greeted, "Hey Tobias!"

He startled and turned his head toward the door. "Kid."

She walked to his desk and watched a few detectives straighten and spring to life with smiles and a few snickers. Did women visit Tobias often at the precinct? She studied his desk for an answer, but he didn't have any photos. Not like the other desks.

With zero views into his personal life, she scanned over Tobias's work. There wasn't much to see. What appeared to be crime-scene photos, important documents, and file folders were mashed into uneven stacks.

Marisol propped her hip against the cluttered desk. "I didn't think you'd be working today of all days."

"Putting in overtime. I must say, this is a pleasant surprise." Tobias leaned back in his chair, extending his legs and crossing his arms behind his head.

"I had to file a report. Someone um..." Marisol hesitated. First, because over her lifetime, she had developed a survivor's instinct for under-embellishing the truth. The tactic prevented people's polite intrigue from becoming pity. Last because she liked how he smirked as she struggled to cook up a half-truth. She pulled her stocking cap firmly in place and said, "Someone pickpocketed my phone."

Tobias maintained his relaxed posture when he cracked, "That sucks."

Marisol rubbed the inside of her wrist and wanted to say everything. "He's you. Just admit it!" But if her instinct pointed her in the wrong direction—that the Patron Saint wasn't Tobias? She'd be a girlish fool. Now, if her instinct pointed in the right direction...? Without the dress, she felt a babbling rush of nervous energy. "What are you working overtime on?"

"Cross-checking some of Narcotic's work with mine in hopes of getting a conspiracy charge thrown in Izzy's way."

"Cross-checking? You don't look like a pencil pusher." As a heavyweight, he looked more like the guy who swung the ax that felled the tree that became the pushed pencils.

"Welcome to actual police work."

She nodded to the piles. "All this thanks to my tip?"

"Sure." Tobias sat forward and ran his hands over his face. "I'm gonna sound like a jerk, kid, but getting Izzy? It wasn't because of your tip."

The news hit like a gut punch. "Oh."

Tobias hunched over in his chair, resting his elbows against his knees. "I've been getting outside help, but the work never ends. I mean, Izzy'll make bail tomorrow. And when he's on trial, he'll be a first-time offender sentenced to piddle and squat. He'll be out on parole in no time. And this whole mess?" Tobias gestured to the piles on his desk. "It's like there are chess boards within chess boards. We thought we had ourselves a king, but he's someone else's pawn." Tobias grabbed a baggy containing a burnt shard of Varian pharmaceuticals packaging from his desk. He smacked it against his palm before flicking it back on the messy pile.

"Who do you think Izzy's working for?" Marisol asked.

"I'm thinking this city's gangs are all working together, at least, to sneak a pretty sizable and quality drug supply under our noses. You gotta admire it. A United Nations of heroin. Just don't tell Narc I did their jobs for them. They hate it when I do that. My only joy is the big pain in my lieutenant's ass I'll become Monday."

The belligerent patient from a few days ago and his ominous warning echoed through her head. That "the Bloodsucker" controlled everything in the city. "It wouldn't be this Bloodsucker guy I've heard about?"

The color drained from Tobias's face. "What do you know about that?"

"Nothing. Only what that patient said." She shuddered. Izzy, the man she believed orchestrated the pain and frustration of the Westside, took orders from someone far more powerful? It would be best to not think about it. She crossed the room toward a whiteboard full of names to distract herself. Most of the names were written in red. The ones named John Doe and Jane Doe stood out the most to her. "Lots of names," Marisol said.

"Those are our cases," Tobias said.

How many names had Caz put up there? "Lots of red."

Tobias walked to the board and tapped against the names. "Those are the ones we haven't solved yet. Once they're solved, we put them here in black. They stay there until the end of the quarter."

Marisol tensed, feeling how close he stood to her. "Does the black ever outnumber the red?"

"Someday it will, but there always seems to be more. That's how it is in Shadowhaven. It's hopeless, really. Best I can hope for is a decent clearance rate and one less body buried in the mass grave south of town."

She couldn't believe him. Not after the last two days. Not after a wipe of a tear. Not after a kiss on the wrist. The Patron Saint's actions vowed to make her world a better place. She turned and faced him. "If Izzy messed up that easily, he'll do it again. And out on parole? He'll get more time, and you'll never have to worry about him again." Marisol smiled. A tiny spark in his eyes lifted the gloom off his expression. Now would be the time to say it—she knew who he was. She parted her lips and breathed in.

Her phone rang. Work. They'd ask her to cover someone else's shift. She'd say no—she was so close to her Patron Saint... but emptied savings and couch cushions. Defeated, Marisol resigned to picking up her phone and another shift. "When do you need me?"

"In half an hour," the scheduling nurse squawked on the other line.

"In half an hour?!" The evidently eavesdropping officers pricked up to attention. Civilians in police precincts had an expected level of decorum, which Marisol wasn't displaying. She sighed away her frustration. "I'm on my way."

Marisol pulled her sweatshirt aside before she tucked her phone in her jeans. Sweatshirt boyfriend accused her of being too distant and busy to make anything work. One-sided. Too much work. And she couldn't blame him. Her romantic relationships yielded to either a crisis at work or a crisis at the Novotny household. Falling head over heels for a weirdo in a mask who could swoop in as her schedule saw fit seemed all-the-more reasonable. "I got to head to work."

"I'll walk you to your car," Tobias said.

"I don't own a car."

"Then I'll give you a ride."

"It's not that bad of a walk."

"It is in this weather without a good coat."

She untied the sweatshirt from her waist. She wasn't a child who couldn't dress for the weather. As she pulled the sweatshirt on, she said, "See? I'm okay." But the sweatshirt knocked her stocking cap askew, exposing the white bandage on her head.

"Doesn't look like it." Tobias indicated the bandage.

Marisol shrugged. "What I get for opening a medicine cabinet in the dark." Her face warmed from the lie.

"C'mon, kid. I'll take you in one of our unmarked cars. City's best taxi. As an honest taxpayer, you've already bought it, so you might as well accept." He put on his trench coat that hung off a hook.

She nodded like a bobblehead. A shot of alone time prickled in her throat like a cheap whiskey. Warm and giddy, she followed him outside to a maroon, four-door gas guzzler. The muscle car stood out among the parking lot's basic sedans with its long, smooth body and fat grill. If the car moved forward, backwards, and braked as planned, it would impress her. That it reached freeway speeds in split seconds or power steered around tight corners was gibberish to her. When Tobias started the car and revved the engine, she flopped into the passenger seat with an eye roll. Was that necessary?

In the close quarters from the passenger seat, she picked up his faint scent. The night before, she felt close enough to taste him—like burnt air molecules leftover from a lightning storm. Nothing like that in the car. Here, Tobias smelled of artificial pine.

Tobias maneuvered the car through traffic. When the driving became less hazardous, he asked, "What made you become a nurse?"

"Fell into it. My sister needed the tuition money for a good high school, so I dropped out of med school and landed on my feet."

"You were studying to be a doctor." Tobias tapped his fingers against the steering wheel. The tapping crescendoed into a loud slap. "Damn, I knew you were too smart for me."

Maybe she should follow Annie's advice. "I suppose I could go back to school, but I like being right in the trenches with people, where I know I make a difference." She looked out the window at an old woman waddling to the bus stop with a pull-cart of groceries. The car zoomed by, and she watched a gangly teenager cradling a basketball. The vapor of his breath trailed behind him like car exhaust.

At a stoplight, Tobias asked, "How is Caz your brother? You seem like you're not cut from the same cloth."

She pulled her hands inside her sleeves, afraid Tobias saw in her skin and the pattern of her veins the same hands that Caz had, the fists that crunched bones, the grip that swung bats against bodies. And the finger that pulled triggers.

She stared at the glove box. "When the dock jobs dried up, he felt like Dad wasn't even a man. Enforcing for the Shadows gave him purpose. It made him the tough guy. I'd like to say that he made the wrong decision—that he should've handled life like me, but I didn't have my greatest role model let me down. Another roll of the dice, it could've been me."

The light turned green. "More evidence that I shouldn't make you angry."

"I'm not an angry person." She recoiled, squeezing her limbs together to take up less space. She'd spent her whole life listening to others label her with negative words she was somehow supposed to be flattered by—angry, outspoken, and fiery. But a worry lingered. Was she an angry person?

"I know that, but you could kick my ass." As he rubbed the top of the gearshift, he added, "And I just might let you."

Finally feeling that same heat from last night, she sat higher in her seat. "I wouldn't do that out of anger."

Tobias's mouth twitched at the corners as if he was holding back a smile. "You hungry? We passed a corner store that has the best microwaves in the whole city. Nuclear grade. It shaves off a whole ten seconds of cooking time."

Once she accepted the offer, it wasn't long before they sat on the hood of the muscle car with piping hot cups of noodles in their hands. Stationed on the top floor of the hospital parking ramp, she saw all the people who entered and exited the main entrance of the hospital.

Below, a silver roadster shined like a mirror and stuck out from the dirty street. Someone had strategically parked the car as close to the hospital's entrance as legally possible. The tires appeared centimeters away from the tow zone. Tobias whistled. "Who do you think drives that? Not sure if it takes stupidity or cajónes to street-park that kind of car."

Marisol laughed. "There's only one person in this city that I know has that kind of money and cajónes. Vincent Varian." From their brief interaction last night, Vincent seemed too in control to be completely stupid. Vincent couldn't simply be a fool. As she looked at the shiny, expensive car below, daring to be vandalized or sideswiped, she had a suspicion that Vincent wanted people to think he was stupid. She scratched the inside of her wrist. "What do you think about the Patron Saint? The guy that dresses up and fights crime?"

Tobias guzzled the last bit of noodles stuck to the bottom of the cup. A lone straggler dangled from the corner of his mouth, which he heartily slurped. He wiped his lips with the back of his hand and squinted toward the distance. "I suppose you reap what you sow. If our city makes people desperate, they're going to resort to desperate measures."

"I heard he's a part of a super-cop program."

Tobias huffed out a laugh. "That's a yarn. We can barely pay overtime, let alone a fancy schmancy super-cop program."

She set her cup of noodles on the car hood as her nerves finished off her appetite. "Would you do it? Dress up and fight crime?" Her heart beat faster as she braced in anticipation for the answer.

Tobias looked at her and smiled. "I do every day."

Marisol checked her watch. Her shift would start soon. *Dammit, Tobias, I know it's you.*

Screech! A speeding car from the street below split her eardrums. As she searched for its direction, Vincent Varian exited the hospital and waltzed toward his silver roadster. A black town car bounced over the curb and stopped on the sidewalk with a familiar, rubber-burning squeal. Vincent jumped back to avoid the car.

Tobias sprang from the hood of the car and watched the dumb show with a clenched jaw.

The passenger window rolled down. Vincent shook his head while two burly men in puffy coats exited the backseat and encroached behind him. Between the car and the two men, he couldn't bolt forward to his car or run back to the hospital. One man struck Vincent on the head while the other shoved him inside the black town car, which sped away from the hospital.

"Call 911!" Tobias entered the unmarked car. The engine started, and he turned on his lights and siren.

Her hands shook as she dialed 911. "I'm at the Varian Family Hospital. There's been a kidnapping."

The maroon muscle car crashed through the parking barrier and swerved onto the street.

In the hospital, she wheeled a chair under the shared television on the patient floor. Nothing had come over the dispatch. She stood on the chair to reach the button to change the channel. Maybe the news caught wind.

Nurse Rossi greeted her. "Long time no see."

Desperate channel clicking robbed Marisol of her ability to vocalize niceties. She simply nodded and grunted.

"Picked a good day. Vincent Varian stopped by with an armload of coffee gift cards for the staff. Said it was for Shadowhaven's true finer people." Rossi held up a gift card. "You look like you've seen a ghost."

"I just saw some people kidnap Mr. Varian." She flipped through all the channels. No coverage yet.

Rossi helped her down from the chair and hugged her. "You're freezing. Change into my spares. They arrived fresh from laundry and will warm you right up. I'll check with first responders over dispatch to see if they heard anything."

In the locker room, Marisol ran her hands under the hot water of the sink and splashed her face. Her breath steadied, and she grabbed a fresh set of scrubs from the laundry cart. At her locker, she removed her cold layers and stuffed them inside.

A shiny object caught her attention. She reached in and drew it out. She gasped. It was Abuelita's necklace with its clasp fixed. Marisol looked around. He had been here. The necklace's comfort melted away her fear, and she held in her heart that he would make everything all right.

Outside the locker room, the EMTs wheeled a man in a puffy coat with a pair of gardening shears stuck in his thigh into trauma surgery. The man screamed about being attacked by a monster. She recognized him as one of the men who had kidnapped Vincent.

"I'll take garden shears. You've had enough of craziness." Nurse Rossi followed the EMTs deeper into the hospital.

Spared, Marisol settled into double-checking the medicine log.

"I know you're not supposed to play favorites."

She jumped at the gruff voice.

Tobias leaned over the counter. "But his name is on the hospital, and I told him I knew a good nurse." He turned around and nudged Vincent Varian forward. Vincent held a bunched-up dress shirt to the back of his head. Dots of blood sullied his white, V-neck undershirt.

"Really. I'm fine," Vincent said.

She shook her head. Only Vincent Varian could use a head injury to charm. "Come with me, Mr. Varian. I'll clean you up."

She guided Vincent to the table inside a private exam room, and she washed her hands, put on her gloves, and greeted his dopey smile with a sigh. His siren allure had nothing on her Patron Saint.

She wheeled a stool over to him and sat down. "Mr. Varian, I'm going to clean your wound. The doctor will then examine you to see how we can help you."

"I insist you call me Vincent."

"All right. Vincent."

"It's head wounds all around, I see." He arched his eyebrows and pointed to the Steri-strip on Marisol's head.

She jerked her gaze away from Vincent as the truth of her violent mugging dared to surface. "Lost a battle opening a cupboard. I'm such a klutz." She prepared gauze with a sterile solution. "You need to lie face down."

"Gladly."

She moved the dress shirt from his wound and dabbed at the dried blood. "It's strange. I thought with how much you bled, you would for sure need stitches. They barely made a dent."

"I heal quickly thanks to a daily vitamin infusion. You should try them."

"I'll consider them the next time I get hit over the head," she said with an outpouring of sarcasm.

"When you lose another round to a cupboard."

"Right." She patted his wound dry.

Dr. Foster came in and repeated Marisol's surprise of Vincent not needing stitches. Shining lights in his pupils, the doctor checked for a concussion and asked Vincent basic questions to test if something worse happened to his head. Marisol tried to hold back an astonished expression when he said he was thirty-three. He had seemed younger to her.

"Do you remember how you hit your head?" Dr. Foster asked.

"Struck from behind." Vincent raised his arm and gestured the blow to his head.

"Do you remember what happened after your injury?"

"You wouldn't believe me if I told you."

"I'm an ER doctor, Mr. Varian. You might be surprised about what I'm willing to believe."

Vincent's chin trembled. "They were going to... to..." His voice quivered. "To cut my fingers off with gardening shears if I didn't tell them my secrets. Whatever those could be." He rubbed his face in his hands and whimpered.

Dr. Foster looked at Marisol with pointed eyes, directing her to "do something." Vincent let out a high-pitched hiccough, and his shoulders heaved. Marisol rolled her eyes, grabbed some tissues, and walked over to Vincent, patting him on the back. She handed him the tissues. Instead of taking them, he gripped her hand. He straightened with his composure completely regained. Marisol wrinkled her nose, puzzled as she watched his emotions quickly turn. His eyes weren't even red from crying.

With his sudden resolve, he continued the story. "Once they knew the police were on them, they pulled into a parking garage. Said they were going to switch cars to throw them off. Out of nowhere, a man in a dark cape and mask jumped on the hood. He dented the whole thing. It was inhuman. He punched right through the windshield and ripped the driver from the seat. The car crashed into a wall, throwing me from my seat. I'm not sure if I blacked out, but the next thing I remember is Detective Quinlan pulling me from the car."

Marisol flickered a smile and yanked her hand away from Vincent's. Tobias had to be the Patron Saint.

"I'm glad you're safe, Mr. Varian. You may have an unconventional story to tell, but you don't have a head concussion. Nurse Novotny will tape you up, and you'll be good to go." Dr. Foster left.

Vincent lay back down on his stomach. Marisol taped the cut on his head.

With his chin against his arms, he asked, "Do you think my story is unconventional?"

"Actually, I don't." Marisol glided away on the stool. She looked down, unsure if she should admit it. "I've seen him myself. The Patron Saint."

Vincent sat up. "Do you think he's the real deal? The man you saw?"

"I don't know. This city can wear on you, you know? And I think whatever he is…"

Marisol paused, remembering the repaired necklace in her locker. She rolled closer to the exam table. "He gives me hope." She looked into Vincent's eyes.

Vincent gulped. He blinked, and then his serious expression turned into a smirk. "You lied to me earlier. About your head."

Marisol scooted back. "How did—?"

"Ticks you pick up from people when you deal with a lifetime of sycophants. Lack of eye contact. Strained smile. I see it a lot. People who want something from me tend to lie—"

"I don't want anythi—"

"You didn't want me to worry about you." The glee he took from catching her in a lie chafed worse than his pompous mug sunk in pity.

"You're my patient with a bleeding head wound. Of course, I didn't want you to worry about me."

"Another explanation is that you're protecting yourself because you think I wouldn't give a shit if you told me what really happened. Lying saves the sting of unexpressed sympathy."

"Or my bedside manner doesn't consist of regaling patients with my problems." Marisol stood and tossed her gloves into the waste bin.

Vincent moved toward her. "Or you like to jump to conclusions about me. You think I'm a vapid rich guy."

"Aren't you?" Marisol cranked the dispenser for a sheet of paper towel, tore it away, and turned on the sink.

"I find it interesting that you care about what I think." He leaned against the sink counter.

"I don't." She vigorously scrubbed her hands and made an effort not to look at him.

"She doth protest too much."

Marisol shut off the sink. "Someone mugged me last night. Satisfied? He didn't make out with much, but it was enough to be annoying." The percussive sound of the dispenser and the loud ripping of the paper coincided with her growing irritation. "I wasn't even that scared, so don't even give me that pitiful look. I stupidly thought I could fight him off but lost. Voila!" She pointed to the bandage on her head. With the truth exposed, Marisol turned her eyes away, afraid to look at Vincent and see his concern. She wadded up the paper towel and threw it away, but she struggled with opening and closing the lid.

The memory of the mugging traveled like a tremor through her body and tightened in her throat. Not to mention that between Dad's financial woes and a new phone, she'd be having a rough time until payday. It all came for her at once—the fear and the struggle—and she wasn't going to break down, certainly not in front of Vincent Varian.

"I'm sorry." Vincent craned his neck. His eyes offered her sincere concern.

She fought the urge to cry the best way she knew how. Marisol met his concern and lashed out. "What do you want from me?"

With the same energy, he replied, "What I want is one less person in my life sparing my feelings. I thought you had more guts than that."

Good. Keep pissing me off. Anger stopped the whole on-the-verge-of-crying thing. She rolled her shoulders back and put her hands on her hips. "Is this a favorite sport of yours? Irritate the poor nurse?" She stared into his eyes, imagining fire flaring from them and scorching him.

Vincent cracked a haughty grin.

Tobias stuck his head in the door. "She taking care of you?"

Vincent's gaze didn't leave Marisol's. "She's terrifying."

Tobias put his hand on top of Vincent's head. "Now that's what I call a patched-up head. You did good, kid." He winked at her, and she, heating with a blush, nibbled her lower lip. "I have more questions about your little incident, Mr. Varian. Come with me." Both men headed out the door. If Tobias straightened his stooped posture, he'd stand a head taller than Vincent. But if he did? It'd give away how much of the Patron Saint he was.

"Wait!" Marisol blurted. The cocktail of anger and flirtation mixed into half-formed ideas: Add more fuel to the heat, get under Vincent's skin. She brushed past Vincent and pulled Tobias by the necktie to bring his head lower. "You did good, too, old man." On her tiptoes, one hand pulling on his tie, the other caressing his neck, she kissed Tobias.

The first touch of her lips tasted as sweet as vanilla. Her mouth opened for more. More burned like a shot of good whiskey, and warmth prickled from her lips, down her throat, across her chest, zinging straight to the dark pit inside her.

Tobias backed away, eyes big and mouth agape. He scratched the back of his neck and laughed. "Well..."

She overdid it. Her lips moved to muster an apology. She never could quite gauge when she'd been too much. The last bit of his tie slid from her fingers. "I'm sor—"

"I could use a kiss," Vincent said as his lips curled into a feline's smile.

"No!" She overdid that too—the volume this time. All because her belly fluttered at the chance of using Vincent to draw out the real version of Tobias.

Tobias shoved Vincent out of the room, gaze fixed on her. "See? Ass kicked."

She rolled her eyes to hide the blush that for sure emerged.

"Call me," he said as the door closed behind him.

She felt like champagne poured with abandon, bubbling over. She had another chance. A chance to really kick Tobias's ass with a kiss and devastate him with her lips and tongue. Another chance couldn't come soon enough.

At the end of her shift, Marisol put on her fixed necklace. But she noticed something else folded inside her locker. She pulled it into the light—a brand-new, black cashmere coat. She whipped off her sweatshirt and threw it in the Lost and Found box. The silk lining glided over her arms as she pulled on the coat. It was tailored perfectly to her body, tapering at her waist and flaring out around her legs. She zoomed through the hallway. The coattails caught in her manufactured wind.

She had become a superhero.

10

Marisol's apartment door whacked a small box across the entrance like a hockey puck. Another present? From him? The anticipation was enough for her to forget she had used the stair railing to pull her post-shift, heavy limbs up the steps. She kicked her door shut behind her and scurried after the box. She scanned the box for a sign from the sender, but whoever delivered it left it unlabeled. She ripped away the paper, revealing a flat white box that could fit a necklace. She popped the top off and saw a note. It read, I'm sorry. I was a jerk. Consider this an escalation. — A.

She ripped away the tissue paper to reveal a leather domino mask with satin ribbons. Annie used her spare key to leave a nice joke. Marisol shook her head and laughed.

thanks for the little gift! apology accepted, Marisol texted.

After a happy emoji, Annie sent, *when we left for the ball, did I do anything weird with my notes?*

no on counter like always.

not there... looking

go home!

the lab is my home

They both needed a Workaholics Anonymous meeting if those existed.

Marisol set her phone down on her nightstand and picked up the mask. In the reflection of her bedroom's elongated mirror, she hovered the mask over her face to preview what could be. Yet beyond her reflection, she sensed something else. It was a vision of herself running through the city and leaping over walls. She had become like him. Her heartbeat pulsed in her ears. To quiet it, she stuffed the mask into the box, burying it under the shards of tissue paper. Masked vigilante adventures could wait until after bedtime. She should send that in a message to Annie too.

After changing into an old XL T-shirt, she climbed into bed and pulled the blanket around herself. It brushed against her cheek. The sensation reminded her of his warm kiss, his gloved hands. The blanket against her bare skin skimmed the other places she wanted to feel his touch. Her pulse drummed again in her ears, echoing through her body. Pressure twisted below her stomach, and heat pooled between her legs.

She sat up in the bed and turned her bedside lamp on. She grabbed her phone, selected Tobias, and typed, *you up?*

As soon as she hit the send button, she tossed her phone on the nightstand. What was she thinking? She turned off the lamp and pulled the covers over her head.

Her phone rang. Holy shit! He called her. "Hello?" she answered.

"I am up. Thanks for asking."

"You're probably wondering why I messaged you."

He exhaled. "To continue where we left off?"

She toyed with her fixed necklace. "And to thank you for what you did today."

"My pleasure. You know, I was raised believing nothing good happens after midnight."

"Me too." Looking at the mask through tissue paper, she said, "Good thing I only want to do bad things to you." She froze in a wince. Too much. Again.

"Christ, kid. I'll be right over."

One hurdle jumped, another on its way: their nervous first kiss. She needed to feel that edge with him again, achieved by the assured energy of body-hugging formal wear and armored costumes. "Can I make a request?"

"Anything."

"This might come across as kinky or objectifying, so you can totally say no, but I was wondering if you could—"

"Wear my uniform?"

She would've said costume, but uniform cast his vigilantism as a calling. "How'd you know?" she asked. The tension in her body shifted from bracing nerves to the richer pang of desire.

"It would be ungentlemanly for me to share why I know, but that request alone is a pretty G-rated kink."

"Is that a reverse psychology tactic to make me go crazy on you?"

"Is it working?"

She rubbed her thighs together. "Come over and find out. I'll meet you outside."

"Yes, ma'am." He ended the phone call.

She scrambled to put on some more clothes, adding black jeans and combat boots to her giant t-shirt, and climbed out her window onto the fire escape. Each boot stomp rang against the grates of the escape. She figured the roof was her safest bet to meet him, unsure how she'd buzz someone in full mask regalia into her apartment.

She sent Tobias a message. *You'll know where to find me.* After she tightened her mask, she flicked up the hood of her new coat and strapped her fingerless kickboxing gloves tight around her wrists. If he wanted crazy, she would give it. She wandered to the roof's edge from the opposite side of the escape. Would the Patron Saint arrive from that direction? The distance between her roof and the neighboring rooftop below was the equivalent of the long jump she had landed in high school track. But many years later? She surveyed the distance to the alleyway below and rubbed Abuelita's cross pendant. The Patron Saint might handle jumping from massive heights, but she needed a risk assessment chart. And the muscles of her teenage self. She shook her head—Ow! Her head still hurt from the mugging. She backed away from the edge and headed to the fire escape.

She leaned against the guardrail and looked at the steps back to her apartment's window. Inside warmth, safety, predictability. Outside…?

A woman screamed from the alley over. Common sense said head inside and call 911. But Marisol Novotny turned around and entered a dead sprint, the skirt of her coat whipping behind her. When she reached the edge of the roof, she jumped across the alleyway, landing on her butt on the opposite rooftop. Plumes of vapor escaped her mouth, her breathing heavy. She landed the jump, but she had become like them—a crazy person in a costume who, if she chased one more bad idea, would appear on the other side of the emergency room.

A man yelled, "Shut up!" and she heard a familiar crack—the sound of a punch meeting cartilage. Followed by a woman crying. Also familiar. Marisol recognized the breaths and pauses between whimpers. It was the cry of someone fighting against it, telling herself to stop. Someone who thought no one would ever hear her or care.

Marisol must save her.

She approached the roof's edge. Across the way, a woman in a mini dress staggered down the fire escape, carrying a pair of high heels. She had a bloody nose. A pot-bellied man followed her.

Marisol darted to a ladder bolted into the building's bricks. She slid down it, avoiding the rungs. She skipped the last story and jumped to the ground with the grace of a cat. Not really. Instead, she crashed into a group of garbage cans, thrashing loud enough to stop the woman and man midstep.

Sour rotting garbage filled her nose. She'd try mouth breathing from now on. Marisol flicked a scrap of God-knows-what out of her hair and pulled her hood back over her head.

"Hey!" Marisol called out. She jumped to grab the steps of the fire escape. "That's not how you treat a lady."

"Mind your own business, you freak!" the man shouted back. He pulled the woman's hair. "See the trouble you get us in?" The woman grimaced.

"This is my business." Marisol lifted her body up the first stair. She ran up, up, and up the stairs until she reached the landing. There, she lowered herself into a fighting stance.

The man watched her and guffawed. He loosened his hold on the woman, who dove to cower behind Marisol. The man reached to grab the woman, but Marisol met him with a left hook. He stumbled back and flipped over the railing, falling the short distance to the ground. Flat on his back, he groaned. Marisol stared at her fist, in awe that it could bruise and break bones. She was too much. And she loved it.

She turned to the bloody-nosed woman who had curled into a ball, shivering. Task one: stop the blood. Marisol ripped away some of the lining of her coat. She handed the cloth to the woman, who blotted the blood collecting over her upper lip. Task two: get her to safety. Marisol asked, "Do you want me to call the police?"

The woman shook her head. "I'm working."

"Do you have a safe place to go to?"

The woman nodded.

"All right, go back inside. Hire a cab to take you there."

"What about the john?" the woman looked to the ground, where the pot-bellied man struggled to stand.

Marisol stretched her neck on each side. "He won't be your problem anymore."

The woman ran back up the steps and crawled back inside the window.

The man rubbed his backside. Marisol raised her fists again, prepared to attack or defend.

The man pointed a stubby and hairy finger in her direction. "When I'm done with you, you'll be shitting blood!"

"I'd like to see you try." She jumped to the ground, finally nailing a graceful landing. The flick of her hands said, "Come at me," and she shifted her weight, readying to fight.

He swung his doughy arms wildly and clumsily at her, which she avoided easily with a bob and weave. She could end it with a haymaker, but she drew out the fight, wanting the Patron Saint to find her. She parried and blocked, bobbed, and weaved. "You can show up anytime!" She called out to the night.

"Who are you talking to?" the man asked. He caught her by the lapels of her coat and shoved her into the ground.

Marisol scudded across the wet pavement and rolled back to standing. She hit the man with an uppercut. He wobbled back and wiped blood from his lip. Marisol stood straight with her hands on her hips.

The man gasped, and his eyes grew wide. He ran down the street screaming.

"That's right!" Marisol chuckled and gloated as she turned around... right into the wall of the Patron Saint. "You!"

"That was really stupid," he said, low and husky.

"How long were you watching?" Which point should embarrass her—the fall in the garbage or her tumble to the ground?

He held up his right hand to stop her from speaking. With his left hand, he looked as if he was checking the time, and a blue light glowed at the wrist. His voice became brash and nasally as he spoke into the commlink on his hand, "Griggs? This is Quinlan. I lost track of a perp heading in your direction. Around 10th and Lewis? Short, bald, slightly overweight. See him? Yeah? Good."

He snapped the commlink off, looked at her, and huffed. "Nice mask." He brushed past her and finessed his way up the ladder, back toward her apartment.

She followed him. "Thought I should show you what you bring out of me."

Over his shoulder, he said, "I'm not... a hobby."

The chill from him stung. Earlier he seemed into it. She ran after him, pulling his cape to stop him. "What's with the hot/cold routine?"

"I want you far from danger." He growled, revealing the beast hiding behind his cool control.

Marisol chortled. "That's sweet, but I work in an ER. I'm surrounded by danger."

"Not that kind. There are bad people out there."

She raised her chin. "I can handle it."

He ran his gloved thumb over the Steri-strip on her head. "I'm sure you can."

She pressed her hand against his right side, above his hip. "I pulled a knife out of you. If we do the math, I think 'knife' is greater than 'a little bump on the head.'" Her fingertips traced a line up his torso, over his chest.

He stopped her hand. "Marisol."

"Kiss me." She reached up to his face and closed her eyes, expecting the kiss he owed her. He pulled her sharply by the waist. She gasped and opened her eyes. With his free arm, he revealed what looked like a gun and fired it. A zipline cable launched over the rooftop. It hooked securely to an opposite ledge of her apartment building, confirmed by a taut vibration of the cable. With her in his grasp, he jumped off the roof, and they glided over the street far below.

She braced for the crash into the opposite building with eyes screwed close. And what was that? A scream? Was she a damsel tied to the tracks? So much for playing the hero...

Her feet kissed the ground. Eyes open, she was on her apartment's roof again. He let the rope retract back into his device.

She slugged him in the shoulder. "You should warn me when you do something like that!"

His lips curled into a wicked smile. "What are you going to do about it?"

She gripped the shoulders of his cape and pulled him toward herself. Her mouth crashed into his, and her teeth grazed his lips. He opened his mouth, and the soft touch of his tongue invited a deeper kiss. He tasted like burning atmosphere, zapping her to attention and vibrating her skin.

Marisol let go of his cape, and his mouth left hers. They stared at each other. Their heaving breath formed into one icy cloud above them. Here on the edge, she wanted to "do bad things" like running her hands up his naked torso, scratching flames across his chest, huffing swirls of smoke off his burning skin, and watching those stained-glass eyes roll into the back of his head when she gave him the little death.

What the Hell? She pulled off her mask, terrified of the side of her that hungered for him.

Marisol looked at the mask and then at him. Their wild gaze locked. He hooked his fingers between the buttons of her coat and pulled her back to him with a groan. She devoured his mouth, sucking and biting his lower lip.

She wanted to pull him down, dig her knees into his arms, and pin him as she kissed him. But she couldn't budge him.

Instead, they awkwardly staggered across the rooftop in a tangle of limbs. He pushed. She pulled. He pulled. She pushed. A little too hard. His back hit the colossal HVAC unit, knocking his breath away.

His eyes widened, as if the dual sensation of pain and pleasure confused him. It was like the kiss at the hospital all over again, a hot start with an anticlimactic finish. She took in a breath, preparing to say sorry.

He inhaled and growled, resuming their kiss. His hands moved from her waist and down her backside. After he lifted her, Marisol wrapped her legs around him. He spun her so her back dented the metal wall of the unit. He leaned his weight into her. She squeezed him with her thighs, hoping to feel that he needed her as much as she needed him. But like the mask, the uniform hid the man underneath. He rocked his hips into her. The erotic friction shocked like a live wire. Marisol opened her eyes, drawing a sharp breath.

She studied his face, caressing his jawline. Under her fingers, he felt unblemished and smooth. She finally noticed the small cleft in his chin. Charming, she chuckled as she kissed it. Her fingers traced up from his chin to his mask, and she toyed underneath its edges. He jerked his face away and dropped her to her feet.

He held his mask in place. "What are you doing?"

"If we are about to do what I think we're about to do, why not as the real you?"

"I'm not ready." His gaze drifted down.

She lifted his chin. "That's kind of adorable." She kissed him on the cheek.

He broke from her embrace and moved to the edge of the roof.

Marisol, unsatisfied, reached out for him. "You're leaving? Now?"

"It's almost dawn. What else are we going to do?"

She arched an eyebrow. What did he think?

"That was a purely rhetorical question."

"Okay. When can I see you again?"

"Tomorrow, here, at sundown." He kissed the inside of her wrist. "But the mask stays on." He smirked, and with that, he jumped down from the ledge and out of her life.

She twirled in place and sat down on the wrought-iron bench, bending to pick up her mask and stuff it in her pocket. Her phone vibrated against her hand. She checked it. It beeped incessantly from a slew of missed calls. The first one was from Annie. Marisol sprung back to her feet and walked down the fire escape, redialing. Straight to Annie's voicemail. "I'm heading to your lab right now. You really need to start charging your phone."

As she headed toward the hospital, she occasionally stopped herself and smiled. She'd lick her lips to savor the Patron Saint. She'd touch her cheek, reliving the burn of his skin against hers. Tomorrow, she'd offer the other parts of her that yearned to be explored.

Marisol swiped her badge to enter the building. She clamped down her widening smile as she rode up the elevator and turned the corner of the hallway. She should just shout her good news—how the weight of his body felt oh-so right against hers, or how his mouth tasted almost metallic. As she neared the light of Annie's lab, Marisol added a skip to her step. "Annie, you won't believe—"

Marisol turned the corner. The sight through the window froze her.

Annie wasn't alone.

Ì𝔫ʈ𝔢𝔯𝔩𝔳𝔡𝔢

You ask, "What are you doing here?" and wipe at your eyes with the back of your arm and sniffle. Drama already visited you tonight. Shattered glass on the counter? An empty mouse cage? What trouble did you get yourself into, little girl?

You eye my partners, the monstrous yet dim-witted Yevgeny and the volatile yet small John-Boy. You inch back and rub your lower back. You're nervous. No need to be, my cherub. You've always been a good little girl. "I'm giving lab tours for interested parties. I'd ask you the same question."

You whisper, "I came to feed the mice."

I explain that I know this seems odd and unnerving in the middle of the night. I like to give tours when the labs are quiet. With everything empty and silent, we are more apt to see its potential. All lies, but it's that potential that I want to talk to you about.

You remain quiet, and the gaze from behind your glasses bounces from one person to the other.

I say that we all heard the rumors—that Vincent Varian has a secret side project. What could it be, I've often wondered. I've heard it all. Super cop program? Alternative energy? But I never once heard about perfection in a pill. Could this be the secret project? I sit in your office chair and put my feet up.

You shift your weight. The broken glass from the cage crunches underneath you. Better get on your knees. Clean it up. Wouldn't want my sweet little girl to get hurt. Then you murmur, "Oh. I was just talking. You know how people talk at parties."

But you're not like other people. You like it when I say that to you. I see how you twitch your mouth and lick your lips when I say it: There's no one like you. You're special, my cherub.

I remind you, "You said within the year. And I believe you even said, 'under-promise, over-deliver'?" You gasp. Red splotches travel down your neck. "What is in that little head of yours?" I imagine that freshly slapped look spreads to your breasts.

And in that tiny, quiet voice, you say, "I'm afraid it's only in my head. I was talking hypothetically last night."

"No!" I say with a clap. "What is Vincent Varian hiding?" The other morons who tried the kidnapping schtick bungled their jobs. But you never bungle a job. You're my dependable girl.

You say, "I barely talk to the guy; let alone know about any secret projects. I'm just a lab lackey." You rub your lower back again. "You're on the board. You'd know more than I would."

I was afraid of this. No one understands emergencies anymore. What if I told you something bad's going to happen? "A lot of Shadowhaven's people are going to get sick. They might die. I believe it has something to do with what was stolen from the W.H.O. in Manila? Would your pill be hypothetical then?"

"No." You look to the ground. My sweet little girl's ashamed from holding back. But the soul of someone else possesses you. You add with more volume than I thought you were ever capable of, "But you need to wait at least a year, especially to pass human clinical trials. People over ambition. That's what I always say."

Oh, I get it now. The research is stuck. You need a little force to get it out. So, I reach into my pocket, pull out my mask, put it on, and... you whimper.

I say that I am a part of some people. Powerful people. You don't want to do anything stupid, do you?

You shake your head. The exaggerated shake of a child who hates being disobedient. Because if you did something stupid, you would have to contend with far scarier people.

You wipe your nose. "Is that why you took my files? My notes?"

I didn't take your files, which means someone got to them first.

"Is that why you killed Dr. Varian?" you ask.

What are you talking about?

"If this is an attempt to suppress my work, you needn't bother. I'm not dying for this! I'll give you all that I have. Just let me leave."

"Where is it?" I hiss out my question like a popped tire.

"It's in my lunch bag in the mini fridge."

John-Boy checks the refrigerator and grabs the pink polka-dotted lunch bag. He opens it and pulls out a vial of serum.

"That's what I was talking about at the party. I should warn you. It's very new. It has had no clinical trials. Okay? I'm leaving now." You tiptoe to the door, even though Yevgeny waits for you there.

I say, "Not so fast. We want to see a trial. On John-Boy here."

There you go, rubbing your back again. It's beautiful to see what you do when you're scared. John-Boy rolls up his sleeve.

II

Unexpected Visitors

A giant stood near the door. His physical opposite sat at the counter island with his sleeve rolled up. A man in a fully hooded mask that obscured his face hovered near Annie. She raised a syringe, flicking it.

Just as Marisol's trembling fingers touched the glass, a white rat dropped from the ceiling, landing on the small one's face. He shrieked as the rat mauled his cheek. Annie shook the syringe and stabbed the masked one in the neck with it, who collapsed. Annie pulled a gun from her waistband on the giant.

Marisol ran to the door and tried to open it, but the lab's security protocol kept it locked on the outside. Only Annie could let her in. Marisol pounded on the door. Annie turned to face Marisol, and the gun went off, striking the arm of the giant. Annie reeled from the kickback and stared at the gun.

"Annie!" Marisol screamed as she shook the door.

The masked man staggered to his feet and pulled the syringe from his neck, crushing it in his hand. The small man wrestled the rat from his now chewed-up face and wrestled the gun from Annie's grasp. As they fought for control, a bullet hit the ceiling, sprinkling bits of tile over the melee.

Marisol kicked at the door handle, trying to bust it open. Through the window, she saw the masked man aiming the gun. The giant seemed indifferent to the scene as he wrapped paper towels around his bicep. Chewed-face threw Annie to the ground behind the counter. White-hot fire flashed from the end of a gun. One. Two. Three. Head. Heart. Lungs.

Marisol's mouth opened, but nothing came out. A silent scream. She pressed her hand against the glass, wishing she had every superpower at once—just like the movies or some fairy tale. She'd shatter the glass with her voice, snap their necks with her mind, and turn back time to save her. And she would shatter the glass and snap their necks all over again. Instead, her shock paralyzed her, and she watched Annie's lifeless arm stretch past the counter on the ground.

Annie was dead.

The turn of the door handle snapped Marisol's attention back to the figure behind the door. Light reflected off the saliva dripping from its teeth; the round circular rows pulsed toward the empty abyss of a maw in the center. Nothing recognizably human. Just teeth and teeth and teeth. The Bloodsucker. Marisol backed away from the door. The men scrambled to the door. She needed to run. Why couldn't she move? All she could do was watch the monsters bound closer and closer.

"Get her, John-Boy!" the Bloodsucker howled.

The voice rattled her out of paralysis, and she sprinted down the hallway. She pushed her hands against the fire exit, but a force pulled her in the opposite direction. No! She thrashed against the arms, kicking and clawing. She and John-Boy stumbled into the wall and against the elevator buttons, activating it. She elbowed the mauled spot on his face. John-Boy threw her to the ground. When she looked up, she saw the barrel of a gun and focused on the Bloodsucker's hungry, eyeless face. Marisol raised her hands over her face. "Please."

Out of the dark, the white rat landed in the middle of Bloodsucker's mask and gnawed. He wailed. There was a man under the mask, after all. Marisol crawled to her feet and hesitated. How could there be a killer rat to the rescue? It almost resembled the mouse from the day before, but that wasn't possible.

John-Boy tackled her to the floor and dragged her by her hair. She struggled against his grip to free herself. The Bloodsucker ripped the rat from his face and threw its body against the wall. He fired a shot at it, exploding the small body into bits.

"How many bullets do you have left, boss?" John-Boy asked; his spittle hit her cheek.

The rat didn't stay in bits for long. The bits collected like goo poured into a mold, forming back into the white rat. Fully repaired, it shrieked. Marisol hiked up her shoulders as her eardrums stung from the unholy screech.

"What the fuck?" The Bloodsucker adjusted his mask.

They stood dumbstruck at the living dead rat. She pried herself away from John-Boy's grasp. The elevator door dinged open. She ran to it, finding it an empty shaft. The Bloodsucker fired the gun. *Click.* He was out of bullets.

She bolted to the fire exit but felt hands pull at her hood and hair. They dragged her back to the open elevator doors. The Bloodsucker motioned for the other two to let her go. She trembled, watching his blood stream out of the hole in his face like a forked tongue. The Bloodsucker clicked his tongue as he moved his head near her face. With each click, his teeth pulsed toward her. A patch of bloody skin poked through the empty maw. Only a mask. Just cloth and plastic. How could cloth and plastic encapsulate terror?

He gave her a sharp shove.

She fell into the elevator shaft, flailing. She grabbed at the steel cables. Her hands ripped open as the cables burned into her grip. She crashed into the stuck elevator car and rolled off, falling again until crunch—the sound of her body hitting the ground.

The darkness swallowed her. Her ears rang, and her neck muscles strained. Was she screaming? She couldn't hear through the ringing. Pain surged from the right side of her body, which choked the breath from her.

She was as good as dead.

12

Not Good At These Things

Marisol gasped as if she forgot how to breathe. After blinking away the dots in her vision, her gaze followed bars of light drawing a grid up the elevator shaft. The grid shrunk into a halo at the top floor. It must've been morning.

The icy chill of the concrete floor dug into her back. Could she move? She wiggled her fingers and her toes. Ow! Breathe. Each sip of air she took begged for respite from the pain. Moving would not be easy.

Would someone hear her if she cried for help? Her dry and sticky tongue stuck to the roof of her mouth. She managed to whisper, ripping her lips apart.

"Help."

The empty hiss of white noise mocked her. She swallowed, but the parched gulp stuck in her throat.

She had to save herself.

The dots in her vision formed into an aura, clouding her search for escape. From under a desperate blink, she spotted a ladder out of the pit. She propped on her elbows and dragged herself an inch. More pain racked her body but not the throb of her broken leg. It was the sharp peel of her skin when she crawled out of the puddle of her own blood. She collapsed.

He found her earlier. Could he find her again? She grazed her hand against her chest—a feeble touch of her abuelita's necklace. "Help me."

The cables in the shaft groaned, pulling the weight of the elevator car. Someone was there. If she yelled, they'd find her, but she couldn't. She reached into the pocket of her coat and grabbed her keys. Shallow, desperate breaths chased the pain away. She inched closer to a vertical metal beam and struck her keys against it. It rang.

The elevator stopped. The bars of light danced above her. She dropped to her back. With every blink, her eyes grew heavier. Dying felt like resisting a nap on a bed of dry ice.

The doors thundered, wrenching open. Tobias emerged from the parted doors. "Somebody's here!" He jumped to the ground and dropped a crowbar at his feet. "Marisol!"

Tobias kneeled beside her and pressed against her carotid artery, checking for her pulse. "Get me a stretcher. She's alive!" He whipped his tie off and tied it around her thigh. "Stay with me, Marisol. Stay with me."

She moved her lips, but they made no sound. With a final push from her lungs, she whispered, "Where were you?"

She awoke in a hospital room. From the angle of a patient, it felt unfamiliar. A sling elevated her leg. A fiberglass cast wrapped from her knee to her foot. She reached to touch her encased leg, but the dull jerk from the tubes in her hand stopped her. An IV of blood and saline solution leashed her to the spot. Boop. Along with an EKG monitor. She was stuck but not in pain. Thanks, morphine.

To her other side sat a bouquet of white and pink lilies. Marisol untucked the card from the plastic prong. "Godspeed. Tobias." It hurt to be charmed. It meant she was worthy; a worthiness she couldn't feel with her body and mind devastated by trauma. A gentle rapping sounded from the doorway.

"Some people are real cheese balls." Tobias leaned against the doorframe, draining a small Styrofoam cup of coffee.

"Thanks." She nodded toward the bouquet.

A weak smile flickered across Tobias's face before he crushed his cup and tossed it in a small waste bin near the door. "We could've set you up in a better place. Nothing but weak coffee here."

Here, abscess-yellow paint decked the walls unlike the institutional blue walls of the Varian Family Hospital. "Where am I?"

"St. James. Far on the Eastside. I swear you won't burst into flames." He stepped farther inside the room. His dress shirt was disheveled and stained with blood.

She was afraid to know whether the blood was hers or... even worse, Annie's. "You should wear a clean shirt when you visit a lady."

"Hey, you owe me a tie, kid. We were attached. It was the last good thing my ex-wife gave me." He ambled around, looking everywhere but toward her bed. "You're already a legend at the precinct, surviving that fall." At the window, he bent a couple of blinds to peer outside; his back turned to her. "We'd been there for hours before we found you."

"What's up with that, man? I thought we had a thing going. I save you. You save me," she teased, but it came out hoarse. Her savior had been too late.

He faced her, his eyes shining with tears. "I got you, though."

"Annie? Is she?" Gunshots echoed in her memory.

"Gone." His voice became a whisper.

Marisol closed her eyes as hot tears rolled out of them.

"I swear I will get him." He brushed his fingers at the foot of her cast.

Within her mind, she saw the twisted tableaux again—the giant, the little guy, and the teeth.

"There were three. Didn't security cameras see them?"

"They were wiped. Did you recognize them?"

"No. I never saw them before, and the Bloodsucker, he was... in a mask. Looked like a sea lamprey." Last night's violence snaked through her brain, numbing her.

Tobias nodded his head, but his face twisted. "Shit." He stuck his head out the door and scanned both directions of the hall. With a lowered voice, he turned back to her. "The Bloodsucker? Once he knows you're alive, he'll be after you."

"Good thing I have you to protect me." In fact, he felt like the only thing around keeping her from living in the unending feedback loop of blood, screeches, and teeth.

"It would be better if we move you to a safe house. Our department will probably put you in a bedbug infested hovel, but we should get you there after they discharge you."

"Will I be able to go to Annie's funeral?" She stiffened as she awaited the answer.

"I don't know."

"Her parents depended on her to translate for them. They'll be so lost when they learn..." She hiccoughed. Her parents would be so defeated as they searched for answers. But there was only one answer. Someone murdered Annie.

"I'm sorry." He sat on the edge of her bed and looked down.

Family. She gripped her sheets as a sob heaved in her chest. "I can't leave. My dad will get himself in trouble, and my mom can only hold so much together. Without me—"

He held her hand. "I'll check in on them. I'll keep a special eye out. Just for you."

Marisol rubbed her fingers across his calloused knuckles. She focused on his hand and not his face, afraid that he would see a heat of shame wash over her when she asked, "What about us?"

He cracked a weak laugh. "Probably couldn't visit you, anyway." He sighed, now serious. "So I don't compromise your location."

"What if you came in disguise?"

"You're a funny one, kid." He interlaced his fingers with hers. "I don't know. I have a way of screwing these things up."

These things being relationships, of course. "You, too, huh?"

"Even when I thought you stood me up, I never cursed your name. And knowing you were..." Tobias drew her hand to his lips and kissed the space between her knuckles.

Stood up?

Strange. As strange as the kiss on top of her hand. In a mask, he would've kissed the inside of her wrist.

The conclusion she'd been afraid of loomed like a knife in the dark. "Could you come closer?"

Tobias bent over her. She placed her hands like a mask over his face, parting her fingers so his eyes peered through them. "Your eyes. They have brown flecks in them."

He nuzzled into her palm. "Yeah. I told you. It's my sectoral heterochromia. My eyes are blue and brown in spots."

Tobias was never the Patron Saint.

And not only had she been a fool, but she had also dragged his feelings into it. She traced her thumb over the edge of his square jaw, tainted with graying stubble, and dropped her hands from his face.

Both sat with their heads bowed. The heart monitor beeped over and over again.

Any second now, one of them would talk.

Tobias sighed. "I'm going to grab some more coffee." He headed out of the room but looked back from the doorway. "I'm your personal bodyguard."

She closed her eyes and nodded. Tears clawed down her face. A part of her always knew Tobias wasn't him. It's why she sought the hero and not the man. She ached, a dull throb of betrayal. Her Patron Saint fought for her, saved her—except for this one time. The one time when she needed him most. She felt for her necklace, only finding her bare skin.

Footsteps thumped into the room. She opened her eyes to see an officer standing at the foot of her bed. He appeared half the size of Tobias. A bandage covered one of his round cheeks. His wading-pool size eyes were bloodshot. She flinched as she recognized him. It was Chewed-face, John-Boy rather, from the night before.

"Came to finish the job, bitch."

Marisol searched for a hole to escape in. Nothing. She had one resource left. "Tobias!"

As if she conjured him herself, Tobias appeared in the doorway. "Can I help you, officer?"

John-Boy stared at her, smiling and baring his crooked yellow teeth.

Tobias adjusted his untucked dress shirt, revealing the gun in his holster. "Officer? I'm talking to you!" His fingers twitched at his hip.

The giant, the second one from last night, crept up behind Tobias.

She screamed, "Look out!"

The giant wrapped a wire around Tobias's neck and dragged him into the hallway.

As John-Boy lurched, she grabbed the vase of flowers and threw it at him. He reeled, howling and holding his face. The vase welted his unblemished cheek. She scrambled to unhook her cast out of the sling.

Through gritted teeth, he said, "I was told to make it look like an accident. Now? I'm really going to make it hurt."

Marisol fell out of her bed; a blinding pain shot from her broken leg. She writhed among the mess of flowers and water. The tangle of tubes pulled at her hand. She ripped them away and smoothed her thumb over the medical tape. The flatlining monitor wailed while Marisol crawled to the corner.

Crash! Bits of glass scattered on the floor. The Patron Saint flew into the room through the window, swinging by a cable.

John-Boy froze. "What the—"

The Patron Saint landed on his feet and stood between Marisol and John-Boy. He swung bolas above his head, cast them, and wrapped them around John-Boy's ankles. As he struggled against his bindings, John-Boy fell to the ground with an oof. As he wriggled on the floor, the Patron Saint attached his cable to John-Boy and shoved him out the window. The cable pulled taut as he dangled outside, screaming.

Gunfire echoed down the hallway. The monsters were still coming for her. The Patron Saint picked Marisol off the floor. She gripped her arms around his neck as thundering footsteps pounded closer to the door. Please be Tobias. Please...

A wheezing mass stumbled and held itself up in the doorframe. Tobias Quinlan. Thank God.

The Patron Saint carried her to the doorway. "I must get her out of here."

"Move fast... backup will... be here at... any moment. Can't trust... my own," Tobias ordered.

"You two know each other?" she strained her eye muscles, looking from Tobias to the Patron Saint.

Tobias rubbed his throat. "Acquaintances."

A howl came from the direction outside. The Patron Saint turned his head, eyes glowing. "You'll have to fish the little fake policeman out the window."

"And fill out... paperwork... about the dead big one."

"I will take her to safety. Do you trust me?" the Patron Saint asked.

"Do I have a choice?" Tobias answered.

Orderlies and nurses bound to the hall and cowered. Nothing like a dead body and the Patron Saint to induce paralysis.

The Patron Saint nodded. "Hold your breath if you want to remember this, Quinlan." He dropped a gas canister to the ground. A wall of smoke separated them from Tobias. The Patron Saint raced with Marisol in his arms out the fire exit and up the stairs.

She warmed with reverence. He hadn't abandoned her. "Where were you?"

He flinched and mumbled, "I busted the window out of a home of a family choking on the fumes of their space heater. Stopped some hooligans harassing a jogger in the park. A stabbing. A robbery. But I didn't... not when you needed me." He stopped running. "I made a mistake, but I swear from now on that no one will ever hurt you again."

Of the three promises she had heard today, she wanted his to come true the most. "How?" she asked. Because he's all-powerful—radioactive or alien?

"I'm taking you to a safe house."

"Will you and I finally be getting some one-on-one time?"

He clenched his jaw. "I'm sorry."

"It's okay. I'm physically broken, suffering some serious grief and abandonment issues. And anyone I have contact with seems to be targeted by murderers. I only need a kind, familiar face. Even if it's behind a mask." She caressed his jawline.

"No. I'm sorry for this." The Patron Saint raised his hand to her face. He blew powder into it. She breathed in and...

13

. . . breathed out, opening her eyes. She had teleported into a bed. Where? Unknown. Shadows cast the room in a dark haze. Her hands glided over cool satin sheets. Her broken leg rested on a mound of firm pillows. More pillows hugged her neck and shoulders.

In the low light sifting between the slats of the window shutters, she fumbled to turn on a lamp at the bed stand. The bed stand displayed prescriptions with her name on it. A plastic bag of her keys, cross necklace, and phone rested on the stand. She opened it and took out her phone. It appeared unharmed by her fall, but the battery was dead. She had to figure out where she was the old-fashioned way. But first, she fastened the chain of her necklace around her neck and touched the pendant.

The luxury of the room jarred her. It had wood paneling with carved filigree. When Tobias mentioned a safe house, he made it sound like a roach motel. Not this. She couldn't quite remember how she got here. Did Tobias drive her? The morphine fogged her memory.

What time was it? Hell, what day was it? The funk emanating from her and the griminess of her hair indicated awhile since the hospital… since her leg broke in a fall… since the monsters murdered Annie. She flinched three times, reliving the explosion of gunfire that took Annie's life. She rubbed where a cold sweat gathered at her nape. Her hands trembled. "You don't have time for this." She needed to figure out where she woke up.

She discovered a wheelchair propped against the far corner of the bed, dragged her body into it, and wheeled around the room. Through a doorway, she entered an ensuite, palatial bathroom with a glass-encased shower, a deep bathtub, and a sprawling vanity. There, unopened designer-brand necessities had been arranged in neat rows.

She brushed her teeth, tied her hair up, and cleaned herself, administering the worst sponge bath ever, as her experience with them was never self-inflicted or impaired. Clean enough, she looked in the mirror. The cut on her temple had faded into a sallow, yellow bruise. But that wasn't the most pathetic part of her appearance. The hospital gown was.

She pushed herself back into the bedroom toward a double-door wardrobe. In it, she found sleeveless undershirts, striped boxers, and black socks still in their packaging. Plaid flannel shirts hung off padded hangers. They were too small to fit Tobias. She broke open the plastic packages. One glimpse of the hospital gown, and whoever these clothes belonged to would forgive Marisol for borrowing them.

Putting on clothes prodded her bruises and muscles, reliving the pain experienced by her body. Her broken leg continued to throb with a constant dull pain. The side of her body that slammed against the elevator car had dark purple bruises pooled around her ribs and underarm. When she pulled on her shirt, each bruise stung. She wiggled into a pair of shorts and lassoed a single black sock on her bare foot. Luckily, putting on a flannel didn't require copious amounts of pain or effort.

Physically spent from dressing, she popped a dose of Percocet. She dry-swallowed the pill, and it forced its way down her esophagus. She wheeled back into the bathroom and cupped her hands under the sink, sipping to wash the pill down. Now she was ready to explore.

Her bedroom door opened to a hallway of windows stretching from floor to ceiling. The place overlooked a lake reflecting the warm pink hues of the setting sun. Dusk. The view would have been exhilarating had she been there under more positive circumstances.

She heard a faint sound of old jazz that must have been coming from a record player, as the sound crackled with age. Either she resided in a haunted house or shared the space with an old man. She tensed as she continued down the hallway, unsure of who or what would listen to such music. Wherever she was, she was far from Shadowhaven.

The hallway opened to a living room with a vaulted ceiling that blended into a dining area and open kitchen. The living room belonged in a time capsule. Thick curtains covered the windows, blocking the waning light of the evening. Tables and bookshelves made of dark, heavy woods brimmed with trinkets and shrouded the open living room with a cave-like appearance. Everything matched a red-white-and-blue color scheme, from the floral patterns of the rug and pillows to the plaid upholstery of the sofa.

Old, beautiful, and lush objects surrounded her, yet she felt no curious wonder. Her heart carried a heavy weight. The weight of Annie's death. The weight of living in fear.

A baritone voice said, "Welcome to the safe house."

She turned her wheelchair toward the direction of the voice. Vincent Varian stood behind her. She asked, "What are you doing here?"

"This is my grandfather's—actually, my—vacation home. I'm usually never here." Vincent recounted in his affected prep school accent.

She touched Abuelita's necklace. "Is this a sick joke?"

"I don't think so? Detective Quinlan needed a place off the books because he said he can't trust his own people. Not after the hospital attack." He put his hands on his hips, resting his thumbs in the loopholes of his jeans. "I, too, am in hiding after my kidnapping incident. The whole world thinks I'm gallivanting in London or Paris. I can never remember which." Vincent laughed.

Cue an unimpressed eye roll. "Point me the direction home. I'm out of here."

"We're a little over an hour west of Shadowhaven. In the Micah National Forest." Vincent pointed in a vague direction. "I think if you head that direction, you'll make it, eventually. The terrain makes it a little iffy. Especially in a wheelchair."

"I'll order a car. I can survive a couple of goons after me."

Vincent looked her up and down. "Barely."

"My family needs me, all right? My dad's real stupid with money—"

"If it's money that's bothering you, let me know what you need. I'll take care of it. It's not worth risking your life over money."

"You can write a check and fix it?"

Vincent nodded. "Like that." He snapped his fingers.

Marisol held her face in her hands. "That's so patronizing."

"I didn't mean to insult you."

"You would have to matter to insult me."

"Marisol." His face deflated. "Can we simply agree to be nice to each other while we're stuck here?"

His imploring face brought on a wave of guilt. She had aimed for cold but landed on cruel. It would be better to avoid all feelings in isolation. She ignored his request with a sigh and wheeled herself toward her bedroom. The quick movement exacerbated her pain. She sucked in a breath as she cradled her side.

"Ice and Epsom salt will help the bruises. I can get those for you," Vincent called after her.

She glared over her shoulder. "Don't you have people to do that for you?"

"I don't tend to keep maids and butlers around."

After another roll of her eyes, Marisol continued to head toward her room. "I can't do this." Time had already ticked away as the Bloodsucker roamed Shadowhaven while she sat stuck on her ass, barely able to move. Her pulse drummed in her ears again, and the mounting anxiety squeezed her chest. Confined. Doted upon. Anything would be better than this situation. Her ribs brushed against the arm of her chair. A sharp pain stabbed into her.

"Why?" Vincent's sharp and serious eyes poked at her vulnerability the way the wrong movement prodded at her bruises.

Her sinuses stung, threatening tears. "I'm gonna get those bastards that killed her."

Vincent turned up the side of his mouth. "With the other foot?"

Marisol had the sudden urge to roll into his shins until they bled. Seated with a puffed-up chest, she looked ridiculous—as intimidating as a kitten. If she found the Patron Saint and had him champion her rage, she would be an unstoppable force. "I have powerful friends."

"They must be very powerful, letting you get hurt like that." Vincent's acerbic tone suggested her Patron Saint caused her pain, and she would not allow it.

She clenched her teeth. "You know nothing about them. Or me."

"I know they wouldn't be good friends if they encouraged you to pursue vengeance."

A sardonic laugh escaped her mouth. "Did you gain that bit of wisdom from writing a check?" Her tears blurred her vision like tempered glass.

Vincent turned his gaze away from her.

"Do you know who I am? I'm from the Westside, motherfucker. My brother murdered people. Didn't even need a gun. He beat a man to death so bad that the cops had to use the guy's tattoos to identify him." She cracked a knuckle, though her chin trembled. "And the same blood runs through my veins. Are you shitting yourself now, rich boy? Me and everyone I know will fuck you up if you try to stop me." Raw pathways of tears streamed from her eyes. She waited for his inevitable freak out. Too much work, he'd say, and he'd demand she leave.

But Vincent crouched and looked up at her. "I'm sorry. I can't imagine what you're going through. But I made a promise to Quinlan to keep you safe. If it means I suffer your wrath, so be it."

"Just... leave me alone," Marisol said with a tinge of regret as she blinked away tears. She rolled to her room and resolved to lie in bed and stare at the ceiling. Anything. As long as she avoided Vincent.

She dragged herself from the wheelchair onto her bed. Until the numbing effect of the painkiller lulled her to sleep, she grabbed a pillow to scream into it. The muffled scream turned into crying, and the crying turned into wails. Between sobs captured in the fibers of the pillow, she begged time to run backwards, to un-hear the gunshots, to see Annie one more time. She punched the pillow and threw it across the room. It landed without fanfare; its feather filling cushioned the impact.

She looked at the dent in the pillow. She couldn't even do grief right. Sobs racked her body as she longed for the stone-faced dignity of a widow at a funeral. Sputtering and sniffling, she wasn't the strong and brave woman she imagined herself to be. She stretched out on the bed, lying on her good side. The weight of her cast pressed her body farther into the mattress. She imagined Abuelita's soft hands rubbing her back, the way she had when Marisol was a child. Her sobbing subsided into gentle hiccoughs, and then she closed her eyes to sleep.

Drums rumbled as she put on her mask and boxing gloves. String instruments repeated a driving, repetitive song in minor keys. She ran into Annie's lab. The music shifted into major key, and she knocked the gun out of the Bloodsucker's hand before he pulled the trigger. With a gut punch and a hook to the jaw, she had defeated him. Annie grabbed her and told her to run. Horns blasted a victorious wall of sound. Evil didn't win today. She and Annie headed to the elevator doors, pressing the button to escape to their safety. The doors opened into an abyss.

Before Marisol turned around, Annie's face morphed into rows of circular teeth, pulsing toward the mouth in the center. Marisol recoiled and lost her footing. She fell into the darkness, screaming Annie's name before hitting the bottom with a jolt.

Outside her body, she watched herself bleed out. She moved her lips and tried to call out for help. Shock paralyzed her. Darkness bound her. Her fear demanded a scream, but more darkness poured into her mouth like motor oil and drowned her.

She was numb and alone.

"Marisol!" Vincent shook her awake.

Her breathing strained. She inhaled short spurts of air. Upon exhaling, her breath felt trapped within the muscles of her neck. She flailed, trying not to suffocate. Her hands struck against Vincent's body.

"You're having a panic attack. Look into my eyes and breathe."

She found his eyes, even in the dark. Marisol braced her palms against his shoulders. Still, she only took sips of air.

"I'm going to hold you. You need to listen to my breathing and copy it." Vincent embraced Marisol. She couldn't move; she could only focus on her breath. Through her desperate gasps, she tried to listen to Vincent's breathing. Her high-pitched wheezes drowned the sound out.

Then, against his body, she felt her rapid heartbeat vibrate back to her. Where was his heartbeat? She searched for it, squeezing tighter, and finally felt a slow, steady heartbeat, like ocean waves hitting the beach on a clear day. She listened to his breath. Deep and calm. She synchronized the pace of her breathing, as his strong arms pressed her against his solid body.

She curled against him. "Vincent? I'm scared."

"Then I'm not letting you go yet." He rested his cheek against the top of her head.

He held her so close, even though she was a mess of grimy skin and oily hair. She said, "That's stupid. I haven't showered."

"I don't care." Vincent stroked the back of her head.

"I'm disgusting."

He shrugged.

"You can't be nice to me. I don't deserve it."

"Of course you do." He adjusted his embrace and settled back onto the bed, and she lay down in his arms.

She nuzzled her head into the crook between his collarbone and shoulder. He smelled faintly sweet and woodsy, like sandalwood. Before she fell asleep again, she could smell a trace of electricity about him, like the atmosphere during a lightning storm.

Interlude

sOMETHING'S cHANGING IN mE. i nOTICE IT fIRST aFTER thAT rABID rAT bITe. nO bLOOD. bUT wHEN iZzY'S gETAWAY dRIVER sHOOts mE, AND mY bODY bECOmes sWISS cHEESE? THE cHANGE IN mE pUSHES oUT THE bULLETS lIKE WORmS cRAWLING tHROUGH THE dEAD.

tHAT dOCTOR mADE mE A gOD.

i aLMOST fEEL bAD FOR kILLING hER.

wHEN tHIS cITY iS tORN aPART BY THE cOMING pLAGUE, IT wILL bE mE lEFT sTANDING. i'LL pUT THE rUINS bACK tOGETHER IN mY iMAGE. tHEn tHE ciTY wILL bE A pLACE tHAT dOESN'T nEED TO bE rEScuED BY cOSTUMED fREAKS.

pEOPLE wILL sEE mE AND kNEEL.

FOR i aM tHEIR sAVIOR.

yET, eVEN wHEN i sTAnd IN THE rOAD, i sTILL dOUBT mY pOWER. hOW dOes IT fEEL, iZzY, wHEN i pUNCH yOUR gETAWAY cAR? mY fIST cRUNCHes THE fRONT eND, aND THE tIRES sCREAM lIKE A sTUCK pIG. The sHATTERING gLASS mOVES mE lIKE tHE tINKLING oF cHURCH bELLS. yOUR cAR fLIes oVER mE AND rOLLs TO THE rIVERBANK. THE sMELL OF bURNT rUBBER AND sMOKE gIVEs mE A hARD-oN.

yOUR dRIVER cRAWLS oUT, nO lONGER hUMAN-sHAPED. i aDMIRE hIS vIGOR. i aDMIRE tHAT hE sTILL fIGHTS eVEN AS hIS bODY liEs bROKEN. tHAT fINAL gASP OF aIR wHEN i rIP hIS bARELY bEATING hEART FROM hIS cHEST! yOU pROBABLY kNOW tHAT bLOOD lOOKS lIKE iNK IN THE dARK. jUST AS yOU mIGHT kNOW tHAT THE mETALLIC sMELL OF bLOOD mAKES yOU hIGH.

wHEN wILL i sMELL yOUR bLOOD, iZZy?

mY mOUTH wATERS.

i bREak oUT THE pASSENGER wINDOW, dESPERATE TO kNOW wHAT A gREAT mAN'S hEART fEEls lIKE IN mY hAND.

bUT yOU aRE gONE. sWALLOWED bY tHE rIVER pERHAPS?

THE cITY wILL tHANK mE bECAUSE i sAVED tHEM FROM yOU. AND then i'LL sAVE tHEM FROM THE pOLICE, THE gANGS, AND THE mASKED vIGILANTES. i'LL dEMAND tHEIR fEALTY OR tHEIR dEATH. wHAT sHALL IT bE, sHADOWHAVEN? pROSPERITY OR pLAGUE?

wHAT sHALL iT bE?

14

I Thought Billionaires Owned More Things

The sun was out when Marisol opened her eyes. Patches of golden light made their way into the room from behind the shutters. Still asleep a pillow's length away from her, Vincent breathed deeply, his back moving up and down with gentle inhales and exhales. His golden hair caught flecks of sunshine.

Something was wrong. She sat up, trying not to rustle the bed. The back of his head was perfect. Yes, that's what was wrong with it. Hadn't she taped a wound there a few days ago? There wasn't even a scratch. Perhaps his cut was buried under the waves of his hair that almost curled into angelic tendrils. She grazed the pads of her fingers over those waves, barely smoothing over the stray wisps. He remained undisturbed, so she combed her fingers through, searching for a flaw.

But the Patron Saint.

She retracted her hand, overcome by a rush of complicated shame. Complicated because she wanted to touch the back of Vincent's head again. Ashamed because in that wanting, she broke the covenant her kiss made to her Patron Saint. And of course, referring to a rooftop make-out session as a covenant was something she'd have to unpack if she had time for therapy or a good self-help book.

For now, she had to stow her complicated shame away because she accidentally nudged Vincent awake.

Vincent flipped over to face her and nestled against the pillow. "I'm sorry. I didn't mean to stay here."

"It's okay. I needed it. Your grip, it's like a thunder vest for a dog."

He propped his chin on one hand and smiled. "You're a dog in this scenario."

"No." Marisol smacked him with a pillow. "Only admiring your therapeutic benefits." Oof! Too much movement. She cradled her side. "Speaking of which, where do you keep your Epsom salt?"

He jumped from the bed and headed into the bathroom. The weight of sleep creased his jeans and white t-shirt. The quiet calm of earlier dissipated as Vincent opened and shut cabinets, gathering supplies. More noise followed—running water and ripping packages.

Once Marisol joined him in the bathroom, he handed her a roll of plastic cling wrap and a cast protector. "For your leg." With a hurried crack of the packaging, Vincent opened a roll of fresh gauze and soaked it in a wash bowl cloudy with Epsom salt and water. "We'll wrap this around your bruises once you've cleaned up."

Marisol struggled to bend far enough to wrap the plastic over her foot, finding her once-dependably flexible hamstrings a new source of disappointment. She silently cheered as she secured the plastic wrap, bunching it at her foot. But attempting to wind the plastic around her leg freed it from its hold. Back to square one. In the corner of her eye, she caught Vincent tapping his foot before he asked, "Do you need help with that?"

"I think I have it figured out." Marisol tossed a limp streamer of plastic far from her target.

Vincent commandeered the plastic wrap and circled it around her cast with seamless precision. As soon as he wrapped around the bottom of her thigh, he gave her the roll. "You rip it." Marisol tore the plastic off and sealed it against her skin. Vincent grabbed the humongous plastic Christmas stocking of a cast protector and guided it up her leg. "I'd double-check if it seals." His fingers met hers just above her wrapped thigh.

Heat rose to her face. That was a part of her thigh she wanted the Patron Saint to know, not the siren allure of Vincent. "If your fingers come up any higher, I'll break your hand."

Vincent arched a single eyebrow and raised his hands up as if he surrendered to her threat. She sucked in her cheeks to stop a smile from forming. Proper grief limited her smile supply, and smiles weren't going to be handed out so easily. At least not until he turned his back.

She wheeled to the massive, walk-in shower and eyed the tiled bench at the back that offered a place to sit and a ledge to prop up her leg. However, the shower frame was far too narrow to fit her wheelchair through. "I drag myself across the floor and sit up there to shower? This isn't exactly ADA compliant."

"Right." He scratched his chin. "I could carry you?"

No, no, no, no, no. Way too intimate, Varian. Might as well offer her a sponge bath.

Oh no.

The alternative was a Vincent-assisted sponge bath. Yeah... NO.

"Fine," she said. A passionate protest would've amused him too much. She pulled off her flannel shirt and stretched her arms above her head. Welts formed tight knots on the underside. She checked them to see bruises pool together at her ribs in a blackish purple hidden by her undershirt. Vincent's eyes bugged. "It's not as bad as it looks." Marisol hugged herself.

He looked at her like he did in the hospital: with pity.

"All right. It's bad, but I'm alive, aren't I?" A vision of Annie's pooling blood and lifeless hand overtook Marisol's body like a fever chill. "Help me in the damn shower already."

Vincent nodded and kneeled at her side. Marisol put her good arm around his neck while he wedged his arms under her thighs. He lifted her without grunting. She kept her gaze behind his shoulder. Better to not make a thing of this anymore than she had. Though she cursed her autonomic system for sending blood to places she had no business mentioning in the same breath as Vincent.

He set her down on the tiled bench and pulled the shower head down, handing it to her. "Everything you need—soap, shampoo—is here. I'll make something to eat. It's afternoon. Would you like breakfast or lunch?"

"Surprise me."

He left the shower and tossed a towel over the glass wall within her reach. "When you're done and dressed, I'll help you get back in your chair."

"Vincent?" Marisol called out. The blur of him through the glass stilled. "Thank you."

He tapped on the doorframe and shut the door behind him.

Finally alone, Marisol flung her undershirt over the shower wall. She wiggled out of her boxers, tossing them toward the same spot. Turning the shower on, she welcomed the warm spray over her skin. One layer of grime washed away, and she felt human again. A few more rinses, and she'd start believing compliments.

A good memory floated into her head—the Patron Saint. She was with him on the rooftop when his body and his heat overpowered the winter cold. He ripped off his mask, revealing the man underneath.

Tobias.

Couldn't be him, though. He left her, albeit necessarily, on the lurch. Her Patron Saint would handle her situation unhindered by danger and distance. Who could this super cop be? A famous actor moonlighting as a superhero for research? Not her worst idea. No, she saved that for the next thought, intruding with blunt force.

Vincent.

To her horror, she imagined the rest of their tryst mask-free. Her imagination turned the Patron Saint's kiss into Vincent's electric kiss. Or, when she thought of black-clad Vincent's body grinding into her on the rooftop, she instinctively rubbed her thighs together. That thought bubble needed to pop. Now. "Transference," she muttered before switching the heat down and splashing her face with cold water. That explained her feelings, transference, when a patient mistakes a caregiver's attention as romantic. Transference because there was no way Vincent was...

She scraped her case of transference off, scrubbing until her skin became raw and pebbled under the cold water. After turning the shower off, she even impressed herself when she yanked down the towel off the shower's wall, wrapping it around her. With her newfound spryness, she could drag herself the short distance to her wheelchair without Vincent's help. She lowered herself to the floor, butt barely hovering above it, and distributed her weight between her good leg and arms. A few more scoots, she would be home free.

Another scoot and her hand slipped. Her elbow cracked against the floor. Before pain registered in her synapses, the back of her head hit the tile. Great, after all she'd been through, this was how she'd die? But it was the sharp jab to her dignity that hurt the most, especially as Vincent darted to the bathroom.

"Hell's bells!" He jerked his gaze to the ceiling. And cursed like a grandpa—a great-grandpa.

"I slipped."

"I'm trying not to see it." Vincent draped a towel across his forearms. Eyes to the ceiling, he scooped his arms underneath her and pulled her off the floor. "You're ice cold."

Marisol's loud breath wavered between her trembling and probably blue lips. "Hot water is bad for bruises. It could burst more blood vessels." A layer of Egyptian cotton towels was not enough protection to guard her from admitting why she really needed a cold shower—stupid, sexy Vincent-induced transference.

Dripping and shivering, Marisol accepted another dry towel around her shoulders. Vincent's soaked T-shirt clung to him, revealing compact muscles. Middleweight but with those muscles? He could pack a heavyweight punch. Hell's bells, indeed.

Marisol pointed to his T-shirt as she squeezed her wet hair into the towel. "Sorry. I got you wet."

"I don't care." He piled more towels around her, patting at her arms and shoulders as if she wasn't capable of drying herself off. Vincent unsealed the protector bag and pulled it off her cast. He draped it over the edge of the shower wall. "Sorry," he said, "please don't break my fingers." A corner of his mouth curled into a smile.

Marisol wouldn't follow through on her threat. He had been quick enough about removing the cast protector; it didn't give Marisol time to keep her defenses up. She unraveled the plastic wrap from her leg and wadded it. "You have a good bedside manner."

"Must've learned it from my dad." He cleared his throat as he placed a white terrycloth robe next to her. "Dinner's almost ready. I could serve it to you in your room."

Eat alone? With her current luck, she'd cut herself with a spoon. Even if she surrounded herself in bubble wrap, eating alone would leave her with only her thoughts, which opened her up to the living nightmares. "I'd rather eat with you." And judging by his wet T-shirt, she was trading avoiding the nightmares with uncomfortable, one-sided sexual tension. She tightened a towel closer around herself.

Vincent pulled at his T-shirt and wrung a few drops of water out of it. He cleared his throat again and left.

After wrapping the Epsom salt gauze around her ribs and right underarm, she slid into the bathrobe. It tingled against her skin with a pattering of static shocks. Straight from the dryer. It smelled of Vincent, a faint scent of sandalwood.

Dressed in a clean shirt and shorts, Marisol kept the robe on. The warm scent of sandalwood comforted her, but another smell wafted into her bedroom. Marisol wheeled out into the hallway, following the scent of cumin and chili to the kitchen.

In a dry T-shirt and jeans, Vincent moved around the kitchen with the same fervor as he had in the bathroom. He ladled soup into a bowl and set it at an empty place at the table. Marisol rolled up to the table and set her brakes.

She recognized the aroma. "Pozole?"

"Yes. No fresh ingredients, but it will make-do."

"You made it from scratch?"

"Relatively."

Marisol dug in. The flavors of hominy, cumin, jalapeno, and a hint of lime reminded her of Abuelita's cooking. "You're a good cook."

"You're too kind. I emptied cans and heated them. And a weak attempt at that. "

With a full mouth, Marisol said, "Don't be so modest." She held her hand over her face, forgetting her table manners. "You won't give my abuelita a run for her money, but you're good."

"Thank you."

"Her food was the best. Cooking was how she loved. She barely put up with my dad, but I knew she loved him when she'd make kielbasa and dumplings."

Vincent smiled. Although she was far from home, she had pieces of it with her—the spice of the food and the warmth of his smile.

A sudden snap sounded from the record player and called her to attention. She had tuned out the music until now. After a grainy whisper, the needle settled on a smooth groove and jazz music played faint and low. The jazz singer's alto voice was beautiful but raspy, as if her grief and exhaustion came out with each note. The music unsettled Marisol and reminded her she was in a strange place. She pulled the robe closer around her. "What's with the music? Figured you'd be listening to something more contemporary."

Vincent chortled. "You're right. The music belonged to an old friend of mine."

"Grandpa's home and a friend's music. I thought billionaires owned more things."

"I suppose I'm atypical." His spoon pinged at the bottom of his empty bowl. Vincent walked to the giant record player swallowing up half the living room. "I'll change the music, but we're limited to ol' Leonard's tastes, I'm afraid."

"Leonard is your friend?" she asked.

He nodded.

Leonard was the old man in the painting hanging back at the estate. "And grandpa," she noted. She loved her abuelita, but they weren't friends. If she dished to Abuelita the way she did to Annie, the old woman would pinch her as a stern reminder to be a lady, whatever that meant.

"We spent a lot of time together until he died. A little over a year ago, actually. A hundred and five years old, yet I was like a father to him."

"You mean, he was like a father to you."

"Right. Today's excitement is getting to me." He stretched his arms above his head and seemed to focus on the living room full of objects. "He turned this place into his escape. Being here makes me feel like he never really left, in a way."

The objects that kept Abuelita's presence alive were at Marisol's childhood home in the closet-sized bedroom. Pictures of Abuelita's favorite saints hung from the walls, and in its corner, stood a small table overcrowded with candles in various stages of life, from a pool of wax to an untouched candle with a singed wick. Marisol fidgeted with her cross pendant, moving it up and down the chain on her neck. What objects would remind her of Annie? A stack of magazines? A beaker?

Her attention drifted back to Vincent, who changed the music and put on an up-tempo number with a bouncing and plucking jazz guitar. "I believe I found just the thing."

Marisol expressed her approval with a rhythmic nod. Vincent's shoulders relaxed, as if his entire fate relied on that nod. Now, he moved with graceful speed from the living room to the kitchen. He cleared the table and washed the dishes. While he worked, Marisol wheeled over to a shelf of old and hard-bound books. She squinted at the titles. Only a few letters were recognizable among other rune-like shapes. She touched the book's spine. "These books, were they Leonard's as well?"

He called back from the sink, "Yes. They're Russian translations of some classics. Dracula, Frankenstein, Phantom of the Opera."

She took in a short breath. "You can read Russian?"

"I can read a lot of languages. I can read one to you."

With that prep school affectation? "Sure. A little later maybe." She ran her finger along the edge of the shelf, zigging and zagging around the trinkets of a by-gone era. "Don't take this the wrong way, but you don't seem like the womanizer that everyone says you are. You're too..." She searched for the word in his face. "Sentimental."

He dried his hands on a dish towel. "Really?"

"The records, the books, the comfort food? Definitely sentimental."

He stepped out of the kitchen and held out his hand. "Dance with me."

Scratch sentimental. He was delusional. "Um—" she gestured to her wheelchair.

"Activity will be good for you. Help you recover faster."

And now she knew why patients scowled at her when she'd say that exact same thing. "I'm not objecting because of that. I can't—"

He took control of the wheelchair and pushed her into the hallway, riding the back like she was a shopping cart.

Marisol braced for the impact of the wall at the end of the hallway. "Vincent! We'll crash!"

He wheeled her in a circle, skidding her to a stop. He held out his hand. Marisol scrutinized the eager expression on his face. Surely, he was pranking her. But she found only sincerity in his twinkling eyes and silly smirk. She took his hand. He grabbed her other hand and swiveled her in alternating, sweeping arcs down the hallway.

She surprised herself as her hips swayed, despite being bound to a wheelchair. "I'll give you credit. You can make a set of wheels dance."

"I practiced with children recovering in the hospital." He rolled her under his arm in a turn.

"That's sweet." Wait, he hadn't danced with the kids since she worked there. "But you don't do it anymore?"

He shrugged.

"A dance would mean more to them than a well-lit photograph."

"Hm." The grip of his hand loosened.

She sensed he was closing himself off from her. She pulled him in to face her. "Think about it. You and the kids smiling? A genuine story? If you danced at your so-called ball, you'd make serious bank."

"It wasn't the greatest environment for dancing. Too many egos in the room."

Marisol chuckled. She remembered the ball and Annie standing in front of the board. They laughed at her when she mentioned the potential of her research. She mentioned her research at the ball. Then the Bloodsucker got her. Marisol gripped the arms of her chair.

Vincent stopped swiveling her around to the music. "What is it?"

The Bloodsucker had to be at the ball. "I think I know who the Bloodsucker is."

15

CABALLEROS FOR JUSTICE

Vincent tossed a legal pad on the dinner table. Marisol wheeled to the table. He took a seat and spun the legal pad to face him. He started to sketch. The pencil scratched swift lines onto the pad, reconstructing the layout of Vincent's ballroom.

Marisol interlaced her fingers and stretched her palms outward. A satisfying click of her joints announced she was ready to work. "Whoever is behind all this, I think they went to your ball."

"We'll try to relive your memory of it."

"Annie always had theories but only would share them with me... until that night."

"What did she know?"

Marisol bit the inside of her cheek, and a knot twisted in her stomach. She made a discovery about Vincent's dad and made a serum from it. And someone killed her for it. Her mind jumped to that fateful night in the lab, as if she opened a door that she wanted to close. She didn't want to re-see the teeth, to re-hear the screeching and the gunfire. What did Annie create? "She thought we could create gene therapy by coding the chemical compounds 'superhuman' traits. Perfection in a pill. Sort of... a sharing of power?"

"Superhuman?" He raised an eyebrow.

"I know, right? Crazy theory." She forced herself to roll her eyes, hoping Vincent studied the sketch instead of her face. Marisol rotated the legal pad and drew stick figures around the room. "She mentioned her theory at the ball to the board and you."

"Anyone seem suspicious?"

"No offense, but you're all weird." She studied the stick figures on the legal pad, remembering Annie rattling off the possibilities of her research. She recalled the snickers and raised eyebrows of the board members. All of them thought Annie was a joke. All but one.

"Which one?" Marisol nibbled her lip. "The board." Marisol dotted above each stick figure. "Dad 'Stache, Jowly Paunch, White Updo, Fluffy Brows, and the Skeleton."

Vincent's expression tightened as if he bit into something sour. He was obviously confused.

"I gave them nicknames. They all thought Annie was a crazy drunk — except one. I can't even see his face." But she could remember the way he made her skin crawl and shuddered. "I just see his terrible smile."

Vincent frowned. "We're not jogging your memory well."

"Trauma's turned my head into a fog. You were across the room. Anyone stick out to you?"

He closed his eyes. "I see it now." Vincent held out his hand, spreading his fingers apart. "I'm in the ballroom, next to the French doors. Whit is across the room at the staircase, posing for more photos. My board, who have names because they're human beings and not fairytale dwarves, is gathered around your friend. Wentworth, Edward, Hillary, Francis, and Ruthven. And then? I see something strange."

Marisol ran a thumb over her knuckles, anticipating a clue that would bring her closer to finding justice. "What is it?"

"I've never seen anything like it. Shining, shimmering, silver. The most amazing woman in a dress."

Marisol crumpled the yellow paper and threw it at Vincent. It bounced off his forehead, landing on the table. "Do you ever take anything seriously?"

"It's my board. They're not exactly criminal masterminds."

Marisol hit her forehead on the table, punctuating her frustration with another bump.

"Give your memory time. It will come back to you. I'll try to send a message to Quinlan about your hunch if I can get phone service out here."

She really needed to punch something. "Great. I can't wait to sit on my ass and twiddle my thumbs while the menfolk figure this out." Marisol exhaled until the last of her breath cooled her lips. In another breath, she might settle for flicking something. "If I could get to the city, I'd tell him. The man who saved you? The real Patron Saint? I know him."

Vincent rolled his eyes and tossed his pen on the table. "If you want justice, the courts should deliver it. Not some souped-up cop."

"Maybe we need to fight crazy with crazy."

"If he's so great, you wouldn't be here. He would've saved you and your friend." Vincent crossed his arms and tensed his jaw.

Why does he seem so angry at him? It's not like the Patron Saint could control the whole world. In Spanish, she repeated something Abuelita said fresh out of Mass: Bad things happen because people choose to do evil, not because good people can't stop it.

"If evil is a choice, where does good even come from? How do you know if anyone, including him, is good?" Vincent asked, confrontationally, sounding like Marisol after Mass without the scolding pinch from Abuelita.

As with any existential question, Marisol didn't know the answer. All she knew is that the Patron Saint sure as hell felt good. "I know he's good," she answered with a purr. Her memory of her last night with the Patron Saint on the rooftop spread heat across her face.

"You have feelings for him."

"Jealous?" Marisol gulped, wishing she could take back the word because, in truth, she wanted him to be.

He stretched back in his chair and tossed the yellow wad of paper in the air. "I can't be. He's an idea. It's like being jealous of Freedom."

She certainly wasn't attracted to an idea, but there was something in the way she wanted the Patron Saint to reach inside her and pull her darkness to the surface—to make her feel like she wasn't holding back. "I think I'm made for someone unconventional." Marisol snatched the crumpled paper from the air and crinkled it in her hand. "I've never been good at relationships. Too much work, they say. And he swoops in, takes my breath away, and disappears into the night. It's—"

"Convenient." Vincent enunciated the t at the end. The sound of his elocution lessons in his voice had returned.

Marisol held out the ball of paper to him. He reached for it, and she snapped it away just out of his grasp. She challenged, "Magical."

"Give it a few days. A week. He'll be a nice story you tell yourself when you look at the sky." He yanked the ball of paper from her and tossed it like a basketball into the bin across the room. "With no danger in the equation, you'll wonder what you ever saw in him."

"It's not like that. When I look into his eyes, I feel that... spark." Damn, she got swept up in some unchecked earnestness. Marisol looked down at her hands, wincing. She braced for his inevitable wise-ass retort. Instead, silence. What was Vincent thinking? Marisol peered up from her hands, her eyes meeting his. His gaze searched hers as he inched closer to her. She tensed, transfixed by the shimmer in his eyes. Was there something on her face? "What?" she asked.

He laughed, mocking and haughty.

"Go ahead. You're not the first person this week to laugh at my romantically challenged life. Annie said—" Marisol pictured Annie laughing and waving a finger at her the morning after she had met the Patron Saint. She would never see those teasing eyes behind those cat-eye glasses again. Marisol's eyes brimmed with tears. "Annie said I have a mask kink—that I'm into masks because I lose interest easily. She said that in a mask, he can be whoever I want him to be." Laughing at herself might fight back her tears, so Marisol pushed out a chuckle that came out more like a defeated sigh.

Vincent's eyes grew wide while he sputtered from holding in laughter.

"At least I'm admitting my potential kink. I'm sure years of prep school wired you into some bizarre humiliation roleplay or spanking fetish." Marisol shifted in her wheelchair, thinking of Vincent's backside turning pink after a slap. Her slap. She had a bad case of transference.

He shrugged his shoulders and rubbed his chin. "Maybe." His mischievous grin faded. "But, you're not alone. As in, you're not the only one who's romantically challenged."

Marisol wiped away the tears that escaped down her cheek with the heel of her hand. "Probably shouldn't let PR play matchmaker."

"I am aware." He cleared his throat. Again. The guy needed to keep some lozenges around. "I haven't wanted to subject anyone to a serious relationship."

"Realized you're too insufferable?" Marisol crossed her eyes in case her sarcasm wasn't thick enough.

"Um." He tapped the table rapidly. He exhaled and looked at Marisol. "I can't have children."

His elegant posture caved. He looked as if this one thing turned his everything to nothing. She gasped. "Oh."

"Been poked and prodded repeatedly all to say, 'case undetermined.' I've wondered whether it's my grandfather's work studying the biological effects of nuclear energy finally rooting into my generation of the tree." He shifted his gaze as it briefly met Marisol's. "I haven't told anyone that before. I suppose I should have you sign an NDA." He looked down, resembling one of Abuelita's pictures of a saint, a being of suffering and serenity.

Marisol hadn't noticed how thick and long his eyelashes were until then. She wanted to touch him—anything—to show he could trust her. "I wouldn't… and you shouldn't let that hold you back from something real. You can have children if you want."

He shook his head.

She wondered at what point in the conversation she'd sound like her mom by listening to protests about becoming a breeder and unquestionably demanding a brood. Children never seemed like something anyone sane or responsible would want. They belonged in a world of plentiful resources and love, a world so far out of reach that Marisol saw it as a tree she'd nurture but never derive shade from. But Vincent didn't seem irresponsible or selfish or anything else she'd use to describe most parents. His need to give love made him wholesome.

She said, "You're not quite as insufferable as I've suggested. You're kind and caring in an empirically attractive package."

"A package that comes with quite a few disclaimers."

"Just a package. Besides, if you're shooting blanks, I know a lot of women who would think that's a dream." And what a dream! Beautifully messy intimacy without barriers, pills, ovulation schedules, or side effects. No latex and chemicals. Just free. The mental rise in her body temperature moved from her face to her belly. She cooled off by blurting, "They're not heiresses looking to merge world power with offspring, but you should try something unconventional. And I'm not talking about the hair color of your date."

"It's better to keep things superficial," he said, leaving her joke unacknowledged, "to stop the inevitable... pain."

"You gotta connect, man. You have to share the pain, or you'll end up..." Doomed like her or worse—hardened like Caz. "End up dead inside. I swear if you hadn't been there for me last night, I'm not sure I would've made it." Uh oh, she left her whole heart out there to be stomped on. She better reel it back, so he didn't get the wrong idea. "And it was just a little bit of connection. A little bit can make a world of difference."

"You never give up, do you?" His observation felt like an unearned compliment.

Marisol avoided him by tracing the pattern of the table's wood grain with her fingers. "I've given up plenty of times. On my career. On people."

"No. I've seen it."

She fidgeted, feeling unworthy. "You barely know me."

"I know enough. You've survived against the odds."

She shifted in her wheelchair, poking her bruises. "Yeah. I'm doing great."

"You've taken care of me."

A bit hyperbolic there, Varian. "I applied basic first aid out of professional obligation."

He dug something out of his pocket and tossed it on the table, a crinkled package of tissue with the last unused one folded inside. It couldn't be... the same fancy tissue she gave him when he almost upchucked off the fire escape?

She wanted to shrink away. It was like when patients who followed the doctor's orders thanked her for their hard work. "It's what nurses do. Anything to clean up the barf, even if it's from a bad hangover."

"A lie. It wasn't a hangover."

The memory, rearranging and reinterpreting itself, spun her brain to dizzying heights.

"That morning, Leonard asked to end the treatments prolonging his life. I needed a moment after we signed the documents and found you instead." He held a breath while his eyes began to shine.

The way she understood that morning dropped out from underneath her, throwing her into a free fall. "Holy shit, Vincent, I'm sorry."

He rubbed his hands together and stared at them. "I'm sorry. I lied because I couldn't bring myself to accept kindness because..." He squeezed his eyes shut. "Kindness makes the pain too real. I'd rather do what I do. Put on the mask and become the fool." Finally, he looked at her with clear eyes but a strained smile.

"It was just a tissue."

"No. Me diste esperanza."

You gave me hope. His low, whisper-like voice tensed inside Marisol's abs. The only one who could bother her that way was him. A notion she couldn't quite place tugged at her.

She reached her hands to Vincent's face to make the mask, to connect. But he couldn't be, not with his average stature and lean frame. She folded her hands into her lap. Of course not.

"You're thinking about something," he said.

Vincent had a way of fishing out the truth, so she might as well admit a part of it. "Your voice. You're not putting on that affectation."

"I don't speak with an affectation."

"You do. I've noticed now that it comes and goes. It's how I can tell when you're performing and being real."

Vincent scowled and clamped his mouth shut. "Hm."

Damn, she touched a nerve again. "I didn't mean to make you self-conscious. I'll put my good foot in my mouth." She released her brakes, backed away from the table to retreat, and wheeled halfway down the hallway. If she kept going, she'd wind up alone with her thoughts. She stopped. "Could you read to me?"

"Not put off by my voice?"

"The opposite."

He cleared his throat. "Any preferences?"

"Something I'll understand."

In her bedroom, Marisol popped a painkiller and heaved herself into the bed. She moved to one side to leave a space for Vincent. She ran her fingers through her hair and slid out of the bulky robe. Sure, he'd just read to her, but it's not like she couldn't try to look her best despite the circumstances. Her primping completed just as Vincent entered her bedroom with a book in his hand.

"What do you have there?" Marisol straightened the wrinkle in the sheet next to her.

Vincent fanned the pages and sat in the easy chair in the room's corner, opening a tattered paperback. He cleared his throat. *The Curse of Capistrano.*

Eyes in the book and butt in the chair across the room from her, he hadn't taken the bait. She adjusted herself again to sit in the middle of the bed, no longer leaving an inviting space. She listened to the tambour of Vincent's voice. His true voice.

For the rest of the night, he read to her. As her eyes grew heavier, she heard him read, *You seek adventure? Here is adventure aplenty, fighting injustice. Band yourselves together and give yourselves a name. Make yourselves feared the length and breadth of the land! And then you shall be caballeros in truth, knights protecting the weak, Señor Zorro said.*

Huh, Zorro. Another masked hero. She drifted off to sleep.

16

Bone Deep

Marisol turned over in the bed. Although due for another round of painkillers, a rush of energy still coursed through her veins, the energy of seeing Vincent.

But he was gone. He had neatly piled his pillow and blankets on the easy chair in the corner. She hated that chair.

Annie, sprouting from Marisol's mind, rebuked her, "Dirty slut. I thought you had a mask thing. Now you're feeling butterflies over Vincent Varian?"

Marisol shrugged, both as a response and as the only sane way to handle her newfound ability of talking to the dead.

Annie apologized, adding, "When I called you a dirty slut, I didn't mean it in the pejorative but in that reclaimed power sort of way."

"I know," Marisol said, as she rolled out of her room. Annie faded away. Unfortunately, the empty quiet of the kitchen and living room reflected the conversation in her head like a funhouse mirror. Everything inside was empty and Vincent-less.

There was only whipping and tapping in rapid succession. She followed the sound and discovered Vincent outside on the deck. His back to the windows, he jump-roped with perfect form—elbows tucked at his hips and forearms parallel to the floor. Sweat streamed down his stick-straight back, darkening the back of his sweatshirt. The rapid whips and taps of the rope played an ode to his balance, speed, and strength. Marisol laughed to herself, enjoying the sight too much.

She knocked on the window and caught Vincent's attention. He threw down the jump rope, jogged to the sliding glass door, and opened it. "Come out. I have something to show you."

The air, though cold, held the promise of spring. She wheeled to the end of the deck, where Vincent pointed. There sat an awkward tower of unfinished wood scaffolding. From it dangled a leather speed bag that had a patch sewn on its side. "I found this among Leonard's things and thought you would like it."

"How did you know that I—"

"There were some kickboxing gloves with your items from the hospital." He presented her gloves and a roll of gauze that awaited her on the deck's ledge.

Marisol hid her smile by looking down at her cast. "Kind of hard to box with a bad leg."

"You're not ready for the ring, but you could work on your rhythm. Give me your hand." Vincent wrapped her knuckles in gauze.

She shifted in her chair, straightening her posture. Vincent's presence unwound her muscles held in a twenty-five-year-long clench. What did that mean? What was he to her?

A man with a tender touch who tucked in the end of her gauze as he prepared her fists for beating the shit out of something. A strange man. A good man. But good things in Marisol's life had the shelf life of a mayfly.

While she squeezed her hands into her gloves, Vincent poised the speed bag at Marisol's sitting height. To concentrate, she licked her lips and raised her fists above her chin. She started with gentle, repeating jabs to understand the new rules of her healing body. She hit the bag with the sides of fists, rotating her arms. Once she found the rhythm, she picked up her speed, hitting the bag with more force.

Old Marisol wouldn't need to be gentle with the bag or herself. Dead friend? Jab. Her killer on the prowl? Jab. Jab. Leaving Shadowhaven and the Patron Saint? Jab. Jab. Cross hit. Throw the entire shoulder into it. The contraption wobbled, rocking from leg to leg. It threatened to tumble to the floor until a miraculous feat of engineering kept it upright.

Vincent flashed a smile. "All right, Lady Dynamite. I think you're ready for your next present." He motioned for her to follow him inside.

Another present? How long would she have to repeat that it was too expensive before admitting she liked it? Then, in the middle of the living room, he handed her a pair of crutches.

She stood and tottered around the room. Mobility. Took the Bloodsucker robbing it from her to get her to miss it. Freedom was better than any overpriced tchotchke she imagined. "Thanks."

Vincent added, "Next will be a walking boot, but surely you'll be back in the city by then."

She'd be back in the city, alone. Annie-less. Friendless and doomed to be alone. She flopped onto the sofa. "Sure."

"I thought you hated it here."

"I hate the situation. I don't hate it here." She rubbed her face in her hands. An idea struck her. "Back in the city, I'd end up crashing at my parents and helping them out despite the bum leg. If you came with me, you could be my thunder vest. You know, help me 'til my leg heals. Whatever you do, I can't have one more friend…" Her breath hitched. Leave, she meant to say.

Silence hovered between them before he asked, "We're friends?"

"Of course." Her gaze lifted, looking him straight in his eyes.

He shifted his sight to the windows. "I can't do that."

"Why not?" Her sinuses burned again. "Not glamorous enough for you?" She blinked away the oncoming tears.

"The paparazzi have a tendency to descend on anyone I give attention to. I'd be... inconvenient."

Inconvenient—the opposite of her Patron Saint. The simplicity of hideaway living had deceived her. Of course, Vincent's visits to her apartment would consist of micromanaging PR teams, minute-by-minute schedules, and intruding photographers. And yet... "You're right about the masked guy. He will end up as another story—some weird factoid about the messed-up city I live in. With Annie gone, I have no one around to keep me from going crazy. And..." She rubbed her lips to give herself a moment, needing to add more bitterness to the sickeningly sweet sincerity clinging to her, she blurted, "I'd rather have a friend around, even if that means life gets a little inconvenient."

He cleared his throat. "Maybe."

She nodded, having said that very same line with loads more of indifference to the occasional moon-eyed chump whom she wanted out of her bed and out of her apartment. The good part about her family was that potential partners rarely entered her life, and for those who did, her family's dysfunction ensured their exit.

Even if Vincent became her friend under the public's eye, she wasn't quite sure what a friendship back in the city entailed. It'd be a strange sight, for sure, but her soul was strange, never quite at home on the Westside but certainly not belonging to the effete assholes with whom she went to school. And Vincent was the *effetest* of the effete. A friendship in the city probably lacked hugs against his chest or tingling touches or borrowed warm robes pinging with static electricity.

And... damn, she'd become the moon-eyed chump.

"The only future you should worry about is what we're going to have for dinner. I'm not promising that it won't be canned and cured, but I can do something extra special."

"Sounds good," she answered, knowing that the one thing she wanted to hear was where you go, I go.

Clean and dressed in only her best flannel, undershirt, boxers, and black-sock ensemble, she hobbled to the kitchen. Vincent's back was to her. He watched over two pots of boiling water. His shoulders were massive under a fitted navy sweater that he paired with tailored gray trousers. Definitely a middleweight with a heavyweight's punch.

"What do we have here?" Marisol nudged Vincent and propped herself up on her crutches to peer over the edges of the boiling pots.

"While you were changing, I found kielbasa in my freezer and the ingredients for dumplings in the pantry." He pointed to the eggs, flour, and butter arranged on the counter. "Potatoes are nearly done. While we wait." He walked over to a small drink cart in the corner. With arms opened wide, he presented a bottle of Perrier in a metal bucket on ice.

Marisol laughed. "You thought of everything."

"I have one more trick up my sleeve." He pulled out a kitchen knife and tapped the blade against the glass bottle. Pop! Marisol squeaked. He poured the bubbling water into two crystal glasses. "Cheers."

As she sipped, the cold, crisp bubbles of sparkling water burst in her mouth. She put down her glass and licked her lips to stave off the sharp sensation. She shifted her gaze up. Vincent stared at her. Swiftly, he set his empty glass down and cleared his throat, his tell. She must be making him nervous. Good.

He returned to the stove and lifted the tall pot of potatoes. His biceps bulged as he carried it to the sink. After draining the potatoes in a colander, his skin glistened from the rising cloud of steam, and a short golden curl drooped over his forehead. Marisol's arms twitched, wanting to reach up and push his hair back.

He asked, "Should I grab a bowl and the electric beater?"

The soul of Abuelita shook her out of her Vincent-induced stupor. She imagined the oft-repeated lecture of how machines took away a food's flavor and loving intentions. "No! We take the potatoes and mash them on the counter with forks, then mix in the egg and flour with our hands as we go."

"On the counter? With forks and hands?" He flared his nostrils, his tone incredulous.

Deep and breathy, she responded, "Afraid to get a little dirty?" She swallowed back the rising embarrassment of her unintentional double entendre.

His doubtful expression relaxed, and the slight turn of his mouth bordered on mischievous, as if he was in on the joke. "No." Vincent conjured a pastry blender and dough scraper from a kitchen drawer and juggled them in the air. "But I balk at hitches in efficiency." He handed them to Marisol.

They rolled up their sleeves. Marisol leaned her weight onto the counter, freeing her arms to work. With the cooked potatoes dumped on the counter, she mashed them using the pastry tools. She sprinkled flour on them and topped them with two cracked eggs. With the blender and scraper, she amassed the ingredients into a ball of dough.

"Boil some more water," Marisol ordered, as she divided the dough and formed half into the shape of a cylinder. The scraper sliced the dough into even pieces. "Do you want to try?"

"Sure." Vincent rolled the dough under his hands, making the shape of a cylinder.

"Don't make it too thin." Marisol guided Vincent's hand to roll the dough under the right amount of pressure. Her floury hands lingered against his. He rubbed his pinky over hers. *Don't be a chump.*

Hiss! Liquid met fire. The water on the stove boiled over. Marisol gathered a pile of sliced dough in one hand and hopped toward the stove. "Cut more dough. I'll add these to the pot." She didn't wait for an objection, favoring the heat of the stove over Vincent's intensity. But new body, new rules. She dropped the dumplings in the water, lost her balance, and stumbled into the stove top. Her fingers caught against the pot's rim.

She sprung back right into Vincent, who lifted her to the sink and ran her fingers under cold water. "Stay here. I'll get the first aid kit."

"No, I'm good. Just wounded my pride. I still can't grasp how much my hands depend on two good legs." The cold water washed the thin layer of dough off their hands.

He rubbed his thumb over her reddened fingertips. "When are you going to start to accept help?"

"At the rate I'm going? Over my dead body."

He turned off the sink. "Better?"

The boiling pot singed her fingertips, so they felt covered in raw pinpricks. "Still hurts."

"I have a Varian family secret for pain."

"Yeah? What's that?"

Vincent cupped one hand under her elbow and pushed against it to present her forearm. From the crease in her arm, he glided his fingers down to her wrist bone. There, he pushed against the spot of her pulse. "The trick is distracting the rest of the nerves." Against her pulse, he placed a kiss.

Just like him.

The rooftop. The kiss. Marisol gasped. She knew.

Vincent broke away from her touch, bounding to the stove. He turned off the burners with loud clicks.

"Vincent." But how could it be?

He sighed, his shoulders tensing up to his neck.

She had to make sure. "Vincent. Come here."

He sidled to her, close enough to graze the top of his hand at her hip. Marisol reached out and pressed her hands against his face, forming the shape of a mask with her fingers. He looked away from her. The blue shimmer of his irises poked through the space between her fingers. Stained glass in the sun. She knew.

Vincent Varian was the Patron Saint.

"It's you."

He drew in a quick breath, as if he was about to say something. Yet he remained silent, managing a shrug.

She moved her fingers down his neck. "I think... I needed him to be you."

The corners of his mouth turned up. His darkened eyes searched her face, stopping at her lips.

Marisol lifted her head to meet his mouth. His true identity was all the more clear to her as he tasted like a thunderstorm: petrichor and air thick with static charges. Goosebumps dotted her arms as her skin sang from little electrical jolts. She pushed her tongue against his, and his arms encircled her waist. The strength of his embrace released her startled gasp. Soon she hummed with delight. She aimed to entice him further, changing the pressure of her tongue to a light flicker and then a strong lunge that he returned. The thrills she chased running and jumping from rooftop to rooftop didn't match her high now.

A twinge from her bad knee warned her. A little too high.

Marisol caught her breath. She rested her forehead against his shoulder. Vincent ran his fingers through her hair and pulled it away from her neck. He kissed behind her ear and down her neck, sucking gently against its tendon, down to her collarbone. His hands slid her flannel from her shoulders. The thin fabric of her undershirt did nothing to block the sudden chilled air pulling her nipples taut. Too high. Her body clenched like a fist, resisting the loss of control. She pursed her lips together and closed her eyes.

He kissed her eyelids, as if starting a reverent ceremony. "How may I please you?"

She popped open one eye. Oddly formal question, but one no one had asked her, even casually: What do you like? She liked the tender sensation of silk braided with the potential energy of leather and shredding power of barbed wire. She liked complex. She liked breaking and reconstructing; a burn followed with a balm.

She opened her other eye and ran her fingers over his belt. "Give it to me bone deep."

He bristled his knuckles against her cast. "I don't want to hurt you."

But what about what she needed? She needed to feel everything—groped, slammed, pounded into. Everything times a thousand just to know she wasn't dead inside. She pressed her lips to his ear. "Pain will remind us that we're alive."

"Hm," he answered like she offered him the sweetest foretaste of pleasure swirling with pain. He scooped her into his arms, carrying her through the hall. As he entered her room, he kicked the ottoman by the chair, and it slid to the foot of the bed.

He lowered her onto the edge of the bed; her bad leg extended on the ottoman. He kneeled before her as if she was his altar. She rubbed his torso with her free thigh, hoping to lure him closer. His body felt so hard and warm between her legs.

He raised his arms above his head, surrendering himself to her. She peeled the sweater from his body. With alabaster skin, he appeared as a monument of strength and symmetry.

Unblemished. Perfect. How? Didn't she pull a blade out of him? But as he looked at her from his place on the ground, the time for answers would be later. Much later...

She wanted to savor him with her mouth and to worship his body. She wanted to kiss the brawn of his shoulders and to run her tongue over the ridges of his abdomen. Yet she was stuck on the altar. Damn him for kneeling. She wouldn't be able to touch or stroke her favorite parts of his body without falling off the bed.

She could only receive his attention. He pulled the black sock from her good foot and traced his fingers up her calf and thighs. At her hips, he pushed her undershirt over her curves, his touch careful of her yellowing bruises. Hot kisses chased after the hem of her shirt. A little skin, then a kiss. He set the pattern forth up her flank and to her shoulder, continuing down her arm to the tips of her fingers. There, he untangled her from the undershirt.

With his face at her hands, she caressed his square jawline and pulled him to her naked body to offer her breasts to his mouth. He indulged her desire by coaxing a nipple between his fingers. His kisses were like a trail of gasoline, and his kneading hands at her breast lit the match. Another pluck. A fire raged inside her, so much so, she arched her pelvis toward him.

"How may I please you?" He took a nipple in his mouth, but his gaze remained on her.

Marisol flung her head back and moaned. "That's good."

"Does it please you when I do this?" He nibbled the inside of her thigh and kissed where his teeth indented her flesh, anointing her with his tongue.

Her muscles wound tight behind her belly, forming into a hollow ache. She sucked in a breath. "Depends."

He nestled his head on her thigh and looked at her with wide eyes. His fingers traced the edges of her shorts. "Depends?"

She nudged his chin with her thigh. "Is that mouth of yours going to go any higher, or are you going to tease me to death?"

He curled his lips into a wicked smile. He kissed her thigh and breathed hot air against her apex. Twisting away, she was unsure if she'd survive. She'd have to demand release. She'd have to tell him to put that wicked mouth to work. She'd have to order him to make her come.

What was that? That inner voice couldn't be her. She closed her eyes, squeezing away her desire. In her self-made darkness, she saw herself in the mask, running through the flames. She was becoming her—a power-drunk creature demanding to be worshiped on her altar. And he was an excellent supplicant on his knees, stroking her through the fabric of her shorts. Oh God.

She propped herself up on her elbows. "Feel how wet you make me."

He pushed part of her shorts aside, exposing her and running his fingers over her bare flesh. His breath hitched, and his ivory skin flushed pink. Was he on the edge like her?

Writhing with every stroke and pluck of her body, she didn't await the answer. She panted and held in a squeal. He laughed, watching her body wriggle and flex under his touch. She feared flying too high and burning. Every squeeze and twist resisted the edge.

"How may I please you?" He withdrew his hands, leaving behind a violent chill that stung against her hot skin.

"You seem to know what you're doing." She whimpered, her body quivering without him.

His tongue teased at the crease of her thigh, a tantalizing preview of what he could do. With her eyes squeezed shut, she breathed deeper and tightened every muscle of her body. He nuzzled again at the inside of her thigh, as if he was waiting to pounce at her command. At her command.

Her eyes opened. She held his chin and ran her thumb over his pouty lips. "Work that pretty-boy mouth on me and don't come up until I scream." She bit her lip and searched his face for approval. Too much, right?

He raised an eyebrow and then yanked her shorts, freeing them off her hips. His arms supported under each of her thighs, arching her toward his face. Every part of his mouth found her. His tongue flickered, prodded, and rubbed flat against her. She bucked. His lips suckled. Her fingers clawed through his hair, pulling at his angelic waves. Her body became a clenched fist, tightening and tightening. Yet she bucked and clawed. Anything to hold off the inevitable snap.

"I want to please you. Let me please you." He panted between delicious laps of his tongue.

The toes of her good foot curled. His words and tongue barreled through her defenses. She deserved to have her pleasure matter foremost. He unearthed in her a long-lost sensation, building and building. Her body went rigid. She tossed her head back. The snap, the snap, the snap! "Vincent!"

Ow.

Ow? Spasms traveled down her leg and bored into her wound. Ow. The orange flames of her vision became white flashes in her eyes. Pain manifested into a visual synesthesia, blocking the edges of her view, not at all like the good ache of being claimed and ravaged. Her muscle tremors peaked into an "Ow!"

"I'm stopping."

Her entire body stiffened into cramped angles. "I just need a moment." Maybe the moment needed to be a minute or—oof!—twenty.

He tightly wrapped her naked body in the sheets. "Breathe."

Right. How had she instructed patients through similar pain but forgot now? Must be Vincent's talent of turning her brain into mush. She nestled in the perfect bevel between his shoulder and collarbone. The sharp pain became a dull pulse.

Their breathing synchronized as she traced her fingertips along the golden hair of his chest and smoothed over the muscular lines of his torso. "Kind of feel like a straight dumbass when I talk a big game but reach my limit right at the first O."

His mouth formed into his feline smile. "You shouldn't feel like a dumbass. I should very, very, very gently," he said before kissing the soft spot behind her ear, "find what your recovering body can handle."

Sounded like a delicious and wicked and great idea—as great an idea as glancing over the trail of golden hair below his navel and under his waistband "We don't have to make this about me." She palmed his erection and felt it strain against his fly.

Vincent hissed and shooed her hand away. "I have a better idea."

"And deny yourself pleasure?"

He hovered his mouth over hers and tangled both of his hands in her hair, effectively pulling her away from his lips. "Whose pleasure is being denied?"

Marisol wiggled her hips to fight the empty need within. The warm breath from his parted lips promised the electricity of his mouth. But the gap between them, barely an inch, was the good kind of wound that left her begging for more. Maybe she could ride along the edge the rest of the night, savor the quieter pleasures, and hold off the loud peaks? She arched into his arm, hoping that hand of his would yank open the sheet and dip lower and lower.

"Turn over," he said with a feather-light rasp.

Her grin widened as she flipped onto her stomach. She heard only the whispering of Vincent's hands rubbing together. His oil-slicked fingers smoothed over Marisol's lower back. He kissed the spot and glided his hands up her back, pressing his thumbs against the tight muscle between her neck and shoulder. The cassia in the oil heated her skin.

Marisol greeted her muscle's release with a grateful hum, and she shifted to rest her cheek on her arm. A massage wasn't exactly what she expected, but it served as an adequate substitute. His hands traced down her sides, applying pressure at the outer edges of her glute muscles. She opened her eyes a little, watching Vincent's perfect, shirtless, shining body move over her. The perfect body that aroused as many questions as it did pleasure. "Can I ask you something?"

"Hm." Vincent ran his hands in a curve at the back of her thighs. His fingers whispered along the crease just under her ass.

"I think most of the time the media said you're out of the country, and you've been busy as him?"

"Is that a question?"

"No, but..." Marisol furrowed her brow. "How do you do it? The media have pictures of you tearing up a hotel in Barbados when I know you were punching baddies in the city."

Vincent inched off the bed. He picked up a computer pad and called up a gossip magazine. He presented Marisol with a blurry picture of himself under a headline:

SOCIALITE SNOGS DIVA

American heir Vincent Varian seen in Notting Hill club locking lips with Della D days after attending gala with model. True love or new notch?

"I play a part to hide the other side of me. If that's not enough, I'll stage a photo. It seems that I'm in London now." Vincent raised his eyebrows and sighed. He had sacrificed his reputation to hide his alter ego. "It is amazing what people will believe with Photoshop and some hired actors. Money has afforded the Varians' privacy."

Marisol shifted onto her back and swiped through various articles on the screen. A lightbulb went off about her earlier conversation with Whit DeWinter in the powder room at the Varian Estate. "Your date at the ball said you seemed like two different people. She was right." She sat up. "Everything that made little sense about you wasn't you at all."

"Right." He lowered his lips to hers.

She could give and deny just as easily. Before their lips brushed, she said, "When they kidnapped you, that wasn't staged with actors. The men even said a Patron Saint attacked them. You said—"

"A half-truth. I saved myself." Vincent tucked her hair behind her ear.

"They didn't say Vincent Varian beat them up."

"That's because I keep an aerosol hallucinogen on me. It looks like pepper spray and disorients a person enough to create images in his head. To them, a Patron Saint did 'beat them up.'" His baritone voice at her ear vibrated down to her core. "Not that they picked the wrong venture capitalist to mess with."

Marisol nudged him away with her shoulder. "Is that what you did to Izzy? He said the darkness came alive and attacked him."

"Not exactly. I called him through a voice box and mimicked someone I had heard once when I surveilled their calls. It scared him enough to come out himself." He mauled her with pecking kisses on her neck.

Marisol pushed his face away, her hand splayed over his face like a starfish. "Who could scare Izzy enough for him to go do a pawn's job?"

Her fingers muffled his answer, "I don't know. Something in the voice, I suppose." As she removed her hand, he kissed the tips of her fingers. Between kisses he added, "But I did light his drug supply on fire and smoke-bombed the getaway car. Siccing the police on him was the bow on the package."

Marisol yanked her arm away. "You also broke his nose." That the angelic beauty she faced could inflict such violence tempted her like honeyed words, searing into her a desire only he could fulfill. The sheets rustled as she rubbed her thighs together.

His gaze fixated on her lips. "Sometimes you have to apply pressure."

She remembered Tobias chucking a shard of burned Varian packaging on his desk. She turned away from Vincent. "They're using your company name to get drugs in this city."

"Yes. I've been working with Quinlan to figure out how."

"How long have you worked with the police?"

"I work with Quinlan, not the police. For a few years now."

"You called the police dispatch through that device in your suit."

"I know how to manipulate the police to achieve certain outcomes." He wrapped his arms around her waist and nibbled at her shoulder.

She faced him. "Like tying up bad guys outside a precinct?"

"One way." He growled, revealing his alter ego hidden underneath.

His explanation reminded her of the night she first met him. "Not too long ago, I pulled a knife blade out of you. Your body should look like a human pincushion. Instead, you look airbrushed. How?"

"Are you sure you can handle my secrets?"

"You haven't chased me away yet. And if that secret is an increased healing factor? Spill it and get me out of this cast."

He slid both hands down the calf of her good leg. "I like you helplessly unable to move from my clutches." He grazed the sole of her foot, tickling her.

After a few tortured wriggles, she ghosted her fingertips down his chest to his abs and teased the waistband of his pants. "Aren't you curious about what I can do to you when I have two good legs?"

Vincent held her hand against the flat plane of his stomach and leaned toward her mouth. "Hm."

"Hm indeed." Her lips parted to close the gap between denial and indulgence with a kiss.

"Get dressed and pack your things."

She jolted as if she overestimated the rise of a stair. "That's not where I thought this was going."

He sprung off the bed and pulled on his sweater. "Follow me when you're ready. I need to show you something."

If a secret vigilante identity wasn't enough to interrupt sexy time, what the ever-loving hell did he have to show her?

17

Family Secrets

Marisol popped lukewarm pieces of dumplings and kielbasa in her mouth as she hobbled around and collected her things. Not an ideal means of eating, but at least she ate. With the way Vincent stormed about the place preparing to leave, she doubted he ever did.

She inventoried her clothes and supplies and discovered she had lost her gorgeous new cashmere coat to medical waste. It was cut off at the hospital after soaking in her blood. Other than her necklace, the survivors of the attack were her now-dead phone, keys and keycard, fingerless boxing gloves, domino mask, and boots. Despite a quick, softening polish from Vincent, the leather of the boot still felt stiff from her blood. Yet she felt grateful to put at least one foot in a shoe. The rest of her things, including her medicine, she shoved into a garbage bag, the suitcase of champions.

She borrowed an old army green field jacket, cinching it tight at her waist. Dressed and ready to go, she followed Vincent and entered the garage underneath the house. The door thundered when he opened it, revealing a vast tunnel.

Another one of Annie's theories proved true. *The underground tunnel.* Marisol pulled the collar of the coat closer around her throat. As Vincent helped her into the seat of his roadster, she couldn't take her eyes off the tunnel. "That tunnel doesn't lead to a secret lab, does it?"

Vincent shut the passenger door before answering her. After entering the driver's side, he sank into his seat and answered, "No." He dug out a pair of gloves hidden in the inner pocket of his brown leather bomber jacket and squeezed his hands into them. Even driving had to be a theatrical production.

Marisol held in a laugh. "You wear driving gloves?"

"They help with a steady grip."

"I look like Tiny Tim, and you look like a Ken doll."

Stone-faced, he buckled himself in and started the car. With a push of a button, the car lit up and hummed with electric power.

The car charged through the tunnel. Marisol gasped as the dotted line of lights turned into a single streak. They approached nothing but a dark abyss. Vincent stomped his foot on the accelerator. The car shot up onto a winding country road lined with giant trees stretched toward the moon, but their tops slumped over in defeat. The engine hummed. Tires screeched. The silver roadster weaved between the reflective stripe in the middle of the road and its edge. After gaining traction, the car straightened. Vincent said, "The tunnel was a shortcut."

Rain intermittently tapped against the windshield, and soundless lightning emphasized the widening spaces between the trees. A storm arrived as soon as they returned to civilization mere miles from Vincent's estate. To Marisol's relief, they arrived at the back of the estate, far from the front's towering pillars and ominous Latin message.

A sudden worry struck Marisol as the car arrived with bombast, speeding down the driveway. "Will they come after us here? This is your home after all."

"I anonymously submitted a staged photo from Europe. It helps that the paparazzi spotted another me outside the country. Plus, it takes over two people to make this place seem inhabited."

Vincent drove his sports car into the garage. He pulled the car into a space next to a larger town car and put it in park. "What do you think?"

Marisol looked around. There was only enough space for another car, fitting her vision of a suburban garage, not one belonging to a palatial estate. "I thought your garage would be bigger."

Vincent smirked. A door in the floor opened to a ramp below. He jerked the gear shift into reverse and slammed the accelerator. The tires squealed as they backed onto the ramp. Marisol braced herself against the dashboard. Vincent maneuvered the car backwards into a dark and endless garage, outrunning bright overhead lights as they turned on in succession. Vincent gripped the wheel and pulled it in one direction, spinning the car 180 degrees. He hit the brakes and slammed it into park.

The last of the lights clicked on, illuminating an endless underground garage. The sudden brightness hurt Marisol's fluctuating pupils. Through squinted eyes, she observed a motorcycle and hulking sports utility vehicle. A grid of metal compartments lined the walls of the garage. "Big enough for you now?" Vincent asked, the side of his mouth curling. He tucked his gloves back into his jacket as he left the car.

"You're showing off." Marisol pulled herself out of the sports car and propped herself against her crutches. Her gaze traveled over the expanse of the basement. The mountain of secrets stretched out before her and drew her in a trance. She almost forgot to step forward with her crutches. A sweaty squeeze of the handles brought her back to the present. "What's all in here?"

Vincent touched a metal compartment. It lit white-hot under his fingerprints. The compartment unlocked with a click and opened, revealing a row of armored suits and capes. In the unforgiving bright lights, they looked more navy and gray than black.

"Your suits aren't black," Marisol said.

"Night isn't pitch black, you know." He pushed the compartment, and it receded back into the wall with a click.

Marisol bit into her cheek, devising a plan of later pulling his chest hair or digging her nails into him. Something to make him pay for being such a smartass. Or would he enjoy that too much? Go the opposite way. Make him suffer by being gentle.

She studied the unending grid of the compartments. "What else do you have in here?"

He opened another compartment. A rack of random outfits jutted out. Among them a neon vest, hard hat, and a tie rack of... facial hair? "Reconnaissance clothes." He hung his jacket and closed it, opening another one immediately after. "Night and heat vision goggles. Gas masks." Then he slammed the drawer shut and opened another one. "Smoke bombs. Concussion grenades."

Her stomach somersaulted. "Weapons." Vincent's nightlife wasn't the brutish simplicity of punches and bloody noses. It was all-out warfare.

But it was across the underground space where she warily eyed a vault door with a small window. Inside of it, something glowed blue. "What's in there?"

His pupils darted, unfocused. "Other weapons." He told a half-truth just like she'd done before.

Perhaps he's rich and radioactive... "We're not sitting on some nuclear warheads, are we?"

He scoffed and shook his head. "Of course not! I use nothing that's lethal... on purpose."

Marisol swallowed to hold herself back from asking if he had killed anyone. A tight sensation in her chest revisited the times Caz had returned home with a rehearsed calm. She didn't want to know the answer to that nagging question. "Is this what you needed to show me?"

Vincent pocketed something from one compartment and elbowed the button to an elevator. The doors soundlessly glided open. "It's upstairs."

Marisol hobbled into the elevator. She squeezed his hand as they rode up, staving off the anxious notion that recently, she had bad luck with elevators. She closed her eyes and teleported back to the lake house where all life's sharp corners had been sanded smooth by Vincent. The elevator arrived on the second floor with a gentle stop. She opened her eyes.

"We're in the eastern wing. Follow me." He kept an ever-widening lead over her as they moved through the hallway.

The ceiling soared above them, supported by sharply arched wooden buttresses. Thick tapestries hung from the walls, billowing into strange shadows among the limited celestial light from the windows. The dust particles clung to the inside of her nose. She sneezed them away. Yep. Definitely didn't keep maids and butlers around.

Their footsteps echoed as they proceeded down the cavernous hallway. They passed through a towering archway. Its height reached Heaven, but she felt dread and wonder, as if she entered Hell. He prowled farther ahead of her. "Vincent, slow down!"

Thunder roared and lightning cracked, strobing the hallway in blue. He stopped. Blue light emphasized his back muscles tensed in vigilance.

She hobbled, catching up with him. Breathless, she said, "You're being weird and not in that usual charming way."

Though still, he stood with the rigid energy of prey caught in a predator's trap, too frozen with fear to play dead.

"I do it too," she said, soft and low. "When I'm afraid someone won't like what they see." She was a moment from touching him, to bringing him back to the Vincent she knew. "Ask to meet my family, and I'll be a real dick."

His shoulders moved as he breathed deeply. Lightning struck close, practically blinding her and charging the air with static. In the brief shutter of darkness, he picked her up. Her crutches toppled to the ground.

This was his plan, right? Goosebumps traveled up the nape of her neck. Right?! He rushed her along the hallway. Only through flashes of lightning could she see his face—all angles and muscle. Sharp and cruel.

They passed the grand staircase of the ballroom and entered the west wing. This wing was a wicked parody of the other side. Sheets covered the windows rather than thick curtains. Tapestries peeled off the walls, shredded by time. The air smelled musty, as if the rain rotted the home's insides. Broken furniture cluttered the hallway. Vincent charged and kicked through the mess, heading to wherever he was determined to take her.

"Put me down," she demanded, but to her escalating fear, Vincent tightened his grip around her.

He kicked open a set of double doors and entered a dark room. A flash of lightning revealed the place to be a study, and he set her down on a desk. She squeezed herself tightly together to shield herself as he broke furniture around the room, gathering objects. He arranged his tools in a line next to her on the desk—syringe, scissors, circular saw, and a bedpan. If she escaped, she'd manage three hops to the door before he'd catch her—to do what? With those tools, what was he going to do to her?

Just under her legs, he opened a drawer. The top of his hand brushed against her thigh. Her breath hitched. Even silent and terrifying, he had that siren allure—maybe even because he was silent and terrifying. He pulled out something metallic and slammed the door shut.

After crossing the room, he grunted, turning the lights on with an old brass lever. The sound of the electricity buzzed and crackled. The light fixture above them flickered on. It pulsed from dim to bright and back again.

"I can fix you." He drew a vial from his pocket. "All I have to do is inject you with this regenerative serum. But it isn't perfect. You can build a tolerance, and if you get hurt again, it won't work as well. Subsequent doses have unseemly side effects."

"Is that what you have to tell me?" She sighed, allowing her breath to return to normal. "A bit dramatic but—"

"No." Vincent held the scalpel to his other hand and sliced it open.

Marisol froze. Blood dripped from the deep cut, but it gradually shrunk in size. Then it faded to nothing. His palm returned to unblemished perfection. Her eyes burned with tears as her gaze moved from his hand to his expressionless face. How?

Her throat squeezed tighter. "You're superhuman." The words came out like a whisper.

"I am," he answered with an icy resolve.

Her breathing became loud and shallow. "I need a moment to think." Another layer of Vincent peeled away, bringing her closer to his true center. She would accept new, world-destroying information about him the way the dying accept death. The secret side project? The rumored super-cop program? Marisol remembered the old shopkeeper patient saying the Patron Saint was stronger than any man. And his kiss—being around him electrified her, standing her hair on end, a psychosomatic response. But now? What if Dr. Varian didn't just experiment with nuclear energy? What if—Marisol's mouth went dry—this Varian man was the nuclear experiment? Rich but radioactive. "You said your grandfather worked in nuclear power and researched its effects."

"Sort of."

"You're a result of that research."

He chortled, thick with derision. "I'm not."

That left... alien? "What are you?"

Vincent bounded to the other side of the study. He tore down a tapestry, revealing a gargantuan painting of a look-alike ancestor. He was dressed in armor, with a ruffled collar around his neck. His wavy golden hair coiffed at his ears, and a Van Dyke beard framed his haughty pout. He posed with one hand on a globe. In the other hand, he held a helmet.

"With the strength of ten men, I am above the ravages of time and disease. I am deathless. My name is Vicente Vasquez. I'm over 500 years old." Saying his name, his real name, unearthed a long-dead Spanish *ceceo*, sounding a lisp on the c and z of his name.

The floor felt like it warped beneath her. Her limbs seemed boneless. Vertigo and anemia hit all at once. Immortal. Annie hadn't mentioned a fourth option. Marisol caught herself against the desk. She breathed out, "Oh."

18

Everything You Touch Dies

Rain drops continued to patter against the window. They confirmed, to Marisol's relief, that she could still hear. She and Vincent waited in silence for so long, she had doubted it. How long had they been like this? Her, with her eyebrows raised, rolling Abuelita's pendant in her fingers? Him, with his brawny arms crossed over his chest, leaning against the corner? He had bowed his head.

Her brain registered his words in slow motion.

Pieces of his 500-year-long story sounded through—"Sixteenth-century expedition for the Queen Regent to the New World," "drinking from the Fountain of Youth," "exploitation, betrayal, and death." The last words he said before bowing his head swam to the surface of her mind. "It wasn't supposed to be permanent. One drink gave us the power of the gods but took our human gifts. To create life, for instance, a condition set in place to ensure we'd return the power with another drink.

But we shed blood in the Fountain's waters and destroyed it. For that, I can never age or die. I am cursed with eternal life until the balance of Justice is restored to the world."

Tiny vibrations rumbled the room as the thunder faded. "So..." She wasn't sure what to say next, waffling between "What's it feel like to be America's first villain?" and "If magic is real, what else is—fairy tales, legends, God?" But her voice breaking through the tinny pitch in her ears said, "There are others like you."

He lifted his head enough to say, "There is no one like me."

She finally let go of the pendant. "How so? You said—"

"Our bodies can handle damage, but we still need to take care of ourselves. If we are too reckless and take on damage too great, we can become..." He paused and sighed. "Permanently affected."

"That's why you needed the blade out."

He tipped his head. "Only the curse holds the others together. Barely human. They're waiting in cryostasis for the day I can fix them. They're stored down below."

Marisol recalled the vault glowing blue. "The weapons."

He nodded.

"You'll fix them when you lift the curse?"

"The curse will never lift! I've spent lives trying to undo the viciousness of humanity, to restore

Justice. I've tried to learn from our mistakes—to stand by those crushed between our wars and revolutions. I can't do it. It's never enough." He pounded his fist into the wall, cracking the marble.

Marisol adjusted the belt of her coat tighter, as if it would protect her. "How will you fix them, then?" The question she really wanted to ask was how he was going to fix himself before he became some thing held together by the rotting sinews of an everlasting curse.

"Aut inveniam viam aut faciam." Lightning flashed and thunder drummed, its rumbling strength ever closer in the distance. "I will find a way, or I will make one."

"The words carved on your estate."

"I've placed my faith in science to find my way."

His past lives were all men searching, discovering, and exploring. One of those lives belonged to his father—him, Victor Varian. And... the cells that Annie discovered were Victor Varian's cells. Or Vincent's cells. The cells that she used for the serum to improve the flawed regenerative serum he had already created.

The serum that cured her tumor-ridden mouse only to leave it as a monster, deathless and vicious.

A fire burned inside of her, an anger for withholding the truth from her. "It hasn't worked." But she felt angry on behalf of her history. Vincent's people created the ripple of death and destruction across early America. They were the reason her abuelita spoke Spanish. The sins of Vincent's people twisted every branch of Marisol's family tree. She saw it in the raw, overworked hands of her mother, the desperation of her father, and the acquired cruelty of her brother.

He talked to the ground. "I should have never acted on my feelings for you. Not when I can't—" He held his face in his hands, his hair caught between his fingers.

Her body spasmed as it felt like another floor dropped out from under her. They bonded over their pasts, over family, food, and the heartbreak of loss. Yet his homes were living mausoleums collecting more and more stuff because he never had to lose anything.

Through clenched teeth, she said, "You lied to me."

"I couldn't bear it," he replied, voice shaking.

He had the nerve to lie to her and snivel because he felt bad? Her darker self, the one too close to Caz, wanted to make ashes of those fake happy memories at the lake house. "Those stories of you and Leonard? You played me! All along you were talking about yourself!"

"It was all true." He heaved a sigh and muttered, "Leonard was an orphan boy whom I offered a future, and in exchange, he helped me but died an old man." He stared outside the window, clenching the muscles in his jaw.

Marisol gasped as if she had emerged from depths of hatred that she swore she'd drown in. No,

Vincent wasn't shut off from loss, he was a vortex of loss, and he would take her with him. She had to escape. But how? "Come here, Vincent." He kept his focus outside, so she vied for his attention another way. "Vicente, ven aquí." She lowered onto her good foot and propped her weight against the desk's ledge.

He looked at her with his brilliant stained-glass eyes.

She untied the coat and let it drop to the ground. "Ven aquí, ahora, Vicente."

He took one step forward.

That wasn't right. He needed to show how contrite he truly felt. "No!" she ordered, "Crawl."

Thunder rattled the windows. Her Vincent dropped to his knees and slinked toward her like a predator. On his knees, he hugged around her waist and nuzzled her belly.

Marisol's knee buckled, and she caught herself on his shoulders. This still wasn't right. "Heal me, Dr. Varian."

He grabbed the syringe on the table, filled it with the serum, and pulled Marisol's shorts down to expose her hip. He hovered the needle over the muscle and glanced at her with a plea that asked, Are you sure?

She answered, "Do it!"

He jabbed the needle into her side and pushed the plunger down. The serum sizzled in her veins like freezer burn. The first blow hit, taking Marisol's breath away as she stumbled back into the desk. She squeezed the edges of the desk and gulped for air. She caught her breath, a sip of respite. Not completely terrible. The pain had been worth it until the stab became a crushing avalanche. Marisol writhed, kicking her good leg. She wanted to escape her body, thrashing and squeezing her muscles.

She blinked rapidly and then felt nothing.

Released from the torture, Marisol relaxed. So did her stomach. She dry-heaved as a warning. Vincent caught the real deal with a bedpan when she vomited. Before she finished wiping her mouth, another wave of pain crashed into her. Her stomach tightened, heaving up what little she had left.

He sawed through the fiberglass layer of her cast and cut away the cotton layer. With a snip, Vincent freed Marisol's leg. A faint scar below her knee was the only sign of her injury. He said, "You're free."

Her veins buzzed with adrenaline from the drug's after-effects. She moved to walk on her new leg, but it took weight like jelly. She fell into Vincent and steadied herself with her arms around his neck. She could have everything now, the pain and pleasure wrapped in a silk, leather, and barbed wire bow. "I want you more than ever."

"Hm." He leaned his forehead against hers.

She approached the edge. With two working legs, she could jump or walk away. What would it be? She could have everything except... "But answer this. If it wasn't for you, would Annie still be alive?"

His chin trembled as he kissed her forehead. "I don't want to hurt you."

She pushed him back yet kept a firm hold of him, fisting the fabric at the neckline of his sweater in both hands. "Answer me!"

"I don't know."

Sobs wrenched from her chest as an unseen rope pulled her between him and Annie. Escape. "I need to go home."

He held her jawline in his thumbs, his fingers threading her hair at the nape. "The Bloodsucker."

She let go of his sweater. "I'll keep a low profile."

"It isn't safe."

She extricated herself from his grip. "How can I be safe with you?" and stood straight on her own two legs. "Everything you touch dies!"

He closed his eyes and stepped back. His resignation twisted like a vise around her chest. But for Annie, she walked out of his study, ran through his ballroom, and left him behind. He'd just become one of those weird stories she had about her city: man-eating sewer rats, immortal cockroaches, and the weekend affair with the cursed superhuman.

With one of Vincent's computer pads, she coordinated a ride two miles up the road from his estate. It would be a spot far enough away to not betray the estate's perceived abandonment. She'd have to leave soon to meet her ride to allow enough time to reach the mile marker.

Before she left, she ripped a commlink off the wrist of one of his suits. If the Bloodsucker happened to sniff around her apartment, she'd make sure Vincent was a click away—for self-defense and nothing more. Maybe when life calmed down, the commlink would end up in a Lost and Found box next to an ex's sweatshirt.

She took off, swinging her garbage bag of things by her side. She caught her reflection in the gleam of a window. Wearing her hood up in oversized clothes, she resembled a teenage version of Caz. She had to come up with a good story to keep her driver from speeding off and leaving her on the side of the road. But when the driver picked her up, he asked, "What is a kid doing out here at night?"

She replied, "Got a little lost. I had to find my own way back home."

Ínterlude

YOU cAN'T sTOP bLEEDING aFTER sOMEONE aLREADY bLED oUT. i wATCH yOU hOLD sOMEONE'S nECK aFTER THE fUN i hAD. i bEt tHAT sTUPID mASK AND cRAZY oUTFIT mAKES yOU tHINK yOU cOULD rEVERSE bIOLOGY. BUT bLOOD cAN'T gO bACK IN oNCE sOMEONE'S dEAD. dON'T lOOK sO sHOCKED. THE wHOLE pILE OF tHEM wERE tWO-bIT gANGSTERS—bORIS bADANOV wANNABES. iF THE rOOM DoESN'T StINk OF bLOOD AND vISCERA, IT wOULD hAVE rEEKED OF bORSCHT AND vODKA. tHEY don't wANT TO wORK FOR mE, sO i mADE sURE tHEY nO lONGER wORKED. cONSIDER mE dOING yOU A fAVOR. tHERE'S A wHOLE lOT fEWER tHUGS TO cAUSE THE cITY tROUBLE bECAUSE i rIPPED tHEM FROM lIMB TO lIMB. im tEMPTED TO sEE wHAT yOUR iNSIDES lOOK lIKE, tOO, BUT i sEe THE fLASH OF bLUE AND rED. i wOULDN'T wANT TO cAUSE aNOTHER sCENE, wOULD i? i'LL sEE yOU aGAIN, mASKED mAN. AND wHEN i dO? mAKE IT A cHALLENGE. pUT UP A fIGHT. kEEP IT eXCITING. wOULDN'T wANT TO sAY THE sPLENDOR iS gONE aLREADY, eSPECIALLY wHEN i hAVEN'T eVEN sTARTED yET.

19

Alternative Lifestyle

Back in her apartment, Marisol returned to normal life, which meant a straightforward shower and putting on her own damn clothes. Normal life also meant a charged phone. A charged phone after a few days of no service meant incessant beeping and rattling from messages, mostly Marisol's mom, dad, and sister, Nicole.

A detective came by, Maria Soledad. He said you're at a safe house. Madre de Dios, ruega por nosotros. Uh-oh, Mom used Marisol's full name and called on the Mother of God and none of the members of the Trinity. She must be freaking out.

A notion confirmed by Dad's curt, *Return your ma's call, Mare.*

Nicole left, *A guy claiming he was a cop called and asked if I knew where you were. All cops are bastards, so I told him nothing, but Mom and Dad said you got into something bad. Please be okay.*

Marisol was due for a day-long session of telling her family vague stories about a safe house and an attack. That included a heap of *I'm sorry* and *It's not that bad* while leaving out the most thrilling details of murder and mayhem. In doing so, she couldn't mention the 500-year-old super-powered billionaire caretaker who worked the third shift as a masked vigilante.

She made it to the last few messages. The phone asked to delete the voicemails left untouched for a few days in her storage cloud. She clicked them.

Hey, it's Tobias. She internally screamed every expletive in existence. She had forgotten about Tobias. The message continued, *Back home now. I'm toying with the bad idea of showing my badge to your landlord in the morning to make sure you're okay. I assumed after that kiss you'd be the type to admit you've got cold feet and changed your mind. Or was this your idea of a crazy kink? Invite a man over and ghost? Anyway, best of luck to you. No hard feelings.* Sure, he said no hard feelings that night. If he knew she invited him over in the middle of the night and sucked face with Vincent before the Bloodsucker shoved her down an elevator shaft, he'd label her the coldest, craziest bitch in the city.

And that label stung with the next message. *Hey, it's Tobias. I just want to talk to you. No funny stuff.*

And the next message. *Hey, it's Tobias. I hope you're not waiting chained up with a whip because a neighbor came down with her dog, took one look at me in uniform, and made sure the security entrance was locked. She probably thinks I'm a stripper. Or some cop gave her a ticket for not picking her dog shit off the sidewalk. Anyway, let me in.*

And the ever hopeful. *Hey, it's me. Buzz me in.*

She debated deleting the last voicemail to never relive the cringe of that night until...

"Marisol."

A short stream of air cooled her parted lips. The voice was Annie's. *I'm having a night of it. I'm in the dark, the electricity's been weird, and that mouse is acting strange. The serum did something to it. It has increased strength and muscle mass. I'd call 911, but I'm not even sure what to say. Do I say it broke out of its cage and attacked the other mice? Because they're dead. Something in the serum made it unhinged. I should've killed it when I stomped on it, but it came right back up. It's my fault. Dr. Varian buried the research for a reason. I don't know what to do. I thought... Hold on, I hear someone.*

If only she had checked her stupid messages before charging into the lab, she could've sent Vincent in to clobber them. What was she thinking? She didn't need—never needed—that sociopath. She could've easily sicced Tobias and the rest of the SPD to stop them.

And that wasn't the only part barbing into her. Annie's mouse had increased strength and advanced healing like Vincent. Those serum results that she alluded to at the ball may have led the Bloodsucker to seek Annie out. Yet the mouse became unhinged, as if a higher power punished them for harnessing magic with science. If Marisol studied the mouse, she could understand magic and whatever happened to the Bloodsucker.

And whatever happened to Vincent. Vincent and his kind eyes, playful quirks, and odd ideas of gifts. She swallowed the lump in her throat. Vincent and his curse that murdered Annie. She dashed out of her apartment on a mission.

First, she needed a mousetrap strong enough to withstand the strength of ten mice. The fool who owned one bought it to catch a rat under the back steps many years ago. A decision that had forced the family to go to food pantries for the rest of the month. She called him "Dad."

She hopped on the bus to her parents' home. The morning bus to the Westside was practically empty. She took a spot near the front across from the one other rider, a woman who wore compression hose and buried her face in the newspaper. The bus hit a pothole. The impact jostled Marisol forward, and she bristled against the newspaper. She noticed the headline:

SOUTHSIDE BLOODBATH

She projected her voice over the roar of the accelerating bus. "Ma'am?"

The woman inspected Marisol from behind her set of tinted eyeglasses. A chain draped from her glasses to her neck and swung whenever the bus hit a bump. She squeezed her handbag to her body with her elbow, probably expecting Marisol to snatch her purse.

"Can I borrow your paper for a minute?"

The woman handed it over. Marisol pored over the paper. According to the article, retaliatory gang violence reigned. Somebody attacked a restaurant that was an alleged front for the Bratva AKA the Russian Mafia, killing eight people. Police determined the Mob did it after a similar attack on them the previous night. If the story of her attack wasn't the actual story, something more sinister and unexplainable happened. Bodies torn apart? That wasn't the modus operandi among Shadowhaven's gangs. Lately, they got along. Before then? It would've been a sloppy shootout.

Below the fold, however, reported a different chaos. In fewer than a hundred words on page two, the news covered the still-missing virus stolen from the World Health Organization's site in Manila. Damn. Buried among the news snippets of page four, Israel Ramirez, aka Izzy, alleged kingpin, missed his court date. Shadowhaven's police were searching for him after finding a smashed, bloody vehicle on the city's outskirts that was registered to a known associate. Double damn.

At least his news made the main section. Annie made the back page of the local section: Gang Violence Linked to Varian Lab Attack. Marisol wanted to light the paper on fire right then and there. It didn't mention either of their names. They were unnamed victims, victims with a single familial connection to the Shadows. Dead Goon, Yevgeny Smirnov, and imprisoned Goon, Jonathan O'Banion, were members of the Mob. The gangs had followed their old rules with the Mob attacking Shadows and vice versa, and the world continued to spin. Violence toward people like Marisol and Annie happened because of the neighborhoods they were from. They only should've chosen a different place to be born. No conspiracy. No Bloodsucker. Nothing. It was an open-and-shut case. She couldn't believe Tobias would peddle such horseshit, but then again, she barely knew him. And what she knew about him wasn't him at all.

She handed the newspaper back. "Thanks." She rang the bell and hopped off the bus. As she neared her parents' house, she saw someone she didn't recognize moving around the front steps.

Had the Bloodsucker found her already? She flipped up her hood and kept her gaze low, fidgeting with the commlink button tucked inside the wrist of her sweatshirt. Triple damn. She lasted all but a few hours before needing Vincent. Maybe she could bolt inside to get the baseball bat Dad kept next to the nightstand instead. She lowered her weight, ready to sprint.

The man was freakishly tall. He bent over and drilled a plank of wood into another one. A construction worker. Phew. She rolled her shoulders back. He was good-looking, too, with the tailored fit of his long-sleeved T-shirt and jeans emphasizing his thickly muscled thighs and massive shoulders. Not Vincent, but still worth appreciating, like a work of art or a sunset. The title of this work? A heavyweight with cropped salt-and-pepper hair.

And... *ohshitohshitohshit*... she just ogled Detective Tobias Quinlan. Watching him work from the sidewalk, she felt something akin to leaving the oven on.

Except the thing she forgot to turn off was a person.

And damn if those voicemails from that night didn't come back to haunt her.

Of course, she greeted the person who scraped her near-dead body off the pit of an elevator shaft with, "What are you doing here?"

The oh-shit feeling wasn't going anywhere soon. At least, not with the way his speckled eyes glowered. "Marisol Novotny. What in hell's ass are you doing here?"

She ground down a dried-out weed poking through the crack of the sidewalk. "I figured the city's safe now that I barely make the paper." She glimpsed back up at Tobias. Vincent looked diminutive in comparison, relying on a costume and mind games to make him the Patron Saint.

Tobias was already an intimidating height and mass, but that just made him Tobias.

Someone needed to smack her and tell her not every white guy with a chiseled jawline looked the same. Tobias's skin tanned from being out in the sun, and the grizzled start of a graying beard hid the telltale jawline. To compare Vincent and Tobias was to compare the Apple of Eden and a decent orange at the supermarket.

Marisol asked, "What are you doing here?"

"I told you I'd look after them."

Quadruple damn.

The door behind them opened a crack. "Tobias, I have fresh tortillas when you're ready for a break."

"Thanks, Mrs. Novotny." He spouted the phrase with such ease, he must've said it a thousand times in the days she disappeared from the city.

The door swung wide open. "Ay Dios Mio, Maria Soledad."

Mom burst from the door, unhindered by the drop to the ground from the missing stairs. She embraced Marisol on the sidewalk. Shorter and stouter than Marisol, she reached up to hold Marisol's face steady with her dry and cracked hands. Marisol scrunched up her face in exaggerated resistance, pretending to hate every kiss Mom planted on her cheek. Mom's tired eyes widened. "Oh, my Maria Soledad. Your father is inside."

Mom yanked Marisol into the house and straight to the kitchen. "Pete! Maria Soledad!"

Dad ran into the kitchen. Without words, he hugged Marisol, suffocating her against his barrel chest with his burly arms.

Released from the safety of Dad's hug, Mom's onslaught began. "Where were you? Why no calls?"

Marisol breathed deeply to prepare for her rehearsed apology.

Tobias entered the kitchen. "She can't compromise her safe house location." Win for him, saving Marisol from the wrath of Mom.

"I'm fine. I worried about you guys, but I guess I didn't need to." Marisol eyed Tobias, who smirked as he lowered himself into a chair.

They gathered as a rag-tag family around the table where Mom had buffed the veneer raw in patches. Marisol picked at a tortilla smeared with butter while Mom piled more on the serving dish, and Dad and Tobias discussed the Rooks' starting players.

Life was working out for them. She didn't need to pull her family from disaster to disaster. For once, she could let them be. Her new problem would be getting Tobias to stop looking at her like she was the buttered tortilla.

After breakfast, she washed the dishes and watched from the kitchen window as Tobias and Dad drilled the last of the stair planks in place. How would Dad get along with Vincent? Vincent would hire someone to fix the stairs, and he and Dad would discuss a famous boxing match in such minute detail that Dad would be confused because it occurred before Vincent's fake birthdate. Better yet, Vincent would superpower his way to building stairs, cooking breakfast, and cleaning dishes so both parents would stare dreamily at him. Or not. They would probably stand in awkward silence before Dad asked Vincent about his money, deduced the rich bitch had a hand in busting the stevedore union, and finally chase him off shouting, "No daughter of mine dates a scab!" You tell 'em, imaginary Dad.

Despite that strange vision, reality proved even more surreal. Mom was sitting at the kitchen table, her legs extended over Nicole's chair.

"Mom, why aren't you at work?"

Mom ran her fingers through the tangled ends of her dark, graying hair pulled into a tight ponytail. "Your dad said I didn't have to work two jobs anymore. Since my back's killing me, I'm finished with the nursing home." She flipped her hair back almost with a proud air about her.

Great, within the week of emptying her savings account to pull Dad from Izzy's clutches, he had already concocted a hairbrained scheme. "He's said that before."

"I haven't quit yet. I'm using up my vacation days. Mainly to worry about you and what happened to your friend, Maria Soledad." This time, her full name reminded her of who the parent was.

Marisol stacked a freshly clean plate on the drying rack, wiping with the efficiency she had learned from Abuelita. While recalling a childhood where work robbed Marisol of Mom's time and affection, a tinge of jealousy emerged. Abuelita's love made do but had never been the same. "Okay, but why are you making them breakfast? You never made me fresh tortillas."

"Unlike you, I find being a wife relaxing."

Marisol had to be strategic about her eye rolling. If she was too obvious, she'd get the shoe, even as an adult. Besides, it wasn't an interaction with Mom without some comment on her love life. "And why are you giving a police detective chores to do around the house?"

Mom shrugged. "He asked how he could help us, and I told him."

"It's odd."

"I guess, but it felt right."

Must've felt right because before life had broken their family into fragments. To feel right was to feel whole, as if their zip code didn't influence her brother's decisions or push her sister away to safety. "Like if Caz was around?" Marisol asked.

Mom sighed and nodded. She scratched a red spot on her hand where her skin had reacted to cleaning chemicals. Marisol needed to get her new gloves. Mom's tired eyes welled with tears.

Marisol sprang from the sink and hugged her. Mom released a sob. "We were so worried about you. We didn't want to lose another."

"You're never gonna lose me, Mom. Mami." But she couldn't keep such a promise. If anything, the last year taught her that everything was fragile. Yet, could she really tell the truth? Death is inevitable and could happen at any moment. She hugged Mom a little tighter. A lie was better. God, why couldn't Vincent have lied to her one more time? Just say, "No, in fact, I didn't nonchalantly leave my DNA around to send your best friend to her oblivion."

Mom sniffled, her sobbing subsided. "That detective's cute. If I wasn't a married woman—"

"Mom!" Marisol stomped out of the kitchen, playing the role of petulant child. As the door closed behind her, she laughed. Mom had never joked with her.

Outside and away from Mom's jumped conclusions and intrusive questions, she asked for the mousetrap. She could hear Mom already. What's with the mousetrap? Doesn't your landlord take care of that? Pete, her apartment is infested. She should live with us. Thankfully, Dad retrieved it from the basement without Mom noticing.

He presented it to her with the same reverent air of a knight who found the Holy Grail. "What you came for."

"Thanks, Dad." She checked the metal box for weak spots.

"Use a pungent cheese, not that bland crap Protestants always insist on."

"I'm pretty sure Protestants don't eat bland cheese."

"Fooled me."

Marisol tucked the trap under her arm. "Things okay?" Her raised eyebrow showed the full meaning behind her question. Have you seen Izzy? Are you in any more trouble?

"Things are okay. Had someone from that Varian corporation stop by the gym. They helped me fill out a grant to teach boxing as an after-school program. Got the grant. Kids will be comin' in after the weekend, then their parents, and then some money. Finally."

Vincent. He took care of it and not by writing them a check like that. He pulled invisible strings to show that he cared.

She should return to the estate and apologize for leaving. She'd play the role of homebound companion to show her gratitude and be his caged bird. Isn't that what these heroes had in their stories—caretaking sidekicks? Life could be beautiful, like at the lake house. All she had to do was tra-la-la away Annie's life. It could be that easy.

No way. She had a bus to catch and a mouse to trap.

A gruff voice called after her. "Wait!" Tobias pulled on his trench coat. "C'mon kid, you can walk me to my car."

She opened her mouth to protest. She had a plan. It didn't include refrigerator-sized police detectives who had cozied up to her parents.

"What? I'm a vulnerable individual. I need the protection."

She tilted her head, granting him permission to walk beside her.

Tobias let out a long sigh. "Roaches in the safe house scare you away?"

"Actually, our friend did an okay job. Top care. Excellent amenities. I'm thinking about leaving a five-star review."

"Our friend spent a lot of time looking out for you?"

"You could say that." Her mind drifted to list all the ways Vincent looked out for her—food, physical therapy, the other kind of physical therapy. The weight of the memory pulled on her chest.

"It's just... I don't mean to stare... but how the hell are you on two legs, kid?"

That was why he eyed her throughout breakfast. She shouldn't be walking. So she, inspired by Vincent, constructed a half-truth. "The leg thing? A misdiagnosed sprain."

"Baloney."

"Scout's honor. Just a little ice and rest. I'm as good as new."

"I wish I could say the same. I'm on admin leave. Your case is now getting handled by the biggest couple of humps counting down to retirement that our department has ever seen. Sad, really." Tobias kicked a broken piece of the sidewalk. It skipped the surface, hit the base of a parking sign, and bounced to a stop.

"That might explain the bullshit I read in the newspaper. On leave? What for?"

"Procedure. Turns out that when you kill a guy, it gets reviewed. I could be on desk duty, but I may have called my lieutenant a limp dick cuck, and well... they say I gotta go see a shrink to prove that I'm doing alright."

"Are you doing alright?"

He put his hands on his hips and looked toward the end of the block. "I'll get my badge and gun back."

"But are you doing alright?"

"You were bleeding in my arms not too long ago, and you ask me if I'm alright? Jesus, kid." His eyes beamed again. "Not sure if a shrink is right for me. Old habits and all. Haven't been to confession going on... twenty years? Why start now? Especially with someone who can't even claim to talk to God." He scratched the back of his head.

She shrugged. Therapy worked for those who had the time and money for such a "treat." Lacking both became one more thing that separated those who were scraping by from those who were healthily maladjusted. She and Tobias would just have to handle their PTSD through sporadic glib conversations. Wasn't that the true Shadowhaven way?

He leaned back against the passenger side of his weathered sedan and wiped at his cold-reddened nose. "When they identified the body, her mom cried so hard in my chest, I had to change my shirt."

Marisol stiffened. Annie's mom.

"I swear I should be used to it by now—the sound parents make when they find out their child's dead. It's like nature knows everything's out of order and splits the world open with a wail. I'm sure you've heard it before."

She nodded. She had. If it wasn't the most ear-splitting cry wrenched from a single human's voice box, it was a barely audible sigh that sucked out the parents' life force, pickling them from the inside. Had Vincent felt that, watching as people aged and died? What he'll feel when she...

Tobias laughed, but it was small, and he kept his eyes fixed on the block ahead. "And they brought me food. Their kid was murdered, but they fed me."

Marisol propelled herself off the curb and hugged him. Even with the boost, she stretched her arms to reach around his neck. He tensed in her embrace. She vowed to hold on until he relaxed, to thank him for being there when she couldn't.

While he held her, he said, "But the strangest thing happened. When I explained who I was, they told me my partner came to her apartment and asked them questions when they were there. In Korean."

"Your partner is fluent in Korean?"

"The oaf's barely literate in his first language, let alone anyone else's. Not to mention, the bearded man they described in no way fit his fat, ugly mug."

Vincent? Marisol dropped her heels back to the ground. "Our friend made an appearance?"

"I think so." Tobias stared down at her. His big palm lingered on her back. He parted his mouth and sucked in a breath. They froze in the same position as when she had kissed him. He said, "I never expected to see you again. If the SPD suggests you leave, you either don't come back, or you end up —" He lifted his eyebrows. "Anyway, I thought, 'I'll keep an eye on her parents. She'll start a new life far from here, and I'll learn that she's doing okay, and it will be enough.'" His hands left her back.

"Enough?" She crossed her arms. Enough of what?

He scratched the back of his head, paced a few steps, and leaned against the trunk. "I spent my whole life on the receiving end of disappointed looks from the women in my life. My ex-wife. That goes without saying. My own mother even. And I deserved it. I started thinking the job is the only thing that matters. It's the only thing I'm good at. But you have this way of looking at me..."

She twisted her face, confused. "How do I look at you?"

"Like I'm worth a damn. Like maybe there's more to me than the job. Like," Tobias rolled his eyes and continued, "I don't know, like I'm a good man or something."

Still puzzled, she asked, "You aren't a good man?"

"My life's trajectory would suggest otherwise. Since I met you, though, you have this way of seeing me, and I started believing things." He wiped his hand over his face and scratched his stubble. "I prayed for you."

"Prayed for me?" Marisol scoffed. Sure, Mom and Abuelita prayed all the time, papering over problems with superstitious words. But for Tobias to go off-brand and say something sincere? She wasn't sure if she was worthy of such a sentiment.

He recited, "Dear God, shit on me all you want but not on her."

She chortled, heartened by Tobias's lack of finesse. That definitely wasn't a prayer you'd learn during catechism. "Thanks." She walked, continuing toward the bus stop, but his large hand on her shoulder stopped her.

"God, she deserves a good life. She deserves a good man. One who will take care of her, who will never break his promises. Who'll be there for her."

The words were too maudlin. Marisol warned him away from them with a sharp, "Tobias."

He removed his hand and shoved both of them into his pockets, looking at the ground. "I know it's not me. It shouldn't be me. But when the world's best woman looks at me like I'm..."

Marisol searched his face, trying to make sense of him.

He continued, "What I'm trying to say is—"

Then it dawned on her. When she looked at him before, she found glimpses of what she thought was his alter ego. The look? It was Marisol searching for the Patron Saint, and Tobias was on the verge of cutting his heart open. She braced for the impact like a car crash. "Maybe you shouldn't—"

"No. What I'm trying to say is we've only had our moments, kid, and I could live off those moments for the rest of my life." Tobias lifted his eyes. His irises shimmered, fluctuating between brown and blue in the light. "It's enough."

Words of advice echoed through her head. Tell him the truth. Tell him he wasn't the one you looked for. However, after losing his gun and his badge, Marisol couldn't bring herself to cause him to lose his idea of her. "Enough."

From a small turn of his mouth, the creases around his eyes flared like sun rays. "I did think I'd never see you again." He walked to the driver's side and leaned his arms against the roof. "What's with the industrial rat trap?"

"Have you ever had to cover for animal control?"

"A few times back in the day. Why?"

She opened the passenger seat and lowered herself inside his car. "I'd sit down if I were you." He hustled inside and shut the door. "With the SPD trawling the river for Izzy and the brutal attacks on the gangs, it'd be accurate to say Shadowhaven's getting a little freakier than usual."

Tobias nodded.

"It started the night he killed her. Listen." Marisol played Annie's message.

"What does that have to do with the Bloodsucker?"

The attack seemed distant this time, like it happened to someone else on some true crime documentary. Her memories were just the cold hard facts of the case: Before the Bloodsucker and his gang attacked Dr. An Jung Park, she fought them off, the narrator would read over ominous synthesizer music. First with her gun and then with what a doctor knows best, a syringe. Marisol sniffled away the emerging prickles of grief as she thought of Annie—her Annie who only abused the ends of pencils—fighting until the end. "The serum?" she said, "She injected him with that stuff."

Tobias grimaced like he had already exploded a few brain cells trying to understand the most believable part of Marisol's week.

"You've worked with our friend for a few years because you know the goings-on in this city need something a little extra. If we find and trap this mouse, we could get ahead of the game and face the

Bloodsucker prepared." There was an even smaller voice telling her that understanding Annie's mouse meant figuring out Vincent's immortality problem, but that voice needed to shut the hell up because he deserved his tortured existence. Or maybe he didn't. Even exes deserved a little dignity.

Tobias tapped the steering wheel and started the car. "Let's catch ourselves a rat."

20

Zombie Rats And Revelations

Marisol jiggled the spare key in the lock of Annie's apartment door. She nudged it open with her shoulder. Tobias trailed close behind, holding her garbage bag.

Annie's apartment seemed stuck in time. Except for the sunlight through the blinds, it was the same as the night she half carried a drunken Annie inside. A stack of magazines needed to be recycled; a cup of partially evaporated coffee begged to be taken to the sink. Marisol moved to smooth over the crease in Annie's unmade bed. Her hand paused over the sheet. It still felt like Annie lived here, like any moment she'd walk through the door and all Marisol's grief would be fixed.

Tobias sighed and stared at the door. "What are we doing here?"

"She has something we could use." Marisol crossed the bedroom to the closet and groped around the top shelf. Her outstretched pinky brushed against a shoebox. She stood higher on tiptoe. "It should be up here."

Tobias snatched the shoebox with one hand and gave it to Marisol with an annoying amount of ease compared to her tiptoeing and stretching.

"Thanks."

"What's in it?" he asked.

She set the box on Annie's dresser and popped the lid. From inside, she pulled out a tranquilizer pistol and a dart with a feathery end. "Annie would sometimes take work home with her and that included critters that needed tranquilizing."

She led Tobias to the kitchen. There, she fished out a double boiler from a box, filling one pot with water and stacking both on the stove. With a turn of the knob, she fired up the burner. As the water heated, she rifled through boxes, cabinets, and drawers, acquiring a pestle, bowl, and funnel. Tobias handed her the garbage bag of drugs. She emptied it across the counter and popped her bottles of painkillers. The capsule broke open with a snap into the bowl. Marisol ground the other pills with a pestle. Once she collected the powder, she dumped it into the pot nestled over the boiling water. The powder bubbled into a liquid, melting into a potent cocktail that she'd funnel into the dart. If this thing was like Vincent, perhaps enough tranquilizer to flatten ten mice could sedate it. The reinforced trap would hold it.

Tobias loaded the pistol with the dart and extended his arm, appearing to test his aim. "Sure the tranq's necessary? A spring trap could crush the critter as we speak."

"Not this one. When you see it, you won't believe your eyes."

"Access denied," the computer voice said after Marisol tapped her keycard against the alley entry to the labs.

"What?!" Marisol cracked a knuckle, preparing to punch the screen. Did Vincent do this to punish her for leaving? What a petty brick of shit.

"I got an idea." Tobias jogged to the back of his car. On the trunk was a silver foil sticker, a parody of a cop's badge. It said, Coupon for Free Donuts. He scraped the edges with his car keys and peeled the rest of it off. "How long do people look at badges, anyway?" He stuffed the sticker into a plastic window of his wallet.

At the information desk of the hospital, Tobias asked the volunteer to let him inside the labs to review details of the crime. When he said "a mnemonic memory technique," the volunteer nodded, a sign of how much he impressed her. He flicked out his wallet, handed his business card, flashed the silly sticker, and shoved it back inside his pocket.

"I'll see what I can do." The volunteer disappeared into the bowels of the hospital.

Marisol leaned against the desk and tapped her foot. The mousetrap poked into her, stored in a flimsy draw-string backpack. If she were pacing the floor in her scrubs, she'd feel right back at home, but on the other side of things, she felt adrift. "Are you sure this will work?"

"Nope." Tobias scratched the back of his head.

The volunteer returned with an exasperated Dr. Foster.

Their plan was doomed.

Tobias greeted her with a handshake. Her frown did not budge. As Tobias rattled off, "a part of an ongoing homicide investigation," and "mnemonic memory technique," Dr. Foster stood with her arms firmly crossed. Tobias did the business card and badge maneuver. With the way she blinked, there was no way she bought that little piece of foil.

"Follow me," she said. "The labs haven't been open since what happened to Dr. Park. I think the scientists can't bring themselves to come in. Some say they hear strange noises there."

Strange noises? Must be the mouse.

Dr. Foster's key card hovered over the security pad. One swipe, and they'd be in. "Dr. Park was your friend." Dr. Foster smiled and quirked her eyebrows as if she studied a clown expressing sympathy. "Sorry, *is*. I suppose she will always be your friend."

"Yes." Marisol sighed. She needed Dr. Foster off her back as well as that mousetrap.

Dr. Foster swiped the card, and the doors to the lab unlocked. Marisol crossed to the other side while Tobias held the door open. They had made it.

"Wait!" Dr. Foster called after her. Uh oh, did she finally notice Tobias's complete lack of authority? What gave it away? Donut?

Marisol froze, preparing for the worst. "Yes?"

"The system automatically booted you for two no-call/no-shows."

Fantastic to know work held an inverse relationship with her. She did everything for them, and the system spit her out when she was broken and scared. Perhaps her unbridled rage would ruin their cover instead.

Dr. Foster continued, "But I can talk to people and explain your situation. This weekend is the Rooks' Legacy game. Half the city gets blind drunk, and we'll need all the help we can get. Could you work the second shift?"

Marisol's mouth dropped open, so she turned to Tobias for some help out of the situation.

He shrugged.

"I can work," she replied with a wince.

Dr. Foster held out her smartphone and clicked through it. "Great! I'll have the supervising nurse schedule you." She followed them into the lab.

"Sorry. For this mnemonic thing to work, we need as few people as possible," Tobias said.

Suddenly, Marisol and Tobias smelled fishy. Dr. Foster wiggled her nose. "Okay?" Then her pager beeped. She checked the message. "Let yourself out."

"Thank you, Doctor," Tobias said. The doors clicked behind them. Marisol waited for Dr. Foster's footsteps to disappear. Then they tiptoed through the darkened hallway of the labs, lit only by the exit signs and emergency lights.

As they turned the corner near Annie's lab, it felt like someone else's legs carried Marisol as her limbs trembled numb. She placed a shaking hand against the lab's window. Her pulse pounded in her ears. In a blink, she could see pooling blood, Annie's lifeless hand, but in another blink, she saw the sheen of the clean tile. The memory of Annie was washed away. She closed her eyes and rested her forehead against the locked entrance.

Vincent's voice echoed in her memory, soothing her. "You're having a panic attack. I'm going to hold you. Copy my breathing." She could hear his slow heartbeat and controlled breathing. She opened her eyes, that level of control now coursed through her.

Marisol turned the lab's door handle to confirm that the security program kept the door locked. It didn't budge. Of course, security locked it. The only time she was allowed in was when Annie opened it from the other side.

From the inside.

Annie had opened the door to the Bloodsucker. She knew him! Not only knew him but also trusted him enough to open the door of her lab at three a.m. Annie, how could you? And now, Marisol was the asshole, victim-blaming her best friend to absolve her ex of guilt.

A shriek traveled from the hollows of the basement. The mouse. Tobias turned on the flashlight function on his phone and led them down the stairs. Marisol used her phone as a flashlight, too, as they inched down the cave-like hallway toward the screeches.

"If that doc checks in with the precinct, she'll figure out that we're full of shit," Tobias said. They followed screeching noises, but that's what bothered him?

"I'm in mourning, and you're helping me out. The story's got legs. Besides, I know the person whose name is on the building." Though if her keycard situation was any indication, name-dropping Vincent Varian might not be the "Get Out of Jail Free" card she was hoping for. They'd definitely be charged with trespassing and the worst crime of all: admitting she needed Vincent.

"Yeah, know him to be a real tool." Tobias stopped. He furrowed his brow and lifted a finger to his lips. "Sh."

She braced herself yet heard nothing. Then a few clicks, and the heating system thundered through the building. She sighed with relief. "The heating."

Tobias shook his head.

Scratch. Scratch. Scratch.

"What was that?" Tobias shined his flashlight in the direction of the claw sounds. Nothing. He tilted his head toward the sounds and gripped Marisol by the wrist, pulling her down the hallway.

The scratching led them to the door to the boiler room. Tobias jimmied the handle. No movement. It was a dead end.

"Didn't think far enough ahead. Damn." Mouse-duty would have to go to Vincent. She did need him.

Tobias moved his flashlight up and down the walls of the hallway. He stroked his chin and settled the light over a fire extinguisher. Using the base of the extinguisher and brute force, he bent the door handle of the boiler room, busting the door free. "We'll get Mr. Name on the Building to buy a new door."

A stench wafted from the room. It was a wave of sulfur and the bacterial farts of rotting animal carcasses.

"Think it's in here?" Tobias asked. He held a hand to his nose.

She stretched the neck of her sweatshirt across her nose. She moved the flashlight over the expanse of the room. Its beams captured small chunks of fur and flesh. Annie's mouse had been down here devouring whatever poor rodents made their way into the room. "Yep. Definitely looks like it made a home here."

They crossed the threshold into the boiler room. Their phones shut down. Tobias violently tapped the power button to restart his phone. Without a light source, only the faint aura of the exit sign lit the room. She backed into the wall. It served as her guide as she moved in the red-tinted darkness with shaking limbs.

"I think something just crawled over my foot," Tobias announced.

"Don't say that!"

"I'm not saying it to freak you out. Something actually did."

The screen on her phone lightly glowed as the power returned, and she aimed the weak beam toward Tobias.

"It bit my foot!" Tobias kicked his leg and launched an object toward the wall.

She tapped the frozen flashlight function on her phone, and a light finally shot out. She pointed it at the wall.

Annie's mouse stood, its spine crushed from hitting the wall. Its back popped into place, and with hair on end, it arched like an angry cat, releasing a guttural growl of a predator twenty times its size. As it leaned forward, its jaws opened with a screech. Marisol dropped her phone and pinned her arms against her ears. The piercing noise transported her to that night. The light projected shadows of large claws and spiny fur over the boiler room.

"Pick up the light!" Tobias ordered. He raised the tranquilizer pistol and steadied his arm with his other hand.

Marisol ran her thumb over her pendant and shone her flashlight toward the mouse. It rocked its weight back onto its haunches.

"Keep it steady!"

She held her phone with both hands. Another roar. A flash of oversized teeth. The mouse leaped. *Click. Hiss.* The dart met it in midair. The mouse tumbled to the ground on its side. Out cold.

Marisol broke into nervous laughter. "Nice shot."

The intensity of Tobias's glare didn't break.

Her laughing morphed into teeth grinding. She fished the trap from her bag, scooped the supermouse into the steel box, and pocketed the spent dart.

In the dark, Tobias's eyes were as black as a predator's. A sadness lingered in them, too, like he was an apex predator who mourned for his prey. Had his mind taken him back to the hospital when he killed that man? Or some other place and time? He certainly wasn't present in the boiler room. At least, not until he tucked the gun in his waistband and scratched the back of his head. Then his pupils shrunk, and he was a man again.

Marisol wrapped her freezer with duct tape. The satisfying *rip!* suddenly became a disappointing *pfft!* when she reached the tape's cardboard ring.

Tobias pushed the refrigerator back to its spot. "Think that will keep Cujo in place?"

"Sure. Cryostasis ala Novotny. Should hold until I can hand it off to someone more capable." More capable meant Vincent, and her stomach clenched at the thought. She needed something to take the edge off. Marisol grabbed the last of her beers out of her fridge, popped the tops off, and handed one to Tobias.

"To our friend." Tobias clinked his bottle against hers and downed it.

Marisol slid to the floor, resting her back against the refrigerator. "Cujo's a rabid dog."

Tobias grunted as he lowered himself to sit next to her. "I stand by my reference." He licked a drop of beer off his lips. "We make a good team, kid."

"We do." She tugged at her sweatshirt as it suddenly became too warm. In the lowlight of her kitchen, his speckled eyes settled on blue, not like stained glass but enough of an echo of Vincent's shade to psychosomatically fissure her ribs.

Maybe this pain came from resisting good enough. Warming herself in Tobias's heat and bolstered by his strength, she could make the easy choice. He was someone who saved her, accepted her, and protected her and her family. He was someone who could grow old with her. She inhaled his essence: the sweat of hard work with a hint of fried dough, wood shavings, and beer.

He smelled like home.

Maybe, just maybe, she'd never have to admit about mistaken identities or mixed signals. Maybe the mistake was an opportunity.

He sighed, turning his head to face her. He looked at her like he had this morning. The gleam in his eye said she wasn't a freak magically on two legs again; she was a promise.

She rolled the sleeves of her sweatshirt up. Tobias didn't cause the hair on her arm to stand on end. Around him, she sensed her heart going on autopilot, operating with words like should and never want. Around him, she'd rub the scar above her knee and ache for the man who healed her, not the one who found her broken.

With him, there was no magic.

She darted her gaze to the floor. "She had to have known the Bloodsucker."

"What?"

"I couldn't save her because her lab is always locked. She's the one that lets you in. She let him in. She trusted him."

"Like a boyfriend or something?"

"Something. She was pretty tight-lipped about her love life. She got messages from someone but wouldn't talk about it. I guess she was too ashamed to tell me." Her throat tightened. If that were true, what kind of friend did that make Marisol?

He emptied his beer and winced. "That's assuming the security program worked. Data shows something wiped the memory of all the network computers. And I mean all. We're talking from the thermostat to pocket calculators. Security only logged Annie's keycard entry. We didn't know you were in the building until we found you."

Computers malfunctioning or not, the door was locked that night. Of this, she was sure. Everything in her had fought to bust open that door, to break open those windows. Her everything wasn't good enough. She was unable to stop them. That memory she'd carry like a jagged scar. "The door was locked."

He shook the empty bottle in his hand. "Do you got any more of these? I could stick around. Pick your brain for leads. Or find a radioactive spider to bomb and nail in a cabinet."

Marisol eyed the orange and purple sky outside her window. The sun was setting. Night. Night meant Vincent. "No. Those were my last." Her failure felt like it wedged the fissure in her ribs wide. She failed to help Annie and blamed Vincent for it. She picked at the label on her bottle.

"They collected her phone as evidence. I could tell them to unlock and check it. Follow that lead if they haven't already." Tobias stretched and headed for the door. "If you need anything, call me."

She stopped picking the label and attempted a slight turn of her mouth. "Tobias?" She verged on saying it—the truth.

His hand lingered over the dead bolt.

I thought you were him. "I never really thanked you for all you've done."

He turned his head back. His crooked smile cut into his laugh lines. "My pleasure." He flicked the dead bolt and turned the doorknob. "I find it funny that you think all this weird stuff that's been happening lately stems from a zombie rat rather than the obvious."

"What's that?"

"Our friend. I saw him early this morning. He told me you left the safe house, and he needed help keeping an eye out for you. Oh, and his gloves? Had blood all over them."

Marisol squinted. "I'm not following."

"You say magic serum. I'm sayin'—disappearing Izzy? Ripping up the Mob and the Bratva?" Tobias opened the door. "Maybe our friend's getting to be a little too extra for the city." He stepped one foot in the hallway. "Alas, if I see him tonight, I'll send him right over to collect the zombie rat."

The door closed behind him. She ripped the label clean off. Annie may have let the Bloodsucker in, but their mouse misadventure hadn't changed the truth: Vincent was always dangerous.

21

Sálvame

Throughout the evening, the fridge was a source of terror. Marisol jumped at every rattle and hum, even when it was just the ice maker or the ambient noise of the working appliance. Her heart and imagination could suffer only so many more tremors before either would kill her, not to mention that the duct tape she used was off-brand and would only hold a cannibal super-mouse for so long. But getting the man capable enough to handle such a thing required poking a wound that hadn't quite formed a scab. How would she survive making contact with a bad case of the feels? Why, reference pages from her *I'm the Asshole* playbook.

Play one, ask Vincent to come over for mouse storage, initiate a phone call to her sister Nicole, and say something upsetting like, "Is there really a difference between Windows and Linux?" Vincent would arrive right as Nicole was in the middle of losing her shit, and all Marisol would have to do is signal to the freezer and gesture apologetically about really needing to take the call. Mouse would be out of her hands, and she'd barely have to utter anything to him. But Vincent was the ultimate bullshit artist and would see right through the ruse.

Which might mean she'd have to opt for playbook page two: Leave necessary item outside the apartment and give the rejected paramour a short window of time to collect it. Hey, if you want that snarling rodent your DNA created, you have 15 minutes to get it off the curb before some unhoused person places it in their shopping cart. No fuss, but that plan risked the muss of an unhinged lab experiment wandering the city streets. Not just a lab experiment, a bit of Annie and a key to bringing her murderer to justice. Marisol had to try something different, crazy even. To accomplish that, she had to become a new kind of asshole. Luckily, she had a good role model to take after.

She perched at the top of her building's water tower, wearing the canvas jacket she borrowed. She gripped the tower's spire with one gloved hand and adjusted her domino mask with the other. Flicking up her hoodie, she summoned forth her smooth-as-silk alter ego, the one that could confront the Patron Saint without becoming a blubbering idiot. But she still was not-so-smooth, as Marisol had busted out the knee of her jeans climbing the tower. She hit the commlink button at her wrist to call for Vincent. For rabid mouse storage and nothing more.

A burst of glowing blue veins beamed from her fire escape. Vincent already waited for her outside her apartment's window, probably after visiting Tobias to learn about the mouse. As soon as she rubbed her cross pendant, she leaped to the railing. She swung and slid down the tower's scaffolding, soundless—no scraping of flesh or screeching of rubber against metal.

She landed on the balls of her feet. Hiding in the recesses of darkness, he remained still. He hadn't noticed her. She clicked her tongue and shout-whispered, "Vicente."

He swaggered toward her. His cape whipped in the breeze behind him.

She popped up straight, hands on her hips. "I got something getting freezer burn that might interest you. Annie synthesized a serum based on your DNA and tested it on her mouse. It eliminated its tumors, but it had a weird side effect of turning it into a superpowered, deathless killer. Sound familiar?"

He nodded and huffed. Frozen breath swirled around his face.

"But you're not a vicious killer. You're different. A good man?" Her muscles tightened as she awaited the answer. But which part was the question—good or man?

His downcast gaze flickered up, meeting hers. "I try to be."

The answer wasn't reassuring, but it was pure Vincent, living along the blurred edge between a sanctuary and a trap. She wanted to dwell on that edge too. So much that even under a layer of armor, her nipples furled tight.

Remember: nothing more. She rolled her shoulders and averted her eyes, returning to perform as the tough badass extraordinaire. "Based on the security measures, Annie had to have known the Bloodsucker to let him into her lab. The night he killed her, she injected him with the serum. I'm guessing, from the mouse's antics and the latest news, we are facing a criminal mastermind who is closer to us than we realize. And he can now meet your magic superstrength with his own lab-created superstrength."

She shifted her weight to one side and dropped an arm. "I relayed important information. What's next? Wait for you to turn around before I disappear into the night? Isn't that what you do?"

"Sometimes." He turned to jump off the rooftop's edge.

A weird mixture of desire and guilt brimmed to the surface, but instead of saying, *Please don't go,* she called out, "I spent the day trying to hate you."

He stopped but didn't even bother to turn around. "Okay."

How dare he brush her off with a short, noncommittal response! She snagged his cape and yanked him away from the ledge. "Okay? It's not okay." She spun him around to stare right into those stained-glass eyes. "I think of all the shit pies

I've been served, and your finger is in every one of 'em."

He looked down and stepped back—like he did back at the estate. He was giving up on her, and the squeeze in her chest returned. There was no way she could handle his resigned expression again. She had to jostle him enough to care.

So, she shoved him. "You're just going to accept that? Stand up for yourself!" She hurled her might into a punch. He raised his forearm and blocked it. She swung fist after fist into his forearm like it was her punching bag. "Tell me I'm wrong! Tell me you're a good man! Just fucking fight me!"

He caught one of her flying fists in his palm. "Would that please you?"

No, resurrecting the dead would please her. Or maybe finding a gray strand in his golden hair. But of course she answered, "Yes!"

His lips curled into a smile. "You're bringing a butter knife to a gunfight."

Once she extricated her fist from his grip, she'd use it again to wipe his smirk off. "Eat my ass! It's your fault she's not alive! The problem was right under your nose the entire time!" He finally let her go, and she shook her cramped hand out. "You had to know! You could've stopped her from going too far!"

His smile deflated. "I'm sorry."

She threw him a cross hook and another one. "I don't care! You could've saved her! I should hate you for... for everything!"

He dodged her punches, bobbing and weaving. "Then do it."

An iron-like taste filled her mouth, so she lowered her guard to catch her breath. "When I try, I end up only hating myself."

He swept-kicked her legs out from under her, knocking her onto her back. "You shouldn't do that."

The force struck the breath from her lungs, which dissipated toward the sky. Adrenaline and dopamine mixed into a heady rush, like fireworks popping inside her skull. He really just did that? She sipped at the air, collected enough oxygen, and sprang back onto her feet. "How? If I hadn't fangirled over you, I could've seen that she needed my help. I could've been there in time."

Never mind reason. Never mind that she intended for each punch and kick to pummel herself. As if under a spell, her body continued to fight, and he answered the call to battle with fluid flips and turns, dodging her attack. The sparring became a dance; the dance morphed from the jabs, kicks, and blocks of kickboxing into the pushes and holds of wrestling.

They reached a standstill huddling together. Her right hand pushed against his shoulder, and the left gripped behind his neck. His position mirrored hers, bracing and holding. "You did see that she needed help, and you were there," he replied.

Her feet started to slide, and her leg muscles burned as his strength overtook hers. This pissed her off more. He was easily ten times stronger than her and patronized her with a fair fight. Or he cared, and she was locking horns with the only man who dared to take on her bullshit. She pivoted out of the way; he barreled forward and stumbled to regain his footing. Her exhausted muscles could no longer hold back the truth. "Yet I'm still angry at myself!"

Vincent hugged her from behind and pinned her into a full Nelson with both arms held above her head. "Why?"

She attempted to wriggle out and grunted through clenched teeth, "Because today I saw the life I should live, and I didn't want it." She donkey-kicked him away. "I should care that you're dangerous. I should care if you're a good or bad man." And she felt it: that she'd sell her soul if it meant being close to him again. It arrived like a shimmer behind her chest, like spinal fluid reversing to a rhythm of more, more, more. "You're a barbed hook in my guts, and it fucking hurts, but I don't care. Whatever you are, whatever you've done, I want you in my life." Everything in her verged on trembling, crying, or breaking as the ultimate fear of running from him lingered in the air. "Do you still want me?"

"Siempre," he whispered before drawing her into a kiss. The perfect combination of strength and softness in his mouth made her body respond with a swoon. His arms caught around her waist.

Lightning crackled in the distance. They should head inside. She flinched, hugging around his neck tighter.

But she felt no fear.

In each other's arms, they fidgeted out of their gloves. Fingers freed, she pulled him by the shoulders of his cape and nibbled his lower lip.

In his kiss, she savored all that was ancient and powerful. In his kiss, she tasted his destiny—a man seeking Justice wherever he trod. From the salt on his mouth, he was a man who set ships on fire in the Atlantic. From the sizzling electricity of his touch, he was a man who witnessed the spark of Enlightenment. His tender lips belonged to the man who led a quiet revolution of kindness, defending and protecting the vulnerable. Their mouths parted from each other, only to gasp for enough air. It was a sip of pure oxygen, the taste of the freedom he gave to those he carried to salvation. His hands, digging into the flesh of her lower back, were the hands that cut open the barbed-wire fence of a prison camp. His kiss possessed the history of a man who saved all that he could. He was the original. The hero that inspired other tales. But he was real. He was hers.

Click. Click. Marisol released his cape from its clasps. *Click.* She unfastened his utility belt. It dropped to the roof, landing with a metallic timbre that stoked a fire between her legs. He smoothly unzipped her coat and hoodie with one fell stroke. The fire within roared after he shucked off her clothes, dropping her armor into a frenzied pile. The cold felt like nothing against her flushed skin.

He pulled at the thick strap of her sports bra and grunted. She jumped back and out of his grasp. With her arms raised to grapple, she circled him. Eyes glowing and mouth parted, he reached for her, ready to play. She grabbed his arm and twisted it behind him, shoving him face first into the colossal HVAC unit.

Lured by her hunger, she bumped her pelvis against his backside. She desired to drive into him like an animal, to leave him a mindless mess, begging for it again. So she asked, "Want to please me?"

He tipped his head.

"Be still. I'll tell you when to move." She kissed him, skimming his jawline.

She found the zipper at the neck. It purred as she undid it. As she pushed away the armored neoprene of his suit, she admired the rippled muscles of his back and the groove of his spine. She followed the groove with her tongue. He tasted like the city, hints of copper and salt.

He exhaled through his teeth. "Should we head inside? Someone might see us." Thunder pounded closer.

She asked, "Do you need to tap out?"

"No." His grimace softened. "But we need a signal if we do."

She pushed the back of his head. "Like a safe word?"

His leather-clad cheekbone pressed into metal, and he squeezed his eyes shut. "Any preferences?"

She peeled the top layer of his suit off, stopping at his hips. His suit bound his wrists to his body.

"Sálvame," she answered.

"Our safe word is sálvame?"

"All right, Vincent, I'll stop." She backed a few steps, holding her palms out.

He chuckled and faced her. "I said it as a confirmation not—"

She grazed his chest with her fingertips. "You don't want me to stop." He struggled, pulling against his bind. She yanked the wisps of his chest hair. "I told you not to move." *Bam*! She shoved him into the HVAC unit again because she could be dangerous too. Her fingers released him, and she kissed the red marks on his chest, flicking her tongue in the shape of a cross.

She turned her back to him and rolled her hips into him. "I know it hurts to want me so much." The heat of his impassioned breath burned against her neck. Her hips coaxed him again, and she added, "Show m—"

He wiggled free of his sleeves, grabbing her at her hips. He pushed. She braced to resist. They stumbled. She caught herself against the ledge wall, her palms scraping the stone.

Bent over the ledge, her curves ached to meet his solid muscles. Yet nothing. Did he ditch her in a switchy state of submission? Trap her in a big *gotcha* moment before disappearing? She looked back. He hadn't left. He had begun to untie his mask.

Marisol stopped his hand. "Keep it on."

He growled and rocked into her backside. She dug her teeth into her lower lip, riding the high of another unlocked secret: Masks stayed on tonight. She'd have the real version of him, the contradiction. He'd be the hero to save her, and he'd be the villain she conquered.

He reached around and unbuttoned her jeans with rough jerks, pulling them off. He dropped to his knees and pressed his face against her ass cheek. His nose caressed higher and higher. A soft kiss became a bite. His teeth pulled at her underwear, guiding them down her legs where they bound her at the ankles.

His caressing nose and mouth traveled up her leg, reaching their destination with a nibble at her rounded flesh. She closed her eyes and leaned into him. He gripped her cheeks and separated them. His tongue traced over her folds. She stiffened; her eyes popped open in shock. Not ready. Too... He hummed. She quivered from the vibrations of his mouth. Filthy. Another hum and his mouth explored further, his tongue grazing her clit. Too much. She lifted her thigh back to block where his mouth, tongue, nose—the rest of him—dared to go next.

He drew his head back. "Do you need to tap out?" His breath, hovering close, heated and teased her.

Her hands trembled against the ledge. "Um..." She squeezed her thighs together, surrendering to her fears. Too sweaty. Too dirty.

"You can say it."

Danger and desire twisted her insides, wringing them to liquid. If feeling his breath drove her wild, why would she stop him? She steadied her palm and inched her legs apart. "I didn't say the word for stop."

His lips and tongue returned with a vengeance. Possessed with slick heat, she arched her backside. Then his fingers joined his mouth and... my God. Lightning dazzled among the clouds moving above them.

After a prod of his tongue and a circle of his fingers, she gasped and reached back, holding the tie at the back of his mask. Before she caught her breath, he devoured her. Her body fought a tug of war. Her hand, gripping the back of his head, demanded more. Her hips, tilting away, sought to dull his power. But his hold on her meant that the only direction she'd go was his. He mastered her as her supplicant.

She begged, "Please," but she wasn't sure what for—release or respite. His tongue fluttered. Her body seized. "Vincent!"

Marisol let go of his mask and gazed back at him with heavy-lidded, sex-drunk eyes. Pleasure racked her body in ever-returning waves.

He ran the edge of his tongue over his pout and rubbed his lips together. "Hm."

"Hm," she breathed.

But he moved without permission. There must be a consequence.

She bucked into him, knocking him on his back. "You didn't wait for my command." Sitting on the ledge, she dug her boot into his shoulder. "I'm not pleased." Her pursed lips hid a smile. "Put your hands against that wall and don't move."

He moved to the HVAC unit and put his palms in place. She took the moment with his back to her to wriggle out of her boots and unbind her ankles, adding jeans, socks, underwear to the growing clothes pile. She approached him and reached down his leg. He twitched. She steadied him with a hand to his back and used the other to unzip his boot at one calf and then another. "Take off your boots." He stepped out of them. Her fingertips glanced across the brawn of his shoulders and back. At his back, she peeled the rest of his suit away to expose his beauty in entirety.

She marveled at his buttocks with a sculptor's caress. Her hero. After a massage with her thumb, she swung her hand back. The villain she'd conquer. *Crack!* Her hand landed against his backside. His abs pulsed and flexed as he took deep breaths. He turned his head, his profile to her. His aghast mouth closed into a grin. She could face her darkness and create pleasure from it.

Crack! He laughed, deep and haughty. That won't do. The other spanks landed harder and louder until her hand stung. Until he grunted and shuddered. Until he rutted against the wall.

The marks on his skin faded into the unsullied ivory skin of a statue. She tugged at him to turn around. When he did, she licked her lips at the sight. She hadn't really known what to expect from a 500-year-old dick. He had deprived her of it long enough that she wondered if his sculpted, godlike body came with one of those disappointingly flaccid penises that adorned otherwise gorgeous statues. But it was perfectly normal, as in, dusky red, erect, pointing to his navel. Most importantly, ready for her.

She leaped onto him, and he collapsed onto his back. She straddled him, dragging herself over his length. "You want this?"

He hissed out a "Yes."

She crossed her forearms over his chest, digging her elbows into his muscles. "Say please."

"Please."

At his word, she guided him inside her, using the strength of her legs to roll her hips. He pulled her down as he thrust up into her. An ecstatic gasp left her mouth like a ghost in the frosty night air.

Her body spasmed from the deep and full sensation, reveling in another boundary pushed, another dose of his perfection.

He squeezed her fleshy hips with one hand while the other pushed her bra over her breasts. Sitting up, he licked and sucked at each nipple with a hungry lack of precision—slippery and savage.

Another deep thrust, and Marisol flung her head back. Her hair danced around her face.

Between rough breaths, he said, "You're beautiful."

Her silken strands snaked over her lips and brushed across her shoulder blades. Her gaze seared into his. "I know."

Marisol shoved Vincent's mouth away from her breasts and pried his hands off her body. She slid the rest of the way out of her bra and ran her hands over her breasts, delighting in the cooling traces of his saliva on them.

His thumb flickered over her sweet spot, and she writhed backwards, clawing into his thighs. After a few pumps with her hips, she adjusted her weight forward and pinned his arms overhead. "No. Watch me." Her hands glided down his arms and over his chest. She caressed her thighs and dipped a hand between them. At her heated apex, her strokes matched the frantic pace of her rolling hips. "Beg me to use you."

His gaze fixed to where their bodies met. "Use me."

She pulled him out and restrained herself from grinding and rocking. "I said beg."

Lightning forked from the sky to the ground. The slick underside of his cock pushed against her, hoping to return to the snug place deep inside. The tendons in his neck strained as he groaned out, "Please."

She sank down on him. Her thighs slapped against his as she rode him. He inched closer and closer to release with every wild buck of her body. His lips parted in a sigh. There it was—the agony. Now for the ecstasy.

The pressure grew inside her. Every nerve wired into her pleasure. "I'm so close, Vincent. I'm so—"

Something guttural rumbled from his chest to his throat, as if it was the only thing to keep him from exploding apart. She stuck her fingers inside his mouth to muffle his sounds. She couldn't hurt him, but her masked side desired to delve inside—to gag, to mangle, to make him beautiful only for her. Destroying and devouring him passed his power to her. Now she knew why people ceremoniously ate their gods.

His teeth crushed her fingers. The pain challenged her to ride harder and harder. After another squeeze and a moan, his eyes rolled back as he died a little death for her.

His lingering bite released another wave of ecstasy, bolting straight to her core just as lightning struck the spire of the water tower. Her cry blended with the thunder, ricocheting off the buildings until it disappeared into the night. She collapsed. Aftershocks tumbled through her.

A hole ripped into the sky, and rain poured down. Sweat and rain anointed them like deities as they shone in the city lights. Breathless and stunned, Marisol closed her eyes and rested her ear against his chest. For once, his heartbeat raced. For a moment, she had made him an ordinary man. Nothing stood between them now. Unbound and raw, they shared their bodies. And she wanted it again and again and forever.

He carried her inside her apartment and insisted she stay in bed as he cleaned up their mess. He moved around her apartment like he belonged there, like home was with her in the heart of the city, hanging their wet clothes and masks in her bathroom.

Together in bed, her fingers interlaced with his, she admired his soft, pink knuckles. She compared the top of her hand to his. Both belonged together now, lustrous with strength and the last vestiges of youth. How long would it be until her hand looked ridiculous in his? Until his agelessness became noticeable, and he'd have to recycle himself into someone new? Twenty years? Fifteen? Ten?

She wanted to tie him to her bed to stop time, to stop the outside world. Over centuries, she couldn't have been the only one with a bed warm from his body with the sands of time sifting rapidly through her fingers. How did they handle it? "What about other… lovers?" The word spouse itched her tongue, but it would've been presumptuous to speak it.

He kept his eyes closed and stroked the hair at her temples. "Some. None knew what made me different." He opened one eye with a hint of a smile.

"Not even Staci?" Marisol couldn't forget the picture of the timelessly beautiful woman with news reporter hair next to the Victor version of him in his ballroom.

"Staci was my wife on paper but—"

Marisol patted his chest. "Don't feel you have to under-embellish the truth for my sake."

He opened his other eye, and he propped his head up. "Security Transportation and Communication Interface. She's the computer program that operates my security system, vehicles, and commlinks. The woman in the pictures was a robot Leonard put together. Based on a real person. Hence the paperwork. Good for photo ops. Terrible conversationalist." He shrugged away robot clone artificial intelligence the way other people say, "grown apart," cueing her to nod in understanding.

She ignored the massive weight of his life story, which receded into infinity like a mirror reflecting another mirror. "But I know about you." Though there was still so much to know, the notion hit like a stiff drink, buzzing with strength. She was the only one to possess him in entirety. Although he wasn't a possession, it assured her enough that perhaps in another hundred years, he wouldn't be in a similar conversation, lumping Marisol with some.

He held her tighter, drawing his magically dry cape around her. Inside his perfect warmth, she dozed off against him.

She opened her eyes to find Vincent sitting at the edge of the bed, mask back on, and zipping himself in his suit.

She rubbed his back as he jammed his feet into his boots. "Where are you going?"

"Work."

She checked the time. Only midnight. "After that? I'm surprised you're even awake."

"Benefit of super recovery." He kissed her and eased her to the back onto the pillows, tucking his cape tighter around her. "Love you."

Marisol snuggled inside the cape's warmth. What did he just say? She sat up. "What?"

"Um..."

"You didn't say the 'I' of 'I l—'" She dared not to repeat it. The words conjured a superstitious force that would definitely break her heart. "That's like saying, 'Good night,' right? You didn't mean to say—"

"I love you?" He clipped on his utility belt and adjusted his mask. "I suppose I have no right to say it given my circumstances, but I feel it. Overwhelmingly, in fact. Being around your compassion and courage moves me like witnessing someone walk on water." Vincent held her chin between his thumb and forefinger. "And for that, I want nothing but life and joy for you. I will be whatever you need to make that true." He brushed her hair with his fingers so that it gathered on one side. "Let me carry your burdens." He kissed her clavicle. "Let me be your vengeance." He kissed the edge of her jaw. "I will take your anger so that you can have peace. I will be your wrath so you can be our healer. I will bring you the justice you deserve." With a gentle pull of his hand, she faced him, lifting her eyes to meet his. His eyes glowed. "When the Bloodsucker looks into the abyss, it will be me who looks back at him."

A single tear trickled down her cheek. Not a tear of sorrow but of awe, as if she witnessed the beginning of the universe.

He wiped away the tear with his gloved thumb. "I can't give you a future, but I can give you this."

Rendered speechless, she kissed the inside wrist of his tending hand.

"I'll return before dawn." He opened her window and crouched on the ledge.

No. He couldn't just say "I love you" and leave. She had to say something, anything back.

But he jumped out below. Her gauzy curtains fluttered and went still.

22

Feminine Intuition

6:32 a.m. How did his powers work, anyway?

The rules were different with Vincent. There was no threat of death or injury on the job. He wasn't like the police. Was he?

Marisol gulped the last of her now-cold coffee and set the empty cup on the windowsill. Not wired enough, she brewed another pot of coffee.

What if he was okay and at home in his pajamas, relishing in a saved day and the side of pussy he got from her? He beat her in the fuck-and-run race before she had a chance to put her feet on the starting blocks, didn't he?

But he said that he loved her, that crazy son of a bitch. And he wasn't a liar—well, not the kind of man to lie about that. Right? She slammed the cabinet doors shut and smacked around the little, plastic coffee maker, preparing to brew coffee with the same subtlety as she would destroy drywall with a mallet. Coffee-making reached an anti-climactic end with the quiet click of the ON button. The button glowed like Vincent's commlink. Which made her think.

She rushed back to her bathroom. Vincent had set her ripped commlink next to her domino mask. She pressed it and ran to the window, but nothing changed.

She picked up her empty cup and headed to the kitchen for a refill. He was avoiding her, wasn't he?

Whoop! Whoop! Honk! The car alarm blaring outside her window stopped her in midpour—the alarm coming from the once-empty alley. She poked her head out the window. Below, Vincent's motorcycle honked and flashed its lights. All-the-more-strange because it was Vincent's motorcycle without Vincent.

Marisol pulled on her clothes and crawled out onto the fire escape. She jumped down, landing in the alleyway just as someone chucked a bottle in her direction. A string of expletives followed that the shattering alarm—or her city-hardened ears—drowned out. She grabbed the handlebars and whispered, "Shut up. Shut up. Shut up." The handles heated under her palms, flashing white hot.

The alarm stopped. A woman's computerized voice said with a broken inflection, "Mi espíritu recognized."

Marisol would have to have a conversation with Vincent about her disdain for pet names, although my spirit was more-than tolerable and even a little perfect, but first, "Staci, where's Vincent?" she asked the dashboard.

The alarm resumed.

If she wasn't careful with the damn thing, the bottle-thrower wouldn't miss this time. "No need to do that." Another squeeze of her hands shut the alarm off again.

The seat slid back with a hiss of compressing air. A helmet emerged, and the seat clicked back into place.

Marisol craned her neck so hard that she risked a spinal injury. "Want me to get on?"

"Mi espíritu recognized."

"I don't have a Class M endorsement," she said, as if that was the main issue–having the correct license, not an insistent A.I. and a missing boyfriend.

The computer repeated her pet name and lit up. Its electric engine softly whirred. Marisol put on the helmet. She swung her leg over the seat and teetered from foot to foot.

As soon as she steadied the bike, Staci chimed, "Destination determined." Without manipulation, the motorcycle charged forward, screeching to a halt before entering the street.

Marisol fell forward and caught herself against the handlebars. "Warn me before you do something like that!"

"Destination determined." The motorcycle pulled Marisol along into traffic.

Unlike riding the bus, the motorcycle offered no reinforced glass or metal frame between her eating pavement or winding up like a smashed bug on a windshield. She leaned forward and squeezed the sides of the motorcycle with her quaking legs. "Take me to Vincent."

The motorcycle sped up and weaved between cars. Sweat interfered with her grip. Even if she could solidly rev up the motorcycle, she hadn't a clue how to drive the machine. Instead, she relied on it to speed up and stop itself. At least the helmet muffled her screams because she doubted the seat would soak up her pee once the contents of her bladder jettisoned in terror.

The motorcycle zoomed between car lanes, cramming itself between side mirrors and teetering along the broken white lines between lanes. She closed her eyes, as if that would help her grow a shell and buffer against death. Speed vibrated her body as the motorcycle accelerated. Or was that her uncontrollable trembling? Dammit, she peeked. The motorcycle tailgated this car, zigzagged among those cars, and accelerated again. Perhaps Lamaze breathing would keep her from barfing up her heart.

She crossed the giant bridge, an amalgamation of cables, steel, and cement that united Shadowhaven's east and west sides.

The Eastside was rife with the gentrified splendor of large open storefronts and impeccably shining windows. Even the cement was white with promise. Shadowhaven's industrial past was a sucked-out venom. She was near the docks where the row housing echoed the Westside homes—minus the bars in the windows and the bullet holes in the brick. The pitch of the engine lowered as the motorcycle pulled into an alley and stopped.

Marisol dismounted and removed her helmet, clutching it against her hip. "Where am I?"

The motorcycle turned its right blinker on.

Marisol eyed the building to her right. "Is Vincent in there?"

The dashboard read 45 and powered down. Shields emerged like reptilian scales and covered the motorcycle in a metallic gloss.

Marisol sighed. She lost the last shred of her mind depending on a motorcycle that contained the computerized soul of Vincent's fake wife. After following the blinker, she discovered an entrance to an apartment complex. She pored over the dented call box for a clue while she moved her pendant up and down its chain. A peeling label said, "Enter Number and Press *."

She let go of her necklace and entered 45 and pressed *.

A throat cleared over the speaker. "Hello?"

The magic of coincidence dropped her jaw. "Tobias?"

"What do you want?"

"It's Marisol. Buzz me in."

A buzz shook the door as Marisol let herself inside.

Tobias stood in his doorway, brushing his teeth while pulling on a T-shirt. His unbuttoned jeans sat on his hips. He garbled, "I got you coming over at all hours too?" Toothpaste foam gathered in the corners of his mouth.

"Is he here?" Marisol jostled him and entered his apartment.

"Come in. Make yourself at home." Tobias slammed the door behind him. He poked his head in a darkened doorway of his bathroom and spat. "He isn't here," he added as he zipped the fly of his jeans.

"Then I need your help."

"I haven't seen our friend since last night. Right after I saw you." Tobias breezed past Marisol. She picked up his scent. No artificial pine aftershave this time. He reeked of sweat and stale alcohol, the smell of a rough night.

He picked up an empty pizza box off a bizarre, makeshift table made of particleboard and a stack of concrete blocks. In his other arm, he collected multiple empty bottles—beers and a pint of whiskey—and moved to the small galley kitchen, where he put them in an unlined trash can. They landed with the piercing *clank!* of glass falling on glass. The inside of the trash can must've brimmed with empties. He placed the pizza box on the half-closed lid.

There wasn't much more to Tobias's apartment. A worn recliner sagged in Tobias-like shapes. A television, perched on another particleboard-and-cement-block construct, asked Are You Still Watching? He walked back to the living room, switched the television off, and tossed the remote onto his chair. "There's this crazy invention where you can call to say you're coming over at seven a.m."

"Sorry. I can't shake a bad feeling. I last saw him at midnight. When he said, 'I l-'" The words caught in her throat. "But he hasn't returned, and I found his abandoned motorcycle in the alleyway this morning instead." Then she muttered, "Rather, his motorcycle found me."

"This might come to you as a shock, but men can be full of shit."

Marisol scoffed. It would be improper to draw a diagram of last night's rooftop activities. But... "That is not the case."

"Why? A guy never ghosted you?"

A guy never said he loved her, so she said, "He wouldn't do that to me." Her puffed-up insistence was more for quieting her doubts than defending Vincent's honor.

But like a dog or a bee, she sensed that Tobias smelled her fear. He rubbed the stubble on his chin and said, "I know what's going on." He leaned until his lips hovered over her ear. "You're dick drunk." And he laughed at her.

What the ever-loving fuck? Marisol shoved him away and bound to the door. "If you're going to be a pig…"

"That wasn't a denial. What is going on with you two?" His question landed like an attack, and she barely had time to raise her fists.

She swallowed. Time to declare the truth. "We're… seeing each other. It's serious." That wouldn't be enough to get her off the ropes. She'd have to match blow for blow. "What's going on with you two?"

Tobias waggled his eyebrows. "He didn't exactly bend me over a cop car and take me, but I'm tempted to say 'It's serious' just to watch how you squirm."

She made a concerted effort to stay still. "Don't be mean."

He spoke through a yawn of lazily articulated consonants. "Have you checked his last-known whereabouts? You said your apartment. What about his place of residence? You know where that is, don't you? Because you're serious?"

"Like I said, bad feeling. His motorcycle brought me here first."

"Following your feminine intuition." He snorted a laugh and staggered back into the chair.

The attitude. His rough scent. The bottles. His lack of balance. It was like Dad at his worst. "Are you drunk?"

He smacked his lips and looked at her, blinking slowly, with one eyelid out of sync with the other. "I'm... not always like this."

She cocked her head, sensing a half-truth. "Just sometimes?"

Suddenly hoarse, he said, "Too many times."

Her sinuses burned, reliving those anxious moments when things became too unpredictable in the Novotny household thanks to Dad and the bottle.

Tobias inhaled and squeezed the bridge of his nose. In that single breath, he rattled off, "You can't file a missing person's report for him. It would compromise his identity. Even if you could, you wouldn't want to send a couple of beat cops in the direction of our missing friend. That would lead to more problems." He scratched at his stubble. "One of those problems being the Bloodsucker, I'm guessing."

A spinneret of hope pulled her step-by-step from the doorway. "Yes."

"What you have, kid, is a conundrum." He cranked up the leg rest, the delicate spinneret destroyed.

"You won't help me?"

He shut his eyes and rolled to his side. "I can't help you. I don't have a badge. I don't have a gun. I'm as useful as a screen door on a submarine."

Marisol shook her head. She couldn't let him give up. Not "the nice shot." Not the guy with the best clearance rate in the SPD. She charged into the bathroom and flicked the light on.

"What are you doing in there?" he called after her.

She opened the medicine cabinet and found a bottle of ibuprofen. Although the expiration date was cutting it close, they were good. After shutting the cabinet, she noticed in the mirror's reflection a hole in the wall behind her. It was the size of a large fist.

Tobias stumbled into the doorway. Marisol eyed the hole. Dad had plastered the holes he punched in usually a day after a drunken bout. When he had sobered up, he sanded away the lumps. Yet, she always found them. New paint never caught light the same way. She poked at the wall, and a fragment dropped away. Tobias rubbed the back of his neck. "I was planning on fixing it."

She handed him the ibuprofen and darted past him into the kitchen, getting him a glass of water. "Do you have eggs? You need a decent breakfast."

"All I got is mustard." He leaned against the refrigerator and swallowed back the pills with a gulp.

A school picture of a teen girl dangled from a magnet behind his shoulder. Marisol studied it as the upturned corners bristled against Tobias's back. The girl had long, curly brown hair and lightly freckled skin. "Who's the girl?"

"You weren't supposed to see that." His gaze shifted to the bottom of the glass.

Marisol sensed his embarrassment and dug her teeth into her bottom lip to hide a smirk. "Some advice, Quinlan? If she's giving you her school picture, she's too young for you."

He moved the magnet and put the picture in a nearby cabinet. "You've never called me that—Quinlan." The wrinkles in his forehead and the slight turn of his mouth hovered between pain and amusement.

Marisol released her lip. Her smirk faded.

He sniffed. "You've got a good hunch, kid. He wouldn't send you here if things were hunky-dory."

"What do we do?"

"I don't know." He wiped his hands over his face. "He programmed his motorcycle to find you and me. Maybe we can use it to find him."

In the alleyway next to the apartment building, Tobias finished chugging a neon yellow electrolyte drink and chucked the empty bottle into an open recycling dumpster. He bit a giant chunk from a breakfast taquito that had spent the morning on the corner store's roller grill.

Marisol put her hands on the handlebars. The motorcycle was dead, no longer searing in response to her touch. "I don't get it. It worked this morning."

Tobias wiped his greasy fingers on the lapel of his trench coat and gripped the handles as Marisol had. The scaly shields folded into themselves. A serpentine-shaped blue light beamed behind the fenders and wheel spokes. Staci's oddly modulated voice said, "Detective Quinlan recognized."

Tobias's eyes widened. "It's like a video game." He stuffed the last bite of his taquito into his mouth and chewed it as if it was a piece of leather.

Marisol, brimming with two parts alarm and one part jealousy, shoved Tobias out of the way. "Can you take us to him?"

After Staci said, "Mi espíritu recognized," then it repeated, "Destination determined." An abstract grid of a map appeared on the screen, with a bold blue line tracing a path from point to point. The seat opened automatically and elevated another helmet from its recesses.

Marisol put on her helmet and mounted the bike. She flicked her head back and inched forward to make space for Tobias behind her. He strapped on his helmet that looked like a white overturned bowl. The motorcycle rocked under his weight as he took his spot behind Marisol. She said, "I'd hold on tight if I were you."

Tobias hugged around her waist. "Tell me how you really feel, kid."

"Figured I should let you know. I don't have a motorcycle license." Marisol flipped down the helmet's visor.

"I'll report you to the cops."

The motorcycle carried them farther south along the river. They entered a neighborhood of skeletal abandoned homes. Plywood shuttered some doors and windows. But rot and gravity dragged down most of the hollowed-out homes. The road gradually became dirt as time and neglect returned the pavement into something more primitive. They stopped at a faded orange and white dead-end barrier surrounded by tangles of naked, drooping tree branches and bushes. The right turn signal flashed before it powered down again. Marisol and Tobias took off their helmets.

Tobias hung his helmet off the handlebar. "I've worked a couple of cases around here. Practically a goldmine if you're murder police."

Marisol flipped up her visor and huffed. At least Vincent couldn't be a dead body, but he had warned of becoming—how did he say it?—permanently affected. She hooked her helmet on the other handlebar. "The signal pointed this direction." She stepped into the thicket behind the barrier. The brambles snagged at her jeans.

Tobias charged past her, swatting the branches away from his head. In a few more swats and snags, they reached a clearing—a knoll blanketed in dead leaves. A tall chain-link fence bisected the hill overlooking Shadowhaven's crumbling former meatpacking district. The brick building at the base of the knoll was the former Clark Slaughterhouse. Thirty years battered the logo into an impressionist outline. If Marisol squinted enough at the abstraction, she could make out the coyly posed cartoon pig with coquettish eyelashes. The place appeared like any patronized business on the Westside except for the brilliant chrome of the cars set against the dead weeds that wedged apart the broken service road.

Tobias hooked his fingers through the links in the fence. "Could he be in there?"

Marisol nodded, an uncertain feeling knotted into her belly. The motorcycle led them to a location that came with a rusty torture-chamber of possibilities for Vincent. Her intuition and that stupid computer needed to be wrong.

Bam! Bam! Bam! Gunfire echoed out from the slaughterhouse.

Guns and bullets were inevitable "natural" disasters. In other parts of the world, people had earthquake or hurricane plans. She had gunfire plans. Sometimes when growing up, she had to sit in her bathtub until a drive-by passed. Sometimes patients were stitched together with bullets still inside them. Sometimes people died from gunshot wounds. A lot of people had to live putting up with guns. Regardless, with guns and bullets, she had to act; she had to move. But now as the man who loved her could possibly be at the receiving end of the gunfire, she didn't have a plan. Instead, she froze.

Tobias tossed his coat over the fence's barbed wire and lumbered over with the awkward grace of a grizzly bear. At the top-of-the-line post, he reached for Marisol. She pursed her lips to edge out her mounting fear, ignoring Tobias's outstretched hand as she tossed her jacket over the barbs. She climbed with lizard-like speed. Tobias landed with a grunt on his knees. Marisol flipped onto her feet from the top and stealthily walked down the hill toward the building.

"No!" Tobias whispered and pointed along the fence that ended at the riverbank. He ran toward the river. It flowed along the edge of the meatpacking district perpendicular to the slaughterhouse. Marisol followed. He jumped off the bank into ankle-deep water. He motioned toward the large storm drain that trickled into the river.

They were a football field's length away from the building. Traces of a rotten egg odor wafted from the entrance, strong enough to give Marisol pause. "What are you doing?"

Tobias stooped inside the archway, heading into the sewer. "We need to investigate. They're packing heat. Safe to say, we don't want them to see us."

"Why do our adventures involve the worst smells?" She jumped into the murky water. The cold temperature stabbed into her bones as it drenched her boots.

In the entryway, Tobias programmed the map function of his cell phone. "Don't wanna get lost." He led the way down the tunnel. The walls closed in enough that even Marisol walked with a hunch. As the water reached under Marisol's knees, Tobias turned down a tunnel and held out his phone as a light source. The farther they were from the outside entrance, the more the air grew hot and thick. Without a breeze, the putrid stench engulfed them.

Twenty feet ahead, light streaked through a grate. Tobias looked at his phone and whispered, "Bingo." Yet he walked slower, not upsetting the gray water at his shins.

Marisol dug her fingernails into her palms to keep quiet. As they approached the light, Tobias hugged his body against the wall. Faint voices and footsteps pattered above them. Marisol joined Tobias against the wall.

A guttural voice thick with spit said, "I think I found a new favorite toy." She had heard that voice the last time she cowered in the dark. The Bloodsucker.

Meanwhile, a syrupy substance dripped between the grates and plopped into the water. Tobias reached out and rubbed the substance between his fingers. Even in the shadows, Marisol saw his lips move. "Blood."

Marisol pushed by him; the water sloshed around her knees. Her fingers dug into the divots in the wall. She climbed, fighting the weak grip of her wet soles.

Then she heard his voice, raspy and frail, but its sonorous quality was unmistakable. "You're... just a... copy of me."

Between high-pitched wheezes of laughter, the Bloodsucker said, "A copy that's stopped you."

A loud crank followed by a sudden squeal and rumble of machinery shook the sewer walls. The sound covered Marisol's splashing as she slipped down. She scaled the wall again, curling her toes into the uneven brick. Her fingers hooked through the holes in the grate. "Vincent," she whispered.

The oppressive jangling of metal ceased. A single *pop!* followed it, like snapping of latex gloves. Through the grate, she could only make out a fraction of the scene. Vincent swung from a rusted meat hook that pulled him by his iron-bound wrists. The metal chafed his wrists bloody. The grate cut into the creases of her fingers.

She slid back into the water for relief. She heard the *pop!* again followed by—oh, her heart— Vincent whimpering. Again, she climbed and fought through the pain in her hands. Vincent dangled with a mound of chains around his legs. Blood and sweat matted the hair on his mask-less head. He flinched. Her arm muscles screamed in pain as she pulled herself up to get a better look.

Then she heard it again, the dreadful popping noise. His body dropped for a moment. The chains at his feet scraped the floor even louder. Oh God. The popping! The scraping! What was it? The force of the hook and chain wrenched his shoulders from their sockets. She held her breath to stifle a gasp, to hold back the nausea of her flipping stomach. And fell back into the water. No! She leaped up the wall. The tips of her fingers turned purple. She needed to see. Vincent's body jerked up. The magic healing made the dislocation momentary. He was immune to the injury but not to pain. His breath heaved, in-out, in-out and—*pop!* He broke again. And again and again and again. How long could he take this before he became like them?

The Bloodsucker's hooded head turned in her direction. Faceless circular rows of teeth pulsed toward a slimy maw, as if it could sense a mere droplet of Marisol's essence. Plastic and cloth. Just plastic and cloth. It was only an illusion, but the nightmare—only days old—began once more.

The Bloodsucker jerked his head back to Vincent. Good, he hadn't seen her, but there she was again, trapped, doomed to watch, and paralyzed by those teeth.

She took in a deep breath to scream.

Tobias's giant hand cupped her mouth and yanked her down into the water. His fleshy paw muffled her cries. His other arm hooked her under her armpits, dragging her away. What in hell was he doing? Marisol thrashed against the wall of muscle, but he picked her up like a small child. She kicked and flailed wildly, to no avail. The light from the slaughterhouse became a flicker with distance. Vincent, tied up and bleeding, was farther and farther away from her. With another twist down a tunnel, the air became cool and fresh.

If Tobias wouldn't help her, she'd have to do things herself. She only had to wriggle out of his grip. Crunch! She bit into Tobias's palm, held over her mouth, and didn't stop until she struck blood, but he grunted and held her tighter.

Outside the drain, he dropped her into a shallow pool. She faced her captor and seethed, picturing her eyes matching the black feral pupils that bored into her. She wiped the blood off her lips with the back of her hand. And saw red.

23

Selling Out

Tobias held his hand against his stomach and stomped. "Jesus, kid. I need a rabies shot!"

Unable to swallow, she spat away the bloody taste in her mouth. "What were you doing? You scared the shit outta me!"

"Stoppin' you from something stupid."

Marisol kicked wave after wave of water in his direction. "He was right there! He needed us!"

"And what were we going to do? Storm the place like we're invading Poland?"

She sucked in a snippet of air, and whispered, "Useless pig."

He put a finger behind his ear, "I can't quite hear you being a crazy bitch."

Something possessed her to charge at him. She crashed into him. The heels of her hands landed with muted thuds into his thick chest muscles. "Can you hear me now?" She wished the chest she struck was Vincent's. "You let everything break and then call yourself a hero when you shoddily glue it back together!" And he took ineffective blows like Vincent took them. She hated him more. Foam must've flown from her mouth. "You're just a swinging dick with a shit clearance rate!"

He stood expressionless and unmoved, a mountain, and she obviously wasn't a prophet.

She drew back her fist. "A useless..." And swung. "...piece of—"

He stepped back. She slipped on a pile of coagulated dead leaves and muck in front of her and fell onto her knees, smack into Shadowhaven's toilet—her new home.

He kept his sights on the slaughterhouse. "Get up."

Marisol hugged her knees to her chest. The water drenched her jeans and reminded her that after that tantrum, rolling around in poop water seemed like her proper place. "No."

"You'll get dysentery."

"So?"

"Frankly, if you diarrhea yourself to death out here, we'd attract a lot of unwanted attention."

Tears filled her eyes as she tried to bring herself back to reason. "I don't care."

"You damn well do, kid! We're fixers. If you don't like that we put broken things together, why the hell do you work in an ER?"

Her job meant she had mended things for the better. At sixty percent, what the fuck did he or his homicide cronies ever fix than have a name in black for the quarterly statement? The ER would be shut down at a sixty percent success rate. Maybe if he had the balls to walk a beat, there'd be no Bloodsuckers. Or Cazzes. Or any other chewed up people this city spat out. Maybe try prevention instead. To articulate that would mean she'd have to swallow a drop of sewer water. It would be best to keep that bit to herself.

So, she rooted her wet butt to the ground and stayed silent. Icy water numbed her lower limbs. When she thought about it, her actual pain came from her devastated heart. Her inability to save Vincent as he suffered perpetually felt like a cleaver to the chest. But to make it worse, watching him get pulled apart and slowly regenerate was like having the cleaver pulled out over and over, and not knowing if he'd come back as a man or zombie made it worse when she realized...

She hadn't returned those words when it mattered.

She hadn't long to clutch at the phantom pain before Tobias grabbed her by the front of her hoodie and almost lifted her out of the water. "I stopped you from shattering, didn't I?"

Her vision turned into watercolors, blurring Tobias's features into splatters. She ran her fingers over his calloused knuckles to pry him off. Once his grip tightened, her chin trembled. Was he going to shake her? Hit her? Snap her neck? Kiss her?

His face turned bright red. He breathed in through his nose slowly and out again. Then he let go of her and skulked a few steps away, keeping his back to her. "You're good, kid, but you're not that good. To face the remnants of the Mob and the Bloodsucker, we'd need a whole force." He turned and pointed a finger. "And I'd sooner convince my Commissioner I found a unicorn that could fart rainbows than I could get him to use the police to save our good-as-dead friend." By the time he said friend, he seemed defeated, and his posture sank, no longer tall. After a sigh, he continued just above a whisper, "I take the successes where I get 'em. You're alive. It's a good day."

She returned a disgusted snort. Tobias knew nothing. Vincent couldn't die.

His strength came back. "Do you wanna be like Caz? Destined for a body bag or prison?"

Was he kidding? She had spent the last twenty years of her life ensuring she was the antithesis to Caz. She made it this far, striking no deals and owing no favors. But if she couldn't get the police to save Vincent...

Marisol stood and wiped the water from her upper lip. "Sorry."

Without a pause, Tobias shrugged. His eyes turned back to their kaleidoscopic color.

Marisol reached in her pocket and drew out the commlink button. She wished she knew Morse code. She'd tap it to say, "I will save you," or "I'm coming back." Instead, she pushed the button four times.

Each click was for the four words she hadn't said to Vincent.

"C'mon, kid," Tobias said.

They trudged up the hill, climbed over the fence, and pulled their coats from the barbs. "I haven't told you everything," Marisol said. "Our friend is like the mouse. The DNA that Annie synthesized? That was his. He can't die. You think he's good as dead, but he can't die."

Tobias smiled faintly. "So, all this time our friend's been that asshole, Vinnie Varian?"

She crossed her arms. "H-h-how do you know?"

He tied his helmet on and took his spot on the motorcycle. "He was messed up, but I'd recognize his golden hair and perfect face anywhere." As he rubbed the back of his neck, he added, "Besides, a beautiful woman into a rich guy? I've heard taller tales."

Marisol scooched in front of him, putting on her helmet. "It's not like that!" Her shoulders tensed into knots. If she protested more, he'd probably get off from burrowing under her skin with more "astute" observations.

Tobias unlocked the motorcycle with a palm print. Marisol commandeered the controls. "Staci, take us to The Pink Curtain," she ordered.

"The stripper joint?"

"Gentlemen's club," she corrected. The blue line traced in another direction across the computerized map, and they were off.

Once they reached a red light, she eased her shoulder blades down. "Vincent is so much more." The traffic light lasted long enough for Marisol to inform Tobias how their friend was a 500ish-year-old cursed former conquistador. And a pirate, a philosopher, a scientist, a doctor, a freedom fighter. "And the man I—" A passing bus drowned out her murmuring. It was of no consequence. The light had turned green.

They arrived outside The Pink Curtain, a gray, windowless storefront decorated with neon tubes bent in the shape of naked women. Live Nude Girls intermittently flashed. Despite the bright electric signs, the pièce de résistance was a wooden folded sign posted on the sidewalk promising an all-you-can-eat lunch buffet.

Tobias stepped onto the pavement and removed his helmet. "Last year when we took out a portion of the Mob? They really lit into him. Never seen a man face that many bullets and live. I thought it was a ninja thing. But..." He shrugged. "The super thing checks out, but 500 years old?"

"And cursed."

"I thought those guys were radioactive or alien. Like in the comics."

"No, there's another option." Marisol dismounted. Her soaked boots squished. She should have stopped to change shoes, but time was precious. She'd risk trench foot if it meant Vincent would be safe in her apartment, his lake house, or—hell—his creepy estate.

"I remember when he was born. It was all over the magazines back when I had to go to the store with my ma." Tobias knocked on the motorcycle. The seat opened and swallowed their helmets.

"Hired actors. You shouldn't believe everything you read." Marisol tied her hair up into a ponytail and zipped up her jacket to collect herself.

"As opposed to everything from the mouth of an ER nurse?"

She lifted her chin. "But I'm right."

His face beamed as if struck by an idea. "If he's like how you say he is, we could take our sweet time. Wait 'til I get my badge back and serve them a warrant." He rubbed his hands together. "By then, he could superpower himself out of the situation."

"If he takes on damage too great, it can become permanent. Think of all the sick things the Bloodsucker is capable of at a slaughterhouse and ask yourself, 'Would I want to live through that forever?' Because those are the rules we're dealing with." Tobias's forehead creased, an expression of pity. Whatever he thought, it sucked the wind out of her. "You still don't believe me," she said.

The stress lines eased from his face. "I helped duct tape a zombie rat in your freezer." He gestured to the building. "And I like lap dances like any red-blooded American man, but I'm failing to see how this could help our situation."

"When you roll in shit, you get shitty ideas. You said we need a force to fight the Bloodsucker. I know a gang who owes my brother a favor."

He chortled. "You think The Shadows are going to help?"

Marisol opened the heavy door of the entrance. What did he think? She'd ask the dancers in eight-inch Pleasers and a sheet of body glitter to kick down the slaughterhouse doors?

His mouth dropped. "You're serious." He followed her, the mission handcuffing them together.

A host sat behind a window of golden bars, propping her chin on the tops of her hands as if she expected them. She purred in a deep twang, "Welcome inside my Pink Curtain, friends. I'm Mijo Ray, and entry will cost you twenty dollars today." She tossed back her black waves of hair. Light caught her glossy, red lips framed by a meticulously shaped goatee.

"I'm here to see Tiny." Marisol chewed the inside of her cheek before adding, "I'm... Caz's sister."

Mijo Ray clicked her slender, glittering nails together. "As in Casimir Novotny?"

Marisol nodded.

Mijo Ray shook her head. "Shame he's locked up."

Great, Marisol could leverage Caz's history to see The Pink Curtain's owner, Tiny. In the hierarchy of The Shadows, Tiny was second-in-command. Except he hadn't relied on Caz to enforce timely payments or to silence witnesses.

As if this host had zero time for pity parties or excuses, Mijo Ray rubbed her fingers together. "Twenty dollars." Then she arched a flawlessly penciled-in eyebrow in Tobias's direction. "Each." Who needed Caz when Tiny had Mijo Ray?

Tobias edged forward. "Our business is with Tiny."

"Your business is with everyone here, baby. Let me put this in a language even a straight boy can understand. Our day players may be in the minor leagues, but the only way to the majors is with a little practice and money. And I don't care if you're only coming in to use the bathroom. A tit's a tit, even in your periphery."

"You won't make an exception?" Marisol asked.

"You have a wad of nerves asking for an exception, Miss Casimir's Sister, especially considering," Mijo Ray's nostrils flared, "that you smell like shit."

Marisol retreated behind Tobias. A little fresh air at a motorcycle's speed should've taken care of her sewer water problem. Obviously, it hadn't.

"We're a little short on cash." Tobias upturned his eyebrows into a face that must've melted a few hearts in his lifetime.

Mijo Ray leaned forward, peering through her pink, tinsel-like eyelashes. "Your eyes are different colors."

Tobias hunched closer to the golden bars. His tone became husky. "It's a condition. Sectoral heterochromia."

"Is it?" Mijo Ray glided a finger down a strand of her hair. Then she blinked and twirled another finger in the air. "ATM is right behind you, Marlboro Man."

Tobias looked at Marisol. Marisol returned the look, gesticulating toward his back pocket. She finally held up her hands. "I didn't bring my purse."

He scoffed and turned to the ATM. "My head hurts. My hand hurts. You owe me big time, kid." After a few of his forceful button presses shook the machine, he asked, "Ten-dollar fee?"

Mijo Ray batted her eyelashes.

With a beep and a grinding of gears, Tobias had the cash. He passed the bills through the bars of the window.

Mijo Ray plopped two plastic tokens into the small metal tray below the partition. "Don't you worry, my ruggedly handsome friend. Entry gets you a complimentary drink and all the food you care to eat. Not to mention the ladies." Tobias pocketed the tokens and winked at Mijo Ray. She giggled and tossed her hair again. "Ask for Tiny at the bar. I'll let him know Caz's sister is here."

Marisol pulled the door open, entering the club. "Here goes nothing."

A slow-pulsing, bass-heavy song rumbled the floor beneath them. Customers were so dispersed throughout the club, the place appeared empty. Lunch at the gentlemen's club was a lonely endeavor, even with purchased company.

The featured dancer bent and flexed slowly on the main stage, ensuring a customer didn't miss one inch of skin. Her movements revealed sturdy, compact muscles. Yet her tattoos and belly ring emphasized the delicate line dividing Marisol from her. Under another set of circumstances, she would be the bikini-clad dancer spinning upside down on the pole, working through the sting of a friction burn.

Tobias flicked Marisol in her bicep. "You drinking anything?"

Marisol scowled and shook her head. They were on a mission. That meant not getting sidetracked by The Pink Curtain's many vices.

He waved to a bartender who had a mane of spiral curls. She wore a fishnet body stocking and strategically placed pasties. As soon as she approached them, Marisol said, "I have a meeting with Tiny."

The bartender ignored her.

Tobias pushed the plastic tokens across the bar. "A shot of whiskey. Irish. And a shot of rail vodka. The kind that gives you gut rot."

Marisol slammed her fist down. "Now is not the time."

In an instant, Tobias's pupils eclipsed his speckled irises. Instinctively, Marisol clenched her body together to hide from his dark glare. When the shots arrived, he poured the vodka on his injured hand and drank the whiskey in one swallow. He shook the excess liquid off his palm and wrapped it in a series of cocktail napkins he had tied together. While the bartender collected the empty glasses, Tobias handed her a tip. "We're here to see Tiny."

"He's back in the Champagne Room." She gestured to a doorway lined with beaded curtains.

Tobias thanked the bartender and smiled at Marisol. "You can't make demands without sweetening the pot, kid."

Okay, so she flubbed playing a shot-caller. She duly noted Tobias's advice, but not without an eye roll to keep her ego protected and his in check.

Marisol approached the doorway's magenta glow and ran her fingers across the beads. Once she crossed here, she'd sell out to the Shadows. But the air felt too cool behind her. Accustomed to her towering companion hanging close, she spun around.

Someone needed to put him on a leash. She had lost Tobias to the buffet where he heaped chicken fingers onto a plate. Marisol placed her tongue against her upper teeth and whistled. How could he eat at a time and place like this?

He stuffed a chicken finger in his mouth and held out the plate. "Does this look like fifty bucks' worth of food?"

Marisol snapped her fingers and jerked her thumb behind her. Tobias grabbed a piece to-go and set the plate down. As they moved past the beaded curtain, he chewed down on another strip and mumbled, "I've never been to a Champagne Room before."

"I'm happy to be a part of your first time." Fully in control of her innuendo, she flashed a halfhearted smile. In that moment, she pictured a gangly, teenage version Tobias, falsely confident from beer and whiskey struggling to unhook a bra on a ragged couch.

Even in the dim purple and pink lights of the hall, she caught a glint in Tobias's eyes. She recognized the look. It was like Vincent's when he asked, "How may I please you?"

Marisol gulped. "Tiny," she murmured and moved through the last set of beaded curtains.

In the waning violet lights of the Champagne Room, every face became a tinted silhouette. All of Tiny's six feet and 350 pounds waited for them in a velvet booth, though he looked like he lost weight from the last time Marisol saw him. Despite people needing an elephant gun to take Tiny out, a set of baby-faced enforcers stood and flanked around him. If a truant officer braved the bowels of the Pink Curtain, he'd cart off the enforcers to high school. Most definitely with a fight.

Far in the corner, an old man sat, buried in layers of winter clothes. A dancer contorted into a shoulder stand, presenting the old man with a salacious view.

Tiny whistled. She rolled onto her feet and seamlessly gathered her money and top. Tiny held up a hundred-dollar bill. "Go get yourself some new shoes."

She snatched the bill, staring at Marisol. "Fresh meat or what?"

"Or what, you nosey-ass bitch," Tiny said.

"Figured. A little old to be fresh." She tied her top, flicked her hair back, and left.

"Kick her out but not the customer?" Marisol asked as she grabbed a chair, spun it once on its leg, and sat across from Tiny.

"Him? He's too damn old to know what's up. He brings in a couple stacks and just sits there. It takes a pair of jiggling titties and a rolling pussy for him to even register a pulse."

"Better Business would be proud." Tobias settled next to Marisol. She elbowed him to keep him on his best behavior.

"So Mare, what makes you step down from your downtown high-rise to the Westside?"

"Considering my brother is doing multiples at the Hill for the Shadows, I thought I could trade in a favor."

"What's up?"

Marisol leaned forward. "The Bloodsucker and surviving leftovers of Shadowhaven's favorite gangs are holed up at the Clark's Slaughterhouse. They captured a friend of mine, and I can't go to the cops. I need the Shadows to help me fight the Bloodsucker and free my friend."

Tiny laughed until a glob of phlegm interrupted him midroar. He coughed it away. "When we said we'd be looking out for your family after Caz's situation, we meant financially. Like if you needed to get diapers or school clothes or something. If you ever had kids, that is."

Marisol crossed her legs. Not a chance. "The Bloodsucker got rid of Izzy and tore up the Mob and the Bratva. It's only a matter of time before he comes for you."

"And we'll be ready for him. Until then—" Tiny motioned to his boys, who encroached on Marisol and Tobias.

She raised her hands in surrender. "We're not dealing with the same rules. He can't be killed!" Purple light caught the gleam of a brass knuckle. "How do you think he got Izzy?"

Tiny shook his head. One enforcer yanked her to her feet by the hood of her sweatshirt. Tobias reached to grab him. A gravelly voice barked, "She's right."

The enforcers stopped. Tiny turned his head, facing the old man. He stood, possessing the straight spine of someone a quarter his age. The old man tossed his stocking cap, revealing a shaved head. Underneath his coat hid a wiry build. He lifted his sunglasses and uncovered shining onyx eyes, like a shark's. He unwound one layer of the scarf, exposing a broad nose dented in tiny cuts. His thin mustache dusted over his bruised lips, swollen to the point of looking like a pair of slugs pushed together. The "old man" was none other than Israel Ramirez, aka Big Iz, aka Izzy himself.

The chapter Vincent helped her close reopened again, as if Fate had a crack in the bind. What had she expected? The city's pseudo-justice came with bail bonds, hung juries, appeals, parole. It'd take more than a broken nose and a pair of handcuffs to snuff out Izzy. The urge to reopen at least one scab on his face conflicted with her need to save Vincent. She scrunched her hand into a fist and gulped again.

Izzy tipped his head, and Tiny took his place among the enforcers. From his new demoted spot, Tiny bowed his head. For a big ass tough guy, Tiny played the subservient part well. Or was he feeling remorse for lying to her? Izzy adjusted into the middle of the booth. "What's the plan, Mare?"

"Um..." She hadn't thought that far.

Tobias returned to his seat. "I'm glad you asked. Our friend is hangin' by his wrists just off the Clark's old kill floor. Luckily, that spot leads to a loading garage. I'd say we split into two groups. One distracts the Bloodsucker and his minions at the entrance while the other, smaller group escapes with our friend out the garage."

"Good work." Izzy smiled like a shark circling its dinner. "Officer."

Uh-oh, Marisol hadn't contemplated the full extent of dragging an unarmed cop into the lion's den. In plain clothes, Tobias should've slipped under their radar. She touched his elbow, anticipating a bolt to the exit. But Tobias returned Izzy's smile. There was something familiar about it, as if this was a dance that began long before Marisol entered the scene and would continue long after she left.

"Detective Quinlan," Tobias said. Although the lights had turned all the faces into magenta-lined shadows, Marisol swore Tobias's eyes reflected a hint of blue.

Once Tobias showed he wasn't an easy meal, Izzy raised his lips to his nose. His thin mustache bristled under the tip. "Sounds simple enough, but the Bloodsucker punched a hole through Santino's chest. How do you stop that?"

Marisol leaned in, echoing Tobias's stance. "We took out something similar using a hefty amount of tranquilizer."

Izzy licked his lips. "I suppose as a nurse you keep the good stuff on hand?"

"I'm clean out." Another shitty idea—manipulating the hospital records to obtain tranquilizing drugs—gurgled into her mind like some kind of swamp creature.

Tobias jut out his chin. "What about your heroin?"

Izzy shifted his gaze to Tiny and then to the floor. "My heroin? I don't know what you're talking about."

"I'm not a narc, Iz. I couldn't give a rat's ass about your drugs as long as you're not leaving around stone-cold whodunnits."

Too many bad ideas—drugs and murder—curdled Marisol's insides. She swallowed back the tang of bile.

Izzy looked up. "How much would we need?"

Marisol wiped her clammy hands on her thighs and murmured, "For the Bloodsucker? Enough to flatten out ten people."

Izzy nodded. "And his lackeys? Light 'em up?"

Tiny's enforcers beamed with boyish glee at the suggestion.

Marisol sprang to her feet. "No guns. No killing." A chorus of, "They're armed!" and "You lost your damn mind!" met her from both sides of the table.

She silenced them with a slap of her hand in the center of the table. "No one here wants a gang war. There'd be blood in the streets."

Tobias leaned back in his chair and linked his hands behind his head. Purple shadows cast a pall over his face. "What do we do then? Buy them all a Coke?"

If Vincent's motorcycle was any sign, she might have an insider's access to his basement. "Give me an hour. If I don't have the supplies to take them out non-lethally, we can discuss another plan." Marisol stiffened as Izzy and Tobias shared glances. They were different predators, a shark and a grizzly bear, but predators all the same. And out for blood.

"You're on." Izzy eased back into the booth. Marisol wiped her hand on the shoulder of her jacket and held it out. Izzy shook it. "Aren't you glad you're in my pocket?"

Whether she was glad wasn't the issue. In Izzy's pocket, Caz had become a murderer whose fury was for sale, but her fury was righteous. If the city's gutters ran deep with blood, it would be for Vincent.

It would be for love.

Ịฅ†ᴇʀʟᴜᴅᴇ

i hAD sENSED yOU aMONG THE sHADOWS OF THE rAMSHACKLE sLAUGHTERHOUSE. i cOULDN'T hEAR yOU OR sEE yOU, BUT i fELT yOU wITH THE pRICKLING hAIR AT THE bACK OF mY nECK.

wHAT dO yOU dO wHEN dESTINIES cOLLIDE? wHY, sTRIKE IT tHROUGH THE hEART wITH cUPID'S aRROW. i kNOW, i kNOW. IT wAS A rOD OF rEBAR iNSTEAD. IT sHOULD kILL yOU THE wAY bULLETS sHOULD kILL mE, BUT IT dIDN'T. iNSTEAD, IT bROUGHT yOU TO yOUR kNEES. yOU gASPED, mY lITTLE gUPPY oUT OF wATER. AND pULLED oUT mY aRROW FROM yOUR cHEST TO dENY oUR cONNECTION. lUCKILY, i hAD A wHOLE qUIVERFULL, AND i dIDN'T sTOP uNTIL yOU wERE mINE. i pLUNGED aNOTHER rEBAR tHROUGH THE hEART AND hAD mORE FOR yOUR lIMBS. yOU wRIGGLED AND bLED, yET IT sURPRISED mE TO fEEL dISAPPOINTED. yOU dISAPPOINT mE.

i sUPPOSE iF wE oPERATE BY THE oLD rULES, yOU'D bEST mE THE wAY yOU sTOPPED tHOSE mORONS-fOR-hIRE wHO sNATCHED vARIAN, BUT iT'S A nEW wORLD nOW. wE oPERATE BY mY rULES.

yOU aRE lIKE mE. i aM lIKE yOU. yOU sHOULD bE mY wHITE wHALE, BUT yOU'RE nOTHING BUT A wORM ON A hOOK. i aSKED, "WHAT aRE yOU? dID tHAT dOCTOR mAKE yOU lIKE sHE mADE mE?" aWAITING yOUR aNSWER, fRAGMENTS OF rUMORS fELL iNTO pLACE—SECRET sIDE pROJECTS AND sUPER cOPS. "ARE yOU THE sUPER cOP?" nO aNSWER. aLL yOU hAD FOR mE wAS sWEAT AND gRUNTS.

i pULLED aWAY yOUR mASK. AT fIRST, bEAUTY, THE sAME pAIN AND aLLURE mASTERS cAPTURED IN pAINTINGS. oNCE mY aWE fADED, i sAW yOU FOR wHO yOU tRULY wErE—VINCENT vARIAN. mAKES sENSE bECAUSE tHAT sIMPLETON nEEDS TO mOONLIGHT AS sOME bADDIE TO cREATE mEANING oUT OF hIS sTUPID lIFE. "ARE yOU A pART OF A gOVERNMENT pROGRAM? wILL THE pOLICE bE lOOKING FOR yOU?" aGAIN, yOUR fACE wAS sTONE.

i sHOULD kNOW bETTER. iT'S nOT "WHO iS lOOKING FOR yOU?" BUT "WILL aNYONE lOOK FOR yOU?" wILL aNYONE IN tHIS tOWN mISS vINCENT vARIAN, A sELF-eNTITLED sNOB wHO'S A sHUT-iN IN hIS dADDY'S mANSION OR wHO gALLIVANTS aROUND THE wORLD wITH lIKE-aND-sHARE-aDDICTED mODELS? wHEN vINCENT vARIAN gOES mISSING, dOES IT sURPRISE aNYONE? wILL tHOSE mODELS sHED A tEAR FOR yOU iF yOU dROPPED oFF THE fACE OF THE eARTH? tHOSE sHINING eYES wENT dULL wHEN i aSKED yOU tHAT qUESTION.

hOW fLIMSY OF A lEGACY TO hAVE. IT wILL bE fUN TO wATCH IT aLL cRUMBLE bENEATH yOU.

24

Puke And Rally

Gravel snapped under the tire as the motorcycle pulled into the driveway of the estate.

Tobias said, "Pictures don't do this place justice." Marisol gazed back at him. He stared, mouth agape.

"Yeah. Empty, dusty, and full of old crap. Media never seems to report that." She got off the motorcycle and approached the garage door.

She stifled a yawn. Her body demanded rest down to its bones, but her heart answered her exhaustion with a resounding, *hell no!*

She flipped up a keypad. Like the handlebars had earlier, the pad lit white-hot under her fingers, and the doors roared open. The motorcycle carrying Tobias followed her inside like a beckoned dog.

The garage door sealed behind them. "What do you think?" Marisol asked.

Tobias's mouth and eyebrows returned to normal. He stood and looked around, hands on his hips. "A billionaire couldn't afford a bigger garage?"

The ramp opened on cue. Marisol nodded for him to follow her into the black depths. As soon as they reached the end of the ramp, the lights flickered on, one after the other. "Big enough for you now?"

Tobias spun around in both directions. "What is all this?"

"Storage. I say we load up what we need in his SUV." She nodded toward the massive black, matte-chrome vehicle parked in the basement. With the plan in place, she rushed to the metal wall cut into grids. As she touched it, a box lit white under her hand and the compartment opened. "Heat vision goggles." She tossed a pair to Tobias. He juggled to catch them.

Marisol opened another drawer. "His suits." In a row, she saw how Vincent adapted, from navy wool coats and gray tights to midnight blue rubber and charcoal armored neoprene.

After a sweep of his gaze, Tobias's face pinched with confusion. "I thought they were black."

"Night isn't pitch black, you know," she said flatly.

Tobias looped the goggles over his upper arm and leaned against the compartment. "I didn't say it was. I just realized the stories about him, they're not accurate."

"You'd prefer people tell stories about men in blue who fight crime?" Marisol flashed a blink-and-miss-it grin.

"You're funny." But all he did was turn a corner of his mouth and puff a single laugh, as if it hurt to be happy. He squinted and rubbed his chin. Something caught his attention—the glowing blue window of the vault door. "What's in there?"

"500-year-old conquista-cicles," Marisol said as she moved from drawer to drawer, opening them with her touch. Never stopping, ever moving, she fought the creeping need to sleep. She found gas masks, concussion grenades, flash bombs, and tear gas canisters. She gathered them and threw them in the back of Vincent's SUV.

Tobias wiped the window, and the glass squeaked under his hand. Peering through it, he shuddered. "Looks like frozen beef jerky."

"What else do we need?" She emptied an entire compartment's contents into the SUV.

"Bulletproof vests? Holy water?" Tobias paced slowly around the open compartments.

Marisol opened more—one refrigerated compartment containing vials drew her attention with the cool vapor emerging from it. "I may need to do a little digging for specific requests."

Tobias moved to a compartment of weaponry and picked out a black metal stick. "A cattle prod." He smoothed his hand over its length before he swung it in the air. He lunged, stabbing an invisible assailant. "Zzzz," he sounded through closed teeth.

Marisol shook her head. "Men and their toys." She studied the vials—Vincent's regenerative serum, anesthetic, antibiotics, and voila! tranquilizer. Guess they didn't need Izzy as much as he needed them.

While she read the labels, her eyes drifted shut and knees buckled underneath her. She steadied herself against the open compartment. Damn. She had paused long enough to surrender to exhaustion. In a moment, she'd walk her drowsiness off like a kick to the shin.

"Whoa, kid." Tobias dropped the cattle prod and rushed to her side. "You're no good like this."

She slapped her cheek. "It'll pass. How do you think I handle rotating shifts?"

"We're not talking about going through a shift on autopilot."

She picked up a vial of regenerative serum. It was the good stuff that healed her broken leg and churned her insides until she barfed her guts out. Sure, it had unseemly effects, but the resulting adrenaline and endorphins could be the boost they needed. "My leg was broken."

He snorted. "No shit. I used my tie as a tourniquet."

"But he healed it, injecting me with this." She held up the vial. "It initiated cellular regeneration at a rapid speed and pumped me with enough adrenaline, I could leap over buildings. This could be a good night's rest in a bottle."

Tobias licked a corner of his mouth as he held the vial between his thumb and forefinger. "Is it safe?"

"Safe enough," she said, leaving out the shattering pain and vomiting part.

He set the vial back into the compartment. "I don't know. The thought of injecting myself with something gives me the heebie-jeebies."

Marisol nodded. When Tobias looked away, she pocketed a vial and syringe. Taking it later might give her the edge she needed.

They loaded the back of the SUV until it ran out of space. Tobias held on to the cattle prod as if he had yanked it from a stone.

"Now that we have weapons, we need to become walking fortresses." Marisol held up a pair of Kevlar pants in front of Tobias. "These could work." She grabbed the tights and held them over her legs. They needed a little adjusting. "Staci! Do you have any scissors?"

A drawer popped open. Marisol and Tobias cannibalized Vincent's suits, cutting and pulling pieces that fit them.

Marisol stripped down to her sports bra and underwear, using the SUV's windows to study her reflection. In the same reflection, she noticed Tobias's clenched jaw and darkened eyes. After what they had been through, it hadn't occurred to her that he'd want to maintain the barrier of modesty between them. But he looked at her just as he had back at The Pink Curtain. The look said despite his assertions otherwise, this friendship would not be enough for him. Damn.

Tobias broke their trance with a blink and shook his head, chuckling. He gathered his supplies and ducked into the nearest room with a door, the sauna.

Marisol pulled on navy spandex tights and a shirt. Next, she put on a pair of armored neoprene shorts she fashioned out of one of Vincent's suits and secured it around her waist with a utility belt. She wiggled into a bulletproof vest and topped it off with a heather gray hoodie. Suited up, Marisol had easily added fifty pounds to her appearance, resembling a welterweight warming up before a fight. The finishing touches, her domino mask and fingerless boxing gloves, she shoved into the pocket of the hoodie.

Though her knuckles longed to break some goons' bones, she'd wrap them in gauze closer to game time. As she loaded her utility belt with smoke bombs and tranquilizers, she heard Tobias in the sauna room squeezing into his layers. He let out a long sigh. A head taller and equally thicker, he must've struggled to get into anything made for Vincent. Then he retched and spit, his hangover clearly catching up with him. Surprising that he hadn't rallied by now.

Falling asleep on her feet and her burly companion throwing up his lunch? They were the rescue mission no one would ask for.

Marisol drew the vial and syringe out from her damp jeans crumpled on the floor. She needed to take the serum. After loading the syringe, she pulled down her shorts and tights to expose her hip and jammed the needle into her side. She reeled back against the door of the SUV.

Pain stabbed into one side of her stomach as if her insides were on the verge of rupturing. Her agony was unsatisfied until she sank to the ground. *Whoosh!* The pain left as soon as it arrived, but it did not fool her this time. It was the eye of the storm before the next hit.

Her cheeks flushed. She took in a deep breath, preparing for the heave of the empty contents of her stomach. But—what the hell?—she licked her lips and rubbed her thighs together. Her lower abdomen muscles tightened. No pain. Just the opposite.

Her head lolled back, and she moaned. An orgasm? Without a broken leg to heal, did her body react differently to the stuff? Unseemly side effects, indeed, Vincent. As the synthetic pleasure faded, she laughed, touching the light sheen of sweat on her face with the back of her hand.

Tobias's heavy footsteps approached. Marisol jumped up from the floor and threw the used vial and syringe in an empty compartment, closing it. She adjusted her shorts back and turned around.

Tobias strutted in. The thump of his steel-toed boots added more heft to his walk. The too-small Kevlar pants he borrowed were tight around his muscular thighs. Creases pointed like arrows at his crotch. Dear God, she needed to look up. He had cut a T-shirt out of Vincent's suits, his biceps too large for the sleeves. His shoulders and chest were even more massive under a bulletproof vest. His arm muscles glistened like some god touched the earth to bless its warrior. Since when did homicide detectives spend hours in the gym?

She searched his face—did a god come down and touch you?—but a knit ski mask disguised him.

Tobias pulled his ski mask up. "What?"

It wasn't a "mask thing." She dealt with enough masked patients at the hospital to know that was far from true. So, what was it? His stubble shone with auburn flecks, no longer a grizzled gray. How? The retching, the glistening muscles. She grabbed his injured hand and unwrapped it. Her bite had disappeared. She ran her thumb over the smooth skin. "No more teeth marks." She looked at him and narrowed her eyes. Her observation sounded more like a reproach. That's not how she meant it, was it?

His lips parted as he took in a breath. "No," he mouthed.

"You took the serum," she scolded.

Busted. He shrugged. Whatever, they had to save Vincent. She bolted to the driver's door of the SUV.

"No!" Tobias slammed his hand against the door. Marisol shivered, unsure of the side effects he was experiencing. She turned to him, holding her breath.

He smiled, baring incisors of a wild carnivore. "I'm sober. I may never drive something so nice ever again. You're riding shotgun."

Marisol let go of her breath and chuckled. She'd gladly ride as his passenger.

Ínterlude

yOUR bODY tAkes bULLETS AND sTRETCHING. i'M cURIOUS wHAT eLSE IT cAN tAKE. sHOULD i pLUG IN tHOSE oLD eLECTRIC cARVING kNIVES tHEY hAVE lYING IN THE cORNER? cAN wE rEGROW lIMBS? bECAUSE i dON'T lIKE tHIS lOOK FOR yOU. iT'S tOO pLEASANT.

i lOWER yOU TO THE gROUND. lIFT yOU UP BY yOUR gOLDEN cURLS AND cRUNCH! i pIERCE A mEAT hOOK iNTO yOUR bACK. tHEN i lET IT cARRY yOU aBOVE mE, sO i cOULD eNJOY mY wORK FROM eVERY pOSSIBLE aNGLE. mY wORK OF aRT. mINE AND nO oNE eLSE'S.

25

Oп The Ropes

Tobias sat on the edge of the SUV's back bumper, unloading the armor and weapons in Izzy's mechanic shop. Each of the Shadows struggled to pull on a sling of smoke grenades or a bullet-proof vest. Even Izzy looked at the stuff like they were alien artifacts, and nothing ever seemed to shake him.

As they armed themselves, Tobias barked out a plan. They'd block all exits except for the front-loading bay and exit chute in the back. A combination of tear gas, flash bombs, and some other fireworks would keep the minions on the ropes and far from Vincent. Since he was the better shot, Tobias would be the one taking out the Bloodsucker, though everyone had enough tranquilizers, black market and commercial, to weaken him. The name of the game was tranquilize and bolt. "If you're close enough to stick him, run away," Tobias warned.

Marisol wrapped her hands in gauze as Tobias reviewed her role in the plan. Armed with a small portable blowtorch, she would be in charge of freeing Vincent and escaping out the back chute. Tobias assigned this duty to her because, although she easily was a decade older than most of the Shadows, she still was the fastest runner. But the other reason he murmured, "Make sure nothing is permanent."

If Vincent couldn't come out of this intact? She jolted and reached for the pendant buried under her armor. Maybe she should pray away the looming uncertainty the way Abuelita would.

A familiar twang eased her worry. "Hell." Mijo Ray, barely recognizable without her wig and eyelashes, wiggled into a bullet-proof vest. "A girl's gonna break a nail putting on all this before she even gets to smack a bitch." Her nails may have been broken and her glitter rubbed off, but Mijo Ray wore a pair of boots with metal stilettos, as dangerous as they were fabulous. Maybe Marisol would request a similar pair but an inch or two lower.

With the equipment distributed, Tobias shut the trunk of the SUV. Izzy hovered right behind him. "The Bloodsucker had a really nice supplier. Shipped stashes in Varian boxes. Quantity and quality so good that it must be from Vincent Varian himself. He has to be a drug dealer. How do you think he got so rich?"

Marisol stifled a laugh, catching a glow in Tobias's gaze as he presumably held in a smile. "I thought it's because of all that compound interest on his antique pirate gold," Tobias said. Was he joking or actually theorizing how Vincent became so wealthy?

Izzy sighed, loud and exaggerated. "Once we do this, the Shadows will be on our own again."

Tobias kept his back to Izzy and looked at Marisol, rolling his eyes. "My condolences, Izzy."

"What will I get for it?" Izzy asked.

"The Bloodsucker took out your competition. After all this, the Shadows could operate on every corner of the city," Tobias said.

Izzy's eyes beamed as he probably estimated the windfall of being the city's sole heroin supplier. "Sounds beautiful."

"But what you get is an early retirement," Tobias continued.

"Excuse me?" Izzy scowled.

"You go to one of those countries without extradition, live off the money you have stored in your offshore accounts, and I never want to see your face around here ever again. I don't want to hear your name even uttered. As far as Shadowhaven's concerned, you're dead."

Izzy brought his lips to his nose and shook his head.

Tobias added, "Accept it. You're out of the game. There should be nothing better. You aren't leaving in a body bag or handcuffs." Tobias rolled his shoulders back and straightened his spine, gaining another foot in height. He lowered his voice, but Marisol could still hear him. "Because after tonight, if I see you, I'll fuck you up, either with my badge or my boot."

Izzy's gaze traveled over Tobias, from his boots to his head. He extended his hand. "It was nice working with you, Detective Quinlan."

Tobias shook his hand. "All right, let's roll."

The SUV wound through alleys, stopping at the dead end where Marisol and Tobias had been hours earlier. The red-gold rays of sun signaled dusk's arrival. Tobias exited the vehicle, ski-mask lowered. He pulled on a pair of black tactical shooting gloves and slung his weaponry behind him. A gas mask hung off the back of his head, as if a new face grew there.

Marisol tied on her mask, put her grappling gloves on, and flipped up her hood. She was prepared, like the perfect shift when she finished her coffee, stocked her supplies, and readied her beds. When triage had informed them of an entire wedding party coming into the hospital with food poisoning, Marisol stretched her neck and said, "Bring it."

Tiny and one of his teen enforcers hopped out of the back.

"Ready?" Tobias asked the mismatched duo.

Tiny and the enforcer pocketed a couple of Molotov cocktails and nodded.

Tobias and Marisol ripped through the foliage and met a rusted chain-link fence marking the perimeter. Down below was the abandoned slaughterhouse. Tobias held the heat vision goggles like binoculars over his eyes. "I think I see him."

"Show me," Marisol said. He handed her the goggles. Through the lens, she could see orange figures moving about the levels of the slaughterhouse. In the very back, an orange figure dangled over everyone. It had to be Vincent.

Tobias patted her on the back. "Haven't chopped him up yet." He tapped a commlink encircled over his ear. "Okay Iz, we have about twenty mob members. We need you to shock and block. If the Teeth Man comes out, you tranq and run, but I'll take care of him."

Tobias cut a gap in the fence with wire cutters. The group crawled to the other side. They watched from the hill as a fleet of beat-up cars drove abreast toward the slaughterhouse and parked, blocking access to the road out. The only way out for the Bloodsucker's goons was swimming.

The Shadows moved like a quiet swarm around the building, stationing themselves at the exits. Tiny and his enforcer moved down the hill and jumped off the riverbank, heading in the direction of the storm drain.

Marisol and Tobias ran to the rear of the building. They fired grappling hooks from their guns in a synchronized fashion and ascended the slaughterhouse.

They prowled toward a skylight and crouched over it. With the goggles protecting her eyes, Marisol cut a football-sized hole in the skylight with her blowtorch. Sweat from the heat dotted her upper lip.

Tobias palmed a flash bomb in one hand. "I hope these guys know sign language. Never seen one of these suckers go off indoors." He pressed the commlink at his ear. "Shock and block time."

The building roared with the sound of doors opening. Canisters of tear gas rolled in all directions. The mobsters collected into a circle to escape the onslaught. Gas poured from the canisters, fogging the entire room. Tobias chucked the flash bomb through the hole in the skylight. Marisol squeezed her eyes shut. *Bam!* Glass shattered, metal rattled, and she could hear the groans of the injured below. She drew the heat-sensing goggles to her eyes. Some orange blobs weren't moving, the mobile ones tried for the doors jammed by the Shadows. When the exits weren't budging, most of the throng scrambled to the loading bay, clamoring to open the garage door with its rusted machinery. A few stragglers made their way to the storage, toward Vincent.

She squeezed her fist. No one came near Vincent but her. Marisol pushed the commlink button at her wrist. "Tiny, do your thing."

An explosion blasted the grate of the sewer to the ceiling. Fire, licking from the depths below, chased the mobsters to the entrance far from Vincent.

She handed the goggles back to Tobias. He secured them over his eyes and drew a long dart gun from the sling on his back. He steadied it. "I see the Bloodsucker trying to open the front bay. He's the only jabroni not staggering." He fired a tranquilizer. *Ptoo!* "Got him." He loaded the gun with another dart from his belt and adjusted the rifle, and *Ptoo!*

The garage door rumbled open. The fog of the tear gas dissipated. Except the coughing, wheezing minions hadn't expected a wall of Shadows in gas masks ready to beat, bruise, and zip tie them into submission.

Tobias shot another dart. He hissed a yes and slung the gun to his back.

"He's spotted me." He tossed Marisol the goggles.

She pulled on a small ventilating mask over her mouth and put the goggles back on.

Tobias barreled the door to the rooftop open with his shoulder. He drew the cattle prod from his back and moved with cat-like efficiency across the narrow scaffolding of the observation deck. Marisol tiptoed behind, her focus only on the figure hanging in the storage room.

Goons filtered up from the floor, escaping the melee down below. Tobias clubbed one with the cattle prod and then zapped him in the torso for good measure as he writhed on the floor. Tobias zip-tied him to the scaffolding, but another swept in on the attack, appearing like an orange yeti in Marisol's view.

"Go get your man, kid!" Tobias shouted.

Marisol breathed in through her nose. A sudden rush vibrated within her body and mind as if her choices and Fate aligned. Everything about her made sense—from her love of the city to her desire to save people; from her boxing to free-running; from Annie to Tobias to Vincent. She had spent her whole life surviving. "Bring it." An orange yeti with outstretched arms entered her goggled vision.

With the intoxicating effects of destiny bolstering her, Marisol floored the henchman with a left hook, wrangling his gun from his hands and meeting his falling face with a jab. She pitched the gun over the catwalk. Another orange yeti charged her. She bobbed and weaved his swinging hands and hinge-kicked him in the gut. While he bent over, she elbowed the back of his head. With the walkway cleared, Marisol swung her legs over the railing, slid down the scaffolding, and landed on the kill-floor.

Propelled from a lunge, she bolted to the back toward the storage. All thoughts fixated on one, her one—her Vincent. She reached the orange figure raised above her and pulled the goggles from her eyes.

The sight dropped her to her knees.

Vincent hung from a meat hook plunged into his back. Coagulated blood gathered around the giant wound. Stacks of bent rebar, like sinister bangles, pinned his arms behind him. His blood dripped into a puddle.

The plan. What was the plan? "Vincent!" she shrieked, though it failed to rattle him as he weakly nodded.

Marisol ran to the rusted controls, jamming the button that lowered him to his feet. First, she pulled the hook from his body. Vincent dropped to the floor. Her hands steadied. The bleeding man was not Vincent then. He was her patient. And Marisol had a job to do.

She used her small blowtorch to melt away his rebar cuffs. The flame burnt the vinyl layer of her gloves. Blood and sweat trickled toward the heat, landing in sick whispers. The torch singed her fingertips. She had to keep going. Fingers on the verge of blistering, she only managed to cut a sliver through those rebar cuffs. Freeing him would take all night.

The blood. Vincent's wound wasn't magically going away. She took her hoodie off and tied the sleeves under his armpits. As she twisted the knot tight, Vincent mumbled something she couldn't quite understand. She bowed, meeting her ear to his chapped lips.

"Run," he whispered.

Never! He needed her! But her gaze followed a path on the ground to a pair of pointed dress shoes and moved up to the masked face of the Bloodsucker. The teeth and teeth! Throbbing pointed rows froze her. An image of Annie's lifeless hand struck like a lightning bolt. Marisol staggered back.

The Bloodsucker lurched toward her. Marisol sprinted away, the Bloodsucker nipping at her heels. Her nerves frayed to the last thread, making everything grow fuzzy as if she watched herself from the outside. She crawled up a rusted conveyor belt and jumped onto a swinging chain. Rusted metal chafed her fingers raw. But the pain kept her in the here and now. While the Bloodsucker clawed for her, she reached and climbed onto a different chain. Panic did no good. Follow the plan. Break it down. Task one: Aim. She reached into her utility belt and drew a gun.

"You can't kill me." His voice slurred, drool pouring from the corners of his wide mouth.

"But I can put you to sleep." Task two: Fire. *Clink*. A tranquilizer dart injected into his body.

He laughed and reached for her, parting the series of chains, but Tobias zapped the Bloodsucker with the prod and threw him to the ground. "I'm out of tranqs, kid. You get your man and go! Don't worry about me!"

Though the Bloodsucker had taken a huge number of tranquilizers, he was still faster and stronger. A flying punch from him cracked Tobias's cattle prod in half.

Tobias slung the pieces of the cattle prod into the holster on his back and raised his fists. With the Bloodsucker occupied, Marisol jumped down to Vincent, laying on the ground. She pulled him by the sleeves, gaining six inches with every burst of leg muscle. Just like her training taught her—kneel, pull, kneel, pull. A foot. More. She needed to gain more distance.

She looked at Tobias. The Bloodsucker punched him over and over again. Each time, he staggered and raised his fists for more. Kneel, pull, kneel, pull. Her lungs burned. A punch cracked into Tobias's flank. He stumbled, appearing to fight the urge to cradle it. Another few drags, and Marisol and Vincent reached the chute. She elbowed a button, and the door to the chute opened, revealing the SUV waiting at bottom with its trunk open. All she had to do was slide down it to get him to safety.

"The virus," said Vincent. "Get the virus."

What was Vincent talking about? In the corner of her eye, Tobias's arms weakened to jelly. He was on the ropes. He needed to keep his fists up.

Back at the lab, she couldn't save Annie. Could she stomach losing one more friend? "Stay here." She leaned Vincent against the base of the chute and kissed his temple. "Time for a new plan." Marisol tapped the commlink at her wrist. The SUV's trunk closed, and it sped away. She pressed another button on the controls. The old conveyor belt shook, squealed, and moved. She rode it, nearing Tobias and the Bloodsucker.

From the conveyor belt, she pounced onto the Bloodsucker's back and jammed a syringe of tranquilizer into his neck. He flipped her over his shoulders. As she tumbled, she pulled the stupid plastic and cloth mask with her.

On the ground with the wind knocked out of her, she strained for air but saw him—Skeleton Man! Or Stone Ruthven, the man who cornered Annie at the ball. She recognized his pale pock-marked skin, thin lips, and patchy black hair slicked back into gelled chunks. This was the Bloodsucker, the scourge of Shadowhaven? He was just a man, a pathetic man! The fear so easily paralyzed her before now flowed out of her, washing away into the drains where all Shadowhaven's shit seemed to gather.

Bring it! She could do this. She could save everyone.

Ruthven punched Tobias in the chest. "Why can't I kill you?" he asked. Tobias, wobbling, spat a mouthful of blood into Ruthven's face and laughed.

Marisol reached for her utility belt to prepare another dose. Standing up, she aimed, but Ruthven spun around and knocked the drug from her grasp. She countered with a hook, leaving her wide open. Ruthven snatched her by the throat. "I should snap your neck! What have you done to me?"

His grip was weak, but still able to squeeze against her throat. Her heartbeat drummed ever louder in her ears. Tobias attempted to reach for the tranquilizers rolling on the floor, and Ruthven kicked him in his ribs while Marisol dangled.

Black spots dotted the corners of Marisol's eyes. She saw Annie smiling, appearing like record scratches in her sight. Ruthven. Scratch. Annie. Scratch. Ruthven. Scratch. Annie. She could see the dead? Was she dying? This couldn't be how it ended. She had victory in her grasp, but it sifted through her hands.

"Annie," she whispered.

"What?" Ruthven asked, but he stumbled, drool pouring out of the corner of his mouth. He slumped, dropping Marisol.

The SUV backed into the kill floor from the storage room, wheeling around injured mobsters and Shadows, and smashed into Ruthven, sprawling him on the floor, out cold.

A syringe protruded from his ankle. Who got Ruthven with a final shot?

Something heavy slapped against the ground. Vincent drug himself to Marisol's feet. His wrists were raw from bending back the rebar, and blood soaked the sweatshirt tied around his back. An empty vial rolled from his hand.

Vincent was her hero, magnificent yet fragile. Panic set in. Did she lose him? She knelt next to Vincent. Her shaking hands wrapped his wound tighter with her utility belt. She dragged him to the SUV, but she could barely lift his limp weight. She held her hand below her throat. God, please don't leave him like this. Again, she pulled him to the trunk. The tendons in her neck bulged from the strain as she tried. She collapsed. "I need help!" came out in an exhausted wail.

Izzy whistled. The Shadows raced to Marisol. Faces behind masks, they turned to her for guidance, Izzy, Mijo Ray, enforcers all. They counted to three and lifted Vincent over their heads, holding him under each of his limbs. They laid him in the back of the SUV. Marisol crouched by his side, trying to make sense of how to fix him.

Izzy lifted his mask and shouted, "The Teeth Man's moving. We got to go!" The Shadows scrambled out of the entrance.

Ruthven stirred, even with the inordinate amount of tranquilizer in his system. Tobias gripped Ruthven by the back of his shirt and dragged him into the old freezer locker room. He threw Ruthven into the room, shut the latched door behind him, and jammed it with the empty tranquilizing rifle. He staggered back to the SUV and stumbled into the passenger seat.

The hatch of the SUV slammed shut.

"Hit it!" Tobias wheezed out.

"Destination determined," Staci answered.

The driverless SUV sped out of the slaughterhouse, leaving a trail of dust among the blood in the abandoned industrial park.

Marisol and Tobias removed their masks. Marisol's cheeks cooled when air met her tears. She held Vincent, his back leaning against her chest. As she bent her head forward, she breathed in his scent of smoke and blood. "C'mon Vincent. You gotta pull through."

"We should get him to a hospital." Tobias grunted as he held the swollen side of his face.

"Destination determined," Staci repeated, and they slowed down, entering traffic.

Against Vincent's ear she whispered, "You gotta because I love you."

Vincent's eyes rolled into the back of his head, and a hissing sound escaped his lips as he passed out.

26

Count Your Blessings

The car weaved behind multiple secured entrances in the parking garage under the Varian Family Hospital. The SUV charged at a cement wall. Marisol searched for her seatbelt. Without it, she hugged Vincent and braced for impact. If he wasn't half passed out from his own wounds, Tobias should grab the wheel. Open your eyes, Tobias! Open—in a microsecond, the wall ascended magically, revealing a hidden world within.

Weak, incandescent lights illuminated a storage room. Rather, an abandoned storage room strewn with old hospital furniture, laundry carts of faded scrubs and hospital gowns, and other odds and ends yet to be explored. Why did Staci bring them to this forgotten place?

Tobias helped Marisol drag a gurney out from the pile, though he winced and limped as he did. After they opened the hatch of the SUV, they counted to three and lifted Vincent onto the gurney. He flopped like a rag doll.

"How are his vitals?" Tobias asked.

Marisol pressed against the ulnar artery at Vincent's wrist. His pulse, a beautiful, steady rhythm, lulled like lapping water, and his chest expanded gently as he breathed. "They're good."

Tobias opened drawers in search of supplies. He remarked that one drawer had a bloody handprint as he opened it and asked, "Do we need forceps the size of a watermelon?"

"No," Marisol replied, joining him to search for supplies. The first one she opened had expired latex gloves and a thread and needle. Tobias found tape, gauze, and silver nitrate. She collected it in a plastic tub and set it near Vincent's feet.

Tobias opened the latched handle of a buzzing refrigerator. From it, he fished out an old polka-dotted ice bag and held it against his swollen eye. Marisol tested a few pairs of gloves before she finally found a pair that didn't disintegrate.

They needed water, but calcium and lime coated the basement's only sink and choked access to the faucet. The only knob Marisol managed to turn was for cold water. She first sipped the water and then washed her hands with a dried-out block of soap that barely lathered.

Tobias flipped Vincent onto his stomach. From there, Marisol removed his souped-up wetsuit of a uniform, noticing small scars over his torso from bullet wounds and slashes. What had Ruthven done to him? Gloves on, Marisol dried one gash with gauze. As she applied the silver nitrate, she winced as it cauterized the wound. But Vincent breathed and slept. Count on him for making perpetual pain beautiful. She repeated drying and cauterizing until the bleeding stopped.

She stitched him together. When the needle poked through his skin, she pictured him flinching. The pads of her sore fingers stroked affirmations. I will heal you, my love. I will make you stronger, they said. She stitched and caressed, sewed and gentled him until the sewn-up gashes looked like a large fist holding three drooping flowers. She wrapped the strange shape in gauze, binding it over his shoulder with tape. When she finished, Vincent resembled the city's sorriest patient, tied in a hospital gown and a threadbare sheet tucked around him.

On the other side of the storage room, Tobias paced the perimeter and discovered an alcove with a shower head. He turned it on. The pipes puffed and shook before releasing a steady stream. "We got warm water."

Marisol broke away from Vincent's side, ripping up another hospital gown. After gathering the hot water in the plastic tub, she returned to Vincent and wiped his head with her makeshift rag.

While she worked, Tobias lugged a plastic-coated couch from the pile of furniture, hooking one arm under it as the other cradled his ribs. He plopped it across from Vincent's hospital bed, wiped the seat, and collapsed into it, spreading his knees apart and stretching his legs. Settled, he ripped off his bullet-proof vest and loosened the zipper of his neoprene shirt.

Marisol ran the wet cloth over Vincent's hair and dabbed away the blood in it. "We should get him upstairs for better care, though I'm not sure how we would explain him."

Tobias rubbed at his chin. "If his powers work like they should, he just needs some extra time to repair. Who knows how long he hung there?" Scratching the back of his head, he muttered, "Or how long he tortured him?"

She gripped her chest in personal torment. How much longer would it have been if she hadn't trusted her instincts? If Tobias hadn't helped her? She'd clean the blood and grime from his face, neck, and arms until it washed away her guilt for doubting him or herself.

Tobias said, "You need a break, and not a chemically induced one."

She bit her tongue and said, "Hm," which stopped her from saying I'm fine, a lie so oft repeated, it came like a reflex.

"You could use a shower and a change of clothes. Trust me, you're ripe."

Seconds ticked by as she weighed wiping another smudge from his skin against smelling presentable. Draping the pink-stained rag on the bed's railing, she pulled herself from Vincent's side but hesitated after each step. Creating too much space between them, she feared, would somehow lose him again.

But her steps quickened until she made it around the shower alcove, where she found a travel-sized bar of soap among a stack of dust-laden supplies. From her hair to her toes, she scrubbed with the tiny bar of soap. A sudsy touch confirmed her neck was tender from Ruthven's chokehold. Her own ice pack would be great. Though judging from Tobias's bruises, he needed the world's supply of them. She dried off with a bedsheet and changed into faded scrubs. Every pair was too big for her, so the pants pooled at her feet and the shirt slung off her shoulder.

When she rounded the corner of the shower, untangling her wet hair with her fingers, she watched Tobias sit next to Vincent in the hospital bed. He bowed his head, holding Vincent's hand between his palms. Tobias touched his fingers to his head, chest, his left shoulder, and then his right before gently setting Vincent's hand back on the bed. Praying. He opened his eyes and lifted his head. The moment he saw Marisol, he scrambled back to his spot on the couch.

She padded across the basement and joined him, sitting a cushion away. "I needed that." She tugged at the shoulders of her shirt. "Only wish I could wear my clothes. For once."

Tobias opened his mouth, making nothing but a glottal sound. Was he embarrassed because he had been praying? Tension ratcheted with each drip of the faucet, marking the silence like a metronome. The pause between the droplets begged for conversation.

He leaned forward, resting his elbows against his knees. His focus honed on Vincent. "Why'd you change the plan?"

The plan to spring Vincent? She tilted her head. It seemed obvious to her—to save Tobias too.

With his voice low and serious, he continued, "You could've died taking him on. If you followed the plan—"

If she had just left with Vincent, the Bloodsucker would've obliterated Tobias. He had to have known that... Oh God, had he expected to die? She swiveled to face him. "Ever occur to you that you're a part of the plan?"

He moved his gaze to the fizzling light above them, focusing on anything, it seemed, to avoid looking at her. With a grunt, he arched his back into the couch. Still, he didn't look at her. Àpropos of nothing, he said, "I went to an AA meeting once. Hung out at the back because everyone sounded like freaks. You should've heard what they did for a drink. Sure, I went through a divorce, but it wasn't because I was—"

"An alcoholic?"

"Right." He clenched and unclenched his jaw a few times. "But this guy leaves the front of the meeting and sits near the back with me. He asks if I recognized him. When I worked a beat, I saw a lot of faces, and I racked my brain to remember him until it clicked. He was a drunk I had picked up off a curb, and instead of bringing him down, I drove him home to his row house on the Westside. So, I'm drinking watery coffee with this guy, and he tells me he keeps a picture of one of his daughters in a spot to always remind him why he quit. A picture of his eldest daughter, the fighter, who was so smart, fierce, and generous that he couldn't quite figure out how he had any hand in making her. 'She has enough heart to carry this whole city out of Hell on her back,' he said."

The foolish hyperbole sounded like her dad.

"I figured I could do the same—put a picture up and make a promise to myself, to her."

It dawned on her—the picture in his kitchen with the curly brown hair and freckles? "That picture's your daughter! Why didn't you tell me? I'm so sorry. I cracked a joke like a total jerk."

"You can be a total jerk, kid, but I like that about you. It reminds me you aren't perfect."

She turned the corner of her mouth in a crooked smile.

"We had her young, the ex and I, and married because that's what we thought you're supposed to do, but all I left room for were the three w's: work, whiskey, and women. For that, I lost my wife, but I never wanted to lose her. When she was old enough to call the shots, she didn't want to see me anymore, and after a few cases wrecked my visitation weekends, I agreed. She already called her stepdad, 'Dad,' for Chrissakes." He dropped the ice bag, and the thud reverberated through the room. "I couldn't be like that guy at the meeting. He didn't give up. I gave up. Last year, I left her graduation with a married woman only to wind up alone under an overpass, drinking a cheap pint of rye. And I keep thinking that someday I'll quit, someday I'll be good enough to face her, to apologize, to be more than a sperm donor, but when is that someday gonna be, my deathbed?"

Marisol shrugged. Did he want her to feel sorry for him and provide comfort? She wasn't sure if she could. Instead, wariness knotted into her. She hadn't forgiven Dad for his failures and held on to them like her childhood home's plaster scars. And of course, it may be well after his deathbed before she would ever forgive Caz.

He sniffed and brushed his good eye with a knuckle. "But you believe in me when you got no reason to, and I get these crazy ideas like I could call her up, apologize and mean it, and maybe she'll even let me sit in a decent row at her wedding. And it's because of you. How's that for twenty years of pent-up confessions?"

Marisol faked a laugh because there was Tobias, reaching ridiculous conclusions about her again. "That'll be three Hail Mary's. One to mess up, the other for practice, and the final one to forgive yourself because you can be better." The knots inside her loosened.

He lifted his head and caught her gaze with one shining eye. "You're what men write poetry about."

Her lips mouthed, "Oh," and she looked at her hands, hoping some token of appreciation would appear in her palms. But she had nothing. If only regenerative powers radiated from her hands. Not simply to ease the swelling of his bruises with a gentle graze of her fingers, but to hold her hand against his heart, make sure he never experienced an ounce of pain the rest of his life because those were the things he deserved.

But she had nothing, so she studied Vincent and watched his bandaged back rise and fall as he slept. That is, she had nothing but the truth. "I thought you were him," she blurted, as if brevity alone could stop the impact. "When I kissed you, I thought I was kissing the Patron Saint. And the night of the attack? I didn't stand you up because of it. I thought I had met up with you as the Patron Saint, but it was him."

Tobias sighed and stared at the ground. His unobstructed pupil shifted rapidly from side to side, as if he calculated the weight of what she had told him. In borrowed clothes, Tobias easily became Vincent. Both faced an unending battle for Justice, and both needed to stand on the side of good. It'd be simple to say that the good pieces about Tobias made him like Vincent, but something in her said that when Vincent dressed up to fight for Justice, that a part of him became Tobias too.

He scraped his fingernails against his thick stubble. "That's stupid. We look nothing alike."

"Stupid is right." She'd accept stupid. That was enough for her. But for him? "My mom thinks you're cute."

"Me and Novotny women go together like peanut butter and jelly."

"Cinnamon and sugar."

"Coffee and doughnuts."

In the middle of laughing, the horrifying conclusion tensed in every one of her muscles. "But stay away from my sister." It was one thing for Mom to mine ounces of glee watching Tobias replace a lightbulb; it was quite another imagining Nicole vaulting over a problematic age gap with a flirty quip.

He placed his sweaty hand on the top of her foot. The warmth echoed. "It's enough." She listened to his breathing. It synced with Vincent's.

The clamor of the rickety gurney caught her attention as Vincent shifted on to his back and groaned. Marisol sprung to his side.

His eyelids fluttered open, and his irises fluctuated. Finally, he grinned. The pointed corners of his mouth grew wicked and assured. "You love me."

"I do." Marisol smiled and blinked a few tears away. They trickled down her cheeks to her chin. Vincent brushed the underside of her jawline, catching the tears in his hand. When she lifted her chin as he touched it, he moved his fingers to her neck.

"Bruises." He traced the line of her tendon. "I'm sorry."

"Wasn't your fault," she hoarsely said and stared at his feet. If she looked at him, the look he was giving her—the love in his eyes would prod her open, and she wouldn't stop crying.

"I should've known how powerful he could be from your warning. You shouldn't have had to—" Vincent's mouth gaped and then relaxed as the battered Tobias limped to his other side. "Quinlan." Vincent extended his hand.

Tobias shook it. "Vinnie."

They held their handshake. The hair on Tobias's arm stood straight from Vincent's touch. Their eyes darkened and shimmered with a palpable intensity, switching the handshake from a sign of gratitude to a pair of opponents sizing each other up before a fight. Marisol flexed her hand, ready to karate chop them apart. Then Tobias blinked, and they dropped it. Instead of looking ready to rip each other's throats, they smirked.

They had worked together years before she entered the picture. How many news stories hid their collaboration between the lines? She and Vincent had become so intertwined in such a short amount of time that someone knowing him longer, however superficially, aroused a tinge of jealousy. She lifted his hand to her face and kissed the inside of his wrist—their own secret handshake.

"I'll let you two have a moment. I'm showering. No peeking." Tobias raised his eyebrows at Marisol.

She snorted in protest. "Especially you," he said to Vincent.

Vincent lifted an eyebrow and smiled. His lips curled like those of a cat that just cornered a mouse. But in actuality, it was the smile of playboy Vincent Varian, who got whatever he wanted. His amused yet predatory eyes locked onto Tobias until he disappeared around the alcove.

If they were this friendly, now might be a good time for Vincent to know about her mistake. "There was a time where I thought he was you."

"I know."

"You knew?"

Vincent blinked and nodded, emphasizing his long eyelashes. Then his gentle demeanor stretched into a smirk. "For curiosity's sake, when in the timeline did you realize that he wasn't..."

Easy. "At the hideaway."

His smug expression pickled with concern. "We kissed before then."

The confident nod of her head stopped as she winced. That she couldn't—at one time—know the difference between his remarkable mouth and tongue versus Tobias's—ahem!—skills would kind of put a damper on the romantic moment, so she set her gaze on scorching. "Even in the dark, I would know the curves of your lips, the playful games of your tongue, and the little hum you make when I give it to you good."

He flicked his eyebrows up, impressed, and curved a finger into a come-hither motion. She lowered her head to meet his lips. He parted her lips with his tongue, and she met the tempting circling of his tongue with her own.

She knew more than the details of his kiss because he made her feel understood. Within her, a creator wrote a secret code only he could unlock and vice versa. Words like *complete* or *the one* were too reductive, overlooking that life endowed both with independent and whole livelihoods. By intertwining their strengths like rope, they had become indestructible and absolute. And the only word for it was *understood*.

Limb by limb, she joined him on the gurney until her body was flush to his. "Do you also know how much you need me?"

"Hm."

"I want nothing but joy and happiness for you," she whispered, lifting his chin with her hand. "I will be your spirit and share your burdens. I will be your hope when you have seen nothing but darkness. I will turn your wrath to righteous fury. I will help us achieve the Justice that will free you." She ran her thumb over his lips in the shape of a cross, her blessing.

Their knees touched; they lay in perfect parallel, leaving room only for their breath. Marisol motioned with her index finger for a kiss. He obliged all too well, skillfully crushing his mouth against hers. A subtle rocking of his hips demanded more.

She pushed him away. Good judgment said to leave well enough alone. He was injured. Tobias would finish his shower any minute now. But Vincent rubbed under her shirt, from her waist to her hip, grazing under the edge of her drawstring waistband.

Many times before, when life's struggles seemed insurmountable, she'd lose herself, believing her desires were the last to matter. Though the Bloodsucker bruised, battered, and scarred their bodies, he had no claim on them, no place here. Their bodies were theirs alone. Only love belonged here. And she needed to believe it down to her marrow. She touched her nose to Vincent's and nodded.

Vincent kissed a trail from her cheekbone, neck, shoulder, flank. He descended, lower and lower. At her hip, he tugged her pants down with each kiss, slowly as not to make a sound. She lifted her hips enough to lower the waistband under her ass. He kissed the underside of her cheek. Her skin so sensitive, Marisol held her breath to stifle a moan.

Vincent pulled the blanket over her exposed backside. Good, he prevented an unfortunate view if Tobias happened to walk in. She scooted onto her back. He braced himself above her with one arm, the other disappeared under the blanket. His fingers journeyed down the crease of her thigh and honed on the wet heat pooling below. He stroked, glancing over her clit. She hummed and writhed.

"*Sh!*" But a grin accompanied his reproach. This was the game: be quiet and still when she yearned for anything but.

And she was ready to play. As she kissed him, leisurely running her tongue over his, she gathered the hem of his hospital gown and drew it over his waist. His erection poked into her hip. She licked her palm and ran it from his base to the head of his shaft. Her thumb smeared the liquid pearled there. He leaned his forehead against hers and groaned. Loudly.

"You *shh!*" she whispered.

He let out a breathy laugh as he nudged his way into her, centimeter by centimeter. The slow sensation pulled her into a tight ache. She wanted to be filled completely, but he kept the drive of his hips shallow and slow, dragging the flared tip of his cock across the front of her inner walls.

A mist of sweat. A flash of heat. She needed to squeeze her eyes shut to control the devastating torrent. But she watched for Tobias in her periphery. If he found her like this, his heart would break. Wouldn't it?

The muscles inside her fluttered, her orgasm more-than looming. It was going to detonate. From sweet, shallow thrusts. From the ruse of holding back. From being whole and alive... because they saved each other... because she loved him utterly. She loved him, removed from his lake sanctuary and ominous estate. She loved him without the mask, cape, and gadgets. She loved him.

Vincent cradled her head and drove in all the way. Marisol suppressed a cry, biting into the unbandaged flesh above his heart. "Your turn," she breathed into his neck.

"Ay," he rasped. But the shower shut off. Vincent stopped, remaining inside her. The lack of friction tortured her back from reaching the edge again. The once exploded bomb inside defused—for now. Tobias had to take at least some time to dry and dress.

Vincent thrust deeply with deliberate strokes and muted his moans by kissing her temple and ear. Under her grip, his shoulder muscles tensed tighter and tighter. The gurney creaked louder and louder. A final thrust like a jump. Silence like a fall. And then? Landing. Vincent collapsed, pressing his entire weight into her. A throaty sigh, hot against her neck, was the only sound he made as he came. Through the halo of golden curls, she saw a shadow moving in the alcove.

Vincent withdrew. Before she could whimper from feeling empty, he lowered his hand between them. "One more for me." He stroked her in circles, mixing with their sweat, her arousal, his seed into the slickest lubricant. So sensitive, another movement would push her over the precipice.

"I can't," she whispered.

"Can't what?" Vincent pinched her clit between his fingers. Everything in her body drew tight, and she snapped, holding the orgasmic wail in the strained tendons of her neck.

She caressed the back of her calf with his foot. Her lips vibrated with the m of more.

"Will someone please punch me in the other eye?" Tobias asked. He stood at the entrance of the alcove in too-small scrubs, drying his hair with a rag.

Marisol jackknifed up and adjusted her pants under the cover of the blanket. She combed through her hair with her fingers to pretend nothing happened, hiding the shudders as she came down. Embarrassment bloomed next to the not-yet faded fervor smacked across her cheeks.

Vincent found the rag-stained pink with his blood hanging off the rail of the gurney. He began wiping his hands with it, matter-of-factly, like they were smudged spectacles. "Don't feel like you have to knock, Quinlan."

Tobias flopped back onto the sofa. "Would now be a good time to talk about some ground rules when we're sharing close quarters?"

"Any suggestions? I've got nothing." Vincent's eyes glowed unabashedly.

"How about keeping the hanky-panky to a minimum?"

"That was me at my minimum." Vincent licked at his plump bottom lip and rubbed it over his top one.

Marisol raised her hand. "I have a suggestion. How about minding your own business?"

Tobias's good eye sparkled. "Touché."

Damn. Not only did his heart withstand breaking, but that spark also said he enjoyed it. She aimed to dart to the safety of the shower alcove, except the rush of blood from her pelvis back to her limbs almost took her back down, and she wobbled toward the lair's shower and only hiding spot. Of course she cleaned up, put on another pair of pants, but here, she could smile, sigh, laugh as traces of Vincent pinged from nerve to nerve.

When she emerged, Tobias stretched his legs across the cushions and shook out a dusty blanket.

"You're staying the night?" she asked.

The plastic crinkled under his weight as he moved on the couch. "Appears so. I want at least someone around in case I don't wake up, you know, if I happen to be severely concussed."

"That's actually a common misconception. You can sleep with a concussion," she said as she nestled against Vincent in the rickety bed.

"I know, but it'd be wrong to leave."

"It's safer here," Vincent said. "Staci, the lights!"

The room went dark. Marisol closed her eyes and hugged Vincent to her. With Vincent in her arms, she felt blessed.

Ínterlude

wHO kNEW THE mASKED fREAK oUTSOURCED? i gUESS tHERE aRE pEOPLE oUT tHERE wHO cARE aBOUT vINCENT vARIAN. tSK tSK tSK.

bUT mAKE nO mISTAKE, IT iSN'T oVER. i'M eVOLVING. i'LL lEARN. i'LL aDAPT. IN THE eND, IT wILL aLL lEAD TO yOUR dESTRUCTION. I cAN'T dESTROY yOUR bODY, BUT i cAN dESTROY yOUR sOUL. iF IT iSN'T pESTILENCE tAKing oUT tHIS cITY AND yOUR lITTLE wONDER bOYS wITH iT, IT wILL bE wATCHING yOUR aGONY wHEN THE cITY rEALIZES tHEIR sALVATION iS tHROUGH mE. yOU wON'T bE sO sPECIAL tHEN, vARIAN. iS tHAT wHY yOU hID tHAT dOCTOR IN THE dREGS OF yOUR rESEARCH? TO pROTECT yOUR sECRET? bECAUSE THE pOWER rUNNING IN yOUR vEINS cOULD bELONG TO aNYONE? iMAGINE iT, A wHOLE cITY aBOVE dEATH AND dISEASE.

iT'S fITTING tHAT A mAN lIKE mE hAS tHIS rESPONSIBILITY hOISTED uPON mE. i mADE A cAREER OF tAKING mONEY pITS AND bUILDING pROFITS FROM tHEM. tHIS iS THE nEXT lEVEL—LIKE aSCENDING TO THE gODS OF oLYMPUS-lEVEL. i cAN bUILD A wHOLE cITY OF pEOPLE lIKE uS.

sTOP mE, AND yOU'LL bE THE mAN wHO lET pEOPLE dIE IN THE sTREETS. wHAT wILL bE yOUR lEGACY, vARIAN?

27

DEATHMATCH EVE

She liked this. Not the squeezing onto a shared gurney or the catching some *z's* on the lam, but she liked, for once, waking with Vincent in her arms.

She inched even closer to him, inhaling his scent of blood and smoke. Something metallic poked into her. Probably a broken part of the gurney, but when she wiggled away, she uncovered a mound of misshapen metal discs; the fired bullets Vincent's body had pushed out in the night. She sat up. Splotches of dried blood on the sheet traveled from the edge of Vincent's hospital gown. She put her hand against his side.

He turned over and lay on his back, shrugging. "I'm fine now."

She searched his face for a sign of a half-truth. Nothing. "Fine or not, I'll rip him limb to limb." It frightened her how much it wasn't an empty promise. She wanted to pull and chop Ruthven apart. And bring popcorn along.

Vincent laughed haughtily, like he didn't believe her. "I'll admit, I was a little out of it when I hung from a hook. Where is Ruthven?"

"Shut him up in an old meat locker with a sizable amount of tranquilizer and heroin in his system," Tobias answered, sitting up on the couch.

"Would that be enough to stop you?" Marisol asked.

Vincent didn't answer. Instead, he leaped off the gurney and ran to the laundry cart. He yanked on some scrub bottoms and tore off the hospital gown with his bandages, revealing his unblemished torso. While he dug for a shirt, the shifting shadows of his movement revealed a series of scars over his upper back.

The scars lured Marisol, and she walked steadily to him until she touched his back. She ran her fingers over the raised skin, amazed by its design. It resembled a fleur-de-lis. "Is it permanent?"

He shrugged. After a few blinks, he threw on a shirt and sprinted to pick his boots off the ground. He released a piercing whistle, and the SUV lit up. From the driver's side, he fidgeted with compartments, acquiring a ball cap and aviator sunglasses. Not the best disguise, but without the fineries of couture or coiffed hair, he looked normal.

"Where are you going?" Marisol followed him with her legs and arms bent in anticipation, as if he was an expensive vase wobbling on an edge.

"I'm going to put him in cryofreeze." Vincent continued to click buttons and open hidden compartments.

Tobias stood, shoulder slumped toward his injured side. "We're clean out of tranqs."

Another push of a button, and something emerged from the center console. "Won't need them." He held up a remote with one hand and dangled bolas in the other. "How do you stop someone with the strength of me? This time, prepared with magnetic force."

Vincent tossed the bolas, and they wrapped around Marisol. They pinched. Definitely leaving a mark. As she struggled to free herself, Vincent pressed the remote and the magnetic force dropped her to the floor.

Oof.

She was a breathless cockroach on her back. Her middle finger would itch if those damn things weren't cutting off her circulation. This warranted a punishment for sure. Kneeling? Wrists bound behind him with sisal rope? Back muscles rippling as she...

He pressed the remote again. The bolas fell off her body. There was that impish grin of his again.

While Marisol dusted her knees off standing up, Tobias asked, "Why didn't we think of that?"

The electric hum of the SUV engine started. Vincent poked his head out of the driver's door. "You two coming?"

At least the swelling of Tobias's eye had subsided. Marisol could almost see the white of his eyeball. Or rather, the broken-blood-vessel red of it. He moved with a crooked spine, slouching toward his injured side. They'd be the help no one asked for. Which gave her an idea.

"We could at least get some real-deal regenerative serum to beef us up," Marisol said.

"Out of the question." Vincent's sonorous voice echoed through the room. He

continued, "Subsequent doses have highly addictive aftereffects. There's the euphoria, then psychosis. It's basically B'Lee." He must've noticed the absence of gray in Tobias's hair, giving away the first dose.

"I took B'Lee?" Tobias shouted.

Bolting for cover in the alcove again seemed like a good idea. "I didn't know it was that," Marisol said as she fidgeted with the overlong drawstring of her pants.

"You didn't know what drug you offered me?" Again with the shouting.

"In fairness, the serum isn't quite B'Lee. Someone inverted the chemical structures. With B'Lee, you get euphoria and psychosis without the regeneration." Vincent cleared his throat. Of course, Vincent would offer a pill of comfort with an unsettling coating.

Marisol straightened. "How did a version of your wonder drug end up on the street?" she asked. "Parallel thinking?"

"More likely? Dr. Park gave an altered version of the formula to Ruthven. But that isn't nearly as concerning as having a superpowered psycho on the loose. I would like to end the situation sooner than later."

Marisol hesitated while Tobias strapped his battered body back into his borrowed bulletproof vest. She wanted to shake Annie the first time Ruthven entered her lab and accessed the research. But Annie kept Marisol out for that very reason. She bit into her bottom lip. Ruthven would pay for trying to change the version of Annie that Marisol had to hold on to. She dashed to her equipment and suited up. With her boots, utility belt, bullet-proof vest, and gloves combined with their faded scrubs, she resembled an escaped patient.

In the SUV, the dashboard came alive under Vincent's touch. As soon as they entered the light early morning traffic, technicolor computer scrawls traced the bottom of the front window. Staci worked a little harder with Vincent in charge.

The car crawled to the crooked chain-link fences of the abandoned industrial park. The morning sun peeked over the horizon. Marisol wiped her clammy hands on the car seat. If Vincent fell to Ruthven the first time, Ruthven wouldn't fall as easily as she did to a pair of bolas. Vincent switched his aviator sunglasses with his heat vision goggles. The SUV stopped right at the barbed wire entrance to the Clark's Slaughterhouse. "No one's there." He tossed his goggles aside and put his sunglasses back on.

Marisol touched the cross at her clavicle to steady her shaking hand.

The wind lifted a broken streamer of yellow police tape over the mouth of the open garage. Tobias rolled his ski mask to his forehead. "Looks like our stunt caught the SPD's attention."

Did Ruthven rip through the police like he had those gangsters? Marisol might need the other car seat to wipe her hands dry.

Vincent pulled an entire computer screen up on the front window, swiping through various blotters and news articles. "Nothing strange reported besides the arrest of a bunch of zip-tied gangsters with open warrants a mile long. He must've ditched them and broke out before the police arrived." He punched the steering wheel.

"We got him once. We can do it again." Marisol put her hand on top of his.

Vincent grimaced. "*Again* is a little complicated. You know the virus the W.H.O. reported missing recently?"

Marisol asked, "The one the news keeps burying on the back page?"

"He has it."

Her heart dropped. "What does he get from that? This place is his city too."

"He's figuring if enough people get sick, he'll force my hand, and Varian Pharmaceuticals will manufacture Dr. Park's cure-all."

"A city dies. The world panics. He profits. And everyone who can afford it will become deathless rage monsters." Tobias pounded his fist into the car ceiling.

Tobias may understand Ruthven's plan, but it made no sense to Marisol. "But Annie's research disappeared, and what was left died with her."

"So a city dies, and Vinnie and the Bloodsucker duke it out over the rubble?"

The massive SUV all of a sudden felt smaller. "People could be getting sick as we speak!" Marisol reached for the door handle. To do what? Run the streets screaming? Either A virus is coming! or Bloodsucker! Come out wherever you are? Anything to feel helpful rather than helpless.

"It's a weaponized contagion. If he released it already, we'd hear about it within the hour. It's ideal for spreading in a densely populated area. Not just a city but a special event."

"How does a career vulture investor like Stone Ruthven go from co-oped drug deals to bioterrorism?" Tobias asked.

"Easy. Someone hired him." Vincent adjusted the rearview mirror. The mirror reflected the emotionless abyss of his sunglasses in contrast to Tobias's face, crooked with bruises and incredulity.

"You're kidding me." Tobias scrubbed his hands over his face and muttered, "Chess boards in chess boards."

Tobias said this before, back at the precinct. They caught Izzy, a king, only to find he was the Bloodsucker's pawn. That didn't mean... Marisol must've misheard him. "What?"

"Someone with even more influence pointed him in my direction," Vincent added. "But I'd surmise that Dr. Park's serum will make it difficult to order him around."

"Know of anyone with a grudge against you?" Tobias punctuated his question with a smirk in the mirror.

Vincent took off his sunglasses, matching smirk with smirk. "Over five hundred years, it can be quite a long list. Though they tend to die after a while." He tapped an arm of his glasses against his lips.

"But that doesn't matter now, right? If he has the virus, he's going to release it. Where? Public transportation? Schools?" She offered anything to change the focus to what really mattered.

"I was drifting out of consciousness on that hook, but he kept bringing up *legacy*."

She snapped her fingers. "The Rooks' Legacy semi-finals is this afternoon. Everyone in Shadowhaven vies for tickets!"

Tobias's smirk faded. "It would be a perfect super-spreader event for something with a—how d'you put it?—weaponized gestation period?"

"We'll patrol the arena for him." Vincent rubbed his chin.

The reality of the date hit Marisol. She kicked the glove box. "Damn, I go into work today! I'll call in."

"No. If he attacks the game, we'll need our best people at the hospitals. Leave the game to Quinlan and me."

"We'll be canaries in the coal mine," Tobias said.

And so they settled it. Her deathless saint and the man who would die for her were all that protected hundreds of thousands of Shadowhaven's people from the Bloodsucker.

28

Parasitic Infection

She was as equally nervous for the bio-terror apocalypse as she was for her first shift since her life went through the rabbit hole, over the rainbow, and launched her into Neverland. Equal because she hadn't really had any other apocalypses to reference, so this bioterror might as well be like the first time she started working at the ER. Could she stick a vein? Would she find her supplies? But unlike her *first* first day, a new question arose. Would she have enough beds ready if the Bloodsucker succeeded? One problem at a time...

With Vincent and Tobias off to work, she prepared for her job alone, just like her pre-boyfriend life—except this time in the underground hideout beneath the hospital. But when she stepped out of the shower alcove, Vincent waited for her. No mask or cape but still wearing his protective body suit. Like this, he seemed like a mermaid or centaur or other half human/half other creature.

"I thought you'd be en guarde at the arena by now," she said, dressing in her scrubs.

"I'll return there in due time, but I wanted to see you in case—"

"In case the world goes to shit?"

His mouth twitched into a crooked smile. Wordless, he handed her a wrapped box, small enough to hold earrings or a ring—God, if it was a ring, she had a right hook with his name on it. On a day like today, he'd pull a stunt like that?

She tore off the paper and flipped open the lid. It'd be better to get moments like this out of the way.

It was silver... and shaped like a large bean.

"An earpiece," she said. Not exactly the jewelry she had expected. But of course, he operated beyond predictability, didn't he?

He pressed the earpiece; his suit glowed. "It's wired to me so wherever I go, you go." Adding a shrug, he said, "And Quinlan. He has a watch."

Even separated, she would always be by his side. Marisol put it in her ear. "Jewelry isn't allowed on the patient floor."

"I'm sure your supervisor can make an exception. After all, I know the guy whose name is on the building."

"I got something for you too."

"Really?"

Not exactly, but she reached back and unclasped Abuelita's necklace from around her neck. She placed it in Vincent's hand. "My abuelita wore it until she was in hospice. Said it didn't belong in the ground with her. Las semillas de la fe crecen por encima del suelo." Faith's seeds grow above ground. "Not sure if it's lucky but—"

"It's powerful."

"It's what you make it."

He kissed the pendant and tucked it into a small compartment on his utility belt. She began combing her hair into a ponytail, but Vincent stopped her, tying the low ponytail himself. With a few brushes of his hands, he kept the earpiece hidden behind her hair. After he tightened her ponytail, he kissed her neck, below her ear, jawline, and then lips—a kiss so strong she'd jump up on him and forget the whole world-saving business.

"She said something else too," she mumbled between kisses.

"Hm?" His prompt challenged her to keep going as much as it invited her to answer.

She tugged the hair at the back of his head, and he jerked away. "Deber antes que devoción."

Duty before devotion. He nodded, rubbing his lips together. Then, as if he conjured them from thin air, he pulled on his mask and cape. He had completely become him: her vengeance and darkness, her savior and lover. The city's Patron Saint, her saint.

The wall opened, and he stepped to the other side.

She tapped the earpiece three times. His suit pulsed three times with blue bursts of light.

He looked back. "I love you too." Boom! The wall closed.

She didn't know Morse code, but Vincent knew their code. That's all she needed.

A throat cleared in her ear, buzzing her earpiece, and a familiar nasal and gruff voice cut through. "My watch is lighting up. What's up?"

"I'm off to work, old man."

"Vinnie and I will keep it nice and boring for you."

"You promise?"

"A wise woman said my promises don't mean shit, but I'll see what I can manage."

Marisol emerged from the hidden basement onto the sidewalk packed with fans decked in the Rooks 'colors: black and royal blue. Perhaps Vincent disappeared so quickly because he looked like an overzealous fan. She headed upstream against the traffic of people. Cars crawled along, filling the air with smog and the smell of diesel. There'd be no easy escape once people packed in the arena. She touched her clavicle at the hollow where her necklace would rest. Vincent and Tobias had to succeed.

She picked up the pace toward the employee entrance. By the time she entered the emergency room, she was running.

"Novotny! You're back!" the janitor said.

Marisol nodded. She wound through the hall; people greeted her with "Novotny!" as she passed.

Clocking in, she asked, "What kind of day are we having today?"

Nurse Rossi answered without looking up from her smart pad, "Superfans who can't handle their liquor already occupy a handful of beds." As she set the pad aside, she completed a double take. "Marisol!" Before Marisol had a chance to speak, Rossi hugged her tightly. "When we heard about the attack, we thought—"

"I'd retreat with my tail between my legs? It's going to take a lot more to get rid of me."

"They must love you if they make today your first back," Rossi said with the sarcasm of every jaded worker in America.

The bosses may be piss-shitting assholes, but they were Marisol's piss-shitting assholes. Showing up when the world could end was her act of love. She placed her hands on her hips and flicked up her chin. Her invisible cape flapped in a gust of central air. "I go where I'm needed."

But apparently, the sleepiest shift of her career needed her as she monitored saline solution bags and bandaged minor contusions. And—yes—she could stick a vein on the first try. Almost an hour in, and all she practiced was the type of first aid she'd been capable of since elementary school. However, Marisol worked enough ER shifts to treat calm with suspicion. Stillness in the Spring always warned that a storm was brewing.

Her earpiece rattled. "I see him!" Tobias said. He panted, probably running. "Freeze!"

Marisol ducked behind a corner to drown out the beeps and whirs of the hospital. She cupped her hand to her other ear.

"He complied. This is too ea—" Tobias gasped. Marisol dug her fingernails into her palms. "It's not him." After a faint ripping noise—duct tape from flesh?—a man shouted in the background. Tobias's breathing became a wheeze. "There's more of them. He's got those weird parasite masks on people everywhere!"

"On it," Vincent said robotically.

"Holy fireworks! He's got explosives strapped to him. All the Bloodsuckers do." He took a deep breath and shouted, "Everybody clear the area!"

The crowd screamed. A series of loud pops followed.

"Tobias!" Marisol clapped her hand to her mouth.

"Novotny," Dr. Foster said with a sigh, "there you are. Come here! Something's happening at the arena."

Marisol moved to the massive room with curtains partitioning patient beds into temporary cubicles. Patients and medical personnel alike huddled to view the small flat screen television bolted to the corner of the ceiling.

Live footage from the arena showed hives of people scattering to the exits. Some barreled over the chairs. Others stumbled onto the court and ran away with the players.

The sportscaster said, "There appears to be some masked terrorists attacking the arena. People heard shots fired at the north end of the arena."

Rossi gripped Marisol's arm. "Why would anyone do this?"

Marisol could answer a lot after this week, but figuring why was a whole other conundrum. Appearing to brush a strand of her hair, she tapped at the earpiece. No sign of Tobias or Vincent.

"The crowd's moving over there," the sportscaster announced.

Marisol watched the corner of the television. The people parted calmly and synchronized. Darting through the pathway? Vincent on his motorcycle, dragging a gaggle of Bloodsuckers behind him.

"It appears some masked hero tied up the group and is helping the crowd move out of the arena," the sportscaster said.

Marisol snuck a smile.

The broadcast showed Vincent tying the Bloodsuckers around a thick, rectangular column by driving his motorcycle in a circle.

"I transmitted a wave that would calm people. The crowd will leave the arena in an orderly fashion, so no one gets hurt. A quick body scan says none of these decoys have the virus," Vincent announced over the earpiece. "Bomb squad's on the way."

"I swear I came in with this bruise!" The camera captured a giant man in a black trench coat tended by an EMT half his size. "Gonna take more than firecrackers to stop me." Marisol leaned into Rossi as a rush of relief weakened her knees.

The television scrambled into broken pixels. The announcement broke into popping vowel sounds. Digital boxes moved across the screen until they finally settled on an image. Circular rows. Of teeth.

"You think it was that easy?" Ruthven asked. Marisol cracked a knuckle at the sound of that voice.

"He's in the press box," Tobias whispered, tickling Marisol's ear drum.

On the TV screen, the Bloodsucker held up a triggering device that must be harnessed to the explosives strapped to his decoys. "I am a god. I'll be your destroyer." Though Vincent had stunned the crowd with a calming hypnotic wave, her earpiece caught their screams and whimpers from a new round of fear.

The Bloodsucker continued on the broadcast, "But I will be your creator too. It was me who ripped those good-for-nothing gangbangers from limb to limb. It was me who made this place safer. And when I'm through, it will be me you'll thank when I take this city into the stratosphere!"

Crash! Glass confetti sprinkled over the parasitic face on the television. Vincent had stormed into the press box, swinging from a cable. He knocked the Bloodsucker to the floor. The whole crowd cheered. Even a patient on the floor squeezed his fist into a Yes!

In the camera frame, Vincent threw the blue electromagnetic bolas. They locked up the Bloodsucker. "I have a place for bottom feeders like you," Vincent said with a growl while pulling the connecting wires off the trigger. From his utility belt, he drew a small remote. After a high-pitched chirp, the transmission on the television cut out. "The trigger's disconnected," he said over the earpiece.

Marisol's body unclenched, leaving her limbs a clammy, wet noodle. Without the television, the crowd on the patient floor dissipated. Patients limped back to their beds; staff helped them.

Dr. Foster barked, "Have more than enough supplies and beds ready. Patients will arrive from the arena!" But Marisol stood in a daze, concentrating on the melee in her ears rather than the ER.

Vincent boomed through her earpiece. "Ruthven isn't here. Another decoy. That voice was a recording."

Tobias said, "I think I see him. He's in an EMT uniform, that rat fuck!" Rough shuffles jostled over the tiny speaker. Out of breath, he added, "Vinnie? Marisol? It's been nice knowing you." He grunted rhythmically to a running pace, but it became erratic like the chaotic thumping of a struggle. Then static, *click*, and nothing.

"Quinlan, come in. Quinlan?" Vincent called. "I can't reach him, but I can track his movements. How is he moving through the crowd so quickly?"

Marisol said, "If he's after Ruthven…"

"Right. I'll follow his signal. He's heading west, away from the arena."

Marisol inched closer to the blank screen in the room's corner. She begged it to turn back on, to give her answers. Police cars, ambulances, all must be flooding the streets. Not to mention the game-day traffic and fans. If Ruthven moved while the whole city was at a standstill, all attention would be on the arena and… not on the actual target.

What if Ruthven only wanted Vincent to think he'd attack the Rooks' Legacy Game? Where would he plant the virus to hurt the city the most?

"I found him. Quinlan, that is. He's pointing to his wrist. The watch. It isn't on him! Then who is heading west?"

"Vincent, if Ruthven's out to destroy you, where would he hurt you? At the greatest thing you ever accomplished. Your legacy. The—"

"Hospital," Vincent said. "I'm on my way."

With the city in a stranglehold, they couldn't get buses here to evacuate the hospital in time. But she had to keep patients away from Ruthven. Perhaps Fate shone when Vincent built this hospital in the heart of the Cold War. Infrastructure was old and needed updating, but not the bomb shelters below.

Marisol ran to the nurse's station and flicked on the intercom. "Attention. Code 5. Follow the signs down the stairs to the shelter. If you need assistance, staff will help you. I repeat, this is a Code 5."

Dr. Foster ripped the cord from the desk. "Of all the things Novotny, this takes the cake."

"I have it on good authority that the hospital is under attack." Marisol gripped the intercom and tugged it back.

"You have it on good authority?" Dr. Foster's nose wrinkled high enough, Marisol could observe the doctor's frontal lobe.

"I may be a pain in your ass, but have I ever been wrong?"

Dr. Foster stopped, slack-jawed. She looked at the stripped end of the cord she ripped out, threw the intercom down, and pulled the fire alarm. Pointing to another nurse, she ordered, "Get to the intercom in oncology and repeat the message." She wiggled her nose. "You're either right or a felon."

Over her earpiece, Vincent said, "I have binoculars set on his location but no luck locating. The tracker is moving in strange zig zags."

Unable to spot moving through the crowd? How had she and Tobias moved around undetected?

By going underground.

"He learned from us. He's using the sewers!" That she said a little too loud before wheeling a wide-eyed patient in an oxygen mask toward the crowd at the elevators. Marisol felt torn in two as her body ran and cleared patients, her mind honed on Ruthven weaving ever closer toward the hospital.

"I programmed a home team advantage. Staci, enact hospital security."

The computerized feminine voice, the same as the motorcycle, echoed through the halls of the hospital. "Security initiated." The hospital rumbled as metal shutters covered the entrances and windows.

"That won't keep him out, but it will slow him down until I get there." The slow start of the helicopter pulsed in the background.

"We're moving patients to the bomb shelters," Marisol said.

"My computer can access the electronic locks. If you get patients behind the fire doors, that will keep him away from them."

Boom! The shutters bent and crunched at the entrance.

Marisol swallowed. "Hurry." She rushed over to stop Nurse Rossi. "Whatever patients we can't get down in the shelter, you get them past the fire doors and far from here." Rossi hugged her and took off with her oxygen patient.

Marisol jogged to an empty room and stuffed a scalpel into her pockets. Now she needed tranquilizers, anything to weaken the monster behind those shutters. Only this time, she didn't have her brother's gang for back up.

A hand touched her elbow. "What should I do?" Dr. Foster asked.

No, this time Marisol had her hospital gang. "Get me a handful of our strongest people and barricade that entrance with a hospital bed. We need to get ready for what's behind that door!" Boom!

Marisol raced to the pharmacy, swiped her keycard, and filled a syringe with ketamine to its limit. She joined Dr. Foster, two orderlies, and a nurse at the hospital bed they dragged to the door. Her rocketing beats per minute qualified her for a tachycardia diagnosis.

Boom! And the skip in her heart, arrhythmia. Ruthven tore away the shutter like a piece of tinfoil. He burst through the last layer of glass.

But he had no place here.

"Ram him!" Marisol and the staff bombarded Ruthven with the bed, knocking him to the ground. They upturned the bed, and all sat on it to pin him to the ground.

He squirmed under the weight of the bed. Marisol jabbed the syringe in his neck and squeezed the plunger. Ruthven grabbed at his neck; Marisol reached into his EMT jacket and felt a small cylinder in his pocket. She ripped the nylon pocket and held up the cylinder. Strange to see something so sinister appear empty, but behind a thick canister, she had the weaponized influenza.

Ruthven's squirming soon became thrashing. He had already metabolized the tranquilizer. "Run!" Marisol shouted to her ragtag crew, and they scattered behind the security of the fire doors. The doors locked with an electric click.

Marisol sprinted into the elevator and smacked the buttons for the door to shut. Too many buttons. She headed only to the third floor.

Ruthven threw the bed. He stalked toward the closing doors. She shut her eyes.

Ping! Ruthven's fist dented the shut door.

She released her breath, having two floors to collect herself. "Vincent? I got the virus."

"I'm almost there," Vincent's voice assured in her ear. "I'll get you to the thirteenth floor. But first, a little help." The elevator stopped and something metallic encased the car.

She scanned the panel for a button to push. "There isn't a number thirteen."

"It's a dummy floor. It has a ladder to take you to the roof. How do you think I get around in secret?"

The elevator arrived on the third floor, opening to a wall of metal that reinforced the car. Fists thundered against it. Her eardrums shattered.

Ruthven found her, and she couldn't avoid him for ten more floors. Marisol hopped up the elevator walls. She popped open the light on the car with her elbow and crawled through it, carefully placing it back.

Clomp. Clomp. Footsteps below. Then silence. Marisol held her breath.

The ceiling light burst up like an explosion. Marisol crawled over the side and squeezed into the crack between the car and the wall. Something clambered after her. Her back to the wall and legs pressing against the car, she lowered herself and gripped the thin brackets at the underside of the car. The stripped skin of her fingers stung as she dangled over the darkness. Her Hell would always be an elevator shaft.

A low grunt echoed after her. Its source disappeared back into the car. The car ascended to the next floor, arriving with a Ding! Stopping suddenly wrenched her biceps. Nine more floors to go. The footsteps faded down the floor above. She exhaled. "I'm hanging off the elevator car. Please tell me you're close."

"He's in the stairwell. I'll give you a boost. Hold on tight."

She squeezed her abs, lifted her legs, and dug her toes into something to relieve the pressure on her hands. The elevator moved up at a clip, gaining speed with each floor. Six bells.

The elevator gradually slowed with a splintering squeal. The car stopped. She shimmied back between the car and the wall. One hand and foot pressed against the car and the other against the wall. Her limbs trembled from exhaustion, but she scaled up the wall and crawled into an open mouth lined in steel.

The hidden thirteenth floor.

"Follow that tunnel to the ladder. I'll meet you on the roof."

Ahead, a faint sheet of light blemished the dark. That must be the ladder to the roof.

Metal crunched and thundered behind her. She jumped with a start.

"He found me," Marisol whispered.

"According to my tracking, he's looking for you on the twelfth floor. Climb to the roof."

Marisol touched the cylinder in her front pocket and ran to the light. She looked up to follow the light source. It ended in a tiny dot above, the way to the roof. By stairs, the distance would be nothing, but straight up in darkness with her jelly-like limbs? Even she felt the sick throb of vertigo.

She grasped the ribbed rung of the ladder. Plunk! Plunk! Her feet reverberated off the bars.

Halfway there, her lungs felt blistered. She pressed her forehead to the cool metal. While breathing through her nose and out of her mouth, she craned her neck to see the ever-approaching circle of light.

Dark tunnel. Meager light. Her brain hit a scratch in the record again. Her memory replayed her leg snapping from the fall. The phantom pain of it hooked into her gut, causing her "bad" leg to give out like it just happened. "I don't think I can do this," she said.

"I see the roof. Stay where you are."

Her sneakers screeched against the walls while she kicked to find her footing. Helicopter blades thundered above her but farther away, as if she was underwater. Her fingers slipped, and the ribbed metal sliced into her palms.

A small and soft hand grabbed her ankle and placed it on a rung. With her footing regained, Marisol hugged herself to the rung and shook her sore hands out. The hand at her ankle? Where did it come from?

"Annie?" Marisol asked into the darkness below.

A shadow entered the circle of light. It had to be Vincent. Marisol touched the vial and scalpel rolling in her pocket and charged farther up the tunnel. The sun hit her eyes. Something lifted her out of the tunnel by her left arm onto the roof. She blinked away the blocks of darkness to find thin lips and gritted teeth.

"You have something of mine," Ruthven said.

"And you took her from me." Marisol reached into her pocket.

"The doctor?"

"Say her name, you son of a bitch!" She plunged the scalpel below his ribs.

He dropped her. Marisol fell to her knees and scrambled behind the mammoth-sized metal tubes of the duct system that snaked across the roof. She patted her pocket for the cylinder.

Nothing.

She peered over the duct to see the cylinder rolling where Ruthven writhed. *Badum! Badum!* Her heart rose to her ears. She dove for it. *Badum! Badum!* Ruthven pulled the scalpel from his side. Badum! Badum! She pinched the cylinder between her fingers. *Badum! Badum!* He dragged her toward him, raising the bloody scalpel...

Smack! Vincent, hanging from a cable off his helicopter, kicked Ruthven. Marisol's muscles unwound with relief at once. Ruthven stumbled to his feet and ripped scaffolding off the ductwork. He swung the club-like piece at Vincent.

As fluid as a shadow, Vincent weaved and darted to avoid the attack. Midhack, Vincent grabbed Ruthven's wrist in the air and cracked it against the galvanized steel of the duct. His bones shattered into a limp squid. As Ruthven's hand tried to pop back into place, Vincent crunched it in his fist. Pride vibrated through her as her dark savior enacted her vengeance.

With his other arm, Ruthven swung wildly and erratically, wobbling his balance. Vincent led him to the roof's ledge. While Ruthven struggled to center his gravity, Vincent whipped the bolas above his head.

Ruthven attempted to strike, missed, and toppled off the ledge. How would he mend together after bursting like a meat balloon?

But her merciful Patron Saint released the bolas and caught the falling Ruthven. In a last-ditch effort, Ruthven flexed to break the cable, but Vincent tapped the remote at his utility belt.

The magnetic force squeezed Ruthven tighter.

The helicopter hovered above them. Vincent clipped the cable to its landing skid. "I'm taking him home."

"Don't forget your bioweapon." Marisol held up the cylinder.

Vincent tucked the cylinder into a compartment on his belt. With the Bloodsucker bound and dangling off a cable, the virus was in safe hands. She earned the gloat about to escape from her lips.

But Vincent wrapped his arms around her waist and drew her in for a kiss. The impact stung with a jolt of electricity.

Marisol's eyes popped open in surprise. But damn, it was that good kind of unexpected. In the corner of her eye, Ruthven strained and climbed up the building, using only his legs. The wind picked up. The surrounding temperature cooled. Ruthven lowered his head and charged at them. She mumbled a warning against those lips. "Vincent, look—"

Zzzz! Lightning pierced through the sky and hit Ruthven square in the chest.

Their mouths separated. Breathless and wide-eyed, they stared at each other and the knocked-out Ruthven.

"Did we do that?" Marisol asked.

"I think so," Vincent answered with a boyish grin. Boyish. As if in his 500-plus years of living as a superhuman, he finally witnessed something unexplained and miraculous.

Vincent grabbed on to the landing skid and reached out his hand. "You can come with me."

Marisol stepped back. "I have a shift to finish."

"And that's why I love you." He climbed into the cockpit. She tapped her earpiece four times. The helicopter headed toward the horizon.

The door to the roof burst open. Marisol gasped before Tobias fell out of it, winded and holding his chest. "I just ran the whole way. I think... I think I'm going to barf."

"Missed the big catch." Marisol held out her arms. "He was this big."

He spat on the ground and settled into a smile. "You did good, kid."

"You did, too, old man." She hugged him around his neck, standing on tiptoes. Before he could break away, she cupped his stubbled face in her hands. He closed his eyes and bowed his head. She pulled him closer and kissed him gently on his bruised eyelid. His eyebrows perked up.

As he straightened back up, grinning, his blackeye had faded into a wine-colored stain. Yeah right, he couldn't heal that quickly. It had to be some trick of the shadows.

She tilted her head to get him to follow her back inside. "We have a lot of patients to move, old man. You can try the elevator, but I'm taking the stairs."

And there wasn't much to wheeling scads of patients back to their rooms or cordoned areas. Some needed an extra hand squeeze, others an extra hug. Even more needed a heated blanket to make it through the night. A few asked about the big guy who followed her around. Tobias, a friend, wasn't fitting enough, so she told them, "Oh him? He's family."

But no one asked questions when Vincent Varian arrived and offered to help. They were too speechless, including her. The man looked straight out of a fashion magazine with his jeans and jacket curated just for this moment and his angelic hair tousled just so. The scent of sandalwood lingered behind him. That and a tinge of electricity.

The last place Marisol found Vincent Varian before she clocked out for the night was the children's floor. He spun a child in a wheelchair under his arm. The child's mouth burst wide with laughter.

And that's why she loved him.

Epilogue

Deliciously attired in his silk pajama bottoms and untied robe, Vincent led Marisol by the hand into the basement of the estate. He stopped her in front of a reinforced mouse cage. The rabid little creature she had last duct taped in a freezer went about its business running on a wheel.

"I have something that you need to do," Vincent said.

"Give the rodent a name?" Marisol asked.

"No." He turned the handle of the vault with the glowing blue window. Clouds rolled out of the open room of frozen conquistadors as liquid nitrogen met the air. Vincent entered the vault. Marisol followed him, brow knit with confusion.

Held by the cable wound tightly around him, Ruthven shivered in an empty glass tank. Vincent hadn't frozen him yet. Vincent guided Marisol's hand to a lever. "When you pull this, it will start the cryostasis process."

"You don't have to do this!" Ruthven interjected between chattering teeth. Actually, Vincent had to. Ruthven would tear up a traditional prison, and it wasn't like he could face execution. His judgment would come in the future under Vincent's watchful eye.

"I hope you had a good look at your eternity." Vincent tipped his head toward the iced-over beef jerky in human form, the others. "Perhaps not an eternity, but it's been 500 years. Could be 500 more." In dark warrior-mode, steely and aloof, Vincent verged on cruel.

Marisol gripped the lever. "Every day, you should think of her." Vengeance didn't direct her hand, her love for Annie did. "I know I will."

Ruthven spat, "Your friend was no saint. She sold me secrets just to keep her lab open. You'll be cleaning up her little B'Lee mess long after I'm gone."

"We always said, 'People over ambition.'" That info stopped Ruthven's shivering. Marisol added, "Whatever she did, she did it to help people."

"You think I'm the only one you should worry about? More will come, and they won't be as nice as I am!"

"They will reveal themselves in due time," Vincent said. He gestured for Marisol to pull the lever.

Ruthven laughed. "Charlie says, 'Hi.'"

"Do it," Vincent ordered with a sneer.

"For Annie," Marisol whispered before cranking the lever.

Ruthven howled, but the sizzling liquid nitrogen muted him in a microsecond. The process mummified his face, freezing it into a scream. Vincent welded the tank shut. There were four full tanks. Four that waited for the day their immortal lives would end.

On the other side of the vault, Vincent turned the handle close. Marisol watched the mouse gobble a pile of alfalfa pellets.

"She might need something rawer and meatier," Vincent said, putting a hand on Marisol's shoulder.

"The mouse is a she?" She nibbled at her lip. That really wasn't the question she wanted to ask. She breathed and just went for it. "Who's Charlie?"

"As far as I know? Nonsense." He crossed his arms. Marisol studied his demeanor, searching for a tick or subtle smile—a clear sign of a truth or lie. But his attention seemed zoned out. She got nothing from her dark warrior.

She focused back on the mouse. "We should call her A.J. Figured we should honor her. It's all we have left of Annie's work. That and whatever she gave to Ruthven."

"She gave only fragments of information. Ruthven happened to turn the shared half-formula into B'Lee. All the world knows that Ruthven dealt designer heroin. And as far as the lab attack is concerned, the media already ditched the gang retaliation story. They say Ruthven had it out for me. With what I gleaned, he only planned to steal some research to sell to the highest bidder, but he hadn't expected to run into you two so late at night."

"Annie is the most brilliant person I know. If this truth gets out, people will see Ruthven's grimy little hands on her accomplishments."

"No one will ever find out."

She leaned her head against his shoulder. "Can we build a better world with a lie?" She expected Vincent to answer with something sage that offered little comfort.

"It doesn't have to be a lie. We can consult her files, her notes." A glint flickered in his irises, like his internal switch flipped from warrior to lover.

Her worry unwound itself from her body. She playfully smacked him in the shoulder. "You took them!"

"I'd prefer to say, 'Stored for safekeeping.'"

"We could make the serum. Give it to A.J. Maybe it could work like the Fountain. Maybe it could rev—"

Vincent winced. "I've learned not to hope too much."

Marisol held his smooth hands in hers. She imagined both becoming wrinkled and liver spotted. And perfect. "But we can hope a little bit."

He kissed the inside of her wrist. "A little bit is okay."

"How can I not hope with you, my saint?"

His eyes lit up. Actually lit up like his suit. "Saint? Isn't that what they call me?"

"It's what I call you."

"And you? My spirit?" He held out her necklace and smoothed his thumb over her cross pendant, offering it back to her.

Marisol cupped her hand over his and closed his fingers around it. Her necklace belonged to him now. "Something like that."

"You'll need something more fitting to wear." Reaching out his hands, the necklace dangling between his fingers, he closed his eyes in obvious mockery. "I can see it now. Something shining. Shimmering. Silver."

Massive eye roll.

"A knight," he added, opening his eyes.

She smiled with her mouth closed, holding in the stinging sensation of tears. Somehow, he always saw the real her—the fighter, the caregiver, the woman.

She curled her finger to direct him to come closer, so her lips met his. His arms hugged around her waist. *Bam!* Her knees buckled, and she swooned. Bent over her, he broke away from the kiss. "I love you," she said.

"I love you, too, sidekick."

He definitely was getting a spanking tonight.

Vincent's private jet rolled to a stop on the tarmac. Even from the small window in the cabin, Marisol watched as paparazzi and reporters jogged in from behind the hangar. They circled around a parked town car, holding cameras and voice recorders in stiff anticipation.

Tobias stepped out of the car. Over the week, his stubble had grown into a lush beard. He wiggled his shoulders in his new charcoal suit jacket. But Marisol took one look at his tieless throat and shook her head. Tobias needed a tie, though he did look remarkably dapper without one.

Though Vincent offered her a new outfit for the occasion, Marisol insisted on wearing the navy sweater and the black trousers she wore during her first day of med school. That was when she met Annie because Park came right after Novotny during the white coat ceremony. Now, all that was missing was her white coat. And Annie, of course.

Outside, a photographer with an open mouth that could catch flies looked especially goofy waiting for the couple to deboard. Nikon Mouthbreather, Marisol named him.

Her mind drifted back to the ceremony when Annie had asked, "What do you think their names are?" Those were the first-ever words she spoke to Marisol. With a flick of her sloppy topknot, Annie pointed out the med students seated behind them, the R to Z last names.

"I don't know," Marisol answered.

Annie pointed at the guy with the polka-dotted bow tie. "Bowtie McTrustfund."

Marisol chuckled softly. "The Ms are ahead of us." The J-last names were in the midst of receiving white coats and applause.

"Mac's his middle name then. What do you think her name is?" Annie nodded toward the woman with short, choppy hair.

"Pixie O'Cutiecutt," Marisol said.

Annie snorted loud enough to earn a pointed "Sh!" from the M-section. "And her? Librarian Magoo."

"I'm Marisol Novotny," she said, holding out her hand.

"Annie Park," Annie replied, shaking it. "What did you think my name was?"

The messy topknot screamed Sprout, but when My New Best Friend seemed more fitting, Marisol wanted to flatter her line neighbor. Annie's thick-rimmed, cat-eye glasses combined with the updo had reminded Marisol of something retro and chic. All that was missing was a pearl necklace and a refined pose. "Holly."

Annie shrugged. "I'd answer to that." She pushed her glasses up the bridge of her nose. "I thought you'd be a Joan."

"Sh!" Librarian Magoo repeated.

They had behaved the rest of the ceremony.

The stairs unfolded from the plane. Vincent and Marisol descended them as camera bulbs flashed. Her face-swallowing sunglasses blocked the strobing onslaught. The sunglasses were also the most glamorous part of her outfit. Vincent, on the other hand, looked impeccable in a black suit and tie. Reporters shouted as Vincent and Marisol walked to the town car.

"Do you think your stocks will recover?"

"How does it feel to have a company targeted by the Bloodsucker terrorist group?"

"And to have your C.O.O. in cahoots with them?"

"Critics say you're dating an essential worker to gain the public's approval after the Ruthven fiasco. What do you say to them?"

Marisol slid into the protection of the car, but Vincent stopped at the passenger door and turned around. He tucked his sunglasses in his suit jacket. "I would tell those critics that I bought the weak shares back from my board to make my company mine again, so that we no longer sacrifice the good of all people for the greedy interests of the few. Our mission will always be for a more just world, and my love is proof of this goal." He opened the door. "Excuse me, I have a memorial service to get to. Please respect the bereaved and keep your distance."

Marisol moved over as Vincent entered the car.

His stained-glass gaze moved to Tobias, who snuck in from the other side. "Quinlan."

"Vinnie." Tobias's left eye twitched, and he shifted to show the badge at his hip. He didn't even need it today when he was off duty.

The two men stared at each other until the pause became nine months pregnant. Tobias blinked, and they shook hands, gripping the other by the forearm. Maybe Vincent should add a sidecar to the motorcycle?

"How was your trip to Thailand?" Tobias asked.

"Not a whole lot of sightseeing. Spent most of our time on the beach." Marisol and Vincent's skin were far from sun-kissed. One of those statements was obviously a lie. "Did you hear W.H.O. reported that the missing virus was due to a computer error?" Marisol asked.

Tobias snorted. "And all this time they said it was stolen."

Marisol dug into her shoulder bag and took out a wrapped box. "Before we forget." She handed it to Tobias.

With a leery squint that bounced from her to Vincent, he took the box. He ripped open the tissue, and there it was—a tie. Silk, gray, and speckled with navy fleur-de-lis.

"You said I owed you one. Thought it might go well with taking your daughter out for coffee."

Tobias's smile faded as soon as it formed. He put the tie on. "I'm a kept man."

The town car drove them to a brownstone. A small group of people in black dress clothes gathered at the bottom steps in animated conversation.

Marisol practiced the Korean phrase Vincent taught her. How sad it is to lose a daughter.

"Eoyo." Vincent lifted his slender fingers to accent the final syllable.

Marisol recited it awkwardly and slowly and definitely not with the right syllable accented. The group on the stairs parted, recognizing Vincent. The trio marched up the stairs and entered the home. Hot cooking oil and green onions wafted from inside. Marisol took a deep breath and crossed the threshold; Tobias and Vincent trailed close behind.

Boisterous people gathered on the patio out back and spilled into the hallway. In disheveled dark dress clothes, they ate, laughed, or played cards. To her right, the somber living room felt heavy with reverent silence.

Incense filled the room with sweet air. A gold-framed, poster-sized photo of Annie the day she had become a doctor stood propped on the table. She wasn't wearing her glasses, and her hair was down and smooth, not in her typical updo resembling a fern. Annie had hated the photo, claiming that the pink blouse and light gray suit jacket made her look like a real estate agent. But her smile and eyes said doctor. For that, Marisol loved the photo. Sorry Annie.

Wreaths of white chrysanthemums surrounded the table. Mourners had piled loose ones on the table under Annie's photo.

Annie's parents, eyes outlined with raw pink, stood at the side of the table. Her father wore a striped band on the arm of his suit. Marisol pursed her lips together to stop them from trembling. Vincent squeezed her hand. Tobias gave her a thumbs up. Together, they laid three chrysanthemums at the edge of the mantel, stepped back, and bowed. While tilting forward from her waist, gravity drew the tears from her eyes. Marisol sniffled and wiped her cheek before kneeling and touching her head to the floor, worshiping the ground at Annie's feet. Marisol stifled a laugh at that notion before standing.

She faced Annie's parents, handed them the other chrysanthemums, and bowed again. She repeated the phrase she practiced ending with eoyo.

"Thank you," Annie's mother said, and she continued in her language.

"We lost a daughter. You lost a friend. How sad for everyone to lose her," Vincent translated.

So true. Annie longed to help people with her research, but the pinnacle of her work was a rabid mouse and her murderer, frozen in Vincent's basement. There had to be something else. A better way. A better story.

After an hour, Annie's parents joined them in the backyard. Pictures of Annie and Marisol hung from clotheslines. Her parents finally had moved everything out of her apartment and found the pictures of the vacations they took together and the nights out and in they had. The pictures stared at her as she picked at the soup, rice, and pickled tofu the family offered her. Tobias's bowl never stayed full. He turned a glass of soju liquor but never turned down seconds of food, or thirds, or fourths, or…

Annie's dad said something and smiled weakly. Vincent translated, "It's hard to feel a broken heart with a full stomach." Realizing her grief-suppressed appetite may come across as rude, Marisol shoveled the rest of the rice in her mouth, filling her cheeks like a hibernating rodent.

I can't believe they're watching you eat. I've come back from the dead to die of embarrassment again, she heard Annie say. Marisol choked on the last bit of rice.

"You're a doctor too?" Annie's mother asked.

Marisol dislodged rice stuck to the sides of her throat. "No. Nurse."

"But you help sick people," Annie's mother continued. She pointed to the pictures and said something Marisol didn't understand.

Vincent translated, "She said that food is medicine, but happy memories are like—baegsin jeobjong?—an inoculation. They make a heart stronger, so it cannot break from grief."

Vincent drew an invisible line with two fingers across the table, a signal that Marisol ate enough food to be polite. Marisol hugged Annie's parents and prepared to leave. As Tobias helped her into her jacket, Vincent said something to her parents.

One of Annie's cousins, who overheard, asked Marisol, "I will find a way, or I will make one. Didn't Hannibal say that?"

"I'm not sure." To her, it would always be Vincent's prayer, guiding him to end the curse. And now? She could accept Annie's story as written... or make a new one that worked.

Marisol blurted, "I'll build a clinic in her name!" Annie's parents froze. "I have the money!" She caught Vincent in her gaze. "Or rather, know someone with money. Her clinic won't just heal the sick or fix the broken, but inoculate them if you will, so people will be strong enough to help themselves." She knew the perfect place for it on the Westside. Some real estate that freed up right after Israel Ramirez disappeared for good.

Vincent translated, and Annie's parents nodded. Marisol continued, "Annie wanted to create a just world. In a just world, no one stands alone. In a just world, we will stand together."

The trio left the funeral in the town car. Before it rounded the corner, Marisol peered back at the brownstone through the back window. Annie waved goodbye from the stairs. When Marisol blinked, she was gone.

Perhaps Annie's spirit found its way to the afterlife.

ΠEW ÌΠTERLVDE

I run past the Westside Boxing Club overrun by young men learning how to give and take a punch. The baby-faced teen Dad coaches on how to give a good jab is one of Tiny's enforcers. Perhaps boxing means there was one less enforcer on the street; one less boy who'd become a man like Caz. And if Tobias's stats are any indication, it's not a silly hope.

I hop from parking post to parking post and run past my childhood home. In a lawn chair at the top of their new front steps with legs extended, head basking in the sun, Mom has a day off. I better leave her alone.

I catch my breath in front of Izzy's former sandwich shop, which is currently under construction. It's gutted to the studs, far from becoming Annie's clinic, but the renovation is underway. That's not the only place getting a makeover. I run to find my hero in our new home, a lair under the Varian Family Research Hospital and Clinics.

Together, we protect our city straight from its heart.

We serve Justice. We stand by those who have no one. We amplify the voices of the unheard. We lift those who are tread upon.

I am his spirit, and he is my saint, awesome and beautiful. He is also my shadow, flawed and mysterious.

Together, we will be unstoppable. Together, we will tip the scales toward a just world.

Tobias's gruff voice blasts into my earpiece, "Hey guys? We got a real whodunnit here."

Trouble's coming for my city? There'll be a reckoning from the Silver Spirit and her Patron Saint.

Acknowledgments

Plenty of people rooted for me or helped me see this project to its end. First and foremost, my husband scheduled family activities around my writing schedule and, on numerous occasions, soothed me in my artistic despair. My writing life would not be the same without author Leigh Michaels. Her wisdom, incisiveness, and time were blessings to my craft. From her romance writing class, I met a strong group of writers whose feedback for well over a year made this book stronger—shoutouts to Kristy, Cathy, and Michele. But there were two classmates who were there for me above and beyond: Ellen Merriss and Meredith Miller. Ellen had the personality of a cheerleader and never let me forget that, despite how dark and disgusting I was getting, I was writing a romance. My lodestar in the group, however, was Meredith, my pen pal, confidante, and brilliant critic. I hope I only mildly annoyed her with all those emails. Once I freed this book from my own developmental hell, Matt Sieren offered me the morale-boosting beta read I needed. Finally, I have quite a few budding adults in my life who want the best for me. Though some would rather see Vincent and Tobias as a couple, I owe a lot of this book to their unwavering belief in my ability.

But I truly need to thank myself. I've been through many wringers while writing this book including a pandemic, job change, cross-country move, a parent with a cancer diagnosis, deaths in the family, and a senseless tragedy back home that shook my very foundations. I am on the other side of these with a book and a smile on my face, and I did it in spite of being my worst critic. I was worth the work.

About The Author

Jonesy Elise is an Iowa transplant living in the Bay Area with her family and dog. She enjoys pumpkin spice lattes, raccoon/opossum memes, roller-skating awkwardly, participial phrases, and the strange space where high-brow and low-brow culture intersect. *Saint of the Shadows* is her debut novel.

Follow her on Instagram or Facebook. Please review and share her book with others. Look out for the sequel, *Deus Ex Umbra*, coming soon... ish.